A FIRESIDE BOOK
Published by
Simon & Schuster Inc.

New York
London
Toronto
Sydney
Tokyo
Singapore

LOOKING
FOR A
RAIN
G·O·D

An Anthology of
Contemporary
African
Short Stories

edited by

Nadežda
Obradović

SIMON AND SCHUSTER/FIRESIDE

Simon & Schuster Building
Rockefeller Center
1230 Avenue of the Americas
New York, New York 10020

Copyright © 1990 by Nadežda Obradović

Designed by Chris Welch
Manufactured in the United States of America

10 9 8 7 6 5 4 3 2 1
10 9 8 7 6 5 4 3 2 1 Pbk.

Library of Congress Cataloging in Publication Data
Looking for a rain god : an anthology of contemporary
African short stories / edited by Nadežda Obradović.
p.   cm.
1. Short stories. African (English) 2. Africa—Fiction.
I. Obradović, Nadežda.
PR9348.L6   1990
823'.010896—dc20   89-48685
                                            CIP
ISBN 0-671-70179-7
0-671-67177-4   Pbk.

Acknowledgments

Grateful acknowledgment is made to the following for permission to reprint their copyrighted material. Every reasonable effort has been made to trace the ownership of all copyrighted material included in this volume. Any errors that may have occurred are inadvertent and will be corrected in subsequent editions, provided notification is sent to the publisher.

"The Madman" by Chinua Achebe from *Girls at War,* copyright © 1972 by Chinua Achebe. Reprinted by permission of the author.

CONTENTS

PREFACE

The Nobel Prize for literature award in 1986 to Wole Soyinka of Nigeria provides evidence that the world is becoming more and more aware of the worth of the work of African writers.

This collection, intended both for the initiated scholars of African literature and even more for general readers, attempts to assemble some of the most representative short stories written in English by Africans (one story, though, was originally written in Arabic). The collection speaks in particular to those readers desiring to get familiar with some new, fresh, different, non-European viewpoints.

Though literary merit was the main criterion, the editor wished to present writers of different regions, sexes, and generations. The stories included originate from ten African countries and cover a variety of topics ranging from madness—in "The Madman" by Chinua Achebe—through traditional customs—as in "Looking for a Rain God" by Bessie Head.

The emphasis in this volume was laid on well-established authors who have gained world acclaim, but certain less-known authors have been included. Several of the stories included were written by women. Women writers in Africa started publishing later than men, have been fewer in number, and have been given less critical attention. This seeming paucity is understandable given that the opportunities for education, travel, and work are less available for women than they are for men. Women have had to overcome real, though sometimes invisible, barriers of public opinion that holds their place is traditionally at home, with children, looking after a family. Nowadays, though, they are emerging on the international literary scene, raising their voices against political and economic repression and racism, offering their points of view.

English is not the mother tongue of these writers and the issue of whether a foreign language can effectively express African aspirations has long been raised. But we will not enter into the discussion here, nor try to answer the question: Can a literature develop properly in a tongue which is not deeply rooted in culture, a language that is not indigenous?

Every author has his own stance, but there are a large number of them who have attempted to forge a new, more African English—to Africanize the English, making it more useful to their outlook and their topics.

We do hope that the reader of these stories can gain insight into everyday life in many African countries. It has not been easy to make these selections; so many promising young authors are missing from the collection. But what we have here does in some measure show that African authors are becoming increasingly conscious of the role they are to play in their society and in the world, that this literature is deeply committed and rooted in African soil. And, that more and more they turn to African sources in order to look for the real, authentic values of their people. It is just a small step toward opening wide the doors of this rich, fresh genuine literature.

Nadežda Obradović

THE MADMAN

||||||||||||||||||||||||||||||||||||||||||||||||||||||||||||

by Chinua Achebe

Chinua Achebe *was born in 1930 in Nigeria. He studied at the Ibadan University and was the first director of the Nigerian Broadcasting Corporation. His first novel,* Things Fall Apart *(1958), received widespread fame and was translated into thirteen languages. His subsequent novels,* No Longer at Ease *(1960),* Arrow of God *(1964),* A Man of the People *(1966); and collections of short stories,* The Insider: Stories of War and Peace from Nigeria *(1971) and* Girls at War *(1972), confirmed his world reputation and he became the most famous writer not only of West Africa but of the entire continent. His works have become obligatory literature at universities in the United States, England, France, and Australia. His latest novel is entitled* Anthills of the Savannah *(1988).*

Along with the English publishing company Heinemann, he founded the famous African Writers Series, which played a pioneering role in propagating African literature throughout the world. Achebe also published two collections of poetry, Beware Soul Brother *(1971) and* Morning Yet on Creation Day! *He was the editor of the Nigerian literary periodical* Okike, *and also wrote children's stories and a book of essays.*

H E WAS DRAWN TO markets and straight roads. Not any tiny neighborhood market where a handful of garrulous women might gather at sunset to gossip and buy ogili for the evening's soup, but a huge, engulfing bazaar beckoning people familiar and strange from

||||||||||||

far and near. And not any dusty, old foothpath beginning in this village, and ending in that stream, but broad, black, mysterious highways without beginning or end. After muc wandering he had discovered two such markets linked together by such a highway; and so ended his wandering. One market was, Af<u>o</u>, the other Eke. The two days between them suited him very well: before setting out for Eke he had ample tim to wind up his business properly at Af<u>o</u>. He passed the night there putting right again his hut after a day of defilement by two fat-bottomed market women who said it was their market stall. At first he had put up a fight but the women had gone and brought their menfolk—four hefty beasts of the bush—to whip him out of the hut. After that he always avoided them, moving out on the morning of the market and back in at dusk to pass the night. Then in the morning he rounded off his affairs swiftly and set out on that long, beautiful boa constrictor of a road to Eke in the distant town of Ogbu. He held his staff and cudgel at the ready in his right hand, and with the left he steadied the basket of his belongings on his head. He had got himself this cudgel lately to deal with little beasts on the way who threw stones at him and made fun of their mothers' nakedness, not his own.

He used to walk in the middle of the road, holding it in conversation. But one day the driver of a mammy-wagon and his mate came down on him shouting, pushing and slapping his face. They said their lorry very nearly ran over their mother, not him. After that he avoided those noisy lorries too, with the vagabonds inside them.

Having walked one day and one night he was now close to the Eke marketplace. From every little sideroad, crowds of market people poured into the big highway to join the enormous flow to Eke. Then he saw some young ladies with water ots on their heads coming toward him, unlike all the rest, away from the market. This surprised him. Then he saw two more water pots rise out of a sloping footpath leading off his side of the highway. He felt thirsty then and stopped to think it over. Then he set down his basket on the roadside and turned into the sloping footpath. But first he begged his highway not to be offended or continue the journey without him. "I'll get some for you too," he said coaxingly with a tender backward glance. "I know you are thirsty."

Nwibe was a man of high standing in Ogbu and was rising higher; a man of wealth and integrity. He had just given notice to all the ozo men of the town that he proposed to seek admission into their honored hierarchy in the coming initiation season.

"Your proposal is excellent," said the men of title. "When we see we shall believe." Which was their dignified way of telling you to think it over once again and make sure you have the means to go through with it. For ozo is not a child's naming ceremony; and where is the man to hide his face who begins the ozo dance and then is foot-stuck to the arena? But in this instance the caution of the elders was no more than a formality for Nwibe was such a sensible man that no one could think of him beginning something he was not sure to finish.

On that Eke day Nwibe had risen early so as to visit his farm beyond the stream and do some light work before going to the market at midday to drink a horn or two of palm wine with his peers and perhaps buy that bundle of roofing thatch for the repairs of his wives' huts. As for his own hut he had a couple of years back settled it finally by changing his thatch roof to zinc. Sooner or later he would do the same for his wives. He could have done Mgboye's hut right away but decided to wait until he could do the two together, or else Udenkwo would set the entire compound on fire. Udenkwo was the junior wife, by three years, but she never let that worry her. Happily, Mgboye was a woman of peace who rarely demanded the respect due to her from the other. She would suffer Udenkwo's provoking tongue sometimes for a whole day without offering a word in reply. And when she did reply at all her words were always few and her voice very low.

That very morning Udenkwo had accused her of spite and all kinds of wickedness on account of a little dog.

"What has a little dog done to you?" she screamed loud enough for half the village to hear. "I ask you, Mgboye, what is the offense of a puppy this early in the day?"

"What your puppy did this early in the day," replied Mgboye, "is that he put his shit-mouth into my soup pot."

"And then?"

"And then I smacked him."

"You smacked him! Why don't you cover your soup pot? Is it easier to hit a dog than cover a pot? Is a small puppy to have more sense than a woman who leaves her soup pot about . . . ?"

"Enough from you, Udenkwo."

"It is not enough, Mgboye, it is not enough. If that dog owes you any debt I want to know. Everything I have, even a little dog I bought to eat my infant's excrement keeps you awake at nights. You are a bad woman, Mgboye, you are a very bad woman!"

Nwibe had listened to all of this in silence in his hut. He knew from the vigor in Udenkwo's voice that she could go on like this till market time. So he intervened, in his characteristic manner by calling out to his senior wife.

"Mgboye! Let me have peace this early morning!"

"Don't you hear all the abuses Udenkwo . . ."

"I hear nothing at all from Udenkwo and I want peace in my compound. If Udenkwo is crazy must everybody else go crazy with her? Is one crazy woman not enough in my compound so early in the day?"

"The great judge has spoken," sang Udenkwo in a sneering sing-song. "Thank you, great judge. Udenkwo is mad. Udenkwo is always mad, but those of you who are sane let . . ."

"Shut your mouth, shameless woman, or a wild beast will lick your eyes for you this morning. When will you learn to keep your badness within this compound instead of shouting it to all Ogbu to hear? I say shut your mouth!"

There was silence then except for Udenkwo's infant whose yelling had up till then been swallowed up by the larger noise of the adults.

"Don't cry, my father," said Udenkwo to him. "They want to kill your dog, but our people say the man who decides to chase after a chicken, for him is the fall . . ."

By the middle of the morning Nwibe had done all the work he had to do on his farm and was on his way again to prepare for market. At the little stream he decided as he always did to wash off the sweat of work. So he put his cloth on a huge boulder by the men's bathing section and waded in. There was nobody else around because of the time of day and because it was market day. But from instinctive modesty he turned to face the forest away from the approaches.

The madman watched him for quite a while. Each time he bent down to carry water in cupped hands from the shallow stream to his head and body the madman smiled at his parted behind. And then remembered. This was the same hefty man who brought three others like him and whipped me out of my hut in the Afo market. He nodded to himself. And he remembered again: this was the same vagabond who descended on me from the lorry in the middle of my highway. He nodded once more. And then he remembered yet again: this was the same fellow who set his children to throw stones at me and make remarks about their mothers' buttocks, not mine. Then he laughed.

Nwibe turned sharply round and saw the naked man laughing, the deep grove of the stream amplifying his laughter. Then he stopped as suddenly as he had begun; the merriment vanished from his face.

"I have caught you naked," he said.

Nwibe ran a hand swiftly down his face to clear his eyes of water.

"I say I have caught you naked, with your thing dangling about."

"I can see you are hungry for a whipping," said Nwibe with quiet menace in his voice, for a madman is said to be easily scared away by the very mention of a whip. "Wait till I get up there. . . . What are you doing? Drop it at once . . . I say drop it!"

The madman had picked up Nwibe's cloth and wrapped it round his own waist. He looked down at himself and began to laugh again.

"I will kill you," screamed Nwibe as he splashed toward the bank, maddened by anger. "I will whip that madness out of you today!"

They ran all the way up the steep and rocky footpath hedged in by the shadowy green forest. A mist gathered and hung over Nwibe's vision as he ran, stumbled, fell, pulled himself up again and stumbled on, shouting and cursing. The other, despite his unaccustomed encumbrance, steadily increased his lead, for he was spare and wiry, a thing made for speed. Furthermore, he did not waste his breath shouting and cursing; he just ran. Two girls going down to the stream saw a man running up the slope toward them pursued by a stark-naked madman. They threw down their pots and fled, screaming.

When Nwibe emerged into the full glare of the highway he could not see his cloth clearly anymore and his chest was on the point of exploding from the fire and torment within. But he kept running. He was only vaguely aware of crowds of people on all sides and he appealed to them tearfully without stopping: "Hold the madman, he's got my cloth!" By this time the man with the cloth was practically lost among the much denser crowds far in front so that the link between him and the naked man was no longer clear.

Now Nwibe continually bumped against people's backs and then laid flat a frail old man struggling with a stubborn goat on a leash. "Stop the madman," he shouted hoarsely, his heart tearing to shreds, "he's got my cloth!" Everyone looked at him first in surprise and then less surprise because strange sights are common in a great market. Some of them even laughed.

"They've got his cloth he says."

"That's a new one I'm sure. He hardly looks mad yet. Doesn't he have people, I wonder."

"People are so careless these days. Why can't they keep proper watch over their sick relation, especially on the day of the market?"

Farther up the road on the very brink of the marketplace two men from Nwibe's village recognized him and, throwing down the one his long basket of yams, the other his calabash of palm wine held on a loop, gave desperate chase, to stop him setting foot irrevocably within the occult territory of the powers of the market. But it was in vain. When finally they caught him it was well inside the crowded square. Udenkwo in tears tore off her top-cloth which they draped on him and led him home by the hand. He spoke just once about a madman who took his cloth in the stream.

"It is all right," said one of the men in the tone of a father to a crying child. They led and he followed blindly, his heavy chest heaving up and down in silent weeping. Many more people from his village, a few of his in-laws and one or two others from his mother's place had joined the grief-stricken party. One man whispered to another that it was the worst kind of madness, deep and tongue-tied.

"May it end ill for him who did this," prayed the other.

The first medicine man his relatives consulted refused to take him on, out of some kind of integrity.

"I could say yes to you and take your money," he said. "But that is not my way. My powers of cure are known throughout Olu and Igbo but never have I professed to bring back to life a man who has sipped the spirit-waters of ani-mmo. It is the same with a madman who of his own accord delivers himself to the divinities of the marketplace. You should have kept better watch over him."

"Don't blame us too much," said Nwibe's relative. "When he left home that morning his senses were as complete as yours and mine now. Don't blame us too much."

"Yes, I know. It happens that way sometimes. And they are the ones that medicine will not reach. I know."

"Can you do nothing at all then, not even to untie his tongue?"

"Nothing can be done. They have already embraced him. It is like a man who runs away from the oppression of his fellows to the grove of an alusi and says to him: Take me, oh spirit, I am your osu. No man can touch him thereafter. He is free and yet no power can break his bondage. He is free of men but bonded to a god."

The second doctor was not as famous as the first and not so strict. He said the case was bad, very bad indeed, but no one folds his arms because the condition of his child is beyond hope. He must still grope around and do his best. His hearers nodded in eager agreement. And then he muttered into his own inward ear: If doctors were to send away every patient whose cure they were uncertain of, how many of them would eat one meal in a whole week from their practice?

Nwibe was cured of his madness. That humble practitioner who did the miracle became overnight the most celebrated mad-doctor of his generation. They called him Sojourner to the Land of the Spirits. Even so it remains true that madness may indeed sometimes depart but never with all his clamorous train. Some of these always remain —the trailers of madness you might call them—to haunt the doorway of the eyes. For how could a man be the same again of whom witnesses from all the lands of Olu and Igbo have once reported that they saw today a fine, hefty man in his prime, stark naked, tearing through the crowds to answer the call of the marketplace? Such a man is marked for ever.

Nwibe became a quiet, withdrawn man avoiding whenever he could the boisterous side of the life of his people. Two years later, before another initiation season, he made a new inquiry about joining the community of titled men in his town. Had they received him perhaps he might have become at least partially restored, but those ozo men, dignified and polite as ever, deftly steered the conversation away to other matters.

MARUMA

by I. N. C. Aniebo

I. N. C. Aniebo *is a prolific Nigerian writer who was born in 1939. Aniebo was trained as a career army officer and served from 1959 to 1971. His first novel,* The Anonymity of Sacrifice, *was published in 1974, followed by* The Journey Within *in 1978, and a collection of twenty-two short stories entitled* Of Wives, Talismans and the Dead.

T HE ROUND MUD HUT *with its conically thatched roof is like the twenty-three others in the village of Okoro. It sits in the center of a walled-in compound, and is dwarfed by the empty, clean spaces, and the tall coconut, orange, pawpaw, palm, and oha trees around it. The presence of these fruit and vegetable trees underscores the age of the hut. The hut was built in 1850, by the grandfather of the present occupant who is now the oldest man in the village, and as a result, the justice of the peace. The hut, built of red clay polished to a high shine, has only two rooms, a bed-sitter with two narrow mud beds, and a kitchen-cum-storage area-cum-chicken coop. On these mud beds on a night in 1926, three men sat drinking palm wine.*

"Cold nights are the right times to drink with friends," Ibealo said. His keen little eyes twinkled in the glow of the hearth fire as he glanced from Oji to Amah, both of whom sat opposite him.

"If you do not depend on your friends for companionship," Oji said. He drained the contents of his gourd cup in one draught. Lifting the gallon jar of palm wine onto his dark lean thighs he refilled his cup. "We have almost emptied this." He set the jar down gently.

A cold, wet wind lifted the matting that served as the door of the hut and rushed in, dampening and then fanning the hearth fire into an angry blaze, ridding the small room of smoke. The room was now filled with the clean, wet smell of the downpour that had taken over the afternoon and early evening, stopping only to let the washed moon step out in cold, triumphant splendor.

Oji shivered as the wind hit him and when it ceased, he dropped the sum of his thoughts into the new silence.

"It is no use, Ibealo. Just as you cannot bring my wife back to life, you cannot reconcile Amah and me."

Ibealo grunted. Oji was not sure whether the grunt had been in agreement or otherwise, so he kept back the rest of what he was going to say. The quarrel between him and Amah was nothing new. During their initiation at the age of ten, they had tried to see which of them would fetch more water for the rites from the stream two miles away from the village. Neither won. From the time they could wield the large hoe, they had dared each other into back-breaking tilling. Neither won consistently.

And when Oji married the most beautiful maiden in all of the seven villages that made up their town, he found out that Amah had tried to win the same girl's affections and failed. Amah then spread the rumor that Oji's wife had lost her virginity to him before she married. They had a confrontation, a terrible fight which Oji won, and which became a figure of speech; the war of Oji and Amah. But, looking back on it all Oji wondered if he had really defeated Amah, who now had a large family of two wives and eighteen children. And what had he, Oji, to show for his life? In concrete terms, nothing. Before long his only daughter, Maruma, would be married and so lost to him forever.

Amah, having now drained his cup, picked up the gallon jar.

"I suppose you have given up," he said to Oji and receiving no answer refilled his own cup. Turning to Ibealo he added, "What is left now will only fill a cup."

"Thank you," Ibealo said. Upending his cup, he picked up the wine jar and shook it vigorously. The contents barely filled his cup with thick, milky wine rich in fermenting yeast. "May the spirit of the wine chase out that of altercation," he prayed.

"Ofo!" Amah said loudly.

Ibealo emptied his cup in one drinking motion, and poured the dregs on one of the small logs of the hearth fire. He wiped his mouth with the back of his hand, and slowly got up, his bones creaking noisily. Stooping, he went into the back room and soon returned with a fresh jar of palm wine. He set it down next to Oji, sat down and said, "This is for you."

Oji looked surprised, but Ibealo's smile told him nothing. Amah wore his usual scowl.

"May you not die before your time," Oji said, hiding his confusion behind the traditional form of thanks. Again, following tradition, he filled Ibealo's cup first, then Amah's and finally his own. Setting down the wine jar he said as his heart suddenly accelerated for no apparent reason, "He that brings wine, brings life. May more come from where this came!"

"Ofo!" Ibealo said.

There was a special silence, filled with the crackling of the hearth fire and the distant hollow barking of dogs. Oji's heart continued to beat fast. And yet he could not tell why his heart behaved so, like that of a child waiting for the initiation ceremony to begin. His mind went back to that time, the smarting of the whip lashes, the heavy pounding of his heart threatening to burst out with prohibited cries of pain, the darkness of the night inside and outside the hut of the spirits . . .

"Oji, we have been worried about you."

He was not surprised. He had been expecting a statement like that, but why had he thought of the initiation?

"I know you won't believe it," Amah said with a forced smile. "I have been worried about you."

"But why?"

Amah and Ibealo exchanged glances. Then Ibealo said, "We think it is time you got another wife. I'm prepared to help you with the bride price if that is what has been holding you back."

"I can help too," Amah quickly added, "if only to provide the wine that will be needed for the ceremonies."

Oji gulped down half his wine in an effort to rekindle the warmth that was gone from his stomach. It did not work. He drank the rest quickly and refilled his cup. If the wine was a gift to him, he might as well enjoy it. He leaned back against the wall. *Chukwunna!* How many times did he have to tell them he did not want to marry again? But they would never give up, always coming at him in ever-changing groups to plead the same cause! It was not as though he was a profligate who should be made to settle down. He had married early and ended up with only one of his seven children surviving and his wife dead. Ha! He had been alone with his daughter for just four years, yet they all made it sound as though it had been for ever.

"What do you say, Oji, *oke osisi?*" Ibealo asked. "I bet you have forgotten your praise-name."

"How can I?" Oji said suddenly laughing at such a ridiculous statement. He could never keep his anger against Ibealo for long.

"You deserve that praise-name," Ibealo said. He refilled his cup, the deliberation of age in his movements. "You are far and above the strongest, and the most masculine tree we ever planted."

And like the tree, Oji thought, the most alone. But he said with careful modesty, "Without your nurturing, I would not have grown strong."

"Nonsense! I merely fed what was there already, and gave it a chance to send its roots far and wide and deep into Mother Earth. And remember, I fed the same things to my sons, yet none of them took root."

Oji hid his face in his cup. Ibealo and he had been through *oku nmuo*. That was what marriage did to you—it put you through *oku nmuo*. Why then should he remarry and go through it again? No!

"*Oke osisi*, what about reproducing the thing I fed?"

"I tried. You know I tried and failed."

"Perhaps you tried with the wrong tool."

"No, *okaa ome*. No."

Once again, Oji hid his face in his cup. He could not really say his wife had been the wrong tool. She had not been a tool at all. She had been the most loving, the most feeling human being. Admittedly they had had to adjust to each other, but then he felt it was he who had caused the most problems. He had been jealous of her beauty, goodness and intelligence. In his youthful callousness, he had wanted her for himself alone. He had wanted to own, possess and if possible absorb her into himself. She had not let him.

"Oji, even an *oji* eventually gets too old to bear fruit."

"I know. But I cannot do what you ask of me."

"Why not? You are still in your prime. Even when you do have white hair like mine, I know you can still do it."

"I agree *okaa ome*, but I can't."

"Why?"

"Because he is afraid," Amah said flatly.

Oji turned to him startled. He had almost forgotten all about him, and seeing his fat, broad face stirred his anger again. Not wanting to control his anger this time, he took fresh note of those aspects of him that always annoyed him—the mean little eyes, the stubborn jaw almost carried by a bull neck, the barrel chest that sat abruptly on lean hips and legs. Age had turned Amah's assets into liabilities.

"What did you say?" Oji asked.

"I said you are afraid!" Amah replied slowly and deliberately.

"Of what?" Oji asked. Anger was not only in his head now but also in his blood and eyes.

"Of women. You are afraid they will enslave you . . . as your wife did."

Oji threw his wine dregs into Amah's face and was about to grapple with him when Ibealo's voice cut him down.

"You have insulted me," Ibealo said.

"You should have let him get at me," Amah said, wiping his face.

Oji rested his back on the wall and kneaded his large hands together. It dulled the edge of his anger and kept him from speaking.

||||||||||||||||||||||||||||||||||||||||||||||||||||||||||||||||||||||||||||||||||||||||||||||||||||||||||||||||||||||||||||||||||||||||||||||

"Why don't we stop hiding behind words and tell him what we have in mind?" Amah asked. He picked up his cup from the polished clay floor and filled it with fresh palm wine.

Oji stopped kneading his hands and waited.

"You have insulted me," Ibealo said.

"What did you expect from a hero?" Amah asked. "Well, *okaa ome*, if you won't say it I will. After all he threw the wine in my face, so I am entitled to say whatever is on my mind. Oji! Look at me, Oji! Yes, look at me. No one wants to force you to marry again. You can remain unmarried forever if you like. What we are worried about is Maruma, who looks after you better than a daughter and a wife. I say it is time you let the girl marry."

In one fluid movement, Oji rose and walked out into the washed clarity of the moon. The cold made him aware of his near-nakedness. He had on only his *ugboro*, a thick strip of cloth worn in such a way that it looked like underpants. He should have worn his army great-coat. But he had not thought of it, just as he had not thought Ibealo would ever invite him to dinner to discuss Maruma's future.

He lengthened his stride at the thought of Maruma. He hoped the poor child had gone to bed. She was always waiting up for him. My poor Maruma, why would people not mind their business? When she turned sixteen two years ago, he had told her to start thinking of marriage. He knew how people were, and how they would talk! She sulked for days and only became her normal playful self after he promised never to mention marriage again. Her reaction had been a revelation and he had been surprised that he had welcomed its import.

Walking into his compound, Oji saw light streaming from his hut. "Oh, my poor child," he muttered. He stooped and entered his hut through the low doorway covered with the usual matting. He was enveloped by the warmth from the blazing fire. Maruma, her covering kicked aside, was asleep on the mud bed to his left. Her dusky, straight back was toward him, and her only article of clothing, a string of large, red beads, glinted round her waist.

The sight of her so fascinated him he stood there tall and straight and lean, savoring the room's warmth, and the brightness of the new mat on his bed to his right, and the straightness of her back. And the longer he stood there, the more often his eyes strayed to her back, scudded over her bare buttocks and rested for a while on her doubled-up long legs and full thighs.

As though she sensed him, Maruma stirred. Then she turned on her back, her legs flung apart, and moaned,

"Nnamu!"

"I am here, my child," Oji said and went to her.

Maruma had been sitting on the low kitchen stool for almost an hour now. She had never felt as listless as this before. Every now and then she uncrossed her stretched-out long legs and gathered her skirtlike blue loincloth between them. She then recrossed her legs at the ankles, and placed her clasped hands between her dark, plump thighs as though she were cold. This last action often reminded her that before long she would not be able to place her hands that way. Her belly had grown so big that although she was only five months pregnant, she looked full term.

"Better get up and fetch firewood before father comes home," she said to herself, but she did not move. Instead, she sighed and tenderly began to rub her bare stomach, concentrating on the slow, mesmeric, circular motion of her hand. Her usually recessed navel was beginning to open out, and she let her hand go over it often. She liked the tingling sensation it sent through her. She felt it had a life of its own, probably connected to that of the baby in her womb.

For no apparent reason, tears suddenly filled her eyes, rolled down her cheeks and spattered on her swollen breasts. The drops were warm, but she felt so detached they might have been someone else's.

Then from far away the thought that triggered the tears came to her mind. If her father would only talk to her today! If only they would have the heart-to-heart talk they used to, so she could tell him she did not mind the condition she was in. She wanted so much to reassure him that she was aware and approved of what they had done, and had been doing, until the cursed *Oku-ekwe* masqueraders sang it into the night and to the ancestors! She wanted to let him know that she knew of his anguish and feelings of uselessness at not having a surviving son to carry on his name! She wanted to tell him of the decision she had made a long time ago—to be the one to carry on the family name.

But deep inside, she knew their heart-to-heart conversations had ceased forever. All she would get from him now would be the mono-syllabic responses she had been getting for some time. And the way he now averted his eyes whenever they met made her feel ugly and evil. After those encounters she often wondered whether she had changed that much. Looking into her mother's hand-carved mirror had failed to reassure her. Not that the mirror lied. No, she mis-trusted her eyes. They always showed she had not changed that much, for all she ever saw was merely the plumping out of her lean, angular face, small neck, and when she lowered the hand-held mir-ror, her puffed-up body.

She was sure those little changes could not have caused her fa-ther's strong aversion, an aversion that had gone to the extent of not wanting to sleep on the same bed with her. To her, sleeping with her father was the most cherished privilege she had claimed soon after her mother's funeral.

She could easily recall how shocked her father had been that first time he woke to find her beside him. She had slipped into his bed in the early hours of the morning and had not slept too well after that. She had been so apprehensive of his reaction she had kept awake till he opened his eyes and saw her. She smiled bravely, and tried hard to control her quivering lips as she watched different expressions chase themselves across his heavy face.

Finally, he sat up and she pretended not to see his eyes run over her from head to feet. She was glad she had put on her loincloth before getting into his bed. It made her feel less vulnerable.

Feeling that she had to make him say something, she said tremu-lously, "You were calling me in your sleep, and . . . and . . . I came and touched you. You were hot and shivering. You had fever so I stayed."

But he still said nothing. After what seemed ages, he got up and went outside. He stayed out so long that while waiting for him she dozed off and on. When he came back, he stood at the door and looked at her in a queer way. She sat up feeling guilty.

The day had already broken completely, and she felt lost and disoriented. She always liked to watch the sun rise in the cool mist of the morning. It often helped to set her feet firmly on the day. But with the sleep still in her eyes, and the bright sunlight stabbing at them, she felt she had slept through many days and nights, and would soon go back to sleep some more. It was like being dead, or rather waking up dead.

Since her father had continued to stand by the door, she finally stood up. The room had spun suddenly and she leaned against the wall to prevent herself from falling. Then a pain started at the base of her neck, throbbing like a heartbeat. She could stand his gaze no longer. She said sharply,

"Father, why do you look at me like that? Did I do wrong to try to keep you warm?"

"No," he said after a while. "But don't do it again." He went out immediately and did not return till the sun had hidden itself.

And she had been doubly surprised the night she found him in her arms. How wonderful things had become after that night.

But everything was changed now, and her eyes would not tell her what it was in her that had caused the change. She wished she had given in to her old urge to gouge them out. Lying eyes, stupid cow-like eyes that saw nothing. It would be better if they were blinded forever so that her father would have to take care of her always. He would no longer evade her. He would be her eyes, eyes that she could trust implicitly.

Her mother had pointed out how untrustworthy her eyes were.

"Maruma, you have no eyes. If you did you would see what we

are telling you. But why should I be telling you this when I know you are different from all of us?"

The day she surprised her mother with a strange man made her realize that her mother was not the only one who thought she saw differently. Everyone, except her beloved father, had laughed when she said what she had seen.

"Your eyes see things other eyes don't see," they had said, and some of the children had made up a quick song about cow eyes that saw more than human eyes.

After that incident of the strange man, she and her mother no longer disguised their mutual hatred of each other. Maruma turned to her father for companionship and protection from her mother's sudden rages.

"Please don't talk about that changeling of a child," her mother once said to a friend, as Maruma hid, listening behind the barn. "Do you know I nearly lost my life giving birth to her? And *that*, after I had given birth to six children without any trouble? She never meant me to be alive now. That was why I gave her that name, *Maruma*, 'do things intentionally'! Everything she does, she does intentionally. Right from the time she was conceived. The only one she cares for is her father. That is why she resembles him so much. You know I have this feeling that she and I are going to fight to the death and beyond."

"*Ahudie!*" the friend had exclaimed.

"Do you know who Maruma really is? Do you know who is reincarnated in her? Do you know? She is Oji's mother. Yes, that's who she is, Oji's mother. After abandoning him at birth, she comes now to reap where she did not even help burn the bush and prepare the land for the hoeing. Now you see . . . ?"

Maruma had been listening so intently she had not been ready to run away when her mother and friend came out of the barn and discovered her. That afternoon she received the severest beating of her life.

The clucking of her hen leading its brood home dragged Maruma back to the present. She was dismayed at how late it was. Drawing up her legs, she began to push aside the ashes from the fireplace, picking out the unburnt wood charcoal at the same time. In her hurry she raised a great deal of ash dust that soon settled on her cropped black hair and broad back. She did not bother about this, for she had to have the evening meal on the fire before her father returned from the farms.

After she had heaped the charcoal on top of crisscrossed dry twigs, and moved the three blackened stones on which the pot rested back into place, she remembered she had to go to the farms nearby to collect firewood. The thought so drained her of all energy, she resumed her former sitting position. Waves of weakness, originating from her head, made her feel as heavy as a basketful of new yams.

She closed her eyes, squeezing them tight in an effort to stop the flow of weakness. It did not work. Resuming her thoughts about her mother, she asked herself as she had done many times before whether she really was the reincarnation of her father's mother. There was no way of knowing the pure truth. If she was indeed her father's mother then her pregnancy was a good thing. A good thing?

Yes, a good thing. She was sure her baby would be a boy. She looked forward already to laughing at the masquerade that had made her a butt of its jokes, for her son would grow up to become a member of the masquers, and avenge his mother.

Ah-a! The night the masquerade had sung in front of the compound had been the turning point in her relationship with her father. That night they had gone to bed earlier than usual, having worked hard at the farm, clearing, burning and hoeing. Her father, in his considerate way, had roasted a big yam for their supper and forbade her to cook anything, not even the heated oil with which to eat the yam. They had used palm oil straight from the *ite nkpa*, spiced with small red peppers and salt.

Far into the night she had been pulled back from her dreams by a consistent, high-pitched, raucous cry. At first she thought a parrot had flown into the hut, but she soon recognized the peculiar singing of *Oku-ekwe*, the one to whom all secrets were made known, and who in turn spread it to all.

Although that had not been the first time she had ever been wakened by the masquerade, she felt very apprehensive as she listened to its song. Her heart beat so painfully loud she was afraid it would wake her father. But she stayed as still as she could, staring up into the darkened roof, wondering why the all-seeing *Oku-ekwe* had not seen her mother and the strange men!

Then she heard it, and her fears were realized. The masquerade was singing a song with her name, and its followers sang the chorus interspersed with shouts of laughter which in the still night sounded obscene and ill-intentioned.

> *Have you seen Maruma lately?*
> *At the farm or at the stream?*
> *Have you seen her walking?*
> *Like a duck about to lay eggs?*
>
> *We have seen, we have seen!*
> *We have seen Maruma walking*
> *Like a duck about to lay eggs.*
>
> *Softly now, softly, have you seen?*
> *The pride of Oji, the mighty tree?*
> *Have you seen her walking,*
> *Like a duck about to lay eggs?*

The masquerade's followers sang their chorus with a great deal of laughter, howling like dogs at a full moon.

> *So you have all seen Maruma?*
> *That is good, but tell me,*
> *Did you notice her breasts swinging?*
> *And the skirt that replaced the maiden beads?*

The followers howled before singing the chorus, and as soon as they had done so, the masquerade sang:

They say, but do not say I said,
The mighty tree is responsible.
Some people are so greedy,
They will even eat their own excreta!

And the followers shouted and shouted with laughter, and praised the masquerade's song and impromptu lyrics, before singing the chorus. Then the masquerade went inexorably on:

And in the olden days, before,
I say before the lepers came,
We knew what to do to human dogs,
To cleanse our earth of their footprints.

And the final chorus was like a mournful dirge:

Yes, yes, before the lepers came,
The mighty hollow tree would have been cut down,
And all its diseased roots dug out of Mother Earth,
Yes, yes!

That morning, Maruma's father neither answered her greetings, nor looked at her. And from that day he never allowed her in his bed. His overreaction to an ordinary song confused her, and the loneliness she felt afterward made her wish for death and blindness. She also noticed that the villagers and most of her relations avoided her as though she were a leper.

The squeal of the gate opening on wooden hinges made Maruma get up quickly. She leaned against the dividing wall till a sudden spell of dizziness passed. She chided herself for forgetting that she was pregnant. Picking up a machete and a short piece of rope from the alcove in the front room, she went outside. Her father was putting down a long basket, full of new yams.

Maruma stood and looked at him. He had aged considerably in

the past few months. He now had a stoop and his face had taken on the weary, humorless cast of old age, brought on by toil and worry. Maruma felt a rush of tenderness for him and thought the baby within her moved in sympathy.

"Welcome, father," she said, loudly.

He did not respond, but simply glanced at her, the setting sun painting his face a wooden hue of such solidity it looked molded. He bent down, picked up his basket and went into the barn.

With a heavy heart, Maruma went out through the main gate and toward the farms. Bitterness and despair were a sharp taste in her mouth. She blamed it all on her mother.

"That witch!" she muttered under her breath. "One of these days I am going to come to the land of the dead and teach you a lesson."

By the time Maruma got to the nearest farm one and a half miles away, the shadows had grown and there was a chill in the air. Quickly, she started picking up the dried twigs strewn around the farm. She needed just enough wood to cook dinner with. Tomorrow, she could go to the forest and cut real firewood that would last.

She had almost filled the crook of her left arm when she bent down to pick up what she promised herself would be the last twig. But it was not a twig. It was a snake. A long black snake that was cold to the touch and wriggled about, but did not run away.

She dropped the twigs she had collected, her heart beating violently as she stared around her.

"Oh, my father!" she cried.

She seemed to see snakes everywhere. Suddenly she uttered a strangled cry and clutched her throat as though someone were trying to choke her. She was afraid to move a step from where she stood lest she step on the snakes.

"Father!" she cried as soon as she found her voice. "Father, please come! Father, oh father!"

At first no one answered, then she heard her name spoken in whispered derision. The voice sounded like her mother's. In fact, it *was* her mother's voice and she was calling her, laughing at her.

Maruma looked, stared into the darkening gloom to see where her mother was calling from. But she saw nothing. The voice seemed to come from all directions. Every twig, every standing shrub, was a bunch of twining snakes.

Maruma stood stock-still, looking straight ahead of her. She was resolved to remain like that till her father rescued her. She knew he would come looking for her very soon. Had he not seen her leave? Perhaps he was on his way right now. He loved her so much he would not rest till he found her. Should she shout to guide him to where she was? No, it would not help because she would not be heard above her mother's mocking laughter that had grown enormously in volume. The very air itself was filled with the sounds of this hideous laughter...

Then, suddenly, there was silence. Darkness had fallen completely. There was no moon. There was no wind. Maruma could hear the sound of her heartbeat clearly. Now she could shout to guide her father to her.

Her mother beat her to it, shouting her name from behind her and making her jump with a cry. And then the child in her womb began to laugh in her mother's voice, to laugh and to cry and to jabber. Maruma started running even though it was so dark she could not see the palm of her own hand. But it did not really matter where she was running to, so long as she was on the move. Shrubs, bushes, snakes and her mother in ever-changing shapes, got in her way but she simply pushed them aside and continued stumbling and running. Meanwhile the mocking laughter grew and grew till she was sucked into it.

The round mud hut with its conically thatched roof is like all the others in the village of Okoro. It sits in the middle of a walled-in compound, and is dwarfed by the empty, dirty spaces, and the tall coarse grass around it.

The compound, however, has an air of abandon and desolation. The walls are crumbling in places and the roof of the hut gapes open in certain areas. *The door of the main gate hangs open in a lopsided, forlorn way and even its hardwood frame is covered with mildew and grass.*

They say the compound belongs to the Oji family. They also say the family committed an abomination and as a result Mother Earth took them all back into her womb, cutting off their tainted line.

But at the other end of the village there is also another compound in the same state of disrepair. They say this belongs to the family of Amah. They also say the family did not commit any abomination, but Mother Earth took them all back into her womb, cutting off their family line as well.

That is what they say.

IN THE CUTTING OF A DRINK

by Ama Ata Aidoo

Ama Ata Aidoo *was born in 1942 in Ghana. In 1964 she wrote her first play,* Dilemma of a Ghost. *The drama won immediate critical recognition. In 1969 she published her second play,* Anowa. *The following year she published a short story collection entitled* No Sweetness Here. *In 1977 her novel* Our Sister Killjoy *was published. Ms. Aidoo is also a poet but both her poetry and fiction are characterized by unconventional form. No matter which form she chooses to write in, most of her stories share the theme of life in Ghana.*

I SAY, MY UNCLES, IF YOU are going to Accra and anyone tells you that the best place for you to drop down is at the Circle, then he has done you good, but . . . hm . . . I even do not know how to describe it. . . .

"Are all these beings that are passing this way and that way human? Did men buy all these cars with money . . . ?"

But my elders, I do not want to waste your time. I looked round and did not find my bag. I just fixed my eyes on the ground and walked on. . . . Do not ask me why. Each time I tried to raise my eyes, I was dizzy from the number of cars which were passing. And I could not stand still. If I did, I felt as if the whole world was made up of cars in motion. There is something somewhere, my uncles. Not desiring to deafen you with too long a story . . .

I stopped walking just before I stepped into the Circle itself. I

35

||||||||||||||||||||||||||||||||||||||||||||||||||||||||||||||||||||||||||||||||||||||||||||||||||||||||||||||||||

stood there for a long time. Then a lorry came along and I beckoned to the driver to stop. Not that it really stopped.

"Where are you going?" he asked me.

"I am going to Mamprobi," I replied. "Jump in," he said, and he started to drive away. Hm . . . I nearly fell down climbing in. As we went round the thing which was like a big bowl on a very huge stump of wood, I had it in mind to have a good look at it, and later Duayaw told me that it shoots water in the air . . . but the driver was talking to me, so I could not look at it properly. He told me he himself was not going to Mamprobi but he was going to the station where I could take a lorry which would be going there. . . .

Yes, my uncle, he did not deceive me. Immediately we arrived at the station I found the driver of a lorry shouting "Mamprobi, Mamprobi." Finally when the clock struck about two-thirty, I was knocking on the door of Duayaw. I did not knock for long when the door opened. Ah, I say, he was fast asleep, fast asleep I say, on a Saturday afternoon.

"How can folks find time to sleep on Saturday afternoons?" I asked myself. We hailed each other heartily. My uncles, Duayaw has done well for himself. His mother Nsedua is a very lucky woman.

How is it some people are lucky with school and others are not? Did not Mansa go to school with Duayaw here in this very school which I can see for myself? What have we done that Mansa should have wanted to stop going to school?

But I must continue with my tale. . . . Yes, Duayaw has done well for himself. His room has fine furniture. Only it is too small. I asked him why and he told me he was even lucky to have got that narrow place that looks like a box. It is very hard to find a place to sleep in the city. . . .

He asked me about the purpose of my journey. I told him everything. How, as he himself knew, my sister Mansa had refused to go to school after "Klase Tri" and how my mother had tried to persuade her to go . . .

My mother, do not interrupt me, everyone present here knows you tried to do what you could by your daughter.

Yes, I told him how, after she had refused to go, we finally took her to this woman who promised to teach her to keep house and to work with the sewing machine . . . and how she came home the first Christmas after the woman took her but has never been home again, these twelve years.

Duayaw asked me whether it was my intention then to look for my sister in the city. I told him yes. He laughed saying, "You are funny. Do you think you can find a woman in this place? You do not know where she is staying. You do not even know whether she is married or not. Where can we find her if someone big has married her and she is now living in one of those big bungalows which are some ten miles from the city?"

Do you cry "My Lord," mother? You are surprised about what I said about the marriage? Do not be. I was surprised too, when he talked that way. I too cried "My Lord" . . . Yes, I too did, mother. But you and I have forgotten that Mansa was born a girl and girls do not take much time to grow. We are thinking of her as we last saw her when she was ten years old. But mother, that is twelve years ago. . . .

Yes, Duayaw told me that she is by now old enough to marry and to do something more than merely marry. I asked him whether he knew where she was and if he knew whether she had any children—"Children?" he cried, and he started laughing, a certain laugh. . . .

I was looking at him all the time he was talking. He told me he was not just discouraging me but he wanted me to see how big and difficult it was, what I proposed to do. I replied that it did not matter. What was necessary was that even if Mansa was dead, her ghost would know that we had not forgotten her entirely. That we had not let her wander in other people's towns and that we had tried to bring her home. . . .

These are useless tears you have started to weep, my mother. Have I said anything to show that she was dead?

Duayaw and I decided on the little things we would do the following day as the beginning of our search. Then he gave me water for my bath and brought me food. He sat by me while I ate and asked me for news of home. I told him that his father has married another woman and of how last year the *akatse* spoiled all our cocoa. We know about that already. When I finished eating, Duayaw asked me to stretch out my bones on the bed and I did. I think I slept fine because when I opened my eyes it was dark. He had switched on his light and there was a woman in the room. He showed me her as a friend but I think she is the girl he wants to marry against the wishes of his people. She is as beautiful as sunrise, but she does not come from our parts. . . .

When Duayaw saw that I was properly awake, he told me it had struck eight o'clock in the evening and his friend had brought some food. The three of us ate together.

Do not say "Ei," uncle, it seems as if people do this thing in the city. A woman prepares a meal for a man and eats it with him. Yes, they do so often.

My mouth could not manage the food. It was prepared from cassava and corn dough, but it was strange food all the same. I tried to do my best. After the meal, Duayaw told me we were going for a night out. It was then I remembered my bag. I told him that as matters stood, I could not change my cloth and I could not go out with them. He would not hear of it. "It would certainly be a crime to come to this city and not go out on a Saturday night." He warned me though that there might not be many people, or anybody at all, where we were going who would also be in cloth but I should not worry about that.

Cut me a drink, for my throat is very dry, my uncle. . . .

When we were on the street, I could not believe my eyes. The whole place was as clear as the sky. Some of these lights are very beautiful indeed. Everyone should see them . . . and there are so many of them! "Who is paying for all these lights?" I asked myself. I could not say that aloud for fear Duayaw would laugh.

We walked through many streets until we came to a big building where a band was playing. Duayaw went to buy tickets for the three of us.

You all know that I had not been to anywhere like that before. You must allow me to say that I was amazed. "Ei, are all these people children of human beings? And where are they going? And what do they want?"

Before I went in, I thought the building was big, but when I went in, I realized the crowd in it was bigger. Some were in front of a counter buying drinks, others were dancing...

Yes, that was the case, uncle, we had gone to a place where they had given a dance, but I did not know.

Some people were sitting on iron chairs around iron tables. Duayaw told some people to bring us a table and chairs and they did. As soon as we sat down, Duayaw asked us what we would drink. As for me, I told him *lamlale* but his woman asked for "Beer"...

Do not be surprised, uncles.

Yes, I remember very well, she asked for beer. It was not long before Duayaw brought them. I was too surprised to drink mine. I sat with my mouth open and watched the daughter of a woman cut beer like a man. The band had stopped playing for some time and soon they started again. Duayaw and his woman went to dance. I sat there and drank my *lamlale*. I cannot describe how they danced.

After some time, the band stopped playing and Duayaw and his woman came to sit down. I was feeling cold and I told Duayaw. He said, "And this is no wonder, have you not been drinking this women's drink all the time?"

"Does it make one cold?" I asked him.

"Yes," he replied. "Did you not know that? You must drink beer."

"Yes," I replied. So he bought me beer. When I was drinking the beer, he told me I would be warm if I danced.

"You know I cannot dance the way you people dance," I told him.

"And how do we dance?" he asked me.

"I think you all dance like white men and as I do not know how that is done, people would laugh at me," I said. Duayaw started laughing. He could not contain himself. He laughed so much his woman asked him what it was all about. He said something in the white man's language and they started laughing again. Duayaw then told me that if people were dancing, they would be so busy that they would not have time to watch others dance. And also, in the city, no one cares if you dance well or not...

Yes, I danced too, my uncles. I did not know anyone, that is true. My uncle, do not say that instead of concerning myself with the business for which I had gone to the city, I went dancing. Oh, if you only knew what happened at this place, you would not be saying this. I would not like to stop somewhere and tell you the end... I would rather like to put a rod under the story, as it were, clear off every little creeper in the bush...

But as we were talking about the dancing, something made Duayaw turn to look behind him where four women were sitting by the table.... Oh! he turned his eyes quickly, screwed his face into something queer which I could not understand and told me that if I wanted to dance, I could ask one of those women to dance with me.

My uncles, I too was very surprised when I heard that. I asked Duayaw if people who did not know me would dance with me. He said "Yes." I lifted my eyes, my uncles, and looked at those four young women sitting round a table alone. They were sitting all alone, I say. I got up.

I hope I am making myself clear, my uncles, but I was trembling like water in a brass bowl.

Immediately one of them saw me, she jumped up and said something in that kind of white man's language which everyone, even those who have not gone to school, speaks in the city. I shook my head. She said something else in the language of the people of the place. I shook my head again. Then I heard her ask me in Fante whether I wanted to dance with her. I replied "Yes."

Ei! my little sister, are you asking me a question? Oh! you want to know whether I found Mansa? I do not know.... Our uncles have asked me to tell everything that happened there, and you too! I am cooking the whole meal for you, why do you want to lick the ladle now?

Yes, I went to dance with her. I kept looking at her so much I think I was all the time stepping on her feet. I say, she was as black as you and I, but her hair was very long and fell on her shoulders like that of a white woman. I did not touch it but I saw it was very soft. Her lips with that red paint looked like a fresh wound. There was no space between her skin and her dress. Yes, I danced with her. When the music ended, I went back to where I was sitting. I do not know what she told her companions about me, but I heard them laugh.

It was this time that something made me realize that they were all bad women of the city. Duayaw had told me I would feel warm if I danced, yet after I had danced, I was colder than before. You would think someone had poured water on me. I was unhappy thinking about these women. "Have they no homes?" I asked myself. "Do not their mothers like them? God, we are all toiling for our threepence to buy something to eat... but oh! God! this is no work."

When I thought of my own sister, who was lost, I became a little happy because I felt that although I had not found her, she was nevertheless married to a big man and all was well with her.

When the band started to play again, I went to the women's table to ask the one with whom I had danced to dance again. But someone had gone with her already. I got one of the two who were still sitting there. She went with me. When we were dancing she asked me whether it was true that I was a Fante. I replied "Yes." We did not speak again. When the band stopped playing, she told me to take her to where they sold things to buy her beer and cigarettes. I was wondering whether I had the money. When we were where the lights were shining brightly, something told me to look at her face. Something pulled at my heart.

"Young woman, is this the work you do?" I asked her.

"Young man, what work do you mean?" she too asked me. I laughed.

"Do you not know what work?" I asked again.

"And who are you to ask me such questions? I say, who are you? Let me tell you that any kind of work is work. You villager, you villager, who are you?" she screamed.

I was afraid. People around were looking at us. I laid my hands on her shoulders to calm her down and she hit them away.

"Mansa, Mansa," I said. "Do you not know me?" She looked at

me for a long time and started laughing. She laughed, laughed as if the laughter did not come from her stomach. Yes, as if she was hungry.

"I think you are my brother," she said. "Hm."

Oh, my mother and my aunt, oh, little sister, are you all weeping? As for you women!

What is there to weep about? I was sent to find a lost child. I found her a woman.

Cut me a drink . . .

Any kind of work is work. . . . This is what Mansa told me with a mouth that looked like clotted blood. Any kind of work is work . . . so do not weep. She will come home this Christmas.

My brother, cut me another drink. Any form of work is work . . . is work . . . is work!

HEART OF A JUDGE

|||||||||||||||||||||||||||||||||||||||||||||||||||||||||||||||||||||||||||

by R. Sarif Easmon

R. Sarif Easmon, *born in 1913, is a prominent Sierra Leonean author of four plays:* Dear Parent and Ogre, *performed in 1961 and published in 1964,* The New Patriots *(1965),* Mate and Checkmate, *and* Dilys, Dear Dilys. *His novels are entitled* The Burnt-Out Marriage *(1967) and* Genevieve *(1968). A thirteen-year gap ensued before the publication of Easmon's last book* The Feud, *a collection of short stories.*

SIR GEOFFREY ROBIN had had a good day, his second in Sunia. Sitting at dinner, taken a little late at nine o'clock, with his wife Cynthia facing him across the beautiful mahogany table, he felt sure he was going to have an even better night. Life felt good. It always did if Cynthia was a part of it. Her golden hair, falling down to her shoulders, wavy always without art, was as lovely as it was ten years before when, against many who in his heart he admitted were better-qualified suitors, he had won her heart and married her.

He refilled his glass with port.

"You know, Cynthia," he said, waving his hand around the dining room, toward the elegant sitting room, "this is yet another manifestation of the younger Pliny's dictum: *Ex Africa semper aliquid novi.*"

"You're too old-fashioned, Geoffrey," laughed the beautiful blonde. "Too old-fashioned for a man, for a judge, for the modern world—"

"Not for a husband, I hope!" he laughed back.

|||||||||||||

"No, dear. But Latin is becoming a stranger even in Oxford. You must forget your double first and stop quoting Latin at your wife: especially over port and a crab salad. By the way, you'd better go easy with both."

"Western civilization has made an alien of Latin," he grumbled. "That only means something's gone seriously wrong with the world. Pliny's apothegm is still as valid today as it was nineteen hundred years ago."

"You old-fashioned thing!" his wife reproved him again. "Nobody, just nobody, says 'apothegm' these days. Why not maxim? From the day we landed in Africa you've been drilling Pliny in my ear: *'There's always something new out of Africa'*!"

"Well," he grinned, "look around and admit it's very apposite for the time and place in which we find ourselves this week."

She looked around the room. In the light of the kerosene pressure lamp, the dark cream paint of the walls looked lovely. The parquet floor continued into the sitting area. Electric lamps with beautiful shades had been installed in the ceiling and on the walls. But each room was lit with the white lights of a pressure lamp, awaiting the completion of the power station six months from that date. The six dining chairs were upholstered in red. Their servant—the steward they had brought up on "trek"—stood by the mahogany sideboard to one side of the dining room. Another servant, not visible, was pulling the cord of the punkah which sent cooling currents of air down from the ceiling over the diners.

"It's almost incredible, Geoffrey," Lady Robin admitted. (Her husband had been knighted when he became chief justice of Luawaland the year before.) "It doesn't seem possible all this should be happening in this wild African bush. And yet they're always running us British down! But you know, seeing for myself what's happening here in this backward Sunia District, I feel proud to be British. I'm even prouder of you, Geoffrey."

"Who's old-fashioned *and* jingoistic now?" he laughed at her. But at that moment he was proud, too, to be so appreciated. Few men were heroes to their wives. But even at that moment his happiness was spoiled by jealousy. She was so young and beautiful that he felt guilty to be fifteen years older. Always he was jealous and afraid she might be having affairs with younger men. There was Mike Hendrick; Edward Charteris, Henry—He had never had any proof of her infidelity. In secret despair he would tell himself it was because she was too clever for him.

In truth, though, he wronged her. Looking across the table, she thought he looked as always handsome, and his hair, more gray now than black, added to his air of distinction. He looked born to be chief justice anywhere in the world. His nose was large. But that was not noticeable under the high, noble forehead. Eyes black and very brilliant. She had loved him most for his lips. They were almost girlish, exquisitely shaped. She was a little worried about his complexion. It was becoming slightly florid in the last year.

As he picked up the port bottle again she said, with great firmness, "No, Geoffrey. You'd finished the white wine before the crab."

"Then I'll have a little more of your excellent crab salad."

"You've had enough, dear. I shouldn't think port goes so well with—"

"*Please.*"

"Oh, very well."

The steward served coffee and brandy. After which the Robins retired to their bedroom.

There were three bedrooms in the large bungalow. Each one had a bathroom. In the main bedroom, there was a magnificent mahogany double bed. The servant had let down the mosquito net around it. The moon shone through the lace curtains in the large, barred windows.

The couple soon changed for the night.

Lady Robin went to bed straightaway.

Sir Geoffrey slipped his old blue silk dressing gown over his pajama suit.

"Hadn't you better come to bed, Geoffrey?" his lady asked rather crossly. "I know the Vamboi case is very important. But you must have gone over the records of the lower court a dozen times."

"But there are peculiar circumstances in the case, Cynthia. Anyway, this is the very last time I'm reading the records. I'll soon turn in."

He took the records out of his briefcase. He sat down by the dressing table to read them. He was studying them for almost an hour.

That was perhaps a mistake. While he assimilated all the salient facts of the case, it also enabled the atmosphere of Sunia to get him. The two days of court sittings he had dealt with ease with the cases of larceny, rape, etc.: the usual humdrum type to be found on a judge's up-country list. Nevertheless, this case of *Regina* versus *James Vamboi* still worried him. But after the last reading of the transcript he was convinced he could cope. The method of murder was new in the annals of crime. But he would have no need as a judge to bring in the panoply of the occult to explain the features of the case, though these were macabre enough, to be sure.

"It seems a straightforward case to me," he told himself, putting the typescript away in his briefcase and stifling a yawn. He reached out his hand to the pressure lamp on its stand between the dressing table and the wardrobe. He turned the knob preparatory to turning in for the night. "A straightforward case, and I shall so deal with it."

The air began to hiss out of the reservoir of the pressure lamp. But before the judge could take his fingers off the milled head of the knob, a lot of strange things began to happen.

First he was conscious that the door opened. At the same time a coldness entered the room. It was not an uncomfortable coldness, though. On the contrary, it had been a hot night. Now the room felt as if it was air-conditioned.

But why had the door opened? Was it in fact open? Judge Robin's back was turned to it. In spite of this, he was as sure as if he was looking at the panels that the door had opened. To settle the point he turned; or rather, attempted to turn to face into the room.

But he could not move. He could not move his hand from the lamp. Something soft and gentle was holding his fingers to the milled head. Whatever influence it was, though gentle, it seemed to have all the power in the universe behind it.

Then, against his own will, the judge felt his right hand twist, so that he tightened the knob again. But much of the air had escaped from the reservoir. By now the light in the mantle was trembling between a pallid whiteness and the threat of going out altogether. Nevertheless, against all the rules it continued to flicker, and seemed capable of flickering throughout eternity without going out.

"A straightforward case eh, Robin? What asses we judges are."

Judge Robin started at the sound of the voice. His fingers broke contact with the lamp. That voice again! He knew it very well. But he knew it only in the long ago. At a time blurred by sorrow and a funeral. How in the name of goodness could a voice challenge Time and the grave to be so natural? How— But just as the force in the room had willed his hand on the knob of the lamp, so now he felt it bending his mind away from the past. He could have sworn that something willed him to remember that his wife had been an actress, and would sometimes play superb tricks of mimicry on him. He smiled to himself. Without surprise to himself, he found himself gliding toward the bed. He was not conscious of limbs, of muscles, of balance.

The lamp continued to flicker behind him. The moonlight blazed through the curtains, splashing the bed with silver.

Sir Geoffrey saw his lady lying on the far side of the bed. She lay on her side. Her hair was scattered like a skein of gold over the pillow. She was fast asleep. Then the judge experienced a slight shock, not unpleasant. It was at seeing *himself* lying in the bed beside his wife. He too was fast asleep. He lay on his back, staring at the ceiling, the moonlight reflected from his eyes.

Now the judge's heart began to beat rather fast. Still, though excited, he felt nothing like fear. Furthermore, though he knew he was wide awake—never mind that chunk of inertia disguised as flesh pretending to be *him* in the bed—he was convinced he was awake in a way different from all the other three hundred and sixty-four days in the year. His brain was working as if it had kicked away material limitations. He was Mind incarnate. Thus though he was certain his wife was asleep beside his carcass in the bed, he felt no astonishment whatever to hear her voice coming from behind him. Now that he was able to turn, he saw her standing across the room in her all too familiar housecoat.

"Ernest!" she was saying. "How wonderful to see you again after all these years!"

"Yes indeed, Ernest!" Sir Geoffrey echoed her welcome with pleasure. "But why did you not send us a wire to say you were coming?"

Sir Geoffrey wondered if it was Sir Ernest who had come through the door with the coldness. He did not look a cold figure as he stood in the middle of the room between him and Cynthia. He was a tall African with a long, very handsome face. (The ladykiller of the bar he was called in his young days.) He wore a full-bottomed judge's wig and crimson robe and looked immensely distinguished.

He smiled with affability as husband and wife converged on him in the middle of the room. Though they greeted him with such warmth, they did not shake hands. Nor did it strike the Robins as odd that their visitor should walk into their bedroom in full judge's regalia while they were in their night attire. Somehow Sir Ernest's smile and carriage were able to take care of all that. And when he spoke, his voice, a golden one, was full of solicitude.

"Friendship proves itself when friends can welcome each other whatever the circumstances on either side. I've come as a matter of urgency, Cynthia, because I'm not happy about Geoff. This visit is for him, and is not necessarily a social one."

"I suppose you judges must talk shop," returned Cynthia with a smile. "Will you have your usual Black Label whisky, Ernest?"

"No thank you, my dear."

Lady Robin took the only armchair in the room. Sir Ernest sat on the stool, his back to the dressing table mirror. Sir Geoffrey remained standing.

All the while the room remained cold, the light continued to flicker.

"May I smoke, Cynthia?"

"Certainly, Ernest," returned his hostess. "Is it one of your famous scented cigars?"

"Thanks. Yes, it's the same old brand," Sir Ernest chuckled. Judge Robin did not observe where the gold cigar case came from. But there it was in Sir Ernest's hand. He opened it, took out one cigar. He did not offer his host one. He cut the cylinder with a gold pen-knife. The action looked so natural. Though it was cold, and the light was flickering.

Sir Ernest lit up.

The first mouthful of smoke at once embraced the Robins in nostalgia. For Sir Ernest was the first friend they made when they came to West Africa. And, as Lady Robin so well recalled, that distinguished African, famous as a *bon viveur*, always smoked a special brand of Havana, gloriously scented.

"I've come about that murder case you're to try in the morning, Geoff," said Sir Ernest, sitting on the stool, very affable and quite at home. He blew a cone of smoke toward his friend. "Do be careful. Don't be carried away by circumstantial evidence. That has in its time killed as many innocents as judges' consciences. I had a very similar case in this very Sunia some years ago. The result for me, as you'll recall, was disastrous. It looked a straightforward case. I'm sorry to say my summing up to the jury was wrong in toto. Circumstantial evidence, you see. I hope you will—"

He stopped in the middle of the sentence. His eyes were staring with a frightening intensity through and through Judge Robin.

All the time he had sat on the stool Sir Ernest had looked as large and clear as life. But all at once the color began to fade from his robe. The full-bottomed wig became more lacelike. The flesh appeared to evaporate from the face. Soon, only the outline of wig and face remained: till Sir Geoffrey became aware he was seeing the dressing table through the outline figure of a long-dead judge of the Supreme Court.

In one bound he was across the room. He began to pump the lamp as if his life depended on it.

"*Cynthia!*"

"*Geoffrey!*"

The beautiful blond woman leapt up in bed and sought to rush to her husband. She got entangled in the mosquito net—which came tearing down to the floor around her. In frenzy she freed herself and ran across to her husband.

"Geoffrey," she gasped, shuddering, "I—I—I have had the most disturbing dream."

"What was the dream, my dear?"

"I dreamed the late Sir Ernest Williams called on us—"

"Wearing a new judge's robe—"

"With full-bottomed wig—"

They stared at each other, shocked beyond measure at the simultaneous invasion of their collective unconscious.

"And—and—and—" Lady Robin stammered, shivered, "he-he was—smoking—"

She stopped and sniffed the air.

"Have you been smoking, Geoffrey?"

"I'm a pipe man, dear," her husband reminded her. "Besides, with young Geoff at Harrow, I can't afford tobacco *that* expensive."

The room was redolent of scented cigar smoke.

Then he took his lady by the hand and led her to the dressing table.

"Look!" he said softly.

He pointed to the object at one corner of the table. In the brilliant white light of the pressure lamp could be seen cigar ash more than half an inch long, lying on the dressing-table just as the smoker had flicked it off. When Lady Robin touched it it was still warm. It crumbled instantly—and vanished.

"O-O-Oh!"

Sir Geoffrey caught his wife to his chest before she fell to the floor. She had fainted.

Only then as reality exploded on him did his hair stand on end.

But the feeling of terror he had was momentary. The next instant he lifted his wife in his arms and bore her to the bed.

She was not unconscious for long. But it was some time before he was able to calm her fears.

"There must be some *rational* explanation," the judge kept telling himself all through the night.

But if there was an explanation the judge did not find it. Sir Ernest Williams, the then chief justice of Luawaland, had died in very mysterious circumstances. It was in that very Sunia, in the very house pulled down to build this beautiful bungalow. It was on the night following the trial of a notorious case of murder. A juju man had been sentenced to death. The prisoner had maintained his innocence to the end. When the judge passed sentence on him, he had told him calmly he, the judge, would die before his unjust sentence was carried out. Sir Ernest had spent his last night in the old rest house. The next morning, he was found lying on his back in bed, staring wide-eyed at the ceiling. He was stone dead. Two palm leaves were crossed on the pillow above his head. A cowrie lay on the center of his forehead. There was no mark of violence on his body. No blood was spilled. And though he was a man reputed never to have had an illness in life, at autopsy no cause of death was found.

The case the chief justice had tried had been one of the most sensational in the country. It was steeped in juju. Some seven years after the juju man was hanged, even more sensational evidence was raked out of the embers of the case. This evidence proved conclusively that the old case had been one of "ritual murder." Several of the "big men" in the district were involved. Eight culprits were hanged. And the poor juju man who had been judicially murdered had had nothing to do with the case.

This and other matters Sir Geoffrey Robin pondered and worried over through the rest of the night. He made his wife take a sleeping tablet. As for himself, barbiturates gave him a hangover worse than insomnia. In any case, he would never take any kind of sedative if he had a case in court next day. Thus though he put the light out, and lay beside his wife in bed, he did not sleep at all.

He watched the new day dawn. It brought no dawn to his spirits.

He took breakfast. And though, radiant after a good night's rest, Cynthia fussed over him, his breakfast turned out a meal at which the coffee was without flavor, the bacon like pulped newsprint.

He was not feeling his best when he walked the short distance to the new courthouse. It had been completed not three months before. And that was the first time he was coming up on circuit there.

His orderly accompanied him up to his office. He robed there in his office. At half past eight sharp he walked down the corridor into the court room.

"Court rise!"

The judge walked up to the dais, mounted. He bowed first on one side, then the other, took his seat on the rostrum.

The case *Regina* versus *James Vamboi* was called. Wilful murder. Defense counsel entered a plea of not guilty.

"M'lord, gentlemen of the jury. . ."

The attorney general rose in the well of the court, standing by the baize-topped table. The voice boomed through the new courthouse and echoed round the mahogany-paneled walls. Proud of having the finest voice of any barrister in West Africa, the A.G. turned toward the sunlit windows beneath which twelve Africans sat on benches of that aggressively uncomfortable kind encountered only in those two places where men, apart from fools and tyrants, admit they are inferior to their institutions: a church and a court of law.

"I doubt if it is possible to describe the malice and low cunning that motivated this murder. More pertinent, gentlemen of the jury, is that yet again something new has come out of Africa. Look in the dock, gentlemen, at the author of this novelty in ghastliness."

On his rostrum Sir Geoffrey drew himself up. His eyes, along with the twelve pairs of the jury, as well as those of the large crowd sitting breathless in court, surveyed what instead of a monster, looked like a very ordinary human male in the dock. Murmurs and movements blended with the subdued sunlight, which, absorbed in part by the wooden panels that lined the walls, managed to tone down the tropical brightness of the morning. The new courtroom also gave an air of gravity, and seriousness appropriate for a murder trial. The policeman standing beside the prisoner coughed. The crowd in the body of the court stirred more nervously. An usher called, "Silence in court."

The judge's face became less impassive as he surveyed the man in the dock.

That young African, in a cheap gray suit, appeared to be the only person in court unconcerned about the trial. As the judge's eyes were fixed on him across the court, the prisoner raised a steel rat trap to the level of his eyes. He winked and whistled to the inmate of the cage. The rat sat up on its haunchs and chirped back just like a cricket.

"How are we, Robin?" the prisoner asked the creature in the cage. Thereupon he raised his face and grinned across to the judge.

Robin! That was the judge's own name. It echoed round and round in Sir Geoffrey's head as the prisoner again called to his rodent friend.

From habit, the face under the judge's wig that was now turned to the prisoner became as expressive as a cadaver's. Nevertheless Judge Robin's heart was working like a strange machine in his chest. With an effort he made a mental note that he would not allow the goings-on in the dock, however bizarre, to bolster up a plea of insanity.

"Gentlemen of the jury," the attorney general went on, "the facts of the case are these—"

"Just a minute, Mr. Attorney General," said the judge. Though all in court observed him to be making records in the book before him, he was not in fact writing. His heart was racing away so that it almost choked him.

For neither the prisoner's appearance nor his comportment was conducive to the judge's peace of mind. Nor, for that matter, were his recollections of the incidents of the night. Sitting there on the dais, high above the court, and so isolated, he wanted to be detached from the passions and frailties that prejudice judgment in a court of law. Above all, he desired to perform his work that day with a mind more than ordinarily free from distraction.

But that morning, for the first time in his career on the bench, he did not feel he could give his undivided mind to the case in the jurisdiction of his court. That distressed him in the extreme. A true rationalist, justice was his religion. He was so distressed he felt obliged to take the unusual course of ordering an adjournment even before the case properly opened.

"The court," he announced without preliminary, "is adjourned for fifteen minutes."

An astonished court rose and watched him go toward the side door, on his way to his office.

It was a cream-painted, airy place. He locked the door behind him. As soon as he sat down at the desk his distress passed, and his confidence began to return. The view through the window gave onto a rice field, bordering on the little river. The hills rose in greenery beyond. With the sun shining over the whole, it brought to Sir Geoffrey's mind the assurance of the permanence of Nature and natural laws, the permanence of normality. For that his soul most craved that morning.

Besides, this was the first time he was coming on circuit to Sunia District. The region was one of the most backward in West Africa. It had a bad name for juju and witchcraft. Being an Englishman, Judge Robin knew he could rise, as he was expected to rise, above such superstitions. The administration had the greatest confidence in him. And, he admitted with pride, he was deserving of that confidence. He was one of those splendid white men in all the British West African colonies who set up judicial systems equal to what they knew in England. He was determined, too, that this his first major case in Sunia with juju associations would make legal history, and deal a mortal blow to the pernicious superstitions in the country. Such was his resolution when he came down from the capital three days before.

"And that is my resolution *now,*" he told himself with firmness, "never mind what happened last night."

In a matter of seconds he recapitulated all the strange things that had happened in the night.

"That is all past," Sir Geoffrey now told himself. "It is morning, I am in court. The case must go on."

However, Sir Ernest's warning of the night stuck like a beacon in his mind.

"I will be wary of circumstantial evidence," he promised himself.

Finding calm in his heart, he took a grip on himself and returned to the court room.

"Gentlemen of the jury," the attorney general's voice rang around the hall, "the facts of the case are as follows. On the morning of the twelfth of June last, the police received the report of the sudden death of one John Lebbie. The prisoner, James Vamboi, reported the death. The manner of his reporting it drew the suspicion of the officer on duty. There was blood on the prisoner's clothes. And he had said"—he turned with a ponderosity meant to impress toward the man in the dock—"'Cock Robin has killed my Uncle John.'"

The A.G.'s smile gained a tinge of the ominous as he turned it on the jury, "holding it" long enough for the interpreter to translate his words into Sowanah for some of the jurors not acquainted with English.

"Have you ever heard, gentlemen of the jury, of such callousness, allied with flippancy in the presence of death, as a man going to the police station to accuse Cock Robin of murder? As it turned out, the prisoner rationalized this brutality by stating that Cock Robin was not the bird the British brainwashed us to cry over in our nursery days, but his late uncle's pet rat. Cock Robin a rat? Why not Little Red Riding Hood turned wolf?"

"Your lordship." The defense counsel leapt up like a very agitated jack-in-the-box at the table and bawled up to the bench, "Your lordship, I object."

The A.G. regarded him with a stern ferocity, though he sat down for about a tenth of a second.

"To what," came his cold query, "does my learned friend object, m'lord?"

"My learned friend, my lord, is trying to influence you with European suggestions. This is an *African* murder—an alleged one. It has nothing to do with British wolves, riding hoods or what have you."

"Objection overruled," said the judge.

The defense counsel, a short wizened man with a bloated face, gave a knowing glance at the jury. He left them feeling he kept a host of aces up his sleeve.

"Thank you, m'lord." The A.G.'s smile was all urbanity. "Leaving aside this flimsy attempt at an alibi, gentlemen of the jury, let me give you the outline of what the police found at the scene of the crime.

"The murdered man was found in his bed in his bedroom. According to the prisoner, the body had not been moved. There was no sign of violence on the corpse. The right foot lay in a pool of blood, which had soaked through the mattress and congealed on the floor.

"We shall call the family doctor of the deceased, gentlemen of the jury, to inform you about his condition of health up to the day of his death. As a result of this, he had no sensation whatever in the toes of his feet. This fact was known to the accused. He himself had admitted it in the lower court. Thus the right great toe of the deceased became, if your lordship will excuse the classical allusion, his Achilles' heel. Through that toe death came to him. In short, he bled to death through a hole in his toe.

"John Lebbie died in the quiet of the night, in sleep, mercifully without pain. We shall call the pathologist to give expert evidence that the deceased died as the result of the artery in his right great toe being cut across. The wound on the underside of the toe was of a peculiar nature. It was not a cut. It was a gnawed, gouged wound.

"A search of the prisoner's room revealed an old and rusty nail gouge. Rusty, that is, in every part but its business end. This end, contrary to all usage, was not blunt. Oh, no! It was bright as stainless steel, having been filed and honed till it was as sharp as a razor. The width of the gouge fitted perfectly into the furrows left on the underside of the deceased's great toe. The pathologist will inform you, gentlemen, that this instrument could have caused the wound that proved fatal to John Lebbie. My lord, I tender it in evidence."

The court clerk passed the nail gouge turned murder weapon up to the bench. The judge glanced at it, instructed that it be accepted, entered and labeled as Exhibit A.

With satisfaction, the A.G. observed Exhibit A had produced all the effect he had hoped for on the jury. He continued,

"The instrument was to hand. The opportunity came to the prisoner on the night of June eleven–twelve. At any rate that was the night he seized it. He was alone in the house with his uncle. He himself admits all the doors and windows were locked on the inside. No one had forced an entry. He knew John Lebbie would not feel a wound in his toes if even he was awake. He killed him when he was asleep.

"We have proven instrument of and opportunity for murder. A cast-iron case, gentlemen of the jury. It is not for the prosecution to prove motive in any case. In this case, however, motive is plainer than a pikestaff. James Vamboi was broke. He had just closed his account at Barclay's Bank. He was in debt. Creditors were squeezing him. Very hard. He had been used to a profligate life in the capital. He knew he was his uncle's heir. John Lebbie was a very wealthy farmer. His nephew was happy to pay his own debts with his uncle's life."

Here he made a satisfied as well as dramatic pause. He knew the jury were his to the last doubting Thomas.

The A.G. now pulled himself up to his full six-foot height. He was a striking figure in his wig and gown. And to this the grandeur of his peroration—as the jury thought—added further distinction.

"It is not my business, gentlemen, to work on your feelings. The case is stark and brutal enough to have done that in its mere narration. But I have given you only the outline. I shall now call evidence to prove the case."

The police, the pathologist, and the rest of the grim and boring parade took two morning and two afternoon sessions to go to and from the witness box. Every witness was harried and counterharried by prosecution and defense.

The defense counsel, though he looked so mild and harmless— indeed, slightly if not certifiably insane—gave the pathologist a grueling time in the witness box. Expert witnesses are very often so extremely expert they cease to be sensible. It was one thing for the pathologist to say with that brutal confidence of the forensic expert that Exhibit A *could* have caused the wound that killed John Lebbie. It was quite another to show that it actually *did*. In short, while the expert tried to look over defense with godly disdain, the little man had made him look a fool to the jury. Indeed, he was so clever he succeeded in making the "twelve good men and true" believe he had led only one of the dozens of aces up his sleeve to trump the patholo-gist.

What these aces of the defense counsel might have been—apart from suggestion, a psychological weapon that often turns out a damp squib—it would have been difficult for any unprejudiced observer in court to tell. At any rate, as far as the case had gone up to that point, all the evidence that had been adduced had gone, all along the line, against the prisoner. Admittedly it was circum-stantial. Then again the prisoner's levity in the dock, his insou-ciance later verging on the bizarre, had done nothing to secure him the sympathy of the jury.

It is no matter for surprise, then, that all the jurors leaned forward in their seats to stare in wonder at Vamboi when he elected to give evidence in his own defense. As every lawyer knows, this can be a very dangerous procedure for a criminal. He could easily hang him-self. But James Vamboi had no fear. Carrying his rat trap, he moved over from the dock to the witness box.

As he entered the witness box, he flourished the rat trap like a trophy above his head. He set it down on the shelf in front of the box: on top of the Bible, Koran and gris-gris on which witnesses were sworn.

With his long wiry hair standing up all over his head, he looked altogether quite macabre, frightening in his wildness.

Judge Robin fixed his eyes on the rat trap. He went slightly green.

"Is the presence of that rat really necessary in my court?" he asked.

"It's vital for our case, m'lord," defense counsel assured him.

"Very well," Sir Geoffrey conceded, turning greener. "But," he muttered, "I hate the creatures."

As soon as he was sworn—on the Bible—James Vamboi began to spread confusion in court. It was a confusion of tongues. He would speak perfect English, Creole, Sowanah—and then some dialect no one in court understood.

Defense counsel rose to lead his witness.

"Name?"

"James Vamboi."

"Where do you live?"

"At Thirty-five Taranko Road."

"Is that the same address as the deceased?"

"Yes."

"What's your occupation?"

"I'm out of work."

"Did you know the deceased?"

"He was my uncle."

Here defense counsel picked up Exhibit A from the table.

"Do you recognize this nail gouge?"

"Yes. It's mine."

"Did you kill your uncle, John Lebbie, with it?"

The prisoner started. He fixed on his lawyer a look of the gravest indignation. His forehead gathered in a ferocious frown.

"Have you," he asked in fury, "joined the prosecution against me?"

Judge Robin leaned over his desk, above which the punkah was going to and fro, and warned the witness, "Confine your answers to the questions asked."

From the way Vamboi grinned and leered at him Sir Geoffrey was not sure if he had understood him. So he addressed himself to the attorney general.

"Mr. Attorney General, I dread to think what irrelevancies we may be dragged into if we take witness's evidence in the strict, formal way. I suggest we let him tell his story in his own way."

"No objection, m'lord," the A.G. rose to answer. "Only I pray you to keep him tightly in rein."

"Now," defense counsel resumed, turning to the man in the box, "tell the court what you found in your uncle's bedroom that morning you called the police."

James Vamboi first grinned up to the rostrum, as if there was some cabalistic understanding between him and the judge.

"When I went to uncle's room," he began, "I found he was dead. Robin here"—to avoid confusion he pointed to the trap. The judge felt rather squeamish at the implied comparison—as though he were "Robin up there." "Robin here was at the foot of the bed. He— Robin, not my uncle who was already dead—jumped down to the floor as I approached the bed. He left a spoor of blood all along the floor. It was then I saw his fur was all caked with blood."

Robin, he deposed, was his uncle's pet rat. Every night his uncle used to put some dried fish in Robin's cage. He was quite tame. The cage—it was a trap, but of course it was Robin's home, so it could not be a trap to *him*—was in its usual place by the wall in the bedroom. The round door (here Vamboi pointed it out) at the back of the cage was open. He had observed Robin hop back into his cage. He noticed the blood about his uncle's foot. "You know when there's no food about a house at night rats come out of their holes and eat the feet of people sleeping." Robin must have been very hungry, he thought. His uncle must have forgotten to put food in the cage.

"Poor Robin meant no harm. I'm sure he would have preferred dried fish to uncle's toe. I'm sure he meant no harm."

Giving evidence, he looked mad to everyone in court: most of all to the judge.

Nevertheless, from that story plainly told James Vamboi would not budge an inch.

Defense counsel, smiling as if he had laid a booby trap for the prosecution, sat down.

The attorney general tried all his forensic wiles to shake the evidence. But he soon developed the sensation he was battering his head against the Rock of Gibraltar. Finding his sanity confronted with that robust madness from the witness box, the A.G. began to feel he must have become mad by induction. At last he was exasperated to the point of losing his temper: a thing no one ever remembered him doing.

"So Robin did it all, eh?" he sneered, his sarcasm firing on all six cylinders, shooting out the most potent nerve poison for witnesses known to the bar. "Pity," he roared so that his voice echoed from the walls, "pity poor Robin can't talk!"

The judge, the jury, the whole court chuckled at that. But the man in the witness box laughed—loud, and diabolically. Then, leaning over the front of the box, grinning hugely, he told the A.G. in a penetrating whisper:

"A-ha! But Robin *can!*"

The judge sat bolt upright. The court stirred like a giant beehive warming in the morning sun. For five whole seconds the A.G.'s mouth remained agape. Then he roared at the witness:

"Robin can *what?*"

"Robin *can* talk," Vamboi assured him with the simplicity born of confidence—or lunacy. He bent with affection over the cage. "Can't you, Robin?"

Robin's answer was a twitter common to all rats. If he could speak the language of Shakespeare, he was keeping it mighty dark: at least, for the moment.

"Let me take him out of his cage," the witness offered.

"You'll do no such thing!" Judge Robin screamed at him. Once, as a toddler he had been bitten by a rat. He had since had a phobia for all rodents. His breath came rasping out of his chest. The sweat began to pour down his face. "Mr. Attorney General," he asked in a shaking voice, "did the government psychiatrist report this man to be *compos mentis?*"

"Who am I, m'lord," the Crown prosecutor returned with his famous sarcasm, "to question the strange ways of experts?"

The judge muttered that psychiatrists were themselves the best fitted subjects for straitjackets.

But that did not help the situation. So the judge wiped off the perspiration running into his eyes. A cold shiver ran down his spine when he turned from the A.G. to the man in the witness box.

"Tell them," that extraordinary young man was saying, as with affection he wagged his finger at the rat in the trap. "*You* killed the old cock, didn't you, Robin?"

Robin ran twice around the cage, twittering.

"Come on, my friend." The prisoner's exhortation to the rodent now held a note of anxiety, like an impresario being let down by his most renowned prima donna. "*You* killed the old cock, didn't you, Robin?"

And now the words were beating like hammer blows within the judge's head. In all his years in Africa he had never witnessed anything so preposterous as the scene unfolding in his court. This surely was juju on the rampage. If science had pronounced this man sane, then he, Geoffrey Robin, was bonkers. But what was sanity? At once he recalled Sir Ernest's warnings about the pitfalls of circumstantial evidence. He saw him as clearly as he had seen him in his dream: as if he had come to his court to keep him up to scratch. Evidence? What was evidence in the quicksands of juju country? What was evidence when science could vouch for Vamboi's sanity? His, Judge Robin's, was already tottering. Sweating, breathing shallowly through his mouth, he felt powerless to control the scene whose madness now began to gather momentum in his court.

Nor was he the only one there so affected. Hardboiled as the A.G. was supposed to be, master of every court situation he had ever found himself in in twenty years, he was gaping in consternation at the man in the witness box. The jurors were sitting forward speechless, still as wax figures on their benches.

The prisoner exhorted the rat, begged, whined. It was as if the rodent had turned into a god the way he prayed to it. Finally, with anguish and terror, and the sweat pouring out of his face, he bent over the cage sobbing:

"*You* killed the old cock, didn't you, Robin?"

At last sanity returned to the judge's mind. In a flash he saw through the whole situation. The prisoner's story hung together. It was the police who were bonkers to have organized a plot too complex for the criminal's understanding. And with all his high intelligence the attorney general had outbonkered all the rest. But then, though he would not have admitted this to anyone connected with the bar, he knew from experience that star forensic skill sometimes spun reason into such a close spiral it could not tell its backside from its front. The rat-kill-man story was all too unfamiliar and unnewsworthy compared with the man-kill-man one. Damn the police and their circumstantial or other evidence.

"Young man," said the judge. The court knew by the tone of his voice where his sympathy and his judgment lay. "Young man, surely you're not expecting sense and coherence out of a mere rat?"

As soon as he said this Judge Robin knew he had undone the knot that held the macabre situation together in his court. Like an actor behind the footlights, every judge in court is sensitive to the "feel" of that court; the meandering of the jury-mind; above all of his control over the proceedings. Now for the first time in his professional life Judge Robin knew what it was to panic and lose control over his court.

For the words were no sooner out of his mouth than Robin the rat spun around to face him through the bars of his cage.

The attitude of the rodent was less significant than that of the prisoner. Vamboi was standing in the witness box staring raptly at the judge. His stance was rigid, cataleptic. Over the cage he held two palm leaves crossed in one hand, in the other a large cowrie.

The knowledge came to the judge with the impact of a psychological blockbuster: Vamboi was using occult means to impose his will on him. Judge Robin trembled with the wrath of outrage. Practice juju on him—on *him*: the choice product of England's premier university; the inheritor of that enlightened sanity European civilization had taken three thousand years to spawn. Juju on *him!*

But outrage is born of resentment, and implies the will to resist. To his horror Judge Robin found he had no will to resist the waves of suggestion impinging on his personality from across the well of the court. It dawned on him in a flash that Vamboi had the means of willing him not so much to *do* whatever he willed, but to see, feel,

||||||||||||||||||||||||||||||||||||||||||||||||||||||||||||||||||||||||||||||||||||||||||||||||||||||||||||||||||||||||||

and think what Vamboi relayed he should. The realization came to him with a terror that was insupportable. The fellow swiftly oozed and squeezed into his personality so that he felt himself to be possessed by the foulness in the witness box that passed for man. It was a kind of possession by an unclean spirit, a demonic combination between man working through the rat as an instrument of destructive psychological power. Something again new—though so old—out of Africa.

Suggestion. That was it. But how could he—*he*, Geoffrey Robin, double first at Oxford, president of the Union, he!—be suggestible by such a source? That was the last flicker of resistance in him, his last controlled thought. Beyond that his mind was not his to control. But how he could *feel!*

He felt some three hundred and more pairs of eyes around the court riveted like nails upon him. He felt most horribly isolated up on his rostrum. He felt and saw the rat stand on his hind legs. It gripped the bars of the cage with its forepaws and began to shake the cage.

No one else in court saw or heard the cage shake and rattle. A last tremor of thought shivered in the judge telling him the thing was not happening; it was only he himself who was being made to feel it was taking place. But the thought would not stick to reality.

Suddenly Judge Robin felt the air around him to be impregnated with the smell and discomfort of juju. In a twinkling the rat had run from the trap. Across the floor. Up on the rostrum. There it was, sitting at the front of his desk. At that diabolical moment when Robin the rat appeared to swell to the size of a bull gorilla the judge *knew* he was not on the desk at all. He knew it was Vamboi inside him, Geoffrey Robin, making him see the rodent there, pouring his soundless thoughts across to him in waves that almost burst his eardrums.

"Of course," Robin the rat roared, "I *can* talk! And of course, it was *I* who killed the old cock. James has an alibi. You dare hang him and you'll go the way of Sir Ernest Williams. James's alibi?" The rat's eyes became incandescent with malice. "You were on circuit the night Uncle Lebbie died. James spent the night with your wife, Lady Cynthia! *Ha-ha-ha! Ha-ha-ha!*"

The laugh reverberated in thunderclaps around the courtroom.

Overwhelmed by a foreboding and a constriction in his chest, Judge Robin clutched at his throat. His wife, beautiful, charming and much younger than himself, had been an actress. Second only to his phobia for rats was his unfounded fear that she was unfaithful to him. And now he knew that the two greatest aversions of his life had joined to disgrace him in his court. Was it possible that that half-mad Vamboi across the court could, by just holding palm leaves and a cowrie in his hands, invade, permeate and destroy him from within? At that moment of mental anguish he felt the teeth of the rat tearing into his throat. African juju had done its worst. With a gasp of horror the judge fell forward fainting on the rostrum—

"Geoffrey! Geoffrey!" A woman was shouting into Judge Robin's ear. "Wake up!"

"My God, Cynthia!" Sir Geoffrey gasped, sitting bolt upright on the bed.

The bedroom was flooded with moonlight.

Her blond hair scattered over her shoulders, Lady Robin was standing in her nightdress in the flood of moonlight. She still held her husband by the shoulders.

The judge rubbed his eyes in disbelief. For it was not yet morning. He had not gone to court. The case of *Regina* versus *James Vamboi* was still to be tried.

"What a nightmare I've had, my dear!" he sighed.

"I warned you," said his lovely lady, "to go easy with that crab salad at dinner."

Judge Robin burst into gargantuan laughter.

"Really, Geoffrey," his wife protested, "you're behaving strangely."

Sir Geoffrey was unrepentant in his mirth. He was a double fanatic: of detective novels and bridge. Conan Doyle, Agatha Christie, Erle Stanley Gardner, the lot: he had them all almost by heart. Bridge, however, was the joy of his life. For two of his three years at

Oxford he had captained the bridge club against Cambridge.

"Never mind, my dear," he said with a very pleased smile. "I wouldn't have missed the crab salad or the nightmare for a dinner at the Coq d'Or in the West End. I've played the hand of my life: a double, miracle takeout bid against tall detective stories; and the even taller stories that come so frequently out of good old Africa."

EMENTE

by Onuora Ossie Enekwe

Onuora Ossie Enekwe *was born in 1942 in Affa of Igbo parentage. He studied English at the University of Nigeria and earned his PhD in theater arts at Columbia University in 1982. He wrote* Broken Pots, *a collection of poetry, in 1977;* Come Thunder, *a novel, in 1984; and,* Igbu Masks: The Oneness of Ritual and Theatre *in 1987. His short stories and poems have been widely published in Africa, America, and Europe. He is also the editor of* Okike: An African Journal of New Writings.

I T WAS A DULL depressing morning worsened by my indisposition and the hospital environment. Anxious to see the doctor, all the patients crowded by the door; I leaned on a wooden balcony overlooking the open field between the wards and administrative buildings of the General Hospital. It was mildly cold, I remember quite clearly. Before me in a disorganized queue were women standing side-by-side with their children or carrying their babies with sunken or swollen cheeks. Some sat on a bench by the corridor. There were a few old and young men and boys and a number of girls, not particularly attractive. Most of the time, I gazed outside at the lush flowers that edged the small hospital field, my mind wandering with the languid and truant memories of my teenage existence. A feeling of ennui had affected me during my first vacation as an undergraduate—an empty, jobless holiday.

A girl approached this group. She was dressed in her college uniform. I don't know why she attracted me so much, but she was pretty enough to enliven the group. Her lips and legs made me think about love. For a while, I forgot about my indisposition, and about the doctor. I wished to talk to her and to be her friend. I imagined myself in her school on one of their visiting days. She would come smiling into the visitors' room. Sometimes, we might even go out together and do all the things that lovers do, like wandering from the well-lit corridors into dark flower-edged enclosures. There we would sniff and moisten each other's lips. Love is a wonderful thing.

But I noticed that she was uneasy. She inclined forward a little and placed her right palm on her chest just above her breasts that were pushed out like cocoa pods. I felt like going over to her and asking her what the matter was, but my legs would not move. I was wary of female insults. She could rebuff me and make me sicker than I was. Soon, however, it was obvious that she was in pain. She was beginning to sag forward. A couple of people caught hold of her. One of them knocked at the doctor's office door. A nurse opened the door and frowned.

"She's an emergency," one of the patients blurted out. The nurse stepped out of the door and put her right arm around the sick girl's waist and led her into the doctor's room. As I stood there, I wondered what must be wrong, and felt great pity for her. When she came out, about five minutes later, I looked close at her face for the first time. She was still in pain, but seemed to be managing. She was still bent slightly forward, her arm on her temple. As I followed her, I dared not stop or talk to her. Because I did not want people to know I was following her, I allowed at least thirty feet between us. She was hurrying toward the gate leading to the wards. When she got there, she showed her paper to the gate man and was immediately admitted by the latter pointing toward one of the wards at the left of the long corridor between the wards. When I tried to go through the gate, the gate man said, "Wey your admit card?"

"I don't have any. I'm going to see somebody," I said, watching with the corner of my eyes to see which of the wards the girl would enter.

||||||||||||||||||||||||||||||||||||||||||||||||||||||||||||||||||||||||||||||||||||||||||||||||||||||||||||||||||||||||||||||||||||||

"This is no visiting time," the gate man said. "If you want to see somebody come between four and five."

I stood there for a little while wondering what to do. I did not return to the doctor's office. I went straight home to wait till four o'clock when I could see her. I lay in bed and tried to read, but the memory of the sick girl kept bothering me. I tried to forget her by reminding myself that she was after all a stranger, one single individual among blundering, suffering, dying humanity. But there is something terrible in the suffering of young people, especially women, particularly beautiful ones. I looked forward to visiting the hospital to find out what had happened to this girl. I looked forward to seeing her well and happy to see me. Maybe the doctor would soon send her back to school.

At exactly four o'clock, I was at the gate of the General Hospital. As the gate man eased open the gate, my heart began to throb like conga drums. I was going to see this girl as she lay in bed. I would say, How are you? I would tell how I noticed and followed her in the morning. I was assuming that she would respond, that a lonely sick girl would be easily amenable to friendship, but she might very well become rude. You never can tell when a girl has a devil in her. As I came through the main door of the rectangular ward, my legs began to weaken like the legs of a robot made of rubber. Nevertheless, I proceeded. To a nurse sitting in an open space before the main hall, I said, "Where is the girl from the Women's College who was admitted this morning?" The nurse stood up, came toward the corridor and pointed at a bed to which I advanced. The sick girl was in great pain; I could tell right away. Her face was sweaty, and as stolid as a statue hewn out of ebony rock. Her eyes did not perceive me. They glared at me, like the masks of Ikot Ekpene. But, she smiled, or rather, she tried to smile. I wondered why she smiled. Was it part of the sickness —the way in which skulls, shorn of skin, grin at the sky? My heart pounded like burial drums.

"How are you?"

"I am very very sick." My pounding heart relaxed.

"Sorry. . . . What's wrong with you?"

"Tetanus," she replied in a languid voice. *Tetanus* the dreadful disease! My heartbeat missed a little. I felt as if I were standing before a corpse.

"There is nobody who cares for me," she added. "I am all alone." She sounded like one being sucked into a chasm of perpetual darkness and nightmare where she would be totally extinguished. She did not want that to happen. Only another human being could save her.

"What's your name?" I said softly, looking into her face now taking on the dead color of gray marble.

"Emente," she said, tears oozing from around her eyes.

"I will come to see you often," I said, hurriedly, almost panic-stricken. As I left I said to myself: "I won't come here anymore."

II

But next day I stood there, confused and unsure of what to say. My gaze wandered all over the ward, seeing many other girls and young children lying side-by-side in white rows on high beds with deep mattresses and big poles. Finally, I wanted to find out if she had improved since the first day.

"Emente, how do you feel now?"

"I don't know," she said. The words seemed to leak out of her tensed-up body. Her eyes were slowly becoming as dull as weather-beaten pebbles by the seashore.

"I have brought you bread and oranges; shall I put them in your locker?"

"Y-e-s," she said, her voice husky, and dry like languid breeze over sleeping sand.

"Thank you," she whispered, as I put the bread and oranges in the locker.

"I'm all alone here. There's nobody to look after me," she continued, her voice like a ripple in a pond. "My people are all in Uyo. I am alone here. There is nobody to care for me."

"What of your classmates in Women's College?"

"None of them has come, or inquired of me. I'm all alone here."
She was trying to clarify her wretchedness so that I would not abandon her. She was struggling to take hold of me by her willpower. She
was clutching at anybody. She did not care who it was. From now my
romantic zeal was gradually being superseded by mere sympathy.
Much as I was disgusted by the hospital environment including her
degenerating frame, I could not help feeling that she was totally dependent on me. She was no longer what she seemed the first day. Her
face had taken on the ashen appearance of a dead leaf in Harmattan.
Before I departed that day, I assured her that I would be back.

III

I kept my promise two days later. It is futile for me to try to describe
the anxiety which tore at me until my nerves jarred like rusted guitar
strings. After the last visit, I had begun to feel that Emente would die;
after all I had never heard of anyone surviving the dreadful disease
which had waylaid her. I had to go because my conscience would not
tolerate a neglect of a lonely, miserable wretchedly sick girl. If I had
followed her, it would have been easier to forget her. The moment I
spoke with her, I had created a bond which was difficult to break
without doing havoc to my heart. Getting to know people makes one
susceptible to empathy. If you do not want to bother with some people it is best to keep them "off your clouds." She was not on her bed.
She is dead, was the first thought to come to my mind. They have
carried her to the mortuary. Better go home, foolish boy! Go home!
She is dead. You have done your best. My face was flushed with
sweat. It would have been sensible to seek out a nurse and inquire
about Emente but I was too weak to face an announcement of her
death. I could not stand it.

So there I stood perplexed and afraid to ask the fatal question, my
heart athrob, athrob, athrob like a funeral drum. She wasn't dead. I
saw her shuffling along toward her bed; a nurse helped her along by
holding her around the waist. My heart began to relax. "Thank

|||||||||||||||||||||||||||||||||||||||||||||||||||||||||||||||||||||||||||||||||||||||||||||||||||||||||||||

God," I said, smiling as she came near. "I went to the toilet," she apologized. As she lay down on her bed, I inquired "How are you today?"

"I don't know," she said. "I've been very lonesome. Why didn't you come yesterday? There is no one to care for me." Her lips were still and hardly moving. Her words seemed to trickle out.

"I am sorry," I said. "I was very busy. How are you feeling now?" I very much wanted her to recover.

"I'm getting very tired. I am very sick."

"Have you eaten?"

"No."

"Why not?"

"I can't open my mouth."

"When did you eat last?"

"Monday." That was two days ago.

"What of the bread I brought you?"

"It's in the locker."

I had to find a way of feeding her. I hurried outside the gate to a small shop in which were sold things ranging from biscuits to plates. I bought two boiled eggs. When I returned to the ward, I broke one and sliced it to tiny bits. I opened the locker and brought out the bread. Standing near Emente's bed, I asked her to open her mouth. I tore off some bread and put it into her mouth but it could not go through her teeth. Her jaws seemed to have been locked permanently. I tore the bread into smaller pieces which managed to slip through a very tiny slit between her lower and upper teeth. This way she managed to eat a little of the bread. I began to pass the egg slices through her teeth. She ate one egg. All this took about thirty minutes. Afterward, I held a cup of water to her mouth. It made a scratchy sound with her teeth. It was very difficult for her to drink, for her tongue was barricaded within her teeth which were adamantine as steel walls. When I left her that day, I was satisfied that I had done well, but I was down-spirited. I was watching a girl die slowly. Her disease seemed to relish the pain that she was writhing under. Some forces seemed to be bent on annihilating Emente. Slowly they locked her jaws so that she could not talk or eat or drink. Her eyes were becoming glassy. I was afraid, so much so that I decided not to return to her. I did not want to watch beauty metamorphose to ugliness and death.

In four days I was back to the hospital. I had to come. I had been worried. I kept feeling that I had betrayed someone who had confidence in me. At the same time, I wanted to find out what had happened to her. Although I wished she was alive and better, I did not expect to see her alive. She was in a really wretched condition. I felt as if I were looking at a living corpse. Her cheeks were sunken so that the lines of her cranium were clearly visible. Her jawbones and eye sockets stuck out like crags. Her muscles seemed to have been eaten up by the incredible disease. What was left was mere skin which clung plasterlike on the contours of her skeleton. Her eyes turned to me in their sockets. Emente was making an effort to turn her head so she could see me. She could not lift her head since it was twisted backward in the shape of a sickle. Her neck stretched tight, all the nerves taut like piano chords. It seemed that the strange disease had been reshaping her, molding her to a form more amenable to its demonic purpose. Her disease was a dehumanizing disease, so merciless and thorough in its disfigurement, that it also cuts off the victim from humanity by making such a one severely abhorrent to human conception of beauty.

With each attack of this disease, Emente writhed and twisted as she tried to wrestle free from the grips of an invisible demon. Her dilated nostrils and her viscid mouth bore witness to a struggle carried on in the deep and lonely regions. From the look in her eyes, it was clear that she had all but lost the battle for human love. She was lonely humanity being smothered at the gates of hell. I find it difficult to describe the feeling I had at that time. I came closer and looked into her face, into the balls of her eyes where God has preserved the perpetual beauty of mankind.

"Emente," I called. "You will soon get better. You will soon get better. You must try."

"Where have you been?" she said in a voice which sounded as if it was coming through a tiny hold of a cavern. "I have been waiting for you to come. I'm all alone. Nobody is caring for me."

"I am sorry," I pleaded. I did not give any reason. Looking at her was punishment enough for my neglect of her. After that day I was convinced that she would die. I must leave... I must stay away, I decided.

I resolved to forget Emente. This I did until one day, three months perhaps after my last visit, I decided to find out what became of her. I was going to ask the nurses about her, and I was prepared for the worst. If she was still alive, I would apologize and make up by being more responsible and consistent. I was totally ashamed of myself. To run away, and then return after three months to ask about Emente seemed belated, to say the least.

When I walked into the ward I felt a momentary chill. The memory of my visits seemed to be recreating the atmosphere in my imagination. Some other girl was in Emente's bed. "She is dead," I mumbled, feeling sick in my stomach. My head seemed to swell like a balloon. What am I to do? I wondered. As I stood there utterly perplexed, a nurse came walking by.

"Excuse me," I stuttered, hardly thinking. "The girl... the girl ... I mean Emente... where... is she?"

The nurse looked at me as if she had despised me since she was born. I must have seemed pathetic, and comic.

"When was she admitted?" she condescended.

"About... about... about three months ago."

"I don't know what you are talking about," she said. "I have no time to waste listening to somebody who wants to know about a patient he never cared about for three months. You are not even sure when she was admitted," she said, looking at me with enough disgust to last me the rest of my life. I said not a word. I turned and walked away, my heart laden with my guilt.

NOORJEHAN

||||||||||||||||||||||||||||||||||||||||||||||

by Ahmed Essop

Ahmed Essop *was born in India. He studied at South
Africa University. His short stories have been published in
various periodicals and his own collection of stories entitled* The Hajji and Other Stories *was awarded the Olive
Schreiner prize in 1979. Mr. Essop then published a novel
entitled* The Visitation (1980). *He has been widely anthologized.*

W HEN I BEGAN MY career as a teacher, Noorjehan spent nine
months in my matriculation English class. I shall always remember
her as a very intelligent pupil, no more than five feet in height, with
a smooth open forehead, hair auburn shading to brown in color,
parted in the middle and the two plaits gathered neatly by mother-of-
pearl clasps on either side of her face. The beauty of her impeccably
fair complexion was set off by the definiteness of her dark eyes. Her
refined blooming appearance, the wraith of a perfume that seemed to
be her constant companion, her literary sensibility, and that subtle
accord that exists between a gifted pupil and a tutor, always filled me
with a singular happiness.

Then suddenly, in early October, Noorjehan left school. A friend
of hers told me that her parents had decided to keep her at home.
That was all I learned and she was no longer a presence. About a
fortnight later I received a letter from her, brought by a maidservant
to my home.

"You must have wondered," she wrote, "why I left school at this

||||||||||||

time of the year. The truth is, my parents are convinced that I shall soon receive a marriage proposal and that in anticipation I should prepare myself. You will appreciate that I have no choice but to obey.

"Last month the go-betweens of the boy (or man?) interested in marrying me came to have a look at me. At first they spoke to my parents in the lounge while I was told to stay in my room. Later my mother asked me to prepare tea and serve the guests. This was a way of allowing them to scrutinize me. There were two women and a man. One of the women smiled at me and the other asked me a few idle questions.

"After they had left, my father said that it would not be long before I was married. I protested, overwhelmed by the prospect of a sudden change in my life. My mother declared that God would punish disobedient children, and in any case who was I to object to the wishes of those who did everything for the happiness of their children?

"Is it possible for you to come and speak to my father and try to dissuade him from forcing me into a marriage I do not want? Forgive me for troubling you, but could you come?"

I went to Noorjehan's home. She lived in a small semidetached house, the outside painted lime green. Her father asked me to enter after I had declared my identity and offered the explanation that I had come, in the ordinary course of my professional duties, to inquire about the absence of one of my pupils.

"She left for a very good reason," said her father, a tall, austere-looking hawk-nosed man. "Noorjehan is going to be engaged shortly."

I said that perhaps it would be wise to allow her to complete her matriculation before she was betrothed, but he waved an impatient hand at me and said:

"Teachers are understandably concerned about their charges, but parents know what is best for their children."

I then said that it did not seem to me reasonable to provide girls with a modern education and then expect them to follow tradition in their private lives.

To this he did not answer but looked at me impassively.

I left. I did not see Noorjehan while I was in the living room. Outside, as I reached the front gate and turned to close it, I saw her standing at a bedroom window with one hand holding aside the froth of a lace curtain. She smiled tepidly and fluttered her fingers good-bye.

After a few days I received another letter from her.

"I am to be engaged at the end of November. The go-betweens were here again to arrange a time and date. While they talked to my parents I sat miserably in my bedroom. You can imagine my feelings when people are closeted, seemingly for hours, deciding on the course of my life. I felt as if I was living two lives, one isolated in the bedroom and later in the kitchen preparing tea for the visitors, the other captured in the living room, the subject of much talk. All that talk about 'me' gave 'me' a kind of significance that frightened me."

After her engagement she wrote again:

"I was engaged two days ago. My future husband came with his family and friends. He brought the usual gifts (which remain in their boxes, unopened) and presented me with a diamond ring which stands on my dressing table and which I cannot, perhaps never will bring myself to wear. What point is there in telling you what he looks like since he is a stranger to me and I cannot love him?

"After they had left I went to my bedroom and cried bitterly. My mother came and tried to comfort me by saying that a girl must marry and what difference does it make whether she marries now or later, or whether she marries a certain man or some other man? 'I never saw your father,' she said, 'until the day of the wedding, and we have been happy. You are very lucky. His family is very wealthy. Your father is only a shop assistant.'"

Shortly afterward, in another letter, Noorjehan made the following confession:

"However much I would like to please my parents, I cannot see myself being married to a man I neither love nor hate, whose welfare will become an object of my lifelong devotion. Such a marriage for me will be a marriage of self-obliteration. I am just not made for this kind of transaction. For some time now a terrible and desperate longing (growing out of my misery and helplessness) seizes me, the longing for 'my prince' to rescue me. Perhaps this longing for a 'prince' is generated by the memory store in me of the magic world of fairy stories told to me during my sapling days at school; or perhaps I am being silly, romantic and sentimental. But you will admit that the girl who meets her 'prince' in the end is lucky."

After several weeks Noorjehan wrote again:

"My wedding day is to be arranged this coming weekend. I know what it will involve. All sorts of preparations will begin, invitations will be sent out, my trousseau will be in the hands of a busy seamstress, everyone will be excited while I will be regarded as an outsider who has little relation to the event. It is in the wedding trappings and its props that people will be interested. When I think of that day I am seized by a strange indefinable fear, you know the sort of fear that comes to one sometimes in dreams when one senses an oblique danger."

I felt sorry for Noorjehan. I could understand her emotional predicament. I had known her to be a girl of precocious intelligence and sensitivity. Now, under pressure from her parents and the conventions of their society, she was reduced to the level of a sacrificial victim. Marriage transactions, although wilting under the force of twentieth-century changes, were still conducted, and I had known of girls who had been pressured into marriage when they were yet mere slips, hardly ready for its coital demands.

On Friday morning I received a very brief letter from her:

"What must I do? What must I do to escape my fate? There is no one to help me. If only my. . ." The letter trailed off without mentioning the redemptive possibility.

Late in the afternoon I received an urgent message from her to meet her at Park Station at seven in the evening.

It was a cold evening—a chill wind had come up from the south —as I waited for her outside the station. Soon a taxi came to a halt and she alighted. I immediately noticed that she had undergone a transformation in her appearance. She had lost weight, seemed a little older and bore a solemn look.

"Thank you for coming," she said in a soft voice.

She wore a green trouser suit. On her wrists were several silver and brass bangles and she wore a necklace of oyster-white beads.

As I felt that it would be callous to ask her immediately where she planned to go, I said it would be warm in the station restaurant.

We sat at a table next to a window. From where we sat we could see the movements of pedestrians in the street, the beams of glossy cars, the mendicant signs of varicolored neon lights, and frosty streetlamps.

"I suppose no one knows that you have left home," I said in a conspiratorial voice, stirring the sugared coffee.

"Only my teacher knows," she answered, "and he should also know that I am taking the eight-thirty train to Cape Town."

"Cape Town?"

"I have an uncle there. I hope he will help me. And even if he does not, who would want to marry a girl who has run away from home . . . ?"

I drank some coffee, musing what the future held in store for my former pupil and acutely pained by her unhappiness. An inner flow of life seemed to be sustaining her in her flight to seek some other world where she could refashion her life.

"Noorjehan," I said, "don't you think you should tell your parents that you will not go through with a wedding?"

"You know that my feelings don't count with them."

I sensed her inordinate bitterness and disappointment at what her parents had done to her young vulnerable life.

"I must go away," she said softly, sipping coffee.

I looked out of the window at the medley of lights in the street and the rectangular gems adorning terraces of windows.

"When do you intend to marry?" she suddenly asked in a sharp hysteria-tainted voice.

Her question, so irrelevant to the situation and so unexpected, left me looking at her in bewilderment and curiosity.

"Not yet," I said, recovering, "but I intend to get engaged soon."

She went on sipping coffee. I detected a tremor in her hand as she held the cup to her lips. It ignited within me a fervent sense of being implicated in her life, and aroused a strange, almost occult feeling that I was withholding some mysterious power in me to protect her and restore her to happiness.

She looked at her watch and said that half an hour remained before her train arrived.

"Please write to me," I said.

"I promise to keep my teacher informed like a dutiful pupil," she said, forcing a tepid smile and replacing the cup in the saucer.

"Noorjehan, I hope you will be happy."

"Thank you," she said, taking her handbag and standing up. "I think we should wait on the platform."

We walked toward the platform and stood there looking at the movements of passengers and porters, the gliding black engines as they entered the station or departed, the hissing of steam and the glowing of furnaces, and at the swift passage of electric trains.

When the train for Cape Town arrived I found an empty compartment for her. I sat down beside her and spoke of some people I knew in Cape Town.

"I shall be glad to meet them," she said. "I spent some school holidays there once, so I should be able to find them."

"Please go to them if you need any help," I said, taking my notebook out of my pocket and jotting down a few names and addresses on a page.

When I looked up to hand her what I had written, I saw her holding her embroidered handkerchief to her eyes.

"You will be happy again, Noorjehan," I said.

I looked around the compartment, at the green leather seats, the cramped space, the oval mirror above the washstand. She would be incarcerated in here for many hours, carrying with her the memory of unfeeling parents and the fear of an uncertain future in a distant city.

She took the handkerchief away from her face, pushed back a few strands of hair with her fingers and looked at me with her dark moist eyes.

As it was about time for the train to depart, I alighted and stood on the platform next to her compartment window.

Punctually at half past eight the train gave its initial jerk and then began to move slowly. Noorjehan gave me her hand for a moment, then lifted it and shouted in a strident schoolgirl's voice: "Good-bye sir! Good-bye sir!" as the train gathered speed and left the station.

Stunned by the formality of her last words, recalling the academic atmosphere of the classroom, I failed for a moment to register her meaning. Then I was overwhelmed by the rebuke implicit in them, and experienced a trenchant sense of guilt for having been so blind to the romantic image of me which she had conceived.

Her words resonated in my mind as I made my way home. I began to feel that they were not only a rebuke, but a cathartic rejection of me from her innermost self.

BLANKETS

||||||||||||||||||||||||||||||||||||||||||||||||

by Alex La Guma

Alex La Guma (1925–1985) is considered one of the most prolific writers of South Africa. As a very young man La Guma entered into political life in his country, so that from 1950 to 1967 he spent a great deal of time in prison or under house arrest. In 1967 he went into exile to England. He was not allowed to publish in South Africa. His works are entitled: A Walk in the Night (1967), And a Three Fold Cord (1964), The Stone Country (1967), In the Fog of the Season's End (1972), and Time of the Butcherbird (1979). The Afro-Asian Writers' Association awarded La Guma the Lotus Prize for Literature in 1973.

CHOKER WOKE UP. THE woman's wiry hair got into his mouth and tasted of stale brilliantine. The old double bed sagged and wobbled when he shifted his weight, and there were dark stains made by heads on the crumpled gray-white pillows, and a rubbed smear of lipstick like a half-healed wound. His mouth felt parched from the drinking of the night before, and he had a headache.

The woman was saying, half asleep, "No, man. No, man." Her body was moist and sweaty under the blanket, and the bed smelled of a mixture of cheap perfume, spilled powder and human bodies mixed with infant urine. The faded curtain over the room window beckoned to him in the hot breeze. In the early, slum-colored light, a torn undergarment hanging from a brass knob was a specter in the room.

Choker felt ill and angry. The unwashed, worn blanket brushed his face and he smelled it with the other smells, and thought vaguely that he had slept under such blankets all his life. He wished he could sleep in a bed in some posh hotel, under fresh-laundered bedding. Then this thought was displaced by desire for a drink of cold beer, even water. He felt irritable, and thrust the bedding from him.

The woman turned beside him under the blanket, protesting in her half-sleep, and Choker sat up, cursing. The agonized sounds of the bedspring woke up the baby who lay in a bathtub on the floor, and it began to cry, its toothless voice rising in a high-pitched wail.

Choker sat on the edge of the bed and cursed the baby and the woman in his mind. He wondered why the hell he had crept in with somebody else's woman in the first place. And she with a bloody baby, too. The child in the tin tub kept on wailing.

"Ah—" he snapped angrily at the infant.

The woman woke up and looked at him, disheveled, from the soiled pillow. "You made such a noise. You woke the child," she chided.

"Ah, hold your mouth," Choker told her angrily. "Get up and see to your damn kid."

He stood up and walked around the bed to find his shirt and trousers. The woman asked, "You going?"

"Of course, yes. You reckon I want to listen to this blerry noise?"

"Well," the woman said crossly, "can I help it? You knew *mos* I had the child."

The baby kept on wailing. Choker looked at it as he pulled on his trousers and buttoned his shirt. "Babies, dammit."

She asked, in a humbler tone, "You coming back?"

"Maybe. Maybe not. I don't know."

"Listen," she said. "Careful when you come, hey? I don't want my man to see you come here. He got an idea you been coming here. He'll maybe do something to you."

Choker sneered: "Him? Jesus, I'll break him in two with my bare hands."

He laughed, standing hugely in the room. He was a big man, with muscles like bulges of steel wire, and great hands. He was brutal and vicious, and used the thick, ropy, grimed hands for hurting rather than for working.

She said, "Awright, man. But even though he left me, he don't like 'nother man coming here. He may be watching out for you."

"The hell with him," Choker growled. "His mother."

The woman said nothing, and climbed out of the jangling bed to attend to the baby. She sat on the edge of the bed in her limp petticoat and suckled it.

She said, "If you wait a little I'll make a little tea."

"Forget it."

Choker looked at her, sneered and shook his head, and then went out.

He walked along the corridor of the house, past the other rooms, frowning irritably against the nagging ache in his head, and the brittle feeling in his mouth and throat. There were holes in the boards of the floor, and he walked as carefully as his heavy body allowed.

In the morning sunlight, outside the smelly house, he headed for the tap in the dry, hollowed-out area which had once been a garden. He drank thirstily for a few moments, and then splashed his face, drying it on the sleeve of his shirt. He thought, To hell with her, I'll be boggered if I go back to that lot.

Around him were the rows of old, crammed houses and tumble-down boxboard-and-tin shanties of the suburban slum. Chickens and dogs picked their way around among the weeds. He made his way idly through the broken streets and pathways. People avoided him, or gave him a casual greeting and passed on quickly, knowing his reputation. He was a drifting hulk, an accursed ship moving through a rotting sargasso.

Choker was passing a walled-in yard when the three men stepped quickly from a gateway behind him. One of them cried, "That's him," and then, before he could turn, pain speared him with red-hot blades. He felt the pain in his head and the pain in his body almost simultaneously, and he fell, cursing. They didn't even wait to examine him, or to try again, but fled swiftly from the reach of the grappling-iron hands, leaving him to bleed in the roadway.

Choker lay in the road and felt the pain and the trickling of blood against his skin. He wanted to get up, but his legs were suddenly useless, and his arms would not lift his body. He lay there, his throbbing mind stubbornly cursing his attackers, while a crowd gathered, everybody talking excitedly.

Somebody said, "Better carry him off the road."

"I don't want nothing to do with it, hey."

"Well, he can't *mos* just lie about there."

"Better go over to the shop and phone for the am'ulance."

"Okay. Did you see them?"

"Look, pally, I didn't see nothing, man."

"Well, pick him up. Look, Freddy, you take his feet. Sampie, you he'p him. Me and Points can take his arms."

Lying there, bleeding and feeling ill, Choker thought—you all, and then he felt himself being lifted roughly. He thought it was a hell of a thing to be so weak all of a sudden. They were bundling him about and he cursed them, and one of them laughed, "Jesus, he's a real tough guy."

Choker lay on the floor of the lean-to in the backyard where they had carried him. It was cooler under the sagging roof, with the pile of assorted junk in one corner: an ancient motor tire, sundry split and warped boxes, and an old enamel display sign with patches like maps of continents on another planet, where the paintwork had worn away, and the dusty footboard of a bed. There was also the smell of dust and chicken droppings in the lean-to.

From outside, beyond a chrome-colored rhomboid of sun, came a clatter of voices. In the yard they were discussing him. Choker opened his eyes, and peering down the length of his body, past the bare, grimy toes, he could see several pairs of legs, male and female, in tattered trousers and laddered stockings.

A man was saying, "... that was coward ... from behind, *mos*."

"*Ja*. But look what he done to others, don't I say?"

Choker thought, To hell with those baskets. To hell with them all.

Somebody had thrown an old blanket over him. It smelled of sweat and dust and having been slept in unwashed, and it was torn

||||||||||||||||||||||||||||||||||||||||||||||||||||||||||||||||||||||||||||||||||||||||||||||||||||||||||||||||||||

and threadbare and stained. He touched the exhausted blanket with thick, grubby fingers. The texture was rough in parts and shiny thin where it had worn away. He was used to blankets like this.

Choker had been stabbed three times, each from behind. Once in the head, then between the shoulder blades, and again in the right side. The bleeding had stopped and there was not much pain. He had been knifed before, admittedly not as badly as this, and he thought, through the faraway pain, The baskets couldn't even do a decent job. He lay there and waited for the ambulance. Blood was drying slowly on the side of his hammered-copper face, and he also had a bad headache.

The voices, now and then raised in laughter, crackled outside, somewhere far away. Feet moved on the rough floor of the yard and a face not unlike that of a brown dog wearing an expired cloth cap, peered in.

"You still awright, Choker? Am'ulance is coming just now, hey."

"—off," Choker said. His voice croaked.

The voice withdrew, laughing: "*Ou* Choker. *Ou* Choker."

Another voice said: "That burg was waiting for him a long time awready."

"*Ja*. But Choker wasn't no good with a knife. Always used his hands, man."

"That was bad enough, I reckon."

The hell with them, Choker thought. He was feeling tired now. The hard grubby fingers, like corroded iron clamps, strayed over the parched field of the blanket. . . . He was being taken down a wet, tarred yard with tough wire netting over the barred windows looking into it. The place smelled of carbolic disinfectant, and the bunch of heavy keys clink-clinked as it swung from the hooked finger of the guard.

They reached a room fitted with shelving which was stacked here and there with piled blankets. "Take two, *jong*," the guard said, and Choker began to rummage through the piles, searching for the thickest and warmest. But the guard, who somehow had a doggish face and wore a disintegrating cloth cap, laughed and jerked him aside, and seizing the nearest blankets, found two at random and flung them at Choker. They were filthy and smelly, and within their folds vermin waited like irregular troops in ambush.

"Come on. Come on. You think I got time to waste?"

"Is cold *mos*, man," Choker said.

But it was not the guard to whom he was talking. He was six years old and his brother, Willie, a year his senior, twisted and turned in the narrow, cramped, sagging bedstead which they shared, dragging the thin cotton blanket from Choker's body. Outside, the rain slapped against the cardboard-patched window, and the wind wheezed through the cracks and corners like an asthmatic old man.

"No, man, Willie, man. You got all the blanket, *jong*."

"Well, I can't he'p it, *mos*, man. Is cold."

"What about me?" Choker whined. "What about me? I'm also cold, *mos*."

Huddled under the blanket, fitted against each other like two pieces of a jigsaw puzzle. . . . The woman's wiry hair got into his mouth and smelled of stale hair oil. There were dark stains made by heads on the gray-white pillow, and a rubbed smear of lipstick like a half-healed wound.

The woman was saying, half-asleep, "You see? You see? What did I tell you?" Her body was moist and sweaty under the blanket; and the blanket and bed smelled of cheap perfume, spilled powder, urine and chicken droppings. The faded curtain beckoned to him in the hot breeze. The woman turned from him under the blanket, muttering, and Choker sat up. The agonized sounds of the bedspring woke the baby in the tin bathtub on the floor, and it began to cry in a high-pitched metallic wail that grew louder and louder. . . .

Choker woke up as the wail grew to a crescendo and then faded quickly as the siren was switched off. Voices still excitedly shattered the sunlight in the yard. Choker saw the skirts of white coats and then the ambulance men were in the lean-to. His head was aching badly, and his wounds were throbbing. His face perspired like a squeezed-out washcloth.

Hands searched his body. One of the ambulance attendants asked: "Do you feel any pain?"

Choker looked at the pink-white face above him, scowling. "No, sir."

The layer of old newspapers on which he was lying was soaked with his blood. "Knife wounds," one of the attendants said. "He isn't bleeding much outside," the other said. "Put on a couple of pressure pads."

He was in midair, carried on a stretcher flanked by a procession of onlookers. Rubber sheeting was cool against his back. The stretcher rumbled into the ambulance and the doors slammed shut, sealing off the spectators. Then the siren whined and rose, clearing a path through the crowd.

Choker felt the vibration of the ambulance through his body as it sped away. His murderous fingers touched the folded edge of the bedding. The sheet over him was white as cocaine, and the blanket was thick and new and warm. He lay still, listening to the siren.

LOOKING FOR A RAIN GOD

||||||||||||||||||||||||||||||||||||||||||||||||||||||||||||||||||||||||||||||||||||||||||||

by Bessie Head

Bessie Head (1937–1986) is considered by some as a
South African writer because she was born in South Africa
and by others as a Botswanian writer since she chose Botswana as her homeland and became a Botswanian citizen.
She escaped South Africa because she would no longer
tolerate the conditions of apartheid. Her novels are entitled: Maru (1971), When Rain Clouds Gather (1969), A
Question of Power (1974), The Collector of Treasure
(1977), and Serowe: Village of the Rain Wind (1981).
The topics of Head's fiction can be classified into two cate-
gories: Village life, which she knew very well, having lived
in a small village in Botswana; and the feeling of bitterness which, because of being both black and a woman in
an oppressive society, she experienced strongly.

IT IS LONELY AT THE lands where the people go to plow. These
lands are vast clearings in the bush, and the wild bush is lonely too.
Nearly all the lands are within walking distance from the village. In
some parts of the bush where the underground water is very near the
surface, people made little rest camps for themselves and dug shallow
wells to quench their thirst while on their journey to their own lands.
They experienced all kinds of things once they left the village. They
could rest at shady watering places full of lush, tangled trees with
delicate pale-gold and purple wildflowers springing up between soft
green moss and the children could hunt around for wild figs and any
berries that might be in season. But from 1958, a seven-year drought

||||||||||||
89

fell upon the land and even the watering places began to look as dismal as the dry open thornbush country; the leaves of the trees curled up and withered; the moss became dry and hard and, under the shade of the tangled trees, the ground turned a powdery black and white, because there was no rain. People said rather humorously that if you tried to catch the rain in a cup it would only fill a teaspoon. Toward the beginning of the seventh year of drought, the summer had become an anguish to live through. The air was so dry and moisture-free that it burned the skin. No one knew what to do to escape the heat and tragedy was in the air. At the beginning of that summer, a number of men just went out of their homes and hung themselves to death from trees. The majority of the people had lived off crops, but for two years past they had all returned from the lands with only their rolled-up skin blankets and cooking utensils. Only the charlatans, incanters, and witch doctors made a pile of money during this time because people were always turning to them in desperation for little talismans and herbs to rub on the plow for the crops to grow and the rain to fall.

The rains were late that year. They came in early November, with a promise of good rain. It wasn't the full, steady downpour of the years of good rain, but thin, scanty, misty rain. It softened the earth and a rich growth of green things sprang up everywhere for the animals to eat. People were called to the village kgotla to hear the proclamation of the beginning of the plowing season; they stirred themselves and whole families began to move off to the lands to plow.

The family of the old man, Mokgobja, were among those who left early for the lands. They had a donkey cart and piled everything onto it, Mokgobja—who was over seventy years old; two little girls, Neo and Boseyong; their mother Tiro and an unmarried sister, Nesta; and the father and supporter of the family, Ramadi, who drove the donkey cart. In the rush of the first hope of rain, the man, Ramadi, and the two women, cleared the land of thornbush and then hedged their vast plowing area with this same thornbush to protect the future crop from the goats they had brought along for milk. They cleared out and deepened the old well with its pool of muddy water and still in this light, misty rain, Ramadi inspanned two oxen and turned the earth over with a hand plow.

The land was ready and plowed, waiting for the crops. At night, the earth was alive with insects singing and rustling about in search of food. But suddenly, by mid-November, the rain fled away; the rain-clouds fled away and left the sky bare. The sun danced dizzily in the sky, with a strange cruelty. Each day the land was covered in a haze of mist as the sun sucked up the last drop of moisture out of the earth. The family sat down in despair, waiting and waiting. Their hopes had run so high; the goats had started producing milk, which they had eagerly poured on their porridge; now they ate plain porridge with no milk. It was impossible to plant the corn, maize, pumpkin and water-melon seeds in the dry earth. They sat the whole day in the shadow of the huts and even stopped thinking, for the rain had fled away. Only the children, Neo and Boseyong, were quite happy in their little-girl world. They carried on with their game of making house like their mother and chattered to each other in light, soft tones. They made children from sticks around which they tied rags, and scolded them severely in an exact imitation of their own mother. Their voices could be heard scolding the day long: "You stupid thing, when I send you to draw water, why do you spill half of it out of the bucket!" "You stupid thing! Can't you mind the porridge pot without letting the porridge burn!" And then they would beat the ragdolls on their bottoms with severe expressions.

The adults paid no attention to this; they did not even hear the funny chatter; they sat waiting for rain; their nerves were stretched to breaking point willing the rain to fall out of the sky. Nothing was important, beyond that. All their animals had been sold during the bad years to purchase food, and of all their herd only two goats were left. It was the women of the family who finally broke down under the strain of waiting for rain. It was really the two women who caused the death of the little girls. Each night they started a weird, high-pitched wailing that began on a low, mournful note and whipped up to a frenzy. Then they would stamp their feet and shout as though they had lost their heads. The men sat quiet and self-controlled; it was important for men to maintain their self-control at all times but their nerve was breaking too. They knew the women were haunted by the starvation of the coming year.

Finally, an ancient memory stirred in the old man, Mokgobja. When he was very young and the customs of the ancestors still ruled the land, he had been witness to a rainmaking ceremony. And he came alive a little, struggling to recall the details which had been buried by years and years of prayer in a Christian church. As soon as the mists cleared a little, he began consulting in whispers with his youngest son, Ramadi. There was, he said, a certain rain god who accepted only the sacrifice of the bodies of children. Then the rain would fall; then the crops would grow, he said. He explained the ritual and as he talked, his memory became a conviction and he began to talk with unshakable authority. Ramadi's nerves were smashed by the nightly wailing of the women and soon the two men began whispering with the two women. The children continued their game: "You stupid thing! How could you have lost the money on the way to the shop! You must have been playing again!"

After it was all over and the bodies of the two little girls had been spread across the land, the rain did not fall. Instead, there was a deathly silence at night and the devouring heat of the sun by day. A terror, extreme and deep, overwhelmed the whole family. They packed, rolling up their skin blankets and pots, and fled back to the village.

People in the village soon noted the absence of the two little girls. They had died at the lands and were buried there, the family said. But people noted their ashen, terror-stricken faces and a murmur arose. What had killed the children, they wanted to know? And the family replied that they had just died. And people said amongst themselves that it was strange that the two deaths had occurred at the same time. And there was a feeling of great unease at the unnatural looks of the family. Soon the police came around. The family told them the same story of death and burial at the lands. They did not know what the children had died of. So the police asked to see the graves. At this, the mother of the children broke down and told everything.

Throughout that terrible summer the story of the children hung like a dark cloud of sorrow over the village, and the sorrow was not assuaged when the old man and Ramadi were sentenced to death for ritual murder. All they had on the statute books was that ritual murder was against the law and must be stamped out with the death penalty. The subtle story of strain and starvation and breakdown was inadmissible evidence at court; but all the people who lived off crops knew in their hearts that only a hair's breadth had saved them from sharing a fate similar to that of the Mokgobja family. They could have killed something to make the rain fall.

A MAN CAN TRY

|||||||||||||||||||||||||||||||||||||||||||||||||||||||||||||||||||

by Eldred D. Jones

Eldred D. Jones *is a short-story writer and the editor of the famous periodical* African Literature Today, *which is now published as an annual survey of literature. His works include*: The Novel in Africa *(1971)*; Poetry in Africa *(1973)*; Focus on Criticism *(1974)*; Drama in Africa *(1976)*; Myth, History and Contemporary African Writers *(1980)*; New Writing, New Approaches *(1981)*.
He lives and works in Sierra Leone.

"WELL, I THINK this is very satisfactory"—old Pa Demba, the paramount chief of Bomp, looked at D.C. Tullock with genuine admiration. "I think you have been very generous to Marie. I really do not see how anyone could have been fairer than you have been—one hundred pounds a year for Marie and a good secondary school education for the boy." Pa Demba turned to Marie: "You should count yourself lucky to have had D.C. Tullock for your husband. I have seen many girls who have lived with men like the D.C. for many years, only to be abandoned at the end without any provision. According to this paper, you and your child have been well provided for. And now you are free to marry anyone you wish. I am going to sign as a witness. Do you agree to the terms?"

As Marie nodded in dumb agreement the tears which had stood poised on the corners of her eyes rolled down her chubby brown cheeks. Tullock looked away through the open office window, and gazed unseeingly at the town beyond. The figure of Marie sitting

|||||||||||||

there stroking the hair of her son Tambah who stood between her knees, was to him a silent indictment. She sat scarcely moving except for her hands which moved so slowly and tenderly along the boy's head that she looked perfectly still. She was like a statue of maternity —mother and child. Tullock thought, she and I have shared in the miracle of creation and here I am about to desert her and the boy. But he persuaded himself that it had to be, although even in the moment of decision he could not avoid condemning himself.

As for Marie, she just sat there stroking her little boy's hair—he had fine silky hair—she was glad that he resembled Tullock in that feature at least. She would always remember him by it. She felt no bitterness at Tullock's departure, only sorrow—intense sorrow. She had known from the first that this moment would come. In their type of relationship, parting was as inevitable as death; but like death, when it actually came, it was still something of a shock. She had served her turn with Tullock. They had been happy within the limits of their relationship for eight years. All the women had called her Marie Tullock, although there was no legal bond between them. Now, Tullock was leaving the service to join his father's law firm— the richer for his experience in Africa. Of course he could not take Marie with him. So he had devised this settlement.

In spite of his generosity by prevailing standards, Tullock felt rather cheap in his own eyes. For unlike some others in his position, he had the uncomfortable habit of judging everyone by a single standard. He could not have disentangled himself from a girl of his own race so easily. He knew this, and the very fact that he could shake off Marie without any complications with a gratuity of his own naming, made him ill at ease with himself.

He, too, had been happy with Marie, at least, quite content with her. She was pretty, cooked well, was affectionate but unobtrusive. True she couldn't read Shakespeare—couldn't read anything at all in fact. The world situation left her completely unmoved, for she knew nothing about what happened outside the town of Bomp where she had lived all her life. In fact to quote Prothero—Old Prothero, the father of the provincial administration—"a barbarian, a pretty barbar-

ian, but a barbarian like the rest of them." It was he who had helped
Tullock solve his little problem, although he did not see what the fuss
was all about. He saw no problem. He had laughed at Tullock's
solemnity. "Look, my boy!" he had said, with his hand on Tullock's
shoulder, "I've had a woman—and children—in every district I've
worked in. The only rules are—never get your heart involved and
never move with a woman from one district to another; creates no
end of trouble. After each station, I just paid them off; no problem at
all. Glad of the money they were, too. They were soon snapped up
by the native burghers of the district. Don't let this worry you, boy.
Pay Marie off. She'll forget you soon enough. And as for you, once
on the boat you'll soon forget about her."

Tullock had secretly wondered how one who was so meticulous
over the jot and title of colonial regulations could be so casual over
matters of the heart. But he checked his flow of self-righteousness.
Who was he to judge anyway? He was no better than Prothero—in
fact he was worse. For while Prothero had never thought his relationship with African women came within his ordinary moral code, he
knew that what he was doing was wrong. He had, however, taken
Prothero's advice and had arranged a settlement for Marie. He had
taken infinite trouble to make it legal—an inadequate sop to his
conscience—but he thought it was the least he could do. So here
they were signing the agreement.

Pa Demba signed his name, rose and took his leave, still com-
mending Tullock's generosity. The three who were left sat on in silence. There seemed to be nothing to say. Tullock was overcome with
shame, Marie with grief. Tambah was just bewildered. He knew his
mother's tears were caused by Tullock but he did not know how.

"Well, Marie, this is good-bye."

Marie's eyes welled, her bosom heaved, but she uttered not a
sound. She had dreaded this moment almost as soon as she realized
how much she liked the feel of Tullock's hair; how longingly she
listened for the honk of his horn as he swerved madly into the compound from the office. In her moments of greatest happiness with

him she had always felt the foretaste of this parting in her mouth. Now it was here.

"I have got the court messengers to take your things to your uncle's house. Good-bye, Marie; you know I have to go, don't you?"

Marie nodded and tried to smile. She turned suddenly to the door, grasped Tambah's hand and hurried away. Tullock watched her disappear down the drive without once turning to look back. He knew that a part of his heart had gone with her.

Trevor Tullock's decision to return home was not as sudden as it seemed—the reason had been on his mind for quite some time. He had been engaged for three years, to the daughter of his father's oldest friend—a London stockbroker. Only the omnivorousness of the human mind could have accommodated two such different women as Marie and Denise, even at different times. Marie, African, illiterate, soft and melting, was entirely devoted to Tullock—she lived only for him. Denise was English, sophisticated, highly educated and a very forward member of the central office of her political party. She was intensely alert and held strong convictions on almost every subject, particularly the rights of women. She had made it quite clear that she had no intention of leaving her life in England and burying herself in the wilds of Africa. She was too engrossed in what was going on in England. In her own country she was part of the scene. She was always addressing women's gatherings, organizing demonstrations, canvassing on behalf of the party from door to door, and this sort of work she could not bear to leave. So Trevor had to make up his mind to return home if he wanted to marry her. He had put it off long enough already and had just been helped to make up his mind by a long pleading letter from home. "What would people think?" his mother had pleaded. . . . So Trevor had decided that he could decently put it off no longer.

In the whirl of official farewells and the thousand and one things he had to do to catch the boat, Trevor Tullock had had little time to think of his future life. He had taken it all for granted. On the boat, however, he could not stop himself from thinking. But it was the image of Marie that kept coming to his mind, pushing out that of Denise—Marie sitting with Tambah between her knees. He did not think very much about the boy and even this worried him, for after all he was his own flesh and blood. He tried to shut off thoughts of Marie, but he found it difficult. He tried because he thought it was his duty. But he could not. He tried to drown his thoughts in drink, but that only made him morbid. He began to look forward to his arrival in England—England with its distractions and Denise!

Denise! This intrusion of Denise into his thoughts startled him. Now that he started thinking about her, doubts about their relationship came rushing into his mind. Doubts of the most fundamental kind. Did he really want to marry Denise? He brushed the question aside. It did not matter. He had to. So the boat bore him speedily along to a fate from which his mind equally speedily shrank.

At Liverpool, Trevor leaned over the rails and peered into the Mersey mist, trying to discern the faces of the visitors on the balcony. There was his mother and yes—beside her was Denise.

His mother waved enthusiastically and Denise put up her right hand in a jerky, almost official act of welcome. Her trim tweeded businesslike figure, through sheer force of contrast, brought back the image of the brown, loose-robed, welcoming frame of Marie. His life with her had been relaxed and easy. His home life in Africa had been so dramatically different from his office life. He had never had to argue with Marie. He was always sure of her willing obedience. Denise, on the other hand, had a quicksilver mind. Life with her was a constant mental tug-of-war. That was in fact the very quality in their relationship which had so exhilarated him during their undergraduate days. Now, the thought of a lifetime with her gave him a chilly feeling. The change from one woman to the other was like the physical change he had just made—exchanging the warmth and relaxation of Africa for the chill, bracing air of England. That economical wave of Denise's, symbolic of her detachment and her control over herself, made Trevor realize with horrid clarity that while he had changed, she had not. How had he changed? He tried to think. He had not lost his love for books; he still read them though, now, with a

less belligerent attitude toward their authors than before. No doubt
Denise, with whom he had cut many an author to pieces, would say
that he was less acutely critical; but he still enjoyed reading—probably even more than before. What else? He certainly drank more, and
more often than before. His drinking action was now a hearty swal-
low compared with the old sip and savor of those rather pretentious
wine-tasting parties. He was now more concerned with the contents
of the bottle than with the suggestions on the label. No doubt Denise
would say his palate had coarsened. The more he thought, the more
Trevor saw that life with Denise would now have to be one long
never-ending effort to live up to a life he no longer believed in . . .
"till death us do part."

He braced himself, picked up his bags, and strode down the gang-
way. "A man can try," he muttered to himself, already aiming a peck
at Denise's proffered cheek.

THE WINNER

by Barbara Kimenye

Barbara Kimenye *is from Uganda. Her books* Kalasanda
(1965) and Kalasanda Revisited *(1966) are collections of
short stories about Uganda's village life. She is a prolific
writer of children's books, among which is the famous*
Smugglers. *Data on her personal life is not very accessible
since the author feels that her readers are interested only in
her literary work, not her private experiences. She worked
in government organizations and as a journalist for the*
Uganda Nation.

W HEN PIUS NDAWULA won the football pools, overnight he
seemed to become the most popular man in Buganda. Hosts of relatives converged upon him from the four corners of the kingdom:
cousins and nephews, nieces and uncles, of whose existence he had
never before been aware, turned up in Kalasanda by the busload,
together with crowds of individuals who, despite their downtrodden
appearance, assured Pius that they and they alone were capable of
seeing that his money was properly invested—preferably in their own
particular businesses! Also lurking around Pius's unpretentious mud
hut were newspaper reporters, slick young men weighed down with
cameras and sporting loud checked caps or trilbies set at conspicu-
ously jaunty angles, and serious young men from Radio Uganda who
were anxious to record Pius's delight at his astonishing luck for the
edification of the Uganda listening public.

The rest of Kalasanda were so taken by surprise that they could only call and briefly congratulate Pius before being elbowed out of the way by his more garrulous relations. All, that is to say, except Pius's greatest friend Salongo, the custodian of the Ssabalangira's tomb. He came and planted himself firmly in the house, and nobody attempted to move him. Almost blind, and very lame, he had tottered out with the air of a stout stick. Just to see him arrive had caused a minor sensation in the village, for he hadn't left the tomb for years. But recognizing at last a chance to house Ssabalangira's remains in a state befitting his former glory, made the slow, tortuous journey worthwhile to Salongo.

Nantondo hung about long enough to have her picture taken with Pius. Or rather, she managed to slip beside him just as the cameras clicked, and so it was that every Uganda newspaper, on the following day, carried a front-page photograph of "Mr. Pius Ndawula and his happy wife," a caption that caused Pius to shake with rage and threaten legal proceedings, but over which Nantondo gloated as she proudly showed it to everybody she visited.

"Tell us, Mr. Ndawula, what do you intend to do with all the money you have won . . . ?"

"Tell us, Mr. Ndawula, how often have you completed pools coupons . . . ?"

"Tell us . . . Tell us . . . Tell us . . ."

Pius's head was reeling under this bombardment of questions, and he was even more confused by Salongo's constant nudging and muttered advice to "Say nothing!" Nor did the relatives make things easier. Their persistent clamoring for his attention, and the way they kept shoving their children under his nose, made it impossible for him to think, let alone talk.

It isn't at all easy, when you have lived for sixty-five years in complete obscurity, to adjust yourself in a matter of hours to the role of a celebrity, and the strain was beginning to tell.

Behind the hut—Pius had no proper kitchen—gallons of tea were being boiled, whilst several of the female cousins were employed in ruthlessly hacking down the bunches of *matoke* from his meager plantains, to cook food for everybody. One woman—she had introduced herself as Cousin Sarah—discovered Pius's hidden store of banana beer, and dished it out to all and sundry as though it were her own. Pius had become very wary of Cousin Sarah. He didn't like the way in which she kept loudly remarking that he needed a woman about the place, and he was even more seriously alarmed when suddenly Salongo gave him a painful dig in the ribs and muttered, "You'll have to watch that one—she's a sticker!"

Everybody who came wanted to see the telegram that announced Pius's win. When it had arrived at the Ggombolola Headquarters—the postal address of everyone residing within a radius of fifteen miles—Musisi had brought it out personally, delighted to be the bearer of such good tidings. At Pius's request he had gone straightaway to tell Salongo, and then back to his office to send an acknowledgment on behalf of Pius to the pools firm, leaving the old man to dream rosy dreams. An extension of his small coffee *shamba*, a new roof on his house—or maybe an entirely new house—concrete blocks this time, with a veranda perhaps. Then there were hens. Salongo and he had always said there was money in hens these days, now that the women ate eggs and chicken; not that either of them agreed with the practice. Say what you liked, women who ate chicken and eggs were fairly asking to be infertile! That woman welfare officer who came around snooping occasionally, tried to say it was all nonsense, that chicken meat and eggs made bigger and better babies. Well, they might look bigger and better, but nobody could deny that they were fewer! Which only goes to show.

But news spreads fast in Africa—perhaps the newspapers have contacts in the pools offices. Anyway, before the telegram had even reached Pius, announcements were appearing in the local newspapers, and Pius was still quietly lost in his private dreams when the first batch of visitors arrived. At first he was at a loss to understand what was happening. People he hadn't seen for years and only recognized with difficulty fell upon him with cries of joy. "Cousin Pius, the family are delighted!" "Cousin Pius, why have you not visited us all this time?"

Pius was pleased to see his nearest and dearest gathered around him. It warmed his old heart once more to find himself in the bosom of his family, and he welcomed them effusively. The second crowd to arrive were no less well received, but there was a marked coolness on the part of their forerunners.

However, as time had gone by and the flood of strange faces had gained momentum, Pius's *shamba* had come to resemble a political meeting. All to be seen from the door of the house was a turbulent sea of white *kanzus* and brilliant *busutis*, and the house itself was full of people and tobacco smoke.

The precious telegram was passed from hand to hand until it was reduced to a limp fragment of paper with the lettering partly obliterated: not that it mattered very much, for only a few members of the company could read English.

"Now, Mr. Ndawula, we are ready to take the recording." The speaker was a slight young man wearing a checked shirt. "I shall ask you a few questions, and you simply answer me in your normal voice." Pius looked at the leather box with its two revolving spools, and licked his lips. "Say nothing!" came a hoarse whisper from Salongo. The young man steadfastly ignored him, and went ahead in his best BBC manner. "Well, Mr. Ndawula, first of all let me congratulate you on your winning the pools. Would you like to tell our listeners what it feels like suddenly to find yourself rich?" There was an uncomfortable pause, during which Pius stared mesmerized at the racing spools and the young man tried frantically to span the gap by asking, "I mean, have you any plans for the future?" Pius swallowed audibly, and opened his mouth to say something, but shut it again when Salongo growled, "Tell him nothing!"

The young man snapped off the machine, shaking his head in exasperation. "Look here, sir, all I want you to do is to say something —I'm not asking you to make a speech! Now, I'll tell you what. I shall ask you again what it feels like suddenly to come into money, and you say something like 'It was a wonderful surprise, and naturally I feel very pleased'—and will you ask your friend not to interrupt! Got it? Okay, off we go!"

The machine was again switched on, and the man brightly put his question, "Now, Mr. Ndawula, what does it feel like to win the pools?" Pius swallowed, then quickly chanted in a voice all off key, "It was a wonderful surprise and naturally I feel very happy and will you ask your friend not to interrupt!" The young man nearly wept. This happened to be his first assignment as a radio interviewer, and it looked like it would be his last. He switched off the machine and mourned his lusterless future, groaning. At that moment Cousin Sarah caught his eye. "Perhaps I can help you," she said. "I am Mr. Ndawula's cousin." She made this pronouncement in a manner that suggested Pius had no others. The young man brightened considerably. "Well, madam, if you could tell me something about Mr. Ndawula's plans, I would be most grateful." Cousin Sarah folded her arms across her imposing bosom, and when the machine again started up, she was off. Yes, Mr. Ndawula was very happy about the money. No, she didn't think he had any definite plans on how to spend it—with all these people about he didn't have time to think. Yes, Mr. Ndawula lived completely alone, but she was prepared to stay and look after him for as long as he needed her. Here a significant glance passed between the other women in the room, who clicked their teeth and let out long "Eeeeeeehs!" of incredulity. Yes, she believed she was Mr. Ndawula's nearest living relative by marriage...

Pius listened to her confident aplomb with growing horror, while Salongo frantically nudged him and whispered, "There! What did I tell you! That woman's a sticker!"

Around three in the afternoon, *matoke* and tea were served, the *matoke*, on wide fresh plantain leaves, since Pius owned only three plates, and the tea in anything handy—tin cans, old jars, etc.—because he was short of cups too. Pius ate very little, but he was glad of the tea. He had shaken hands with so many people that his arm ached, and he was tired of the chatter and the comings and goings in his house of all these strangers. Most of all he was tired of Cousin Sarah, who insisted on treating him like an idiot invalid. She kept everybody else at bay, as far as she possibly could, and when one woman plonked a sticky fat baby on his lap, Cousin Sarah dragged the child away as though it were infectious. Naturally, a few cross words were exchanged between Sarah and the fond mother, but by this time Pius was past caring.

Yosefu Mukasa and Kibuka called in the early evening, when some of the relatives were departing with effusive promises to come again tomorrow. They were both alarmed at the weariness they saw on Pius's face. The old man looked utterly worn out, his skin gray and sickly. Also, they were a bit taken aback by the presence of Cousin Sarah, who pressed them to take tea and behaved in every respect as though she were mistress of the house. "I believe my late husband knew you very well, sir," she told Yosefu. "He used to be a Miruka chief in Buyaga County. His name was Kivumbi." "Ah, yes," Yosefu replied, "I remember Kivumbi very well indeed. We often hunted together. I was sorry to hear of his death. He was a good man." Cousin Sarah shrugged her shoulders. "Yes, he was a good man. But what the Lord giveth, He also taketh away." Thus was the late Kivumbi dismissed from the conversation.

Hearing all this enabled Pius to define the exact relationship between himself and Cousin Sarah, and even by Kiganda standards it was virtually nonexistent, for the late Kivumbi had been the stepson of one of Pius's cousins.

"Your stroke of luck seems to have exhausted you, Pius," Kibuka remarked, when he and Yosefu were seated on the rough wooden chairs brought forth by Cousin Sarah.

Salongo glared at the world in general and snarled, "Of course he is exhausted! Who wouldn't be with all these scavengers collected to pick his bones?" Pius hushed him as one would a child. "No, no, Salongo. It is quite natural that my family should gather round me at a time like this. Only I fear I am perhaps a little too old for all this excitement."

Salongo spat expertly through the open doorway, narrowly missing a group of guests who were preparing to bed down, and said, "That woman doesn't think he's too old. She's out to catch him. I've seen her type elsewhere!"

Yosefu's mouth quirked with amusement at the thought that "elsewhere" could only mean the Ssabalangira's tomb, which Salongo had guarded for the better part of his adult life. "Well, she's a fine woman," he remarked. "But see here, Pius," he went on, "don't be offended by my proposal, but wouldn't it be better if you came and stayed with us at Mutunda for tonight? Miriamu would love to have you, and you look as though you need a good night's rest, which you wouldn't get here—those relatives of yours outside are preparing a fire and are ready to dance the night away!"

"I think that's a wonderful idea!" said Cousin Sarah, bouncing in to remove the tea cups. "You go with Mr. Mukasa, Cousin Pius. The change will do you as much good as the rest. And don't worry about your home—I shall stay here and look after things." Pius hesitated. "Well, I think I shall be all right here—I don't like to give Miriamu any extra work. . . ." Salongo muttered. "Go to Yosefu's. You don't want to be left alone in the house with that woman—there's no knowing what she might get up to . . . !" "I'll pack a few things for you, Pius," announced Cousin Sarah and bustled off before anything more could be said, pausing only long enough to give Salongo a look that was meant to wither him on the spot.

So Pius found himself being driven away to Mutunda in Yosefu's car, enjoying the pleasant sensation of not having to bother about a thing. Salongo too had been given a lift to as near the tomb as the car could travel, and his wizened old face was contorted into an irregular smile, for Pius had promised to help him build a new house for the Ssabalangira. For him the day had been well spent, despite Cousin Sarah.

Pius spent an enjoyable evening with the Mukasas. They had a well-cooked supper, followed by a glass of cold beer as they sat back and listened to the local news on the radio. Pius had so far relaxed as to tell the Mukasas modestly that he had been interviewed by Radio Uganda that morning, and when Radio Newsreel was announced they waited breathlessly to hear his voice. But instead of Pius, Cousin Sarah came booming over the air. Until that moment the old man had completely forgotten the incident of the tape recording. In fact, he had almost forgotten Cousin Sarah. Now it all came back to him with a shiver of apprehension. Salongo was right. That woman did mean business! It was a chilling thought. However, it didn't cause him to lose any sleep. He slept like a cherub, as if he hadn't a care in the world.

Because he looked so refreshed in the morning, Miriamu insisted on keeping him at Mutunda for another day. "I know you feel better, but after seeing you yesterday, I think a little holiday with us will do you good. Go home tomorrow, when the excitement has died down a bit," she advised.

Soon after lunch, as Pius was taking a nap in a chair on the veranda, Musisi drove up in the Land Rover, with Cousin Sarah by his side. Miriamu came out to greet them, barely disguising her curiosity about the formidable woman about whom she had heard so much. The two women sized each other up and decided to be friends.

Meanwhile, Musisi approached the old man. "Sit down, son." Pius waved him to a chair at his side. "Miriamu feeds me so well it's all I can do to keep awake."

"I am glad you are having a rest, sir." Musisi fumbled in the pocket of his jacket. "There is another telegram for you. Shall I read it?" The old man sat up expectantly and said, "If you'll be so kind."

Musisi first read the telegram in silence, then he looked at Pius and commented, "Well, sir, I'm afraid it isn't good news."

"Not good news? Has somebody died?"

Musisi smiled. "Well, no. It isn't really as bad as that. The thing is, the pools firm say that owing to an unfortunate oversight they omitted to add, in the first telegram, that the prize money is to be shared among three hundred other people."

Pius was stunned. Eventually he murmured, "Tell me, how much does that mean I shall get?"

"Three hundred into seventeen thousand pounds won't give you much over a thousand shillings."

To Musisi's astonishment, Pius sat back and chuckled. "More than a thousand shillings!" he said. "Why, that's a lot of money!"

"But it's not, when you expected so much more!"

"I agree. And yet, son, what would I have done with all those thousands of pounds? I am getting past the age when I need a lot."

Miriamu brought a mat onto the veranda and she and Cousin Sarah made themselves comfortable near the men. "What a disappointment!" cried Miriamu, but Cousin Sarah sniffed and said, "I agree with Cousin Pius. He wouldn't know what to do with seventeen thousand pounds, and the family would be hanging round his neck forevermore!"

At mention of Pius's family, Musisi frowned. "I should warn you, sir, those relatives of yours have made a terrific mess of your *shamba* —your plantains have been stripped—and Mrs. Kivumbi here," nodding at Sarah, "was only just in time to prevent them digging up your sweet potatoes!"

"Yes, Cousin Pius," added Sarah. "It will take us some time to put the *shamba* back in order. They've trodden down a whole bed of young beans."

"Oh, dear," said Pius weakly. "This is dreadful news."

"Don't worry. They will soon disappear when I tell them there is no money, and then I shall send for a couple of my grandsons to come and help us do some replanting." Pius could not help but admire the way Sarah took things in her stride.

Musisi rose from his chair. "I'm afraid I can't stay any longer, so I will go now and help Cousin Sarah clear the crowd, and see you tomorrow to take you home." He and Sarah climbed back into the Land Rover and Sarah waved energetically until the vehicle was out of sight.

"Your cousin is a fine woman," Miriamu told Pius, before going indoors. Pius merely grunted, but for some odd reason he felt the remark to be a compliment to himself.

All was quiet at Pius's home when Musisi brought him home next day. He saw at once that his *shamba* was well-nigh wrecked, but his drooping spirits quickly revived when Sarah placed a mug of steaming tea before him, and sat on a mat at his feet, explaining optimistically how matters could be remedied. Bit by bit he began telling her what he planned to do with the prize money, ending with, "Of course, I shan't be able to do everything now, especially since I promised Salongo something for the tomb."

Sarah poured some more tea and said, "Well, I think the roof should have priority. I noticed last night that there are several leaks. And whilst we're about it, it would be a good idea to build another room on and a small outside kitchen. Mud and wattle is cheap enough, and then the whole place can be plastered. You can still go ahead and extend your coffee. And as for hens, well, I have six good layers at home, as well as a fine cockerel. I'll bring them over!"

Pius looked at her in silence for a long time. She is a fine looking woman, he thought, and that blue *busuti* suits her. Nobody would ever take her for a grandmother—but why is she so anxious to throw herself at me?

"You sound as if you are planning to come and live here," he said at last, trying hard to sound casual.

Sarah turned to face him and replied, "Cousin Pius, I shall be very frank with you. Six months ago my youngest son got married and brought his wife to live with me. She's a very nice girl, but somehow I can't get used to having another woman in the house. My other son is in Kampala, and although I know I would be welcome there, he too has a wife, and three children, so if I went there I wouldn't be any better off. When I saw that bit about you in the paper, I suddenly remembered—although I don't expect you to— how you were at my wedding and so helpful to everybody. Well, I thought to myself, here is somebody who needs a good housekeeper, who needs somebody to keep the leeches off, now that he has come into money. I came along right away to take a look at you, and I can see I did the right thing. You do need me." She hesitated for a moment, and then said, "Only you might prefer to stay alone . . . I'm so used to having my own way, I never thought about that before."

Pius cleared his throat. "You're a very impetuous woman," was all he could find to say.

A week later, Pius wandered out to the tomb and found Salongo busily polishing the Ssabalangira's weapons. "I thought you were dead," growled the custodian, "it is so long since you came here—

but then, this tomb thrives on neglect. Nobody cares that one of Buganda's greatest men lies here."

"I have been rather busy," murmured Pius. "But I didn't forget my promise to you. Here! I've brought you a hundred shillings, and I only wish it could have been more. At least it will buy a few cement blocks."

Salongo took the money and looked at it as if it were crawling with lice. Grudgingly he thanked Pius and then remarked, "Of course, you will find life more expensive now that you are keeping a woman in the house."

"I suppose Nantondo told you." Pius smiled sheepishly.

"Does it matter who told me?" the custodian replied. "Anyway, never say I didn't warn you. Next thing she'll want will be a ring marriage!"

Pius gave an uncertain laugh. "As a matter of fact, one of the reasons I came up here was to invite you to the wedding—it's next month."

Salongo carefully laid down the spear he was rubbing upon a piece of clean barkcloth and stared at his friend as if he had suddenly grown another head. "What a fool you are! And all this stems from your scribbling noughts and crosses on a bit of squared paper! I knew it would bring no good! At your age you ought to have more sense. Well, all I can advise is that you run while you still have the chance!"

For a moment Pius was full of misgivings. Was he, after all, behaving like a fool? Then he thought of Sarah, and the wonders she had worked with his house and his *shamba* in the short time they had been together. He felt reassured. "Well, I'm getting married, and I expect to see you at both the church and the reception, and if you don't appear, I shall want to know the reason why!" He was secretly delighted at the note of authority in his voice, and Salongo's face was the picture of astonishment. "All right," he mumbled, "I shall try and come. Before you go, cut a bunch of bananas to take back to your good lady, and there might be some cabbage ready at the back. I suppose I've got to hand it to her! She's the real winner!"

BLACK SKIN WHAT MASK

|||||||||||||||||||||||||||||||||||||||||||||||||||||||||||||||||||||||||||||||||||||||

by Dambudzo Marechera

Dambudzo Marechera (1955–1987) *grew up in Zimbabwe. After being expelled from Rhodesia University he was awarded a scholarship to Oxford. The collection of short stories* The House of Hunger *appeared for the first time in 1978 with Heinemann's famous African Writers Series, which was republished in 1980 in Zimbabwe after the country gained independence. The book was warmly acclaimed by critics and readership and it was awarded the fiction prize of Guardian 1979. His second book,* Black Sunlight (1980), *confirmed the writer's gift and exposed his bitterness about urban life in the "House of Hunger"—Rhodesia. His last novel,* Mindblast, *was published in Harare in 1984.*

M Y SKIN STICKS OUT A mile in all the crowds around here. Every time I go out I feel it tensing up, hardening, torturing itself. It only relaxes when I am in shadow, when I am alone, when I wake up early in the morning, when I am doing mechanical actions, and, strangely enough, when I am angry. But it is coy and self-conscious when I draw in my chair and begin to write.

It is like a silent friend: moody, assertive, possessive, callous—sometimes.

I had such a friend once. He finally slashed his wrists. He is now in a lunatic asylum. I have since asked myself why he did what he did, but I still cannot come to a conclusive answer.

He was always washing himself—at least three baths every day.

||||||||||||

And he had all sorts of lotions and deodorants to appease the thing that had taken hold of him. He did not so much wash as scrub himself until he bled.

He tried to purge his tongue too, by improving his English and getting rid of any accent from the speaking of it. It was painful to listen to him, as it was painful to watch him trying to scrub the blackness out of his skin.

He did things to his hair, things which the good Lord never intended any man to do to his hair.

He bought clothes, whole shops of them. If clothes make the man, then certainly he was a man. And his shoes were the kind that make even an elephant lightfooted and elegant. The animals that were murdered to make those shoes must have turned in their graves and said Yeah, man.

But still he was dissatisfied. He had to have every other African within ten miles of his person follow his example. After all, if one chimpanzee learns not only to drink tea but also to promote that tea on TV, what does it profit it if all the other God-created chimpanzees out there continue to scratch their fleas and swing around on their tails chittering about Rhodes and bananas?

However, he was nice enough to put it more obliquely to me one day. We were going to the New Year's Ball in Oxford Town Hall.

"Don't you ever change those jeans?" he asked.

"They're my only pair," I said.

"What do you do with your money, man, booze?"

"Yes," I said searching through my pockets. Booze and paper and ink. The implements of my trade.

"You ought to take more care of your appearance, you know. We're not monkeys."

"I'm all right as I am."

I coughed and because he knew what that cough meant he tensed up as though for a blow.

"If you've got any money," I said firmly, "lend me a fiver."

That day he was equally firm:

"Neither a lender nor a borrower be," he quoted.

And then as an afterthought he said:

"We're the same size. Put on this other suit. You can have it if you like. And the five pounds."

That is how he put it to me. And that is how it was until he slashed his wrists.

But there was more to it than that.

Appearances alone—however expensive—are doubtful climbing boots when one hazards the slippery slopes of social adventure. Every time he opened his mouth he made himself ridiculous. Logic—that was his magic word: but unfortunately that sort of thing quickly bored even the most thick-skinned anthropologist in search of African attitudes. I was interested in the booze first and then lastly in the company. But he—God help me—relied on politics to get on with people. But who in that company in their right mind gives a shit about Rhodesia? He could never understand this.

And Christ! when it came to dancing he really made himself look a monkey. He always assumed that if a girl accepted his request for a dance it meant that she had in reality said yes to being groped, squeezed, kissed and finally screwed off the dance floor. And the girls were quite merciless with him. The invitations would stop and all would be a chilly silence.

I did not care for the type of girl who seemed to interest him. He liked them starched, smart and demure, and with the same desperate conversation:

"What's your college?"

"———. What's yours?"

"———."

Pause.

"What's your subject?"

"———. What's yours?"

"———."

Pause. Cough.

"I'm from Zimbabwe."

"Where's that?"

"Rhodesia."

‖‖

"Oh. I'm from London. Hey [with distinct lack of interest], Smith's a bastard, isn't he?"

And he eagerly:

"As a matter of fact, I have just addressed the Africa Society on the thesis that Ian Smith blah blah blah blah blah blah blah..."

(Yawning.) "Interesting. Very interesting."

"Smith blah blah blah blah blah blah..." (Suddenly.) "Would you like to dance?"

Startled:

"Well...I...yes, why not."

And that's how it was. Yes, that's how it was, until he slashed his wrists.

But there was more to it than that.

A black tramp accosted him one night as we walked to the University Literary Society party. It was as if he had been touched by a leper. He literally cringed away from the man, who incidentally knew me from a previous encounter when he and I had sat Christmas Eve through on a bench in Carfax drinking a bottle of whiskey. He was apoplectic with revulsion and at the party could talk of nothing else:

"How can a black man in England let himself become a bum? There is much to be done. Especially in southern Africa. What I would like to see blah blah blah..."

"Have a drink," I suggested.

He took it the way God accepts anything from Satan.

"You drink too much, you know," he sighed.

"You drink too little for your own good," I said.

The incident of the tramp must have gnawed him more than I had thought because when we got back to college he couldn't sleep and came into my room with a bottle of claret which I was glad to drink with him until breakfast when he did stop talking about impossible black bastards; he stopped talking because he fell asleep in his chair.

And that's how it was until he slashed his wrists.

But there were other sides to the story.

For example: He did not think that one of his tutors "liked" him.

"He doesn't have to like anyone," I pointed out, "and neither do you."

But he wasn't listening. He cracked his fingers and said:

"I'll send him a Christmas and New Year card, the best money can buy."

"Why not spend the money on a Blue Nun?" I suggested.

The way he looked at me, I knew I was losing a friend.

For example: He suggested one day that if the warden or any of the other tutors asked me if I was his friend I was to say no.

"Why?" I asked.

"You do drink too much, you know," he said looking severe, "and I'm afraid you do behave rather badly, you know. For instance, I heard about an incident in the beer cellar and another in the dining room and another in Cornmarket where the police had to be called, and another on your staircase..."

I smiled.

"I'll have your suit laundered and sent up to your rooms," I said firmly, "and I did give you that five pounds back. So that's all right. Are you dining in Hall, because if you are then I will not, it'd be intolerable. Imagine it. We're the only two Africans in this college. How can we possibly avoid each other, or for that matter..."

He twisted his brow. Was it pain? He had of late begun to complain of insomnia and headaches, and the lenses of his spectacles did not seem to fit the degree of his myopia. Certainly something cracked in his eyes, smarting:

"Look, I say, what, forget what I said. I don't care what they think. It's my affair, isn't it, who I choose to be friends with?"

I looked him squarely in the eye:

"Don't let them stuff bullshit into you. Or spew it out right in their faces. But don't ever puke their gut-rot on me."

"Let's go play tennis," he said after a moment.

"I can't. I have to collect some dope from a guy the other end of town," I said.

"Dope? You take that—stuff?"

"Yes. The Lebanese variety is the best piss for me."

He really was shocked.

He turned away without another word. I stared after him, hoping he wouldn't work himself up into telling his moral tutor—who was actually the one who didn't like him. And that's how it was. That's how it was, until he slashed his wrists.

But there had to be another side to it: sex.

The black girls in Oxford—whether African, West Indian or American—despised those of us who came from Rhodesia. After all, we still haven't won our independence. After all, the papers say we are always quarreling among ourselves. And all the other reasons which black girls choose to believe. It was all quite unflattering. We had become—indeed we are—the Jews of Africa, and nobody wanted us. It'd bad enough to have white shits despising us; but it's a more maddening story when one kettle ups its nose at another kettle . . . And this he had to learn.

I didn't care one way or the other. Booze was better than girls, even black girls. And dope was heaven. But he worried. And he got himself all mixed up about a West Indian girl who worked in the kitchen. Knowing him as I did, such a "come-down" was to say the least shattering.

"But we're all black," he insisted.

It was another claret being drunk until breakfast.

"You might as well say to a National Front thug that we're all human," I said.

"Maybe black men are not good enough for them," he protested. "Maybe all they do is dream all day long of being screwed nuts by white chaps. Maybe . . ."

"I hear you've been hanging around the kitchen every day."

He sat up.

I *was* finally losing a friend.

But he chose to sigh tragically, and for the first time—I had been waiting for this—he swore a sudden volley of earthy expletives.

"From now on, it's white girls or nothing."

"You've tried that already," I reminded him.

He gripped the arms of his chair and then let his lungs collapse slowly.

"Why don't you try men?" I asked, refilling my glass.

He stared.

And spat:

"You're full of filth, do you know that?"

"I have long suspected it," I said, losing interest.

But I threw in my last coin:

"Or simply masturbate. We all do."

Furiously, he—refilled his glass.

We drank in silence for a long, contemplative hour.

"They're going to send me down," I said.

"What?"

It was good of him to sound actually surprised.

"If I refuse to go into Warneford as a voluntary patient," I added.

"What's Warneford?"

"A psychiatric care unit," I said. "I have until lunch this afternoon to decide. Between either voluntary confinement or being sent down."

I tossed him the warden's note to that effect. He unfolded it.

He whistled.

The sound of his whistle almost made me forgive him everything, including himself. Finally he asked: "What have you decided to do?"

"Be sent down."

"But—"

I interrupted:

"It's the one decision in my life which I know will turn out right."

"Will you stay on in England?"

"Yes."

"Why not go to Africa and join our guerrillas? You've always been rather more radical than myself and this will be a chance blah blah blah blah blah."

I yawned.

"Your glass is empty," I said. "But take a good look anyway, a good

look at me and all you know about me and then tell me whether you
see a dedicated guerrilla."

He looked.

I refilled his glass and opened another bottle as he scrutinized me.
He lit up; almost maliciously.

"You're a tramp," he said firmly. "You're just like that nigger
tramp who accosted me the other day when we—"

"I know," I said belching.

He stared.

"What will you do?"

"Writing."

"How will you live?"

"Tomorrow will take care of itself. I hope," I said.

And that was the last time we made speech to each other over
bottles of claret throughout the small hours until clean sunlight sli-
vered lucidly through the long open windows and I left him sleeping
peacefully in his chair and hurried to my last breakfast in college.

THE CRIMINALS

||||||||||||||||||||||||||||||||||||||||||||||||||||||

by Stephen Mpofu

Stephen Mpofu *completed his primary and secondary education in Zimbabwe. He was the first black Zimbabwean
news editor of the* Herald *(1980). The collection of thirteen
stories entitled* Shadows on the Horizon *was published in
Zimbabwe in 1984.*

T HEY CAME FOR HER AT this Midlands hospital on a Tuesday
afternoon in 1977. She was off duty and was ironing her uniforms in
her hostel room when the shuffling of feet prompted her to turn her
face toward the door. Her head jerked slightly backward and her eyes
opened wide as the two men stopped near the door which one of
them had half shut. Both men wore fine suits. One of them was big
and he had a black patch over his left eye. The other man did not
look unfamiliar but she could not presently recall where she had seen
him. He was short, stocky and bald-headed. He also wore dark glasses
with silver frames.

The one-eyed man cleared his voice. "I take it you're Nurse
Moyo?" His voice was throaty.

"Yes. . . . Why?"

The one-eyed man nodded to his companion who moved a pace
forward, pushed Nurse Moyo aside with his hand, flung open the
wardrobe door and started to search inside.

"Why? What's the matter?" Nurse Moyo demanded, her eyes
hardly blinking and one hand still holding the hot pressing iron.

"We're policemen," said the one-eyed man. When the other man had moved forward he had shut the door near which he now stood with his big legs wide apart and his clumsy-looking arms poised. Looking at him one got the impression that he wanted to make sure their quarry was safely in the net.

Nurse Moyo stooped to switch off the pressing iron which she then set on the ironing board. Turning first to the man at the door and then to the one half-buried in her wardrobe, she shook her head. "Why are you searching my room?"

"You shut up your big mouth or else I'm going to..." the one-eyed man screamed. He had fashioned a fist the size of the biggest of her three plant pots and he waved it menacingly at her.

Nurse Moyo stepped back out of his range and curled herself in a corner behind her bed. She was a small girl just approaching twenty years of age, and the least she could ever wish for herself was for that pulverizing fist to spoil the good looks of her round, plump face.

From the safety of the corner she watched in horror as the short man ripped open letters which he read cursorily. He searched her clothes and every nook in the wardrobe and as he turned his attention to a suitcase on the bed, Nurse Moyo wrinkled her face. Her mind was reenacting scenes: she recalled an incident one evening. She and another nurse had been returning to the hostel from work. Her companion had pointed to a man leaning against a lamppost behind a tall hedge just opposite the hostel. They had stopped only a few meters from the man. The other girl, who intimated to Nurse Moyo that she was expecting a friend, had coughed purposely. The man, who wore a dark jacket and gray trousers, had swung round and gazed at them for several seconds before walking briskly away. The frames of his sunglasses had glinted in the setting sun as he glanced back three times before the girls proceeded to their hostel. There had been further sightings of a man of the same description, and the similarity in the physical appearance of the man now throwing things out of the suitcase and that of the mystery man, sent a tremor through Nurse Moyo.

The man looked angrier at the end of his search than when he started it. The small room was messy with clothes and bits of paper thrown all over.

"Anything?" the one-eyed man asked as the other pulled a khaki handkerchief out of his trouser pocket and wiped his face and hands.

"Nothing, chief," said the other, "nothing of interest."

The one-eyed turned to Nurse Moyo. "Now you come with us . . ."

"Where to? What have I done?"

"You'll be told at the Charge Office!"

"I must know now what crime I've committed so that my friends know also."

The one-eyed man's face tensed and he made as if to yell, but instead he bit his lower lip and squinted his eye at the girl. After several tense moments of silence he shot out a finger at her and said: "Girl, if you keep on wasting our time like this we're going to throw you out of this room. Do you understand?"

"But what do you want from me, sir?" Her voice shook and she stood with her hands crossed on her chest.

"You're under arrest. Under arrest! Do you understand?"

"Under arrest? What have I done?"

The one-eyed man turned to his companion. "She's very stubborn . . . Throw her out!"

"No! . . ." she raised her hands to keep the short man at bay. "I'm not refusing . . . Please let me change into something."

"Those trousers will be good for you," said the one-eyed man.

Nurse Moyo looked down at her white, billowy trousers which she wore with a striped long-sleeved shirt and white sandals. Then she turned to her bed and as she stretched out her hand the short man grabbed a newspaper which lay beside her sweater. It was yesterday's issue of the daily newspaper.

"Look, chief, look," the man said as he stepped back and showed the newspaper to his boss. He pointed a finger at a news item with a red circle round it. "Today we caught her red-handed."

The one-eyed man took hold of the newspaper and raised it to his eye. He frowned and his lips twitched. "So you were going to send this one away as well?"

"I don't know what you're talking about, sir," Nurse Moyo said. All she knew was that she had marked the item with a red pen rather unconsciously. It had made her angry. Not all of it but the part from Security Force Headquarters in Salisbury (now Harare) which reported that some "*terrorist* collaborators" had been "caught in cross fire" when security forces engaged a group of guerrillas in a rural district near the hospital where Nurse Moyo worked. As she substituted "murdering innocent villagers in cold blood" for "caught in cross fire" she had run her pen round the item and then cast the newspaper on the bed to start her ironing.

The two men eyed each other.

"Let's get moving," the one-eyed man barked the order.

"Yes, chief," his companion said. He turned to face Nurse Moyo and then nodded to her to move.

Nurse Moyo picked up her sweater and her handbag.

The one-eyed man opened the door and nodded to the short man to get out first. "Follow him," he ordered the girl and then followed close behind her, shutting the door as he went.

"Move on!"

"I want to lock the door," Nurse Moyo said, gazing frightfully in his eye.

He mumbled something. She produced a bunch of keys from her handbag, nervously selected the right key and then she took several seconds to insert it in the keyhole.

As they rushed her across an open space toward an unmarked white Peugeot 404 parked near the hedge, Nurse Moyo glanced this way and that, her eyes unblinking.

Moments later her escorts stumbled to a halt and the one-eyed man cried: "Why do you stop? Move!"

Nurse Moyo gasped and rushed her best foot forward. She had not realized that she had stopped. It had all been an unconscious move: she was anxious to be seen being hustled away between the two men.

For as the war intensified people had disappeared, some mysteriously, some in almost the same way she was being taken away, and most of them had never been accounted for. Nurse Moyo reasoned that if someone saw her with her "abductors," and they knew that they had been seen, then the chances of her disappearing, or much less being harmed, would be reduced.

"Why are you dragging your feet?" the short man demanded and he pushed her forward with his hand.

They changed course slightly and made for an opening in the hedge through which they sneaked out. The short man outpaced the others and when he reached the car he flung open the back door through which the one-eyed man shoved the girl and then seated himself beside her.

At the Charge Office they locked her up in a cell by herself.

She was taken for interrogation on the morning of the third day. A man she had never seen led her to a room with long, thick curtains. He was a tall, thin man with protruding upper front teeth and he wore civilian clothes.

Another man sat in the room at a small desk on top of which he tapped with a finger, nodding his head rhythmically with his lips moving silently. When the prisoner appeared, he raised his face and pursed his brows. "Sit over there!" he indicated to a bench in the corner toward which he turned his eye like one focusing a camera lens on a subject.

Nurse Moyo crawled to the bench and seated herself on it with a bump. She had not had a change of clothes and she stank of sweat; holes had developed in her cheeks making her look like a ghost; and her long hair was disarrayed.

The other man had pulled up a chair and dumped himself on it at the door which he had locked.

The one-eyed man drew a notebook from his pocket and laid it on the desk in front of him. He eyed the girl and then lowered his eye to the notebook which he now opened. He pulled out a drawer and took out a writing pad which he handed to the man at the door. Again he cast his eye down and then up at Nurse Moyo, while the man at the door waited expectantly, and he said:

"We're now going to discuss business... the business of your presence here. In other words the reasons for your arrest. Do you understand?"

"Yes, sir," Nurse Moyo said. She looked calm and resigned to her fate.

"If you tell us the truth, if you choose not to waste our time, things will be easy for you, my girl. Do you understand?"

"Yes, sir."

"But if you think you're clever and start playing around, we'll teach you a lesson you'll never forget for the rest of your life.... Do you understand?"

"Yes, I do."

"Fine... Fine... So tell me: For how long have you been a spy?"

The short man's pen screeched on the writing pad.

"I beg your pardon." Nurse Moyo turned an ear.

"I said for how long have you been in the spying business?"

"Ah!... I'm shocked... I don't understand what you mean. I've never been a spy."

"Yes, you're a spy and just now I'm going to show you that you're a fool, you don't think we know what you're doing. As a matter of fact I'm going to show you that we know what most of you at that hospital have been doing... and sooner or later some of you are going to pay dearly for betraying the government. I must tell you at the outset that no *terrorist* can ever hope to rule this country. It can't happen and it won't happen..."

"Honestly, I don't know what you're talking about."

"You bloody well do because you've been sending secrets about our security operations to our enemies who harbor *terrorists*..."

"I've never done anything like that all my life."

"Turn to your left," the one-eyed interrogator gestured with his hand. "Do you see anything on the wall?"

The prisoner craned her head and for several seconds she studied the wall.

"You can't see anything?"

"Yes, these dark spots. . . ?"

"Yes, those patches of blood. Some people have come here behaving like you and by the time I was finished with them, by the time I'd made them shed that blood as a lesson for hiding the truth, they realized their foolishness. . . ." Now, he rose, and turned up the long sleeves of his shirt. "I'm going to give you the same treatment. . ."

"Please don't. . . hurt me." She rolled herself up in the corner.

The interrogator grabbed the notebook and strode forward. He stopped beside her. "I won't hurt you if you cooperate."

Nurse Moyo sat up, watching his every move. The interrogator bent forward until his head was level with hers. He then flung open the notebook to reveal three or more letters stapled to a page. She concluded from their pale appearance that they must be photostat copies. The interrogator drew the notebook closer to her eyes, whereupon she saw on the opposite page a list of three names. The man shut the notebook and withdrew it when she raised her eyes to have a good look at the names.

"Now don't tell me you didn't write those letters?"

"Ah. . . Yes, I wrote them. But who gave them to you?"

"Who gave them to us, you ask?" He grinned, his eye trained menacingly on her. "Who gives God information about what goes on on earth?"

She gasped, out of breath. "Anyway," she spoke with her head bowed, "those letters are completely innocent. . . I mean I wrote them to a young sister at school advising her not to come home at this time because of the situation in the country. . . which is not very good. That's what they were all about, sir."

The interrogator had backed away and was now seated on top of the desk, facing the prisoner. He turned over a few pages and cast his eye on the letters. "In two of the letters you tell lies about our security forces: you say that if your sister comes she might be killed or raped by our soldiers on the way. . . True or false?"

"I advised her so."

"Why?"

"Because I feared for her life. I didn't want her to come and—well—perhaps get into trouble."

"So you admit that you sent military secrets to a country which harbors *terrorists* and is thus at war with us?"

"I admit that I wrote the letters to this young schoolgirl. Like me she knows nothing about what you call military secrets. I wrote the letters, as I said earlier on, purely out of love for her, and if that is what is meant by military secrets then I admit I acted in complete ignorance."

The interrogator laid the notebook on the desk and sat back with a weary sigh. And with no further questions coming presently from the man, Nurse Moyo saw her freedom in sight. Moments later, however, the man at the door sniped a question that nearly made her scream with indignation:

"But who told you, girl, that our security forces rape people?"

Nurse Moyo's head drooped, her hope of freedom virtually quashed. She did not even know how to answer that question. So it initially came as a bit of relief when the chief interrogator said:

"Now tell me something else..." He watched in silence as she slowly raised her hand and looked in his face. "How many secrets have you passed over to the *terrorists* in this country about the movements of our security forces? We know that you people at the hospital feed them, we know that you give them medicines and even treat them when they are seriously ill or when they are wounded..."

Her eyes opened wider. "I don't know anything about what you are saying."

"Nurse Moyo, you're doing the wrong thing in the wrong place," her interrogator said. "Politics and nursing don't mix well and when the time comes we'll show you the truth of it all."

Before the threat in his last words took effect, the prisoner felt rather flattered: she had never at any moment considered herself a politician as such although she had always felt she possessed a political insight superior to that of many men she had come into contact with. Indeed, she felt the same about her interrogator and the other man with him and those others she had interacted with in this place.

For instance, she had not first believed her ears when earlier in the interrogation the one-eyed man had bragged that *"terrorists"* would never rule the country. It had seemed that he had merely been parroting other people's sentiments, but as the interrogation developed it had become clear to her that the views the man had been expressing were truly his own and that they also appeared to reflect the feelings of his colleagues. Still, the question remained unanswered whether these men were entrenched in the "wrong" political camp because of their lack of political foresight, or whether it was because of fanatical loyalty which made them cling to a system whose life-chances they knew little about, or a combination of both. If it was because of the latter reason, she wondered what would happen should the "terrorists" get into power? Was it possible that these people, if the new government decided not to sweep them away into the rubbish dump of history, would move from their old camp to the new camp with the same fanatical loyalty?

The chief interrogator broke the tense silence by rising suddenly. He grabbed his notebook and nodded to the other man who also rose and together they went outside and locked the door.

Nurse Moyo relapsed into fear and despair as she listened to the men's feet shuffling away. And when she heard them coming back some fifteen to twenty minutes later, her body tensed up and she fixed anxious eyes on the door handle.

The shuffling ceased at the door, but she could hear voices. She arched her body forward and waited with an ear to the door.

"Now if she goes . . . what about the list?"

"It's better that she goes so that we can wipe it out properly. . ."

She identified the last speaker as her main interrogator. The knot in her heart had tightened when the list was mentioned. Her own name was on it and the other people listed were a nursing sister and a hospital executive. At first—when she had become aware that her letters had been intercepted—she had thought that perhaps the list had been kept in connection with the letters and, thus, her arrest. But the dialogue between the two interrogators seemed to suggest that her release would not in any way guarantee her total freedom.

|||||||||||||||||||||||||||||||||||||||||||||||||||||||||||||||||||||||||||||||||||||||||||||||||||||||||||||||||||||

She sat up, held her breath, as the door was unlocked and the junior interrogator came in. He left the door ajar.

"Back to your..." he gestured with his head and thumb.

The prisoner sat leaning against the wall at noon, the next day, when the same man came to the cell. "How are you, nurse?"

"Well... not bad," she replied, sitting up.

"I've brought you good news, nurse..."

"Good news?"

"Good news. You're now free to return to your work."

She gasped, and then she rose. "You mean...? You mean... I can now leave this place? Really?"

"Sure, nurse, sure."

She hugged herself with a sudden gush of joy. There was actually such an outpouring of joy that she felt like hugging and kissing her bearer of good news, but his surly face put her off.

"There are formalities to be completed before you leave," he said and indicated with his head and thumb to her to follow him.

"What did he mean by wiping out our names?" Nurse Moyo said and a man seated beside her on the bus held his left ear toward her and said:

"I didn't get you, my daughter?"

"I'm sorry, father," she apologized. "I was talking to myself."

The man grimaced, then turned his eyes in the other direction.

Though now free, Nurse Moyo still felt uneasiness at the back of her mind, an uneasiness which did not go away even when she saw the gleaming buildings of her hospital set against a setting sun. She felt remotely detained even as the other nurses mobbed her congratulating her on her release. They informed her, as they accompanied her to the hostel, that one of them had spotted her being driven away and had alerted hospital authorities, whose inquiries had established her whereabouts. Tears rolled down her hollow cheeks as she listened to their stories. For she had not until this moment felt the deep attachment of the other girls to her, and she felt like a prodigal daughter returning home to the love and warmth of her family.

They were approaching the hostel when one nurse stopped. "Look." She pointed in another direction. "He's still there!"

The rest of the group stopped and looked in that direction. "I wonder why he has been standing there like a guard for so long," another nurse said.

The man had been facing in another direction, but the girls' presence seemed to have drawn his attention, for he turned his head sharply in their direction. It was not quite dark yet and the girls could see clearly that he wore dark glasses.

The girls proceeded to the hostel while he gazed dreamily at them.

For Nurse Moyo, the appearance of the man immediately brought two things to her mind: first, it reminded her of how he had searched her room, leaving it in a terrible mess the other day, and it filled her heart with more gloom as she wondered whether he had been sent ahead of her to "wipe out the list."

By the time she went to bed that night she had already made up her mind what to do with her life. When the other girls called at her room to say good morning the room was empty. All her personal belongings were also missing. A report was made to the hospital authorities, but the inquiries that followed were inconclusive. The hospital only came to know of her whereabouts when she wrote from Gweru asking for a testimonial, and almost immediately afterward to send her condolences after the other names on her interrogator's list had been "wiped out."

Nurse Moyo had just reported for work in the casualty ward one afternoon in early April 1980 when a patient in bed eight attracted her attention. Although he was asleep his eye patch aroused her curiosity and she went round to see his hospital admission card. His case history confirmed her suspicion. The patient had arrived two days ago when Nurse Moyo was having her nights off.

About an hour later the patient in bed eight woke and sat up in bed. He had turned the blankets to one side to reveal his right leg cast in plaster. His case history stated that he had been injured in a land mine explosion. From whichever part of the ward she was Nurse Moyo watched him keenly. When she saw him raising the injured leg with both hands and then lowering it again and again after he woke, she had felt herself choking with anger. However, she had controlled herself and watched the patient's behavior. Most of the other patients were euphoric as they talked about the forthcoming independence celebrations, or compared the past with the prospects for life in a truly independent state. But not so the patient in bed eight. From the gloom on his face he seemed to be in a world of his own. Nurse Moyo thought that perhaps he was in pain, and her call of duty overshadowed her boiling fury and she took painkillers to him.

"Good afternoon, and how are you feeling?" she said as she stopped at his bed.

The patient had been exercising his leg and when he looked up and their eyes met, he dropped the leg and winced, with dismay on his face. A grin formed on his mouth and then his lips trembled.

"I said how are you feeling?" The grin on his face had stoked the fire in her heart and her arms started to tremble.

"Ah . . . Ah . . . not . . . not bad." His eye retreated into its socket as he stared at her. "Do you . . . do you think I'll be all right, nurse— the leg?"

"So that you can be mobile again to murder more people?" she said silently, but seconds later she coughed to steady herself and told him: "Oh yes." Then to torment him she added: "You should be home to celebrate our independence. . . . Wouldn't that be wonderful celebrating our independence at home with everybody else?"

The patient bowed his head. "Well, I suppose you're right."

His indecisive answer summed it all up as far as she was concerned: the man was still as unrepentant as he was when he interrogated her and declared that freedom fighters would never rule the country. Inside she spat a mouthful in his face. When she realized saliva had formed in her mouth, and that she was about to violate a norm, she swallowed noisily.

The patient looked at her and when he lowered his eye he said: "I

am wondering, nurse, whether I haven't seen you somewhere before?" He now appeared helpless and frightened.

"Yes, you're seeing my ghost," Nurse Moyo said and the patient's
eye rolled up with a start. The tray of medicine in her hand shook.
Thoughts were piling up in her head. She had heard that members of
the security forces had fled the country when it became clear that
their government had been defeated in the general election. Was it
not possible that others might still be hiding in the country? If that
was possible what would stop those who had fled recruiting their
colleagues within the country, like this former interrogator, to sabo-
tage the new government? She recalled a story she had heard recently. It said some of the former agents of the old regime had begun
to worm their way into "hiding" in different sectors before the new
government took over power. "Where can one get a magic wand to
neutralize these agents in order to protect our independence?" she
asked herself.

Meanwhile, the former interrogator had seen her lips moving,
and he had fixed his eye on her. When their eyes met a four-letter
word formed on her lips, and she spun round and stalked away from
bed eight, the tray swinging in her hand. "With the criminals still at
large," she soliloquized as she went, "shall we ever be safe?"

SOME KINDS OF WOUNDS

|||||||||||||||||||||||||||||||||||||||||||||||||||||||||||||||||||||||||||||||||||||||||||||

by Charles Mungoshi

Charles Mungoshi *is undoubtedly the best known and the most prolific novelist, poet, and playwright in Zimbabwe. His literary work includes nine books in English and the Shona languages. The book* Waiting for the Rain *was first published in England in 1975, and was awarded the Rhodesia PEN prize in 1976. Only after independence was it published in Zimbabwe (1981), and it became recommended reading for all schools and universities. It was preceded by the collection of short stories* Coming of the Dry Season *(1972), which was banned in Rhodesia. Both books were translated into Hungarian, German, Bulgarian, and French. A collection of verses,* The Milkman Doesn't Only Deliver Milk: Selected Poems, *was published in 1981. The collection of nine stories,* Some Kinds of Wounds, *published in 1980, had a second edition in 1983.*

K UTE PUSHED THE woman gently into the room and before she could sit down on the floor—as I saw she was about to—I quickly offered her a chair. Suddenly the smell of the room changed. The woman carefully sat on the edge of the chair, her hands in her lap, eyes cast down. Kute remained standing in the doorway.

"Okay?" he whispered.

"It's all right," I said.

"Good. Won't be long. A minute to work the windowpane loose —and—halleluja!" He was in sudden good spirits.

"Mind the good neighbors," I warned him.

|||||||||||||

"They call me Cool Cat Kute. And anyway who would hear a thing with that kind of roof-wrecking racket going on? Tell me, Gatsi. How did I go and choose myself a father like that?"

"The ways of the Almighty are mysterious and not to be sniffed at with our clay snouts," I offered him the wisdom of our seven-month friendship.

"Amen. Could we borrow a knife?"

I handed him my all-purpose table knife. "Mind you don't break it. It's the last of its kind in this country."

"Priceless, to be precise," he said, giving it the expert butcher's professional squint. "It's in safe hands." Turning to the woman, he whispered loudly, "Patience. The Reverend Gatsi here will take good care of you. I lost my key and the spare in opening some bright future for me in my father's dreams." He said this last bit nodding toward the sound coming from his father's room down the corridor.

The woman didn't say a thing. He went out to the back where the door to his room was. The smell in the room was growing thicker. I guiltily looked at the window and saw that it was partly open. I couldn't bring myself to open it wider.

Slowly I turned my head toward the woman. She wore a sleeve-less top of some faded, very thin pink material that showed she had nothing to hold up her breasts. She had on a homemade black skirt and her dusty feet were covered by worn-out once-white tennis shoes without laces. Her head was covered in a headcloth that hid almost half her face down to the top of the bridge of her nose so that her eyes were in shadow. It gave her a very mysterious look which I was sure must have appealed to Kute's sense of the sensual. There were deep lines down from the flanks of her nostrils to the corners of her mouth. These lines gave her an old woman's face although I could sense that she was far from being old. In fact, there was a certain subtle awk-wardness in her that made me feel she wasn't even aware that shZe was a woman.

She looked as if she had come a very long way on foot. She looked that dusty and travel-used—a kind of slept-in-everyplace air about her. And she sat in that chair as if she couldn't trust herself to let go and relax, as if she knew that was only a temporary resting place on the long road. And yet, in spite of all this, there was a kind of watchful stillness about her, a kind of relaxation-in-motion that made me feel that she was as much at home in that chair as on her feet or asleep. Walking, sitting or sleeping, her body had erased all the differences and acquired its own kind of separate peace with her mind.

She didn't look at the pot of sadza cooking on the fire, nor around this room which must only have been strange to her with the numerous books piled knee-high against one wall, some cheap reproductions of some abstract paintings, the typewriter, the single unmade bed and the clothes hanging from wirehangers in a corner. She did not even look at me or at anything else except at her hands in her lap. I wondered whether she even saw those hands. The *silence* in her resting hands suggested some deep religious experience in her. Those hands—which were clearly not sweating from nervousness as mine would in the presence of strange people or unfamiliar rooms—gave me a feeling I had never had since coming to the city some ten or so years back. They belonged to the depths of the heart of the country and all that I missed. She reminded me of where I came from and suddenly the smell in the room was clearly a mixture of human sweat and soil and grass and leaves as we carted hay for the cattle. Once I knew what it was, I felt at home in it.

Outside, I heard the scraping of the knife on Kute's window.

"He has lost his key and he is trying to remove the windowpane so that you can get in," I told the woman, for something to say.

She didn't say anything. Suddenly, I felt as if she were accusing me of something. I turned the stove low. I had lost all appetite. Then, remembering home, I felt guilty all over again. I had lost the rural sense of hospitality and she would never forget how I had received her in my house.

"Want anything to eat?" I asked her, trying to cover up. And that was wrong too. You don't ask strangers who come into your house whether they would like food or water. You give them what you have and leave them to say no or to eat.

"I am all right," she said.

"Honestly, I mean—it won't take long—"

"Don't worry, brother." Her mouth gave the faintest suggestion of a smile and she left me to stew in my own guilt.

I took up a novel and tried to read. I read one line three times.

"Where do you come from?" I asked.

"Mount Darwin. Chesa."

I put the book face-down on the table and stood up to look out through the window. Behind me I could feel that she wasn't even taking advantage of this to look at me. I sat down in the chair and picked up the book again.

After some time the woman spoke, "He told me this is his house."

"It's his father's and he is the firstborn, so I suppose that makes it his." She didn't seem to have heard me. I said, "But his father sleeps in his own room and Kute has his own at the back."

"And you are his brother?" she asked with the slightest hint at raising her eyes.

"I am only their lodger." She didn't seem to understand that. "I pay rent to them for this room. We are not related at all."

She didn't say anything to this.

I picked up the book, decided that poetry would be easier in the circumstances. I threw the book on top of the pile of other books and pulled out a much-referred-to, dog-eared paperback edition of Paul Celan's selected poems. His poetry was very difficult yet most of the poems were almost haikulike in their brevity. I thought I would work on the meaning behind the verbal appearance while I waited for Kute. What bothered me was that the words were all quite simple—I didn't need a dictionary for their conventional meanings—yet the way they were used here was beyond me. Words.

"And his mother?" she startled me.

"His mother?"

"Your—your . . ."

I understood. "She is keeping their home out in Manyene Reserve. She only comes to town for two weeks once every year."

We fell silent. I returned to my poetry.

Later, "Is she married?"

"No."

Pause.

"Do you think he will let me sleep here tonight? Only for to-night?"

Down the corridor I heard the snoring reach such a pitch that it was impossible for it to go any higher.

"I don't know," I said. "He might." But then you would have to leave at half past four in the morning, I didn't tell her.

"It won't be long now," she said. "If he would only let me put up here for the night, tomorrow I am sure I shall be all right. I have got a friend in Highfield—that's what he said—Highfield. Do you know where Highfield is? This friend—I have known him for such a long time and I know he wouldn't lie to me. Back home I . . . he . . . he said he would take me to Highfield." Pause. "Is it far from here, this Highfield?"

I could smell the sadza burning but I didn't have the energy to take the pot off the stove. I had turned the flame low thinking it wouldn't need attending to till the woman had left the room.

"Is it far?" she repeated.

"No," I said, suddenly unforgivably angry with Kute. I wondered what he had told her and *how* she had got here without asking for directions.

"This friend of yours in Highfield," I asked quickly, "did he ask you to come to him? Wasn't he waiting for you at Musika bus termi-nus?"

She simply shook her head and said nothing. How the hell could I help her if she wasn't going to talk? I looked out through the win-dow, seeing nothing, feeling a newer kind of chilly guilt creep over me. I was suddenly aware of the depth of my hatred for Kute but I couldn't do anything and I just sat there feeling as if I were keeping vigil in a house of mourning.

"When he left there was no time to say good-bye." She startled me once more. I turned toward her.

"My boyfriend," she helped me although I was sure she could not have read my thoughts. "I didn't even see him. He left word with one of his friends to tell me that should I ever come to Harare I should look him up in Highfield."

"And the number? Where exactly in Highfield were you to look him up?"

"There was no time." She hadn't heard me or she was just dumb. "They came for him the following morning but he had gone."

I was trying very hard to settle in between the lines so I didn't say anything.

"They knew he often came to our place to see me. I am sure they knew he was going to marry me. They know everything out there. They thought I would try and hide him. I wasn't there when they came. They shot my mother and my father. I was at a friend's— Chengeto—where I had put up for the night because of the curfew. Then we heard the shots and saw the flames and the smoke as our home burned down."

"I am sorry," I said and then felt very stupid. I was sinking.

"Chengeto's folks advised me to run away. Just as I was leaving I could see the dust of their cars making toward Chengeto's home."

"Is it that bad out there?" What was I talking about? Or, rather, how do you—what do you say when someone tells you a story like that?

She looked up at me. Her eyes seemed to be points of light coming a long way through a tunnel. "If the soldiers suspect you of harboring or giving food to *vanamukoma* they kill you. If *vanamukoma* suspect you of passing information to the soldiers, they kill you. If your neighbor hates you he can tell either the soldiers or *vanamukoma* that you are a sellout and either way you will be killed." She lowered her eyes. I would have felt easier had there been any kind of self-pity or suffering in her voice.

"So, what did your boyfriend do? Why did they come for him?" I felt it wouldn't be safe for me to ask her *who* came for him.

"Nothing," she said. "He didn't do anything at all. The soldiers just don't feel happy with a young man of twenty doing nothing out there."

"But are you sure that he came here when he ran away?" I felt that it was more likely that he would want to join *vanamukoma* in the bush if the soldiers were after him. He would be safer in the bush.

"Wouldn't it have been safer for him to run into the bush?" I asked seeing that she didn't seem to have heard me.

"He was going to marry me when all this fighting was over," she said, apparently not interested in my question. I felt like someone who had been invited to a party and then found himself ignored by the host. It made my guilty feeling more complex. I felt that she was silently asking me why I wasn't also out there. I looked at my pile of books and suddenly I wished I hadn't let her into the room.

"He was going to marry me," she said. "He would have married me if he hadn't felt that one day he might join the fighters—*vanamukoma*. He was quite friendly with them but they told him to help his old people on the farm. They didn't even recruit him to be a *mujibha*—that's the name for their messengers or spies—local village boys who keep *vanamukoma* supplied with information."

"I know," I said and then wished I hadn't said it. The pinpoints of light from her dark tunnel bored into me but she quickly dropped her head.

I looked through the window. I felt ashamed of the poetry. What was Kute still doing? The scraping had stopped.

"It must be tough living out there," I said, wanting to hear more. It was like a sore which you felt needed scratching.

"We no longer think about it."

"What are you going to do if you don't find him here?"

She looked up at me, but not accusingly, rather pleadingly, as if asking how I could be so cruel—but then I might have been wrong in thinking so because nothing in her showed that she needed my pity. Instead, I could feel deeper silence settling in the room, that kind of silence one senses in places where a human life has been lost—the scene of an accident or some other disaster. A desperate, frightening silence that makes you ask metaphysical questions.

"How far is this Highfield?" she asked after some time.

I heard a tap on the window. I looked up and saw Kute looking in, grinning. I restrained myself from slapping that greedy, meaty grin off his face.

"It's open," he said. He came around to the door and entered without knocking. He handed me the knife. "Thanks, Gatsi," he said. "Keep it safe for future journeys to the land of milk and honey —it's an all-purpose Moses's rod." He nodded toward his father's snoring. "Ask Pharaoh and the Red Sea." He laughed and rubbed his hands.

I didn't look at him.

"Hey, what's going on in here? It's as if you had just buried a dearly beloved."

I didn't answer him.

"All right, Reverend Gatsi. All right. Come on, sister." He was angry.

They went out and Kute's anger reminded him to close the door softly. His father's snores were coming along the corridor like trapped wind in a tunnel. There were slight rustles and soft-footed thuds as they helped each other through the window into Kute's room. I sat in my chair, doing nothing.

Forty minutes later I heard a sound as if someone was crying. I listened hard and heard them coming out. Their shadows passed by my window and I heard their footfalls fade beyond the yard to get swallowed by other footfalls on the street.

Kute came back five minutes later. He entered my room without knocking.

"Silly bitch," he said, sitting on the edge of the table. He wanted my compliments or some kind of comment that would make him feel good. He always felt he wasn't living until someone else told him so. When he saw that I wasn't going to answer him he went on, "Thinks this is a home for the pregnant, destitute and aged." He shook a cigarette from my pack which was lying on the table and lit it. He drew in smoke and filled his cheeks and then blew it out stintingly, afraid to waste good smoke.

"Wanted to spend the night here. Wouldn't accept any money.

||||||||||||||||||||||||||||||||||||||||||||||||||||||||||||||||||||||||||||||||||||||||||||||||||||||||||||||||||||||||||||||||

And does she stink! If the old goat weren't around I would have asked her to have a bath first."

"Where did you pick her from?" I asked.

"The pub." He pulled on his cigarette and began to laugh. "Can you imagine it, man. She was asking for directions to Highfield *in* Highfield! Must have got into town today. Didn't even go to school too. Can you imagine that—in this day and age?" He had a good laugh over that and went on, "'Would you please tell me where Highfield is, brother.' And I took her right to Highfield—here! I told her Highfield was too damn far to get there tonight."

"Did she say what she was doing in the pub?"

"That's her problem. If I had known she was pregnant I wouldn't have bothered with her. Silly bitch."

I was quiet for some time while he smoked and thought over the wrong she had done him.

"Where have you taken her now?" I asked.

"I put her on the street and pointed east, south, north and west and told her this was all Highfield." He laughed. The smoke caught in his throat and he coughed. "You know, Gatsi. I just don't understand these country women. I offered her money and she refused it. And yet any fool can see how desperately she needs food, decent clothes, and if she is going to have a baby—hell. Probably she will throw it down some sewer drain or dump it on some rubbish heap for the dogs."

I looked through the window. "Where did she go?" I asked.

"How the hell should I know? Does her type ever lack places to go to? She just walked straight away from me without looking back—as if she knew where she was going. How the hell would I know where she was heading?"

I didn't say anything.

"You know, I think she was after something more than money. You can never tell in these times. Telling me she has walked all the way from Chesa or whatever place she mentioned—after her parents had been killed and she escaped—who does she think will believe that baboon-and-hare story in these times? Does she look the type that could have walked from Chesa to you? The dirt, the stink and the simple mentality might belong to Chesa yes—but don't let that fool you. She could have run away from home in Harare—her father after her with the old battle-ax for conceiving a bastard—and now she wants to con some fool of a man into keeping her till she delivered and later she will run away again with all his money and clothes and everything—leaving him to look after her bastard. Damn silly bitch!"

He smoked for some time in silence. I knew he was looking at me, waiting for me to say something like "Good old Cool Cat Kute," so that he could really begin to purr, stroking his whiskers and licking his fur as if he had finally landed the record-breaking rat.

"Hey," he said suspiciously, "what's got into you?"

I didn't answer him.

"Well, I got what I wanted out of her—Chesa stink, rags and all—and she can get what *she* wants from someone else. Saved me the trouble of scrounging for cigarette stubs though. Mighty considerate of her. *Kakara kununa hudya kamwe*, as the wise old folks had it. Dog eat dog."

"Kute."

"Yes?"

"You should have given her the money, you know. Forget about lying to her about Highfield. But the money at least."

"Well, she refused it, didn't she? You aren't suggesting that I should have gone down on my knees and begged her to take it, are you?"

"She is not your usual type. Probably she didn't know all you wanted out of her is only *that*."

"Heey! Come on, Gatsi. You know very well what she wanted—a good bed and a man for the night. Then tomorrow she would have come back again—and tomorrow and tomorrow till I was so entangled in her I wouldn't know whether my head comes before my ass or what." He was now pleading with me. He didn't want me to get him wrong. He lived on the actor's habit, the clap of the hand the cry for more.

I kept quiet and turned to look at him.

"Look," he said. "Why this sudden interest in that—that slut?"

"She is no slut. She may be pregnant but she is no slut."

"Does she come from your home?"

"No."

"Then?"

I didn't answer.

"Or you wanted her for yourself?" He had solved the problem for himself. He laughed long and hard. He patted me on the shoulder and laughed some more till tears stood in his eyes. "Guts-less Gatsi! Why didn't you tell me you wanted her? I could have left her all to yourself and gone and found me another tail. Now you are growing up. You are coming to my way of thinking now. That's a good sign. The heavens augur well for a bumper crop in tail this year!" He looked warning. "Tell you what," he said. "When I make my patrol tomorrow we might go together, right? Good Gutsy Gatsi. Man does not live on books alone but on . . ."

"I think you should take it slow," I cut into his sermon.

"Take what slow?"

"You know what I am talking about. Once or twice per week is all right. Not every day."

"What the hell are you talking about?"

I could see dark anger and fear gathering in his eyes like storm-clouds.

"It isn't healthy you know."

"What isn't healthy?" He was hedging, trying to avoid facing it. He knew what I was talking about.

"This won't get you anywhere, Kute."

"The hell you say!" He banged the table with his fist. "Has my old man asked you to interrogate me about this?"

"I don't need your old man to see that."

"O, so you have decided to play savior! With your kind of guts?" he sniggered. "Look, you are just jealous, man. You can't do what I can do and you dream of doing it and when the moment of truth comes you haven't got the guts, right? You wanted that piece of tail and you hate my guts for doing what I have done to her. Why don't you ask me how it's done and I will give you a few elementary lessons, huh, Gatsi-boy?"

"That doesn't change the fact that you won't get anywhere. Look how many times you have been to the doctor. Your seat-hide must be as perforated as a sieve now. Sounding tough and brave doesn't get you anywhere either."

"Hell, man, hell! And what has ever got me anywhere in this rotten world? Third division in form four and everyone at my neck saying I wasn't applying myself. Four years tramping round the country, knocking on every goddamn door for *any* kind of job and being shooed off with a boot in my ass and at home my old man out for my scalp telling me I am not searching hard enough. I would have drunk, taken drugs—anything to jump out of my skin—but that stuff hasn't been good for me. And now you begrudge me the one and only little thing that keeps me going."

As always, the anger was crumbling into his other only weapon that was even worse than the anger. It was as if I had taken off the lid of a sewer-drain manhole knowing exactly what would come out but not quite prepared to take what finally came out of it.

"Listen," I said, "I am only trying to help."

"Yeah? Give me a job then—and money and keep me sane."

"You are getting more than enough money from your old man."

"For my private studies. And he didn't give it to me until he saw you with all those books. He thinks it's the books that get one a job."

"I don't see how else you want to get a better job if you aren't going to study for it."

"So you haven't heard of the university blokes who have been years looking for jobs?"

"They are no reason why you shouldn't study yourself."

"What the hell do you mean I am not studying?"

"Don't fool yourself, Kute. Since you brought those books you haven't touched a single one of them. If your old man had been to school he would know exactly what you are doing to him."

He leaned toward me menacingly and hissed, "You aren't going to let him hear that, are you?"

I said nothing.

"Well, are you?" His nose was only a few inches from my face.

"It's your funeral, Kute," I said, rising to close the window. "But I wish you wouldn't take advantage of your old man in this way."

He leaned back in his chair and brought his hands to face, sighed and looked blearily at me. He said, "You don't know how it is."

"I know."

"No, you don't."

We were quiet for some time.

"Know what," he said. "When I ran into you that day in town —must be six months or so now—and you told me that you were looking for a room, you don't know how good I felt. To have someone—a classmate from way back those years in school—to talk to. Someone like you to confide in, someone who would understand. I knew I could trust you. You were one of those who always understand me. I felt good, I tell you. And the best feeling I ever had in my life was when I knew I could ask my old man—persuade him—to give you a room here. I knew he would know I was moving in good company. I knew he would know that I wasn't as useless as he seemed to think. That made me feel good, Gatsi. To be able to do something for someone, for nothing. I almost cried, Gatsi. It's a thing I have always wanted to do all my life but when you don't have what others have how do you do it? Who will believe you are sincere? I know I don't have your kind of brains. Even in school, but should the luck always come to those who have brains alone? Look at me now, still at the bottom of my class while you are well tucked in that firm of publishers. And my old man believes it's because I am lazy. Do you know that my old man loves you more than me—his own son? Do you know that?"

"No."

"The hell you don't!"

"Listen, Kute. I know how you feel. I have been through something like it too."

"But not four years, man. Four years is too long for any man to be still hoping."

"But you can't just give up like this. You aren't helping anyone, least of all yourself, by being bitter and attacking your father and dropping your studies and chasing tail. You have to face yourself, find what you want to do and do it."

He squinted dangerously at me. "So I was right, huh?"

"Right about what?"

"You are together with my old man. Shit, man. I thought you were my friend. I thought you understood. I persuaded my old man to give you a room here and now you are better than me—his own son!"

"Don't hang your own shortcomings round other people's necks, Kute."

"Dang shortcomings! I know you have been stabbing me in the back since that time you started staying here. Neither you nor my old man has the guts to say it to my face but I know it. I have been too long among people to be fooled by toothpaste-advert smiles."

"You are imagining things, Kute."

"Exactly. And who taught you that word? Let me tell you. It's that pig gruntling down the corridor who would sell his own son for chicken shit."

"You are frustrated, Kute, and that's all. You can't face the real world that's doing this to you and so you turn against those that would—"

"You mean people like you? You are damn right. It's people like you who come messing up things for us unfortunates who should be shot."

"You are not an unfortunate, Kute—"

"The hell I am not! When they have looked inside my head and decided that I am not good for nothing else and what kind of load do you think I always carry round with me if it isn't maths twenty percent; English lit fifteen percent; history forty percent; geography nine-teen percent? They have made my old man and all people I know believe it and now you are pushing it further into my old man's head that I am completely castrated with your books and studies. He really believes it's this shit you are doing in here that makes people and because I can't measure up to it—I am not his son anymore. Do you realize what I am talking about, you squirty worm?"

"Listen. I just wanted to help. Forget all I said. I just worried that you might catch it worse than what you are receiving treatments for right now."

"Just like my father. Now you are the bigger brother that I don't have. Do you know what it feels like to be the big brother in a family of eight and never be able to help your little brothers and sisters just because you have been labeled incompetent by some smart Mr. Know-it-all who has had the further luck of having it believed by your own family?"

"Then prove yourself!"

"Prove my death, you mean?"

"So you want to kill—you would rather kill yourself?"

"Who says I am killing myself?"

"How many times have you been to the doctor for the past half year and he hasn't diagnosed VD in one form or another?"

"So you told my father that too? You are not leaving any stone unturned are you? You want to see me completely destroyed." He put his hands to his face.

"How could I tell him *that?*"

"Sure you didn't when you shout it out like that as if you were the shortchanged tenth wife in a polygamous marriage!"

"Kute."

"Don't Kute me!"

"Listen."

"Listen yourself, Mr. Gutbug! It's me who feels the pricks of the doctor's needle. It's me who is going to do the dying if there is going to be any dying around here. And you won't hear me complaining when I am dead, hear that? Not a single word from me when I am

down and under. I'll be so far away and out of it all that I won't
bother you. Then you can continue with your books all year round,
all your damn precious life. God, I wish I had never met you!"

I looked at him. There were pieces of broken glass in his eyes.

"Please leave me alone with my life, Gatsi, will you? I can't be as
bright as you and you can't do what I can do although no one else
thinks it's anything and when I die you will be king of the world and
cock of the roost and I hope to honest God you drown in your own
piss. So leave my goddamn rotten life alone, will you?"

I looked at him and he turned his face away from me, swallowing
hard. I looked through the window and saw only my reflection in the
glass pane.

"Just stay out of my life," he said, his eyes to the wall but his fists
clenched so hard that several veins bulged out in his neck.

He stood up and, without looking at me, opened the door and
went out, closing the door so silently that the echo of its eternal bang
haunted me for the next three weeks as I tramped from one location
to another in search of new lodgings. I had also given away the bulk
of my books to friends, because I found that it was just too much
useless baggage to lug around with me whenever there was a need to
change lodgings.

A DIFFERENT TIME

‖‖‖

by Chicks Nkosi

Chicks Nkosi *is a newcomer to the literary scene of Swazi-land. The story included here was originally published in the book* Africa South: Contemporary Writings (1980), *edited by M. Mutloatse.*

U MHLATHI OWEHLULA *izimolontshisi zama khafula emab-hunu,* the jaw that defied the force of kaffir knobkerries. Those were his praises.

Whenever one of the old men greeted him with these praises, he would shake his head and say: *"Shiyakhona,* leave it there."

His jaw was crooked and a big scar ran from ear to chin. He was a kind old soul who always greeted us children with a smile, even though the smile was a bit wry because of his disfigured jaw.

Still, we liked him very much, but wondered what it was that had hurt him so badly.

One evening we were sitting around a fire eating *imbasha. Imba-sha* is a word for grains of dry mealies which have been soaked over-night in water. We fried *imbasha* in a *likesi,* the upturned lid of a three-legged iron pot. We had to snatch it off the *likesi* while it was still hot and dancing. Once *imbasha* cooled, it became hard again and unchewable.

We were having our *imbasha* when bold Mncina started telling us about what they used to do when they were *umbutho,* the king's regiment.

"You know Nkambule," he said screwing up his jaw. "You know

‖‖‖‖‖‖‖‖‖‖‖
148

whom I mean?" Yes, we knew whom he meant.

"I was in the same regiment with him. Ho, ho, you boys do not know anything. Ask from this one," he said pointing at his chest.

"You say so, Mkhulu?"

"Yes, I say so. What can you tell me? You whose food is cooked for you by women, and yet have the liver to call yourselves men! *Sukani lapha*, get off. You are nothing. You would never survive a single battle. You would die like flies sprayed with sheep dip."

"What are we supposed to do, Mkhulu?"

"Supposed to do? Listen to them. They ask what they are supposed to do!

"Do you not know that you should defend your king, your women, your children, your country and your cattle? Is that not what a man was made for?

"Do you think that the gods of Mswati made you to live and work for white men and become their kaffirs? You are like women who work for their husbands. You till the fields and do all the odd chores. You work for your white bosses in exchange for money, food and shelter. *Sukani lapha*, get away. You are a disgrace.

"*Thina*, we became regiments of the king. We learned to live a hard life. Nobody gave us food. We had to fend for ourselves. Who would feed you in the field of battle?"

"You say so, Mkhulu?"

The old man did not answer. He looked into the distance, the distance of time.

The firelight showed the skin of his furrowed forehead. It drew tighter and tighter into wrinkles and his eyes shone brighter and smaller as he looked back into the past.

No one could disturb him then.

"Ya," he said after a time. "You cannot understand, children of my children. I lived in a different world. You cannot understand."

"*Hawu* Mkhulu?"

"I was telling you about the scar on . . ." Mkhulu twisted his jaw to indicate whom he meant.

"Yes, Mkhulu. Please tell us. What happened to him?"

||||||||||||||||||||||||||||||||||||||||||||||||||||||||||||||||||||||||||||||||||||||||||||||||||||||||||||||||||

"What happened? He nearly died, that one. But, *hayi*, the man is strong. I tell you, they thought they had finished him. *Ubani yena*, not that one. He got away through the small hole of a rat."

"*Hawu* Mkhulu?"

"*Lalelani nginitshele*, just listen and let me tell you. You see, it all started a long time ago, this trouble with the white people. It started when the great king Somhlolo prophesied that people with white skins, blue eyes and hair that hangs down like mealie tassles would come from the sea.

"King Somhlolo said we should not fight them. We should not spill even a drop of that foreign blood on this land.

"Indeed, long after he of the right hand had gone to join his forefathers, the white people came.

"When they came, they asked for, and were given land by the good King Mbandzeni who was reigning at the time.

"You see, it was our tradition that strangers to a country should be given land and helped to set up home. It was in that spirit that they were given land to pasture their sheep and cattle.

"The white people used to come down to Swaziland in the winter, driving flocks of sheep to eat up the king's green grass.

"Unlike other black people who had come to the country, the whites did not join the Swazi nations. They merely used the privileges and rights of the Swazis without the attendant responsibilities, like serving in the regiments, joining in the collective community work and so on.

"Naturally, we did not like that. We did not like to see those flocks driven down from faraway Transvaal, coming here to devour our grass free of charge. Especially because those animals, the *tiklabu* sheep, were so very tasty to the tongue.

"We decided to have our own back for the destruction of our grass by these animals.

"The white men used to come here with people whom they had dressed up in old torn dirty clothing. These people they called their kaffirs, and that is how we came to call them, *emakhafula emabhunu.*

"Usually two of these men would look after a big flock of sheep. They used to drive the sheep in a long line on the road. One chap would lead the flock and the other would be right at the back.

"The line would extend as far as from here to that antheap." Mkhulu pointed into the dark at an antheap that was about two hundred yards away.

"We studied the way they were driven," said Mkhulu. "We got the kaffirs to get used to seeing us washing in the rivers near the bridges over which they passed.

"The bridges were low and narrow in those days; just wide enough for a wagon to cross.

"As the line of sheep went past over the bridge, we quickly snatched a few, and sat on them in the water. Sheep do not cry so they drowned quietly, and the shepherds went on unaware.

"At the next bridge the same thing happened. Altogether, we found ourselves with over twenty sheep.

"The sheep were normally counted in the mornings to see if any had strayed off or been stolen during the night.

"That gave us the whole night to hide our loot. We never regarded ourselves as having stolen the sheep. We felt we were entitled to repossess some of these animals to avenge the loss of our grass, that's all.

"Anyway, we dug a big hole in the middle of the king's field and buried our sheep in a hole this deep." Mkhulu raised his hand about four feet from the ground.

"We stacked the animals close, wool and all, and we covered the hole. Then early in the morning when you could only see the horns of the cattle, we were up collecting wood and stacking the wood over our secret.

"The Lion of Somhlolo had been pleased to give relish to the regiment, that day we got the sheep. Relish for the regiments meant an ox. It had been slaughtered and hung overnight.

"By sunrise the fire was roaring and we were cutting up the beast, ready to roast it.

"When the shepherds counted their flock that morning, they found over twenty sheep missing.

"The Boer had arrived at the camp with dogs to watch overnight. No dog had barked in the night.

"However, the shepherds remembered seeing members of the regiment bathing in the rivers when they were driving the sheep.

"The Boer suspected.

"Onto his horse, straight to the nearest police post at Bremersdorp.

"When the sun was this high, we saw them raising dust in the distance. The metal plates on their mounts glittered in the morning sun. It was them. It was the formidable mounted police, *zona ngempela izimawundeni*.

"They came with the Boer and his shepherds in tow.

"Yes, the shepherds recognized some of us. We were the ones they had passed as they drove the sheep down the previous day.

"Did we see any lost sheep?

"No. Which lost sheep?

"What are we roasting on the fire?

"Meat.

"Meat? What kind of meat?

"Meat from an ox. There is the skin.

"Can we taste a piece of that meat?

"Sure. Why not? Any piece you fancy.

"After that the Boer and the police held short counsel. They left a few to watch over us and the rest continued to the Great Place. They got permission to search our huts. Nothing.

"They searched the surrounding area. Nothing.

"They gave up the search and came back to join those they had left to watch us.

"We were too busy roasting and feasting on our meat to worry about them and their lost sheep.

"After lingering around a bit, asking stupid questions and getting stupid answers, they decided to go.

"I do not need to tell you that the sheep were roasting beautifully in the earth below the big fire. The coolness of the earth preserved the meat for days and days. Every evening we dug up a sheep or two."

"*Kanti* Mkhulu, you used to be naughty when you were young," somebody said.

"Naughty? Just listen to this one. What do you mean naughty? Can't you see that ours was a mere act of avenging the grass which belonged to the land, grass that was being destroyed by these animals? What are you saying, *kanti bakuthengile*, eh? You have eaten the saliva of the white man."

We all laughed.

"But Mkhulu you have not told us about the one who is like this."

"Ssh," whispered Mkhulu. "He does not like it. Never talk about it again."

He looked about him in the dark to see if anyone was snooping.

"You see," he continued, "most Boers used to come with their flocks of sheep and go back to the Transvaal in summer.

"But there was this one who decided to bring his wife and build a house across the river. He came down with his shepherds, his sheep, cattle, goats, pigs and chickens.

"He was clever. He changed his workers frequently so that we never came to know them well enough to get them drunk and help ourselves to the Boer's animals.

"However, our hearts did not stop bleeding for the king's grass as the animals multiplied. We decided that enough was enough.

"One evening we approached the place about midnight. It was a cloudy and misty night, just the right time and setting for repossession.

"Quickly, we collected a few chickens and sheep. Sheep are easy because they never make a noise and, of course, they are the tastiest."

"What about the chickens, Mkhulu? They are so noisy."

"Boys of today know nothing. We had learnt that when it rains, chickens hide their heads under their wings.

"So, we carried a tin of water with us and as we approached the chickens, we scattered the water over the fowls and the fowls put their heads under their wings.

"Whilst it was still in that position, we would grab a fowl and wring its neck. Not a sound.

"The following day the Boer quarreled with his workers and sent them away. He brought out a new group but he continued to lose his animals.

"But, *lafika ilanga elisilima,* and indeed, when it dawned we did not realize that it was the day that was to make us look stupid with our well-planned designs.

"We used to go in turns to pick up something from the Boer's farm. It happened to be Nkambule's turn that night.

"He had just got inside the fence when he stumbled over a string.

"*Maye babo.* O fathers. The string was tied to a bell on the Boer's veranda. The bell went *kring, kring, kring.*

"The Boer was up, gun in hand. His workers came out carrying lanterns and kerries. They surrounded the whole place. Feet were running and people were shouting; the place was in an uproar.

"The chickens clacked and the pigs squealed and grunted, grousing at the untimely disturbance.

"The night was so dark you could not see your own hand if you put it out in front of your eyes. The mist was thick and it was drizzling and slippery. The lanterns were closing in around the yard.

"He knew he did not dare to try and get out. He was trapped.

"The area in which the Boer kept his animals was fenced in and the lanterns were surrounding it. Nkambule decided at that moment to take off the only thing he had on, *emajobo,* the loin skin covering his front and back below the waist.

"He put his head between his forearms and joined the pigs, grunting and pushing in the dark.

"His shining black body was difficult to detect among the large black pigs, in the dim light of the lanterns. They could not spot him, but they knew he was somewhere in there.

"After waiting for some time in the dampness of the night, the Boer left the others with instructions to *vang hom,* you must catch him, and went back into his house to catch some sleep.

"By this time, if it had been a clear night, the morning star *ink-*

wenwezi would be rising. Before long it was going to be light. Nkambule realized his time was running out.

"Gingerly, he crawled toward the fence. He had his hand out-
stretched in an attempt to feel for the string. He touched nothing.

"He crawled farther and still he touched nothing. He raised his
head just that much. His head found the string.

"He had no time. He jumped over the fence and dashed. He was
just a little slower than the raised knobkerrie in front of him.

"It caught him flush on the jaw.

"He stumbled and fell. He got up and ran on all fours.

"The man behind reached out to catch him. The man's hand
glided down the slippery wet naked body.

"Nkambule regained his feet and ran. *Nango eshona.* But *suka*,
the man behind him was closing in again fast. The thudding steps
were directly behind him.

"Quickly, he squatted on the ground. The chap came upon him
full speed. He tripped over Nkambule's body and fell on his face. He
landed on hard gravel which stripped his flesh into strings.

"Meantime, Nkambule picked himself up and got onto the man.

"*Nangu nyoko,*" he said, bringing his bare foot down hard onto
the back of the man's head.

"The man's front teeth collided violently with the hard gravel and
dislodged.

"Gone was Nkambule."

THE DOUM TREE OF WAD HAMID

by Tayeb Salih

Tayeb Salih *was born in 1929 in the northern part of the
Sudan where he was brought up in a farm community. He
was the head of drama in the Arab division of BBC and at
the time of this writing is working in UNESCO in Paris.
A short novel and several short stories were published
under the title* Wedding of Zein and Other Stories
(1968). His book The Season of Migration to the North
was published in 1969.

W ERE YOU TO COME to our village as a tourist, it is likely, my
son, that you would not stay long. If it were in wintertime, when the
palm trees are pollinated, you would find that a dark cloud had descended over the village. This, my son, would not be dust, nor yet
that mist which rises up after rainfall. It would be a swarm of those
sand flies which obstruct all paths to those who wish to enter our
village. Maybe you have seen this pest before, but I swear that you
have never seen this particular species. Take this gauze netting, my
son, and put it over your head. While it won't protect you against
these devils, it will at least help you to bear them. I remember a
friend of my son's, a fellow student at school, whom my son invited
to stay with us a year ago at this time of the year. His people come
from the town. He stayed one night with us and got up next day,
feverish, with a running nose and swollen face; he swore that he
wouldn't spend another night with us.

If you were to come to us in summer you would find the horseflies with us—enormous flies the size of young sheep, as we say. In comparison to these the sand flies are a thousand times more bearable. They are savage flies, my son: they bite, sting, buzz, and whirr. They have a special love for man and no sooner smell him out than they attach themselves to him. Wave them off you, my son—God curse all sand flies.

And were you to come at a time which was neither summer nor winter you would find nothing at all. No doubt, my son, you read the papers daily, listen to the radio, and go to the cinema once or twice a week. Should you become ill you have the right to be treated in a hospital, and if you have a son he is entitled to receive education at a school. I know, my son, that you hate dark streets and like to see electric light shining out into the night. I know, too, that you are not enamored of walking and that riding donkeys gives you a bruise on your backside. Oh, I wish, my son, I wish—the asphalted roads of the towns—the modern means of transport—the fine comfortable buses. We have none of all this—we are people who live on what God sees fit to give us.

Tomorrow you will depart from our village, of this I am sure, and you will be right to do so. What have you to do with such hardship? We are thick-skinned people and in this we differ from others. We have become used to this hard life, in fact we like it, but we ask no one to subject himself to the difficulties of our life. Tomorrow you will depart, my son—I know that. Before you leave, though, let me show you one thing—something which, in a manner of speaking, we are proud of. In the towns you have museums, places in which the local history and the great deeds of the past are preserved. This thing that I want to show you can be said to be a museum. It is one thing we insist our visitors should see.

Once a preacher, sent by the government, came to us to stay for a month. He arrived at a time when the horseflies had never been fatter. On the very first day the man's face swelled up. He bore this manfully and joined us in evening prayers on the second night, and after prayers he talked to us of the delights of the primitive life. On the third day he was down with malaria, he contracted dysentery, and his eyes were completely gummed up. I visited him at noon and found him prostrate in bed, with a boy standing at his head waving away the flies.

"O Sheikh," I said to him, "there is nothing in our village to show you, though I would like you to see the doum tree of Wad Hamid." He didn't ask me what Wad Hamid's doum tree was, but I presumed that he had heard of it, for who has not? He raised his face which was like the lung of a slaughtered cow; his eyes (as I said) were firmly closed; though I knew that behind the lashes there lurked a certain bitterness.

"By God," he said to me, "if this were the doum tree of Jandal, and you the Moslems who fought with Ali and Mu'awiya, and I the arbitrator between you, holding your fate in these two hands of mine, I would not stir an inch!" and he spat upon the ground as though to curse me and turned his face away. After that we heard that the sheikh had cabled to those who had sent him, saying: "The horseflies have eaten into my neck, malaria has burnt up my skin, and dysentery has lodged itself in my bowels. Come to my rescue, may God bless you—these are people who are in no need of me or of any other preacher." And so the man departed and the government sent us no preacher after him.

But, my son, our village actually witnessed many great men of power and influence, people with names that rang through the country like drums, whom we never even dreamed would ever come here —they came, by God, in droves.

We have arrived. Have patience, my son; in a little while there will be the noonday breeze to lighten the agony of this pest upon your face.

Here it is: the doum tree of Wad Hamid. Look how it holds its head aloft to the skies; look how its roots strike down into the earth; look at its full, sturdy trunk, like the form of a comely woman, at the branches on high resembling the mane of a frolicsome steed! In the afternoon, when the sun is low, the doum tree casts its shadow from this high mound right across the river so that someone sitting on the far bank can rest in its shade. At dawn, when the sun rises, the shadow of the tree stretches across the cultivated land and houses right up to the cemetery. Don't you think it is like some mythical eagle spreading its wings over the village and everyone in it? Once the government, wanting to put through an agricultural scheme, decided to cut it down: they said that the best place for setting up the pump was where the doum tree stood. As you can see, the people of our village are concerned solely with their everyday needs and I cannot remember their ever having rebelled against anything. However, when they heard about cutting down the doum tree they all rose up as one man and barred the district commissioner's way. That was in the time of foreign rule. The flies assisted them too—the horseflies. The man was surrounded by the clamoring people shouting that if the doum tree were cut down they would fight the government to the last man, while the flies played havoc with the man's face. As his papers were scattered in the water we heard him cry out: "All right— doum tree stay—scheme no stay!" And so neither the pump nor the scheme came about and we kept our doum tree.

Let us go home, my son, for this is no time for talking in the open. This hour just before sunset is a time when the army of sand flies becomes particularly active before going to sleep. At such a time no one who isn't well accustomed to them and has become as thick-skinned as we are can bear their stings. Look at it, my son, look at the doum tree: lofty, proud, and haughty as though—as though it were some ancient idol. Wherever you happen to be in the village you can see it; in fact, you can even see it from four villages away.

Tomorrow you will depart from our village, of that there is no doubt, the mementos of the short walk we have taken visible upon your face, neck and hands. But before you leave I shall finish the story of the tree, the doum tree of Wad Hamid. Come in, my son, treat this house as your own.

You ask who planted the doum tree?

No one planted it, my son. Is the ground in which it grows arable land? Do you not see that it is stony and appreciably higher than the river bank, like the pedestal of a statue, while the river twists and turns below it like a sacred snake, one of the ancient gods of the

||||||||||||||||||||||||||||||||||||||||||||||||||||||||||||||||||||||||||||||||||||||||||||||||||||||||||||||||

Egyptians? My son, no one planted it. Drink your tea, for you must be in need of it after the trying experience you have undergone. Most probably it grew up by itself, though no one remembers having known it other than as you now find it. Our sons opened their eyes to find it commanding the village. And we, when we take ourselves back to childhood memories, to that dividing line beyond which you remember nothing, see in our minds a giant doum tree standing on a river bank; everything beyond it is as cryptic as talismans, like the boundary between day and night, like that fading light which is not the dawn but the light directly preceding the break of day. My son, do you find that you can follow what I say? Are you aware of this feeling I have within me but which I am powerless to express? Every new generation finds the doum tree as though it had been born at the time of their birth and would grow up with them. Go and sit with the people of this village and listen to them recounting their dreams. A man awakens from sleep and tells his neighbor how he found himself in a vast sandy tract of land, the sand as white as pure silver; how his feet sank in as he walked so that he could only draw them out again with difficulty; how he walked and walked until he was overcome with thirst and stricken with hunger, while the sands stretched end-lessly around him; how he climbed a hill and on reaching the top espied a dense forest of doum trees with a single tall tree in the center which in comparison with the others looked like a camel amid a herd of goats; how the man went down the hill to find that the earth seemed to be rolled up before him so that it was but a few steps before he found himself under the doum tree of Wad Hamid; how he then discovered a vessel containing milk, its surface still fresh with froth, and how the milk did not go down though he drank until he had quenched his thirst. At which his neighbor says to him, "Rejoice at release from your troubles."

You can also hear one of the women telling her friend: "It was as though I were in a boat sailing through a channel in the sea, so narrow that I could stretch out my hands and touch the shore on either side. I found myself on the crest of a mountainous wave which carried me upward till I was almost touching the clouds, then bore me down into a dark, bottomless pit. I began shouting in my fear, but my voice seemed to be trapped in my throat. Suddenly I found the channel opening out a little. I saw that on the two shores were black, leafless trees with thorns, the tips of which were like the heads of hawks. I saw the two shores closing in upon me and the trees seemed to be walking toward me. I was filled with terror and called out at the top of my voice, 'O Wad Hamid!' As I looked I saw a man with a radiant face and a heavy white beard flowing down over his chest, dressed in spotless white and holding a string of amber prayer-beads. Placing his hand on my brow he said: 'Be not afraid,' and I was calmed. Then I found the shore opening up and the water flowing gently. I looked to my left and saw fields of ripe corn, waterwheels turning, and cattle grazing, and on the shore stood the doum tree of Wad Hamid. The boat came to rest under the tree and the man got out, tied up the boat, and stretched out his hand to me. He then struck me gently on the shoulder with the string of beads, picked up a doum fruit from the ground and put it in my hand. When I turned round he was no longer there."

"That was Wad Hamid," her friend then says to her, "you will have an illness that will bring you to the brink of death, but you will recover. You must make an offering to Wad Hamid under the doum tree."

So it is, my son, that there is not a man or woman, young or old, who dreams at night without seeing the doum tree of Wad Hamid at some point in the dream.

You ask me why it was called the doum tree of Wad Hamid and who Wad Hamid was. Be patient, my son—have another cup of tea.

At the beginning of home rule a civil servant came to inform us that the government was intending to set up a stopping place for the steamer. He told us that the national government wished to help us and to see us progress, and his face was radiant with enthusiasm as he talked. But he could see that the faces around him expressed no reaction. My son, we are not people who travel very much, and when we wish to do so for some important matter such as registering land, or seeking advice about a matter of divorce, we take a morning's ride on our donkeys and then board the steamer from the neighboring village. My son, we have grown accustomed to this, in fact it is precisely for this reason that we breed donkeys. It is little wonder, then, that the government official could see nothing in the people's faces to indicate that they were pleased with the news. His enthusiasm waned and, being at his wit's end, he began to fumble for words.

"Where will the stopping place be?" someone asked him after a period of silence. The official replied that there was only one suitable place—where the doum tree stood. Had you that instant brought along a woman and had her stand among those men as naked as the day her mother bore her, they could not have been more astonished.

"The steamer usually passes here on a Wednesday," one of the men quickly replied; "if you made a stopping place, then it would be here on Wednesday afternoon." The official replied that the time fixed for the steamer to stop by their village would be four o'clock on Wednesday afternoon.

"But that is the time when we visit the tomb of Wad Hamid at the doum tree," answered the man; "when we take our women and children and make offerings. We do this every week." The official laughed. "Then change the day!" he replied. Had the official told these men at that moment that every one of them was a bastard, that would not have angered them more than this remark of his. They rose up as one man, bore down upon him and would certainly have killed him if I had not intervened and snatched him from their clutches. I then put him on a donkey and told him to make good his escape.

And so it was that the steamer still does not stop here and that we still ride off on our donkeys for a whole morning and take the steamer from the neighboring village when circumstances require us to travel. We content ourselves with the thought that we visit the tomb of Wad Hamid with our women and children and that we make offerings there every Wednesday as our fathers and fathers' fathers did before us.

Excuse me, my son, while I perform the sunset prayer—it is said that the sunset prayer is "strange": if you don't catch it in time it eludes you. *God's pious servants—I declare that there is no god but God and I declare that Muhammad is His Servant and His Prophet —Peace be upon you and the mercy of God!*

Ah, ah. For a week this back of mine has been giving me pain. What do you think it is, my son? I know, though—it's just old age. Oh to be young! In my young days I would breakfast off half a sheep, drink the milk of five cows for supper, and be able to lift a sack of dates with one hand. He lies who says he ever beat me at wrestling. They used to call me "the crocodile." Once I swam the river, using my chest to push a boat loaded with wheat to the other shore—at night! On the shore were some men at work at their waterwheels, who threw down their clothes in terror and fled when they saw me pushing the boat toward them.

"Oh people," I shouted at them, "what's wrong, shame upon you! Don't you know me? I'm 'the crocodile.' By God, the devils themselves would be scared off by your ugly faces."

My son, have you asked me what we do when we're ill?

I laugh because I know what's going on in your head. You townsfolk hurry to the hospital on the slightest pretext. If one of you hurts his finger you dash off to the doctor who puts a bandage on and you carry it in a sling for days; and even then it doesn't get better. Once I was working in the fields and something bit my finger—this little finger of mine. I jumped to my feet and looked around in the grass where I found a snake lurking. I swear to you it was longer than my arm. I took hold of it by the head and crushed it between two fingers, then bit into my finger, sucked out the blood, and took up a handful of dust and rubbed it on the bite.

But that was only a little thing. What do we do when faced with real illness?

This neighbor of ours, now. One day her neck swelled up and she was confined to bed for two months. One night she had a heavy fever, so at first dawn she rose from her bed and dragged herself along till she came—yes, my son, till she came to the doum tree of Wad Hamid. The woman told us what happened.

"I was under the doum tree," she said, "with hardly sufficient

||||||||||||||||||||||||||||||||||||||||||||||||||||||||||||||||||||||||||||||||||||||||||||||||||||||||||||||||

strength to stand up, and called out at the top of my voice: 'O Wad Hamid, I have come to you to seek refuge and protection—I shall sleep here at your tomb and under your doum tree. Either you let me die or you restore me to life; I shall not leave here until one of these two things happens.'

"And so I curled myself up in fear," the woman continued with her story, "and was soon overcome by sleep. While midway between wakefulness and sleep I suddenly heard sounds of recitation from the Koran and a bright light, as sharp as a knife-edge, radiated out, joining up the two riverbanks, and I saw the doum tree prostrating itself in worship. My heart throbbed so violently that I thought it would leap up through my mouth. I saw a venerable old man with a white beard and wearing a spotless white robe come up to me, a smile on his face. He struck me on the head with his string of prayer beads and called out: 'Arise.'

"I swear that I got up I know not how and went home I know not how. I arrived back at dawn and woke up my husband, my son, and my daughters. I told my husband to light the fire and make tea. Then I ordered my daughters to give trilling cries of joy, and the whole village prostrated themselves before us. I swear that I have never again been afraid, nor yet ill."

Yes, my son, we are people who have no experience of hospitals. In small matters such as the bites of scorpions, fever, sprains, and fractures, we take to our beds until we are cured. When in serious trouble we go to the doum tree.

Shall I tell you the story of Wad Hamid, my son, or would you like to sleep? Townsfolk don't go to sleep till late at night—I know that of them. We, though, go to sleep directly the birds are silent, the flies stop harrying the cattle, the leaves of the trees settle down, the hens spread their wings over their chicks, and the goats turn on their sides to chew the cud. We and our animals are alike: we rise in the morning when they rise and go to sleep when they sleep, our breathing and theirs following one and the same pattern.

My father, reporting what my grandfather had told him, said: "Wad Hamid, in times gone by, used to be the slave of a wicked man.

He was one of God's holy saints but kept his faith to himself, not daring to pray openly lest his wicked master should kill him. When he could no longer bear his life with this infidel he called upon God to deliver him and a voice told him to spread his prayer mat on the water and that when it stopped by the shore he should descend. The prayer mat put him down at the place where the doum tree is now and which used to be wasteland. And there he stayed alone, praying the whole day. At nightfall a man came to him with dishes of food, so he ate and continued his worship till dawn."

All this happened before the village was built up. It is as though this village, with its inhabitants, its waterwheels and buildings, had become split off from the earth. Anyone who tells you he knows the history of its origin is a liar. Other places begin by being small and then grow larger, but this village of ours came into being at one bound. Its population neither increases nor decreases, while its appearance remains unchanged. And ever since our village has existed, so has the doum tree of Wad Hamid; and just as no one remembers how it originated and grew, so no one remembers how the doum tree came to grow in a patch of rocky ground by the river, standing above it like a sentinel.

When I took you to visit the tree, my son, do you remember the iron railing round it? Do you remember the marble plaque standing on a stone pedestal with "The doum tree of Wad Hamid" written on it? Do you remember the doum tree with the gilded crescents above the tomb? They are the only new things about the village since God first planted it here, and I shall now recount to you how they came into being.

When you leave us tomorrow—and you will certainly do so, swollen of face and inflamed of eye—it will be fitting if you do not curse us but rather think kindly of us and of the things that I have told you this night, for you may well find that your visit to us was not wholly bad.

You remember that some years ago we had members of Parliament and political parties and a great deal of to-ing and fro-ing which we couldn't make head or tail of. The roads would sometimes cast down strangers at our very doors, just as the waves of the sea wash up strange weeds. Though not a single one of them prolonged his stay beyond one night, they would nevertheless bring us the news of the great fuss going on in the capital. One day they told us that the government which had driven out imperialism had been substituted by an even bigger and noisier government.

"And who has changed it?" we asked them, but received no answer. As for us, ever since we refused to allow the stopping place to be set up at the doum tree no one has disturbed our tranquil existence. Two years passed without our knowing what form the government had taken, black or white. Its emissaries passed through our village without staying in it, while we thanked God that He had saved us the trouble of putting them up. So things went on till, four years ago, a new government came into power. As though this new authority wished to make us conscious of its presence, we awoke one day to find an official with an enormous hat and small head, in the company of two soldiers, measuring up and doing calculations at the doum tree. We asked them what it was about, to which they replied that the government wished to build a stopping place for the steamer under the doum tree.

"But we have already given you our answer about that," we told them. "What makes you think we'll accept it now?"

"The government which gave in to you was a weak one," they said, "but the position has now changed."

To cut a long story short, we took them by the scruffs of their necks, hurled them into the water, and went off to our work. It wasn't more than a week later when a group of soldiers came along commanded by the small-headed official with the large hat, shouting, "Arrest that man, and that one, and that one," until they'd taken off twenty of us, I among them. We spent a month in prison. Then one day the very soldiers who had put us there opened the prison gates. We asked them what it was all about but no one said anything. Outside the prison we found a great gathering of people; no sooner had we been spotted than there were shouts and cheering and we were embraced by some cleanly dressed people, heavily scented and with

gold watches gleaming on their wrists. They carried us off in a great
procession, back to our own people. There we found an unbelievably
immense gathering of people, carts, horses and camels. We said to
each other, "The din and flurry of the capital has caught up with us."
They made us twenty men stand in a row and the people passed along
it shaking us by the hand: the prime minister—the president of the
Parliament—the president of the Senate—the member for such and
such constituency—the member for such and such other constituency.

We looked at each other without understanding a thing of what
was going on around us except that our arms were aching with all the
handshakes we had been receiving from those presidents and
members of Parliament.

Then they took us off in a great mass to the place where the doum
tree and the tomb stand. The prime minister laid the foundation
stone for the monument you've seen, and for the dome you've seen,
and for the railing you've seen. Like a tornado blowing up for a while
and then passing over, so that mighty host disappeared as suddenly as
it had come without spending a night in the village—no doubt because of the horseflies which, that particular year, were as large and
fat and buzzed and whirred as much as during the year the preacher
came to us.

One of those strangers who were occasionally cast upon us in the
village later told us the story of all this fuss and bother.

"The people," he said, "hadn't been happy about this government
since it had come to power, for they knew that it had got there by
bribing a number of the members of Parliament. They therefore
bided their time and waited for the right opportunities to present
themselves, while the opposition looked around for something to
spark things off. When the doum tree incident occurred and they
marched you all off and slung you into prison, the newspapers took
this up and the leader of the government which had resigned made a
fiery speech in Parliament in which he said:

"'To such tyranny has this government come that it has begun to
interfere in the beliefs of the people, in those holy things held most

||||||||||||||||||||||||||||||||||||||||||||||||||||||||||||||||||||||||||||||||||||||||||||||||||||||||||||||||||||||||||||

sacred by them.' Then, taking a most imposing stance and in a voice choked with emotion, he said: 'Ask our worthy prime minister about the doum tree of Wad Hamid. Ask him how it was that he permitted himself to send his troops and henchmen to desecrate that pure and holy place!'

"The people took up the cry and throughout the country their hearts responded to the incident of the doum tree as to nothing before. Perhaps the reason is that in every village in this country there is some monument like the doum tree of Wad Hamid which people see in their dreams. After a month of fuss and shouting and inflamed feelings, fifty members of the government were forced to withdraw their support, their constituencies having warned them that unless they did so they would wash their hands of them. And so the government fell, the first government returned to power and the leading paper in the country wrote: 'The doum tree of Wad Hamid has become the symbol of the nation's awakening.'"

Since that day we have been unaware of the existence of the new government and not one of those great giants of men who visited us has put in an appearance; we thank God that He has spared us the trouble of having to shake them by the hand. Our life returned to what it had been: no water pump, no agricultural scheme, no stopping place for the steamer. But we kept our doum tree which casts its shadow over the southern bank in the afternoon and, in the morning, spreads its shadow over the fields and houses right up to the cemetery, with the river flowing below it like some sacred legendary snake. And our village has acquired a marble monument, an iron railing, and a dome with gilded crescents.

When the man had finished what he had to say he looked at me with an enigmatic smile playing at the corners of his mouth like the faint flickerings of a lamp.

"And when," I asked, "will they set up the water pump, and put through the agricultural scheme and the stopping place for the steamer?"

He lowered his head and paused before answering me, "When people go to sleep and don't see the doum tree in their dreams."

"And when will that be?" I said.

"I mentioned to you that my son is in the town studying at school," he replied. "It wasn't I who put him there; he ran away and went there on his own, and it is my hope that he will stay where he is and not return. When my son's son passes out of school and the number of young men with souls foreign to our own increases, then perhaps the water pump will be set up and the agricultural scheme put into being—maybe then the steamer will stop at our village— under the doum tree of Wad Hamid."

"And do you think," I said to him, "that the doum tree will one day be cut down?" He looked at me for a long while as though wishing to project, through his tired, misty eyes, something which he was incapable of doing by word.

"There will not be the least necessity for cutting down the doum tree. There is not the slightest reason for the tomb to be removed. What all these people have overlooked is that there's plenty of room for all these things: the doum tree, the tomb, the water pump and the steamer's stopping place."

When he had been silent for a time he gave me a look which I don't know how to describe, though it stirred within me a feeling of sadness, sadness for some obscure thing which I was unable to define. Then he said: "Tomorrow, without doubt, you will be leaving us. When you arrive at your destination, think well of us and judge us not too harshly."

THOUGHTS IN A TRAIN

||||||||||||||||||||||||||||||||||||||||||||||||||||||||||||||||||||||||||||||

by Mango Tshabangu

Mango Tshabangu *is a former artist and editor. The story we publish here was included in the book* Africa South: Contemporary Writings (1980) *edited by M. Mutloatse.*

W HEN WE RIDE THESE things which cannot take us all, there is no doubt as to our inventiveness. We stand inside in grotesque positions—one foot in the air, our bodies twisted away from arms squeezing through other twisted bodies to find support somewhere. Sometimes it is on another person's shoulder, but it is stupid to complain so nobody does. It's as if some invisible sardine packer has been at work. We remain in that position for forty minutes or forty days. How far is Soweto from Johannesburg? It is forty mintues or forty days. No one knows exactly.

We remain in that position, our bodies sweating out the unfreedom of our souls, anticipating happiness in that unhappy architectural shame—the ghetto. Our eyes dart apprehensively, on the lookout for those of our brothers who have resorted to the insanity of crime to protest their insane conditions. For, indeed, if we were not scared of moral ridicule we would regard crime as a form of protest. Is not a man with a hungry stomach in the same position as a man whose land has been taken away from him? What if he is a victim of both!

We remain in that position for forty minutes or forty days. No one knows exactly. We, the young, cling perilously to the outside of the coach walls. It sends the guts racing to the throat, yes, but to us it is

||||||||||||

bravery. We are not a helpless gutless lot whose lives have been patterned by suffering. The more daring among us dance like gods of fate on the rooftop. Sometimes there is death by electrocution but then it is just hard luck. . . . He was a good man, Bayekile. It is not his fault that he did not live to face a stray bullet.

We remain in that position for forty minutes or forty days. No one knows exactly.

We move parallel to or hurtle past their trains. Most often my impression is that it is they who cruise past our hurtling train. Theirs is always almost empty. They'll sit comfortably on seats made for that purpose and keep their windows shut, even on hot days. And they sit there in their train watching us as one watches a play from a private box. We also stare back at them, but the sullen faces don't interest us much. Only the shut windows move our thinking.

On this day it was Msongi and Gezani who were most interested in the shut windows. You see, ever since they'd discovered Houghton golf course to be offering better tips in the caddy business, Msongi and Gezani found themselves walking through the rich suburbs of Johannesburg. Their experience was a strange one. There was something eerie in the surroundings. They always had fear, the like of which they'd never known. Surely it was not because of the numerous policemen who patrolled the streets and snarled in unison with their dogs at black boys moving through those gracious thoroughfares.

Msongi and Gezani were young no doubt, but this writer has already said that bravery born of suffering knows no age nor danger nor pattern. Fear of snarling policemen was out for these two young black boys. Nevertheless, this overwhelming fear the like of which they'd never known was always all around them whenever they walked through the rich suburbs of Johannesburg. They could not even talk about it. Somehow, they were sure they both had this strange fear.

There was a time when they impulsively stood right in the middle of a street. They had hoped to break this fear the like of which they'd never known. But the attempt only lasted a few seconds and that was too short to be of any help. They both scurried off, hating themselves for lack of courage. They never spoke of it.

In search of the truth, Msongi became very observant. He'd been noticing the shut windows of *their* train every time he and Gezani happened to be in ours. On this day, it was a week since Msongi decided to break the silence. Msongi's argument was that the fear was in the surroundings and not in them. The place was full of fear. Vicious fear which, although imprisoned in stone walls and electrified fences, swelled over and poured into the streets to oppress even the occasional passer-by. Msongi and Gezani were merely walking through this fear. It was like walking in darkness and feeling the darkness all around you. That does not mean you are darkness yourself. As soon as you come to a lit spot, the feeling of darkness dies. Why, as soon as they hit town proper, and mixed with the people, the fear the like of which they'd never known disappeared. No, Msongi was convinced it was not they who had fear. Fear flowed from somewhere, besmirching every part of them, leaving their souls trembling; but it was not they who were afraid.

They did not have stone walls or electrified fences in Soweto. They were not scared of their gold rings being snatched for they had none. They were not worried about their sisters being peeped at for their sisters could look after themselves. Oh, those diamond toothpicks could disappear you know. . . . Those too, they did not have. They were not afraid of bleeding, for their streets ran red already. On this day Msongi stared at the shut windows. He looked at the pale sullen white faces and he knew why.

He felt tempted to throw something at them. Anything . . . an empty cigarette box, an orange peel, even a piece of paper; just to prove a point. At that moment, and as if instructed by Msongi himself, someone threw an empty beer bottle at the other train.

The confusion: They ran around climbing onto seats. They jumped into the air. They knocked against one another as they scrambled for the doors and windows. The already pale faces had no color to change into. They could only be distorted as fear is capable of doing that as well. The shut windows were shattered wide open, as if to say danger cannot be imprisoned. The train passed swiftly by, disappearing with the drama of the fear the like of which Msongi and Gezani had never known.

THE SOLDIER WITHOUT AN EAR

by Paul Zaleza

Paul Zaleza *was born in 1954 and was educated in Malawi, where he graduated from the university in 1976. He has written plays and poems and a selection of his short stories has been gathered in* Night of Darkness and Other Stories (1976).

MANY YEARS AGO, while I was still a student, I did some research for one of my history lecturers. He was writing a doctoral thesis and he was trying to find out the reaction of the people of the country to the two World Wars. It was after I had been to several villages and seen quite a number of people who had participated in or witnessed one of the wars or both that I came to Biwi village. I first went to the chief and briefed him on the purpose of my visit. He was cooperative and directed me to the house of Baba Fule, the soldier who had fought in both wars.

"He is an interesting man. You'll like him," said the chief.

When I got to Baba Fule's house, I agreed with the chief. Baba Fule's house was modest and clean. With its corrugated iron sheets, glass windows and four-cornered structure, it had a touch of the town and was almost out of place in the village. There was nobody outside. I knocked. I was told to enter. I found a very aged man sitting on a chair doing nothing. Save for a few black dots of hair, his head was white. His sunken, nearly blind eyes gazed at me with surprise.

"Who are you?" he asked me. I introduced myself. He sat for a moment, reflecting on where he could have met me or what relationship I had with him.

"Are you Solomon?"

"No, I'm not." I told him that I did not come from his village.

"Then, what do you want here?" I explained the purpose of my visit.

"So you want to write a book about me. Ma, ma, ma! Nanyoni, come and hear what this young man wants to do. He wants to write a book about me. Ma, ma, ma!"

Presently, a very old woman, walking with a stick, with her back permanently bent and thereby having the height of an average twelve-year-old girl, came into the room. She extended her weak, thin and wrinkled arm to me. Her face was so wrinkled that if anyone from outer space saw her before setting his eyes on anyone else, he would form a mean impression of the beauty of human beings. He would think our faces are a collection of mouths with a nose in between and two small eyes for decoration. Baba Fule looked much younger and energetic when compared with her.

"This young man wants to write a book about me," Baba Fule excitedly told his wife. The folds on her face extended, indicating that she was smiling or doing something of the kind.

"Are you at school?" Baba Fule asked me.

"Yes, I am," I replied.

"What standard are you doing?" he asked. Telling him that I was in my third year at the university would not mean much to him, so I told him that I was doing standard fifteen.

"Standard fifteen. Ma, ma, ma, the children of these days. Standard fifteen. Ma, ma, ma."

"What is standard fifteen?" his wife asked.

"As many as the fingers on your hands and the toes of one foot," he explained, smiling, showing his partially filled gums.

"Has he more standards than Josiah and Aleck?" his wife inquired.

"Yes, Josiah and Aleck have twelve standards." Baba Fule told me who Josiah and Aleck were. They were his grandchildren. He had eleven children, three of whom had died while they were still young. The eight were still alive and were gifted with big families as he had been.

"If I count all my grandchildren, they reach sixty-nine, and some of these have children of their own," he said, smiling contentedly.

"Where do they all live?" I asked.

"They live in towns. If they all came back, this village would be too small to accommodate them. But they all come here from time to time. I live with two of my great grandchildren here, a boy and a girl."

"You've been blessed," I said.

"Oh, yes, very much. Everything we eat and wear comes from our children and grandchildren. All we do is sit down, basking in the sun, waiting for the day." He then boasted of the cars some of his children and grandchildren had.

"The world has changed," he said. "In my youth there were no cars, only bicycles, and even then only the very rich could afford them. In fact, only the Azungu possessed them. But these days, even children have bicycles and as for cars, even women drive them! In my youth many children did not go to school. Anybody who reached standard three was considered very educated. But these days, you get almost every child in school. You know, small children this high," he indicated with his stick, "are doing standard three. I finished my standard two at your age." He paused, smiling at me. I was fascinated.

"If it were possible, would you exchange your life of those days for the life of these days?" I asked.

"The life these days is easier and more comfortable. But still I would not exchange the life I had."

"Why?"

"There are many reasons. As boys, we had more fun and adventure in our days than the children of these days. You see, all that the children do these days is go to school from an early age and be stuffed with books in foreign languages and mostly about foreign ways so that they lose their own things. Indeed, now things seem to have no direction, no purpose. You see, in the old days, a man of my age and my family would have left this village long ago and founded his own village and would have been chief. But today, my wife and I are left alone to look after ourselves. I don't complain about my children. They help me. I have some friends who are not in such a fortunate position. However, I still feel something is wrong. It's like a basket weaver exchanging his best baskets for a bag of maize only to find out that it's full of sand." Baba Fule went on telling me about his youth with deliberate emphasis to show how superior it was to our youth. I was too absorbed with the conversation to realize that I had not begun my interview.

"Baba, I would now like to ask you a few questions about the two World Wars."

"Oh, yes, the book. I forgot. Forgive me, my son. I'm feeling cold. Let's go and sit in the sun."

I offered to carry his chair, but he insisted on carrying it alone. The sun was quite high, and the heat was oppressive. I pretended not to mind.

"Come and sit on this side," he told me. One side of his face had no ear. It was a memorable souvenir of his life as a soldier.

"You want me to tell you about my whole life or my life as a soldier?" he asked.

"Your life as a soldier," I replied.

"All right. I joined the army when the Great War broke out between the Germans and the British. I was already a man by then with a family of four. The training did not take long. I first fought in Tanganyika. There, I got the first big excitement of my life. You know what it was?" he asked me, smilingly.

"No, I don't," I replied, smiling back.

"I killed an Azungu, a German. It sounds strange, eh? I don't know how I can explain it. But I was wildly excited. Gradually, shooting them became commonplace. Of course, we also killed the Africans on the side of the Germans, but that was not as exciting as killing the Azungu. Then, in 1916, I was sent to Egypt where fierce battles were being fought. Egypt, as you know, is a land of Arabs. I will always remember it for one thing." He paused as he saw a young boy standing in the *Khonde*.

"That's the boy I was telling you about. Imagine such a young boy in standard five. Richard, come and greet your brother here." The young boy came and greeted me shyly. Then Baba Fule told him to go away. The boy reluctantly left us.

"What was I saying?" Baba Fule asked me.

"You were saying that Egypt is a land of Arabs and you'll always remember it."

"Oh, yes. You see, the Arabs are the ones who enslaved our fathers and grandfathers, destroying our villages and all that. I'm sure you learn that at school."

"Yes, we do," I replied.

"And you know what? Well"—Baba Fule looked around to see if anyone was listening—"you see, I and some of my friends slept with their women. Well, don't write that in the book." He gave a small laugh. I felt slightly embarrassed. But I managed to share his laughter.

"Moreover, for the first time I met a lot of Africans from other countries. It was an unforgettable experience. I remember I had a friend from Kenya. He was . . . well, we can forget that."

"No, tell me," I pleaded.

"It's a very long story," he objected.

"It doesn't matter."

"All right. I'll cut it short. This friend of mine was called Murasa. One day he was in the bush with a small group of soldiers. In the distance he saw white soldiers. He ordered his men to fire. The other side also opened fire. Before long, half of Murasa's men lay dead. Murasa surrendered. You know what happened?" Baba Fule asked me.

"No, I don't," I replied.

"The white soldiers were not German but the British." I gave a sigh. Baba Fule nodded his white head while muttering. "Yes, yes, they were British. And Murasa was sent for trial and later executed. It was a tragic incident." For a moment Baba Fule was silent, as if composing what he would say next. I was fascinated by him. He looked frail and yet his voice was strong and his memory unfolded itself vividly before me.

"When the war ended," Baba Fule resumed, "we came back here. We arrived in March 1919. But we were in for a lot of disappointments. The government had promised us a lot of things when we joined the army, but when we came back things were as bad as they had been before. Most of my colleagues found that their wives had remarried and their land had been taken away. It was difficult to start again, especially in the face of such unfulfilled promises. Fortunately, I found my wife waiting for me and my land unoccupied by anybody. However, I was not all that lucky. Two of my four children had died during my absence."

"Oh, I am sorry," I muttered.

"Well, it's gone now. You know, it's surprising how we forget our troubles. A woman may claim that she will never marry again after her husband is dead, and a short while later she marries and forgets her first husband. Anyway, that's how we're made."

"It's true," I said. "What would you describe as your most important experiences during the war?" I asked him.

"Hm, that's difficult. I enjoyed seeing so many different new places and meeting many different people. Oh, yes, I forgot to tell you this. When I came back here after the war, I and a few other people were called to Zomba. There we were awarded medals by the governor. I was awarded two medals, one for bravery, the other for good conduct. Wait! I'll show you." Baba Fule rose and went into the house. He came out with a wooden, silver-rimmed box. He opened it with a key. There were five medals, all shining brightly and carefully laid in the box. He picked up two medals with care and showed them to me.

"These are the medals," he said, hardly concealing the fact that he was pleased with himself. When he thought I had stared at the medals sufficiently, he laid them back in the box.

"What was I saying again?" he said, after he had closed the box.

"I asked about your most important experiences during the war."

"Oh, yes. Apart from these medals and the other good experiences of the war, there were some things which seriously troubled me and my colleagues. During the war, we became aware that the Azungu, for all their pretenses, were just like us. We fought together. We shared the same hopes and fears. We were all vulnerable to the deadly power of bullets. Indeed, we had the pleasure of killing the Azungu who were enemies of our Azungu. At home they had called us savages and baboons, but in the battlefield we were no different from them."

"You really experienced a lot of things," I commented.

"Oh, yes. We did. The war was tragic, too. I saw many of my friends die. It was horrible. People died like chickens afflicted with *chitopa*. Most of us were disturbed. We were dying for a war which was not ours, which we did not understand."

"Did you leave the army after the war?"

"Yes, but only for a short time. Military life fascinated me and still does. It's the discipline, the order and the sense of danger and adventure. And you see, my son, when you are a soldier, you gradually acquire the greatest mark of courage, the courage not to fear death. I rejoined the army in 1920. But between that year and 1939 when war flared up again, everything was relatively normal.

"The Second World War was more dangerous, with more people and countries involved and with more dangerous weapons. In that war I fought in Burma and India. I was thrilled to see the Amwenye in their own home. When they are here, these people are respectable. You should see them at home. They are very poor. They live in deplorable conditions. The way they pile on top of one another is amazing. One man can have as many as twenty children."

At that moment, a girl with a pot of water on her head entered the house. Baba Fule called her.

"Margaret, come and see your brother here." She came and greeted me with her eyes staring at the ground and some of her fingers in her mouth.

"Put some water on the fire and make us some tea," he told her.

"Yes, *agogo*," the young girl said, leaving.

"What was I saying again? I've a bad memory these days. It's the toll of age."

"You were talking about the Amwenye you saw in Burma and India."

"Oh, yes. Now, my experiences in that war were essentially the same as those of the first Great War. The only difference was that everything was on a bigger scale. However, there was one thing that was fundamentally different. Do you know what it was?"

"No, I don't."

"Try and guess."

"I've no idea."

"Have you learned about the Second World War at school?"

"Yes, I have."

"What did they teach you?"

"It was a war between Britain with her allies and Germany with her allies."

"Yes, that's right. But, I mean, what did they give you as the reasons for the war?"

"There were many. But, basically, they were fighting against Hitler who wanted to dominate the world."

"You're clever, young man. That's it. That's what I wanted. This is what disturbed some of us. The British were fighting against domination and yet they dominated us. Was it not only reasonable for us to do the same?" I had read and heard about this contradiction and its implications. What fascinated me was to hear it fresh from one who had actually fought in the war.

"Should I bring the tea outside?" asked the girl.

"Yes, bring it here," answered Baba Fule. The girl brought a teapot and two cups. She poured the tea for us. It was almost midday and the heat was unbearable. However, I forced myself to drink the tea.

"Was I telling you about the Amwenye in India and Burma?" asked Baba Fule after a couple of sips.

"No, you were telling me about what troubled you about the war."

"Oh, yes. In that war, I almost died. A bomb blew up near where we were hiding. A few of my colleagues died, and I was blinded. I was taken to hospital. I stayed there for five months. After that, I was able to see again, and almost immediately I went to the battlefield."

"Hm," I sighed.

"Yes, my son, I've tasted death over and over again so that the idea of dying does not frighten me, not even a little bit."

"So, your experiences were almost the same in this war as in the first?"

"Yes. I was struck by the senselessness of the whole thing in the guise of peace and civilization. The indiscriminate slaughter of human life, destruction of property and social life. I came to the conclusion that it would have been incomparably better if the Azungu had not come here. Our frequent small wars were not so disruptive by any means. You know what, my son?" He looked at me. His eyes shone excitedly.

"No, I don't," I replied, anxious to hear what he wanted to say.

"I don't have your standards. But I've more years and therefore more wisdom. The Azungu have a passion for grand things, be they good or evil." He paused and smiled at me with both his lips and eyes. The girl brought some food.

"No, put it inside. I can see your brother here is perspiring. Let's go inside." I was relieved. It was cool inside. We washed hands and he said a prayer before we began to eat. There were two dishes of relish. He hardly dipped his hand into the dish of vegetables. I wondered how on earth he managed to munch the meat with virtually no teeth in his mouth.

"I forgot to ask you where your home is."

"I come from Lilongwe," I said.

"Which side of Lilongwe?"

"Nathenje."

"You know this man Mchenga?"

"No, I don't."

"You're too young. You wouldn't know him. But I'm sure your parents know him. He is a friend of mine. He also fought in both wars. In the second war he fought in Egypt. And you know what? He saw Churchill himself when he came for inspection of the British soldiers. You should hear him talk about it. It's so amazing. We all envy him."

For a while we ate in silence. When we had finished, he resumed his story.

"The war ended in 1945 and we came back here at the beginning of 1946. Just as after the first Great War, I was awarded two medals for exceptional bravery and good conduct."

Baba Fule opened the box again and took the two medals and showed them to me. I admired him. When I told him so, he was visibly moved and pleased.

"And this medal"—he picked up the remaining medal—"is the one I was awarded in 1957 on retirement for a long and meritorious service. My life is in these medals, my son, my whole life." He was serious.

"I'm very grateful for the assistance you've given me, Baba," I thanked him.

"When is the book coming?"

"It depends. One, two or three years from now."

"I'll be dead by then."

"I don't think so."

"No, my son. I'm a very old man. I don't know when I was born, but when the first missionaries came into the country, I was a boy."

"I would like to say good-bye to *agogo*."

Baba Fule called his wife. She limped into the room. I bade them farewell. I promised that I would come again someday. Baba Fule accompanied me for a few yards. I felt there was one thing he hadn't told me.

"Baba, did you get your ear cut during the wars?" I asked.

"Oh this. Ha! Ha! Ha! No, my son. It was my wife who cut it off one day in my sleep for being unfaithful to her. But don't write that in the book. Go well, my boy."

I have not kept my promise that I would go to see Baba Fule again. But I think it's too late now. I am sure he has departed for the other world together with his wife.

THE SPIDER'S WEB

|||||||||||||||||||||||||||||||||||||||||||||||||||||||||||||||||||||

by Leonard Kibera

Leonard Kibera *was born and grew up in Kenya. He pub-lished a novel,* Voices in the Dark, *and is the co-author of a collection of stories,* Potent Ash.

INSIDE THE COFFIN, HIS body had become rigid. He tried to turn and only felt the prick of the nail. It had been hammered carelessly through the lid, just falling short of his shoulder. There was no pain but he felt irretrievable and alone, hemmed within the mean, stuffy box, knowing that outside was air. *As dust to dust . . .* the pious preacher intoned out there, not without an edge of triumph. *This suicide, brethren . . . !* They had no right, these people had no right at all. They sang so mournfully over him, almost as if it would disappoint them to see him come back. But he would jump out yet, he would send the rusty nails flying back at them and teach that cheapjack of an undertaker how to convert old trunks. He was not a third-class citizen. *Let me out!* But he could not find the energy to cry out or even turn a little from the nail on his shoulder, as the people out there hastened to cash in another tune, for the padre might at any moment cry *Amen!* and commit the flesh deep into the belly of the earth whence it came. Somebody was weeping righteously in between the pauses. He thought it was Mrs. Njogu. Then in the dead silence that followed he was being posted into the hole and felt himself burning up already as his mean little trunk creaked at the joints and nudged its darkness in on him like a load of sins. *Careful, care-*

||||||||||||
184

ful, he is not a heap of rubbish ... That was Mr. Njogu. Down, slowly down, the careless rope issued in snappy mean measures like a spider's web and knocked his little trunk against the sides to warn the loud gates that he was coming to whoever would receive him. It caved in slowly, the earth, he could feel, and for the first time he felt important. He seemed to matter now, as all eyes no doubt narrowed into the dark hole at this moment, with everybody hissing *poor soul; gently, gently.* Then *snap!* The rope gave way—one portion of the dangling thing preferring to recoil into the tight-fisted hands out there—and he felt shot toward the bottom head-downward, exploding into the gates of hell with a loud, unceremonious *bang!*

Ngotho woke up with a jump. He mopped the sweat on the tail of his sheet. This kind of thing would bring him no good. Before, he had been dreaming of beer parties or women or fights with bees as he tried to smoke them out for honey. Now, lately, it seemed that when he wasn't being smoked out of this city where he so very much belonged and yet never belonged, he was either pleading his case at the White Gates or being condemned to hell in cheap coffins. *This kind of thing just isn't healthy...*

But he was in top form. He flung the blanket away. He bent his arms at the elbow for exercise. He shot them up and held them there like a surrender. *No that will not do.* He bent them again and pressed his fingers on his shoulders. They gathered strength, knitting into a ball so that his knuckles sharpened. Then he shot a dangerous fist to the left and held it there, tightly, not yielding a step, until he felt all stiff and blood pumped at his forehead. Dizziness overpowered him and his hand fell dead on the bed. Then a spasm uncoiled his right fist which came heavily on the wall and, pained, cowered. Was he still a stranger to the small dimensions of his only room even after eight years?

But it wasn't the first time anyhow. So, undaunted, he sprang twice on the bed for more exercise. Avoiding the spring that had fetched his thigh yesterday morning between the bulges in the old mattress, he hummed "Africa Nchi Yetu" and shot his leg down the bed. Swa—ah! That would be three shillings for another sheet through the back doors of the Koya Mosque. Ngotho dragged himself out of bed.

It was a beautiful Sunday morning. He had nothing to worry about so long as he did not make the mistake of going to church. Churches depressed him. But that dream still bothered him. *(At least they could have used a less precipitate rope.)* And those nails, didn't he have enough things pricking him since Mrs. Knight gave him a five-pound handshake saying "Meet you in England" and Mrs. Njogu came buzzing in as his new memsahib borrowing two shillings from him?

Ngotho folded his arms at his chest and yawned. He took his mustache thoughtfully between his fingers and curled it sharp like horns. At least she could have returned it. It was not as if the cost of living had risen the way employers took things for granted these days. He stood at the door of the two-room house which he shared with the other servant who, unlike him, didn't cook for memsahib. Instead, Kago went on errands, trimmed the grass and swept the compound, taking care to trace well the dog's mess for the night. Already Ngotho could see the early riser as good as sniffing and scanning the compound after the erratic manner of Wambui last night. (Wambui was the brown Alsatian dragged from the village and surprised into civilization, a dog collar and tinned bones by Mrs. Njogu. A friend of hers, Elsie Bloom, kept one and they took their bitches for a walk together.) Ngotho cleared his throat.

"Hey, Kago!"

Kago who was getting frostbite rubbed his thumb between the toes and turned round.

"How is the dog's breakfast?"

"Nyukwa!"

Ngotho laughed.

"You don't have to insult my mother," he said. "Tinned bones for Wambui and cornflakes for memsahib are the same thing. We both hang if we don't get them."

Kago leaned on his broom, scratched the top of his head dull-wittedly, and at last saw that Ngotho had a point there.

He was a good soul, Kago was, and subservient as a child. There was no doubt about his ready aggressiveness where men of his class were concerned it was true, but when it came to Mrs. Njogu he wound tail between his legs and stammered. This morning he was feeling at peace with the world.

"Perhaps you are right," he said, to Ngotho. Then diving his thumb between the toes he asked if there was a small thing going on that afternoon—like a beer party.

"The Queen!"

At the mention of the name, Kago forgot everything about drinking, swerved round and felt a thousand confused things beat into his head simultaneously. Should he go on sweeping and sniffing or should he get the Bob's Tinned? Should he untin the Bob's Tinned or should he run for the Sunday paper? Mrs. Njogu, alias queen, wasn't she more likely to want Wambui brushed behind the ear? Or was she now coming to ask him why the rope lay at the door while Wambui ran about untied?

With his bottom toward memsahib's door, Kago assumed a busy pose and peeped through his legs. But memsahib wasn't bothered about him. At least not yet. She stood at the door legs askew and admonished Ngotho about the cornflakes.

Kago breathed a sigh of relief and took a wild sweep at the broom. He saw Ngotho back against the wall of their servants' quarters and suppressed a laugh. After taking a torrent of English words, Ngotho seemed to tread carefully the fifty violent paces between the two doors, the irreconcilable gap between the classes. As he approached Mrs. Njogu, he seemed to sweep a tactful curve off the path, as if to move up the wall first and then try to back in slowly toward the master's door and hope memsahib would make way. For her part, the queen flapped her wings and spread herself luxuriously, as good as saying, You will have to kneel and dive in through my legs. Then she stuck out her tongue twice, heaved her breasts, spat milk and honey onto the path, and disappeared into the hive. Ngotho followed her.

Kago scratched his big toe and sat down to laugh.

Breakfast for memsahib was over. Ngotho came out of the house to cut out the painful corn in his toe with the kitchen knife. He could take the risk and it pleased him. But he had to move to the other end of the wall. Mr. Njogu was flushing the toilet and he might chance to open the small blurred window and see the otherwise clean kitchen knife glittering in the sun on dirty toe nails.

Breakfast. Couldn't memsahib trust him with the sugar or milk even after four years? Must she buzz around him as he measured breakfast for two? He had nothing against cornflakes. In fact ever since she became suspicious, he had found himself eating more of her meals whenever she was not in sight, also taking some sugar in his breast pocket. But he had come to hate himself for it and felt it was a coward's way out. Still, what was he to do? Mrs. Njogu had become more and more of a stranger and he had even caught himself looking at her from an angle where formerly he had stared her straight in the face. He had wanted to talk to her, to assure her that he was still her trusted servant, but everything had become more entangled and sensitive. She would only say he was criticizing, and if he wasn't happy what was he waiting for? But if he left, where was he to go? Unemployment had turned loose upon the country as it had never done before. Housewives around would receive the news of his impertinence blown high and wide over Mrs. Njogu's telephone before he approached them for a job, and set their dogs on him.

Ngotho scratched at his gray hair and knew that respect for age had completely bereft his people. Was this the girl he once knew as Lois back in his home village? She had even been friends with his own daughter. A shy, young thing with pimples and thin legs. Lois had taught at the village school and was everybody's good example. She preferred to wear cheap skirts than see her aging parents starve for lack of money.

"Be like Lois," mothers warned their daughters and even spanked them to press the point. What they meant in fact was that their daughters should, like Lois, stay unmarried longer and not simply run off with some young man in a neat tie who refused to pay the dowry. Matters soon became worse for such girls when suddenly Lois became heroine of the village. She went to jail.

It was a general knowledge class. Lois put the problem word squarely on the blackboard. The lady supervisor who went round the schools stood squarely at the other end, looking down the class. Lois swung her stick up and down the class and said,

"What is the commonwealth, children? Don't be shy, what does this word mean?"

The girls chewed their thumbs.

"Come on! All right. We shall start from the *beginning*. Who rules England?"

Slowly, the girls turned their heads round and faced the white supervisor. Elizabeth, they knew they should say. But how could Lois bring them to this? England sounded venerable enough. Must they go further now and let the white lady there at the back hear the queen of England mispronounced, or even uttered by these tender things with the stain of last night's onions in their breath? Who would be the first? They knit their knuckles under the desks, looked into their exercise books, and one by one said they didn't know. One or two brave ones threw their heads back again, met with a strange look in the white queen's eye which spelled disaster, immediately swung their eyes onto the blackboard, and catching sight of Lois's stick, began to cry.

"It is as if you have never heard of it." Lois was losing patience. "All right, I'll give you another start. Last start. What is our country?"

Simultaneously, a flash of hands shot up from under the desks and thirty-four breaths of maize and onions clamored.

"A colony!"

Slowly, the lady supervisor measured out light taps down the class and having eliminated the gap that came between master and servant, stood face to face with Lois.

The children chewed at their erasers.

Then the white queen slapped Lois across the mouth and started for the door. But Lois caught her by the hair, slapped her back once, twice, and spat into her face. Then she gave her a football kick and swept her out with a right.

When at last Lois looked back into the class, she only saw torn exercise books flung on the floor. Thirty-four pairs of legs had fled home through the window, partly to be comforted from the queen's government which was certain to come, and partly to spread the formidable news of their new queen and heroine.

Queen, she certainly was, Ngotho thought as he sat by the wall and backed against it. Cornflakes in bed; expensive skirts; cigarettes. Was this her? Mr. Njogu had come straight from the University College in time to secure a shining job occupied for years by a Mzungu. Then a neat car was seen to park by Lois's house. In due course these visits became more frequent and alarming, but no villager was surprised when eventually Njogu succeeded in dragging Lois away from decent society. He said paying the dowry was for people in the mountains.

As luck would have it for Ngotho, Mr. and Mrs. Knight left and Mr. and Mrs. Njogu came to occupy the house. He was glad to cook and wash a black man's towels for a change. And, for a short time at any rate, he was indeed happy. Everybody had sworn that they were going to build something together, something challenging and responsible, something that would make a black man respectable in his own country. He had been willing to serve, to keep up the fire that had eventually smoked out the white man. From now on there would be no more revenge, and no more exploitation. Beyond this, he didn't expect much for himself; he knew that there would always be masters and servants.

Ngotho scratched himself between the legs and sunk against the wall. He stared at the spider that slowly built its web meticulously under the veranda roof. He threw a light stone at it and only alerted the spider.

Had his heart not throbbed with thousands of others that day as each time he closed his eyes he saw a vision of something exciting, a legacy of responsibilities that demanded a warrior's spirit? Had he not prayed for oneness deep from the heart? But it seemed to him now that a common goal had been lost sight of and he lamented it. He could not help but feel that the warriors had laid down their arrows and had parted different ways to fend for themselves. And as he thought of their households, he saw only the image of Lois whom he dared call nothing but memsahib now. She swam big and muscular in his mind.

Ngotho wondered whether this was the compound he used to know. Was this part connecting master and servant the one that had been so straight during Mrs. Knight?

Certainly he would never want her back. He had been kicked several times by Mr. Knight and had felt what it was like to be hit with a frying pan by Mrs. Knight as she reminded him to be grateful. But it had all been so direct, no ceremonies: they didn't like his broad nose. They said so. They thought there were rats under his bed. There were. They teased that he hated everything white and yet his hair was going white on his head like snow, a cool white protector while below the black animal simmered and plotted: Wouldn't he want it cut? No, he wouldn't. Occasionally, they would be impressed by a well-turned turkey or chicken and say so over talk of the white man's responsibility in Africa. If they were not in the mood they just dismissed him and told him not to forget the coffee. Ngotho knew that all this was because they were becoming uneasy and frightened, and that perhaps they had to point the gun at all black men now at a time when even the church had taken sides. But whatever the situation in the house, there was nevertheless a frankness about the black-and-white relationship where no ceremonies or apologies were necessary in a world of mutual distrust and hate. And if Mrs. Knight scolded him all over the house, it was Mr. Knight who eventually seemed to lock the bedroom door and come heavily on top of her and everybody else although, Ngotho thought, they were all ruled by a woman in England.

Ngotho walked heavily to the young tree planted three years ago by Mrs. Njogu and wondered why he should have swept a curve off the path that morning, as memsahib filled the door. He knew it wasn't the first time he had done that. Everything had become crooked, subtle, and he had to watch his step. His monthly vernacular paper said so. He felt cornered. He gripped the young tree by the scruff of the neck and shook it furiously. What the hell was wrong with some men anyway? Had Mr. Njogu become a male weakling in a fat queen bee's hive, slowly being milked dry and sapless, dying? Where was the old warrior who at the end of the battle would go home to his wife and make her moan under his heavy sweat? All he could see now as he shook the tree was a line of neat houses. There, the warriors had come to their battle's end and parted, to forget other warriors and to be mothered to sleep without even knowing it, meeting only occasionally to drink beer and sing traditional songs. And where previously the bow and arrow lay by the bedpost, Ngotho now only saw a conspiracy of round tablets while a *Handbook of Novel Techniques* lay by the pillow.

He had tried to understand. But as he looked at their pregnant wives he could foresee nothing but a new generation of innocent snobs, who would be chauffeured off to school in neat caps hooded over their eyes so as to obstruct vision. There they would learn that the other side of the city was dirty. Ngotho spat right under the tree. Once or twice he would have liked to kick Mr. Njogu. He looked all so sensibly handsome and clean as he buzzed after his wife on a broken wing and—a spot of jam on his tie—said he wanted the key to the car.

He had also become very sensitive and self-conscious. Ngotho couldn't complain a little or even make a joke about the taxes without somebody detecting a subtler intention behind the smile, where the servant was supposed to be on a full-scale plotting. And there was behind the master and the queen now a bigger design, a kind of pattern meticulously fenced above the hive; a subtle web, at the center of which lurked the spider which protected, watched and jailed. Ngotho knew only too well that the web had been slowly, quietly in the making and a pebble thrown at it would at best alert and fall back impotent on the ground.

He took a look at the other end of the compound. Kago had fallen asleep, while Wambui ran about untied, the rope still lying at the door. Kago wore an indifferent grin. Ngotho felt overpowered, trapped, alone. He spat in Kago's direction and plucked a twig off one of the branches on the tree. The tree began to bleed. He tightened his

grip and shed the reluctant leaves down. Just what had gone wrong
with God?

The old one had faithfully done his job when the fig tree near
Ngotho's village withered away as predicted by the tribal seer. It had
been the local news and lately, it was rumored, some businessman
would honor the old god by erecting a hotel on the spot. Ngotho
hardly believed in any god at all. The one lived in corrupted blood,
the other in pulpits of hypocrisy. But at least while they kept neat
themselves they could have honored the old in a cleaner way. How
could this new savior part the warriors different ways into isolated
compartments, to flush their uneasy hotel toilets all over the old one?

Ngotho passed a reverent hand over his wrinkled forehead and up
his white hair. He plucked another twig off the dangerous tree.
Something was droning above his ear.

"What are you doing to my tree?"

The buzzing had turned into a scream.

"I—I want to pick my teeth." Ngotho unwrapped a row of defiant
molars.

The queen flapped her wings and landed squarely on the ground.
Then she was heaving heavily, staring at him out of small eyes. He
tried to back away from her eyes. Beyond her, in the background, he
caught sight of Mr. Njogu through the bedroom window polishing
his spectacles on his pajama sleeve, trying desperately to focus—
clearly—on the situation outside. A flap of the wind and Ngotho felt
hit right across the mouth, by the hand that had once hit the white
lady. Then the queen wobbled in midflight, settled at the door, and
screamed at Mr. Njogu to come out and prove he was a man.

Mr. Njogu didn't like what he saw. He threw his glasses away and
preferred to see things blurred.

"These women," he muttered, and waved them away with a neat
pajama sleeve. Then he buried his head under the blanket and
snored. It was ten o'clock.

Ngotho stood paralyzed. He had never been hit by a woman before, outside of his mother's hut. Involuntarily, he felt his eyes snap
shut and his eyelids burn red, violently, in the sun. Then out of the

spider's web in his mind, policemen, magistrates and the third class undertakers flew in profusion. He opened up, sweating, and the kitchen knife in his hand fell down, stabbing the base of the tree where it vibrated once, twice, and fell flat on its side, dead.

Then with a cry, he grabbed it and rushed into the house. But Mr. Njogu saw him coming as the knife glittered nearer and clearer in his direction, and leapt out of bed.

Suddenly the horror of what he had done caught Ngotho. He could hear the queen at least crying hysterically into the telephone, while Mr. Njogu locked himself in the toilet and began weeping. Ngotho looked at the kitchen knife in his hand. He had only succeeded in stabbing Mr. Njogu in the thigh, and the knife had now turned red on him. Soon the sticky web would stretch a thread. And he would be caught as he never thought he would when first he felt glad to work for Lois.

He saw Wambui's rope still lying in a noose. Then he went into his room and locked the door.

CALL ME NOT A MAN

||||||||||||||||||||||||||||||||||||||||||||||||||||||||||||||||||||||||||||||||||||||||

by Mtutuzeli Matshoba

Mtutuzeli Matshoba *is the author of a collection of short stories entitled* Call Me Not a Man, *which was banned in South Africa in 1979. He is now working on a novel.*

> For neither am I a man in the eyes of the law,
> Nor am I a man in the eyes of my fellow man.

B Y DODGING, LYING, resisting where it is possible, bolting when I'm already cornered, parting with invaluable money, sometimes calling my sisters into the game to get amorous with my captors, allowing myself to be slapped on the mouth in front of my womenfolk and getting sworn at with my mother's private parts, that component of me which is man has died countless times in one lifetime. Only a shell of me remains to tell you of the other man's plight, which is in fact my own. For what is suffered by another man in view of my eyes is suffered also by me. The grief he knows is a grief that I know. Out of the same bitter cup do we drink. To the same chain gang do we belong.

Friday has always been their chosen day to go plundering, although nowadays they come only occasionally, maybe once in a month. Perhaps they have found better pastures elsewhere, where their prey is more predictable than at Mzimhlope, the place which has seen the tragic demise of three of their accomplices who had taken the game a bit too far by entering the hostel on the northern

||||||||||||

side of our location and fleecing the people right in the midst of their disgusting labor camps. Immediately after this there was a notable abatement in the frequency of their visits to both the location and the adjacent hostel. However the lull was short-lived, lasting only until the storm had died down, because the memory tarnishes quickly in the locations, especially the memory of death. We were beginning to emit sighs of relief and to mutter "good riddance" when they suddenly reappeared and made their presence in our lives felt once again. June '76 had put them out of the picture for the next year, during which they were scarcely seen. Like a recurring pestilence they refuse to vanish absolutely from the scene.

A person who has spent some time in Soweto will doubtless have guessed by now that the characters I am referring to are none other than some of the so-called police reservists who roam our dirty streets on weekends, robbing every timid, unsuspecting person, while masquerading as peace officers to maintain law and order in the community. There are no greater thieves than these men of the law, men of justice, peace officers and volunteer public protectors in the whole of the slum complex because, unlike others in the same trade of living off the sweat of their victims, they steal out in the open, in front of everybody's eyes. Of course nothing can be done about it because they go out on their pillaging exploits under the banners of the law, and to rise in protest against them is analogous to defiance of the powers that be.

So, on this Friday too we were standing on top of the station bridge at Mzimhlope. It was about five in the afternoon and the sun hung over the western horizon of spectacularly identical coalsmoke-puffing rooftops like a gigantic, glowing red ball which dyed the foamy clouds with the crimson sheen of its rays. The commuter trains coming in from the city paused below us every two or three minutes to regurgitate their infinite human cargo, the greater part of whom were hostel dwellers who hurried up Mohale Street to cook their meager suppers on primus stoves. The last train we had seen would now be leaving Phefeni, the third station from Mzimhlope. The next train had just emerged from the bridge this side of New

CALL ME NOT A MAN ▼ 197

Canada, junction to East and West Soweto. The last group of the
hostel people from the train now leaving Phefeni had just turned the
bend at Mohale Street where it intersects with Elliot. The two-
hundred-meter stretch to Elliot was therefore relatively empty, and
people coming toward the station could be clearly made out.

As the wheels of the train from New Canada squealed on the iron
tracks and it came to a jerking stop, four men, two in overalls and the
others in dustcoats, materialized around the Mohale Street bend.
There was no doubt who they were, from the way they filled the
whole width of the street and walked as if they owned everything and
everybody in their sight. When they came to the grannies selling
vegetables, fruit and fried mealies along the ragged, unpaved sides of
the street, they grabbed what they fancied and munched gluttonously
the rest of the way toward us. Again nothing could be done about it,
because the poverty-stricken vendors were not licensed to scrape together some crumbs to ease the gnawing stomachs of their fatherless
grandchildren at home, which left them wide open for plunder by the
indifferent "reserves."

"Awu! The hellions," remarked Mandla next to me. "Let's get
away from here, my friend."

He was right. They reminded one of the old western film; but I
was not moving from where I was simply because the reservists were
coming down the street like a bunch of villains. One other thing I
knew was that the railway constable who was on guard duty that
Friday at the station did not allow the persecution of the people on
his premises. I wanted to have my laugh when they were chased off
the station.

"Don't worry about them. Just wait and see how they're going to
be chased away by this copper. He won't allow them on the station,"
I answered.

They split into twos when they arrived below us. Two of them, a
tall chap with a face corroded by skin-lightening cream and wearing a
yellow golf cap on his shaven head, and another stubby, shabbily
dressed, middle-aged man with a bald frontal lobe and a drunk face,
chewing at a cooked sheep's foot that he had taken from one of the

grannies, climbed the stairs on our right-hand side. The younger man took the flight in fours. The other two chose to waylay their unsuspecting victims on the streetcorner at the base of the left-hand staircase. The first wave of the people who had alighted from the train was in the middle of the bridge when the second man reached the top of the stairs.

Maybe they knew the two reservists by sight, maybe they just smelled cop in the smoggy air, or it being a Friday, they were alert for such possibilities. Three to four of the approaching human wall turned suddenly in their tracks and ran for their dear freedom into the mass behind them. The others were caught unawares by this unexpected movement and they staggered in all directions trying to regain balance. In a split second there was commotion on the station, as if a wild cat had found its way into a fowl run. Two of those who had not been quick enough were grabbed by their sleeves, and their passes demanded. While they were producing their books the wolves went over their pockets, supposedly feeling for dangerous weapons, dagga and other illegal possessions that might be concealed in the clothes, but really to ascertain whether they had caught the right people for their iniquitous purposes. They were paging through the booklets when the railway policeman appeared.

"Wha . . . ? Don't you fools know that you're not supposed to do that shit here? Get off! Get off and do that away from railway property. Fuck off!" He screamed at the two reservists so furiously that the veins threatened to burst in his neck.

"Arrest the dogs, *baba!* Give them a chance also to taste jail!" Mandla shouted.

"Ja," I said to Mandla, "you bet, they've never been where they are so prepared to send others."

The other people joined in and we jeered the cowards off the station. They descended the stairs with their tails tucked between their legs and joined their companions below the station. Some of the commuters who had been alerted by the uproar returned to the platform to wait there until the reservists had gone before they would dare venture out of the station.

We remained where we had been and watched the persecution from above. I doubted if they even read the passes (if they could), or whether the victims knew if their books were right or out of order. Most likely the poor hunted men believed what they were told by the licensed thieves. The latter demanded the books, after first judging their prey to be weak propositions, flicked through the pages, put the passes into their own pockets, without which the owners could not continue on their way, and told the dumbfounded hostel men to stand aside while they accosted other victims. Within a very short while there was a group of confused men to one side of the street, screaming at their hostel mates to go to room so and so and tell so and so that they had been arrested at the station, and to bring money quickly to release them. Few of those who were being sent heard the messages since they were only too eager to leave the danger zone. Those who had money shook hands with their captors, received their books back and ran up Mohale Street. If they were unlucky they came upon another "roadblock" three hundred meters up the street where the process was repeated. Woe unto them who had paid their last money to the first extortionists, for this did not matter. The police station was their next stopover before the Bantu Commissioners, and thence their final destination, Modderbee Prison, where they provided the farmers with ready cheap labor until they had served their terms for breaking the law. The terms vary from a few days to two years for *loaferskap*, which is in fact mere unemployment, for which the unfortunate men are not to blame. The whole arrangement stinks of forced labor.

The large *kwela-kwela* swayed down Mohale Street at breakneck speed. The multitudes scattered out of its way and hung onto the sagging fences until it had passed. To be out of sight of the people on the station bridge, it skidded and swerved into the second side street from the station. More reservists poured out of it and went immediately to their dirty job with great zeal. The chain gang which had been lined up along the fence of the house nearest the station was kicked and shoved to the *kwela-kwela* into which the victims were bundled under a rain of fists and boots, all of them scrambling to go in at the same time through the small door. The driver of the *kwela-kwela*, the only uniformed constable among the group, clanged the door shut and secured it with the locking lever. He went to stand authoritatively near one of the vendors, took a small avocado pear, peeled it and put it whole into a gargantuan mouth, spitting out the large stone later. He did not have to take the trouble of accosting anyone himself. His gangsters would all give him a lion's share of whatever they made, and moreover buy him some beers and brandy. He kept adjusting his polished belt over his potbelly as the .38 Police Special in its leather holster kept tugging it down. He probably preferred to wear his gun unconventionally, cowboy style.

A boy of about seventeen was caught with a knife in his pocket, a dangerous weapon. They slapped him a few times and let him stand handcuffed against the concrete wall of the station. Ten minutes later his well-rounded sister alighted from the train to find her younger brother among the prisoners. As she was inquiring from him why he had been arrested, and reprimanding him for carrying a knife, one of the younger reservists came to stand next to her and started pawing her. She let him carry on, and three minutes later her brother was free. The reservist was beaming all over his face, glad to have won himself a beautiful woman in the course of his duties and little knowing that he had been given the wrong address. Some of our black sisters are at times compelled to go all the way to save their menfolk, and as always, nothing can be done about it.

There was a man coming down Mohale Street, conspicuous amidst the crowd because of the bag and baggage that was loaded on his overall-clad frame. On his right shoulder was a large suitcase with a gray blanket strapped to it with flaxen strings. From his left hand hung a bulging cardboard box, only a few inches from the ground, and tilting him to that side. He walked with the bounce of someone used to walking in gumboots or on uneven ground. There was the urgency of someone who had a long way to travel in his gait. It was doubtless a *goduka* on his way home to his family after many months of work in the city. It might even have been years since he had visited the countryside.

He did not see the hidden *kwela-kwela*, which might have fore-warned him of the danger that was lurking at the station. Only when he had stumbled into two reservists, who stepped into his way and ordered him to put down his baggage, did he perhaps remember that it was Friday and raid day. A baffled expression sprang into his face as he realized what he had walked into. He frantically went through the pockets of his overalls. The worried countenance deepened on his dark face. He tried again to make sure, but he did not find what he was looking for. The men who had stopped him pulled him to one side, each holding him tightly by the sleeve of his overall. He obeyed meekly like a tame animal. They let him lift his arms while they searched him all over the body. Finding nothing hidden on him, they demanded the inevitable book, although they had seen that he did not have it. He gesticulated with his hands as he explained what had caused him not to be carrying his pass with him. A few feet above them, I could hear what was said.

"Strue, *mododa*," he said imploringly, "I made a mistake. I lug-gaged the pass with my trunk. It was a jacket that I forgot to search before I packed it into the trunk."

"How do we know that you're not lying?" asked one of the reser-vists in a querulous voice.

"I'm not lying, *mfowethu*. I swear by my mother, that's what hap-pened," explained the frightened man.

The second reservist had a more evil and uncompromising atti-tude. "That was your own stupidity, mister. Because of it you're going to jail now; no more to your wife."

"Oh, my brother. Put yourself in my shoes. I've not been home to my people for two years now. It's the first chance I have to go and see my twin daughters who were born while I've been here. Feel for another poor black man, please, my good brother. Forgive me only for this once."

"What? Forgive you? And don't give us that slush about your

children. We've also got our own families, for whom we are at work right now, at this very moment," the obstinate one replied roughly.

"But, *mfo*. Wouldn't you make a mistake too?"

That was a question the cornered man should not have asked. The reply this time was a resounding slap on the face. "You think I'm stupid like you, huh? Bind this man, Mazibuko, put the bloody irons on the dog."

"No, man. Let me talk to the poor bloke. Perhaps he can do something for us in exchange for the favor of letting him proceed on his way home," the less volatile man suggested, and pulled the hostel man away from the rest of the arrested people.

"*Ja*. Speak to him yourself, Mazibuko. I can't bear talking to rural fools like him. I'll kill him with my bare hands if he thinks that I've come to play here in Johannesburg!" The anger in the man's voice was faked, the fury of a coward trying to instill fear in a person who happened to be at his mercy. I doubted if he could face up to a mouse. He accosted two boys and ran his hands over their sides, but he did not ask for their passes.

"You see, my friend, you're really in trouble. I'm the only one who can help you. This man who arrested you is not in his best mood today. How much have you got on you? Maybe if you give something he'll let you go. You know what wonders money can do for you, I'll plead for you; but only if I show him something can he understand." The reservist explained the only way out of the predicament for the trapped man, in a smooth voice that sounded rotten through and through with corruption, the only purpose for which he had joined the "force."

"I haven't got a cent in my pocket. I bought provisions, presents for the people at home and the ticket with all the money they gave me at work. Look, *nkosi*, I have only the ticket and the papers with which I'm going to draw my money when I arrive at home." He took out his papers, pulled the overall off his shoulders and lowered it to his thigh so that the brown trousers he wore underneath were out in the open. He turned the dirty pockets inside out. "There's nothing else in my pockets except these, mister, honestly."

"Man!"

"Yessir?"

"You want to go home to your wife and children?"

"Yes, *please*, good man of my people. Give me a break."

"Then why do you show me these damn papers? They will feed your own children, but not mine. When you get to your home you're going to draw money and your kids will be scratching their tummies and dozing after a hectic meal, while I lose my job for letting you go and my own children join the dogs to scavenge the trashbins. You're mad, *mos*." He turned to his mate. "Hey, Baloyi. Your man says he hasn't got anything, but he's going to his family which he hasn't seen for two years."

"I told you to put the irons on him. He's probably carrying a little fortune in his underpants. Maybe he's shy to take it out in front of the people. It'll come out at the police station, either at the charge office or in the cells when the small boys shake him down."

"Come on, you. Your hands, maan!"

The other man pulled his arms away from the manacles. His voice rose desperately, "*Awu* my people. You mean you're really arresting me? Forgive me! I pray do."

A struggle ensued between the two men.

"You're resisting arrest? You—" and a stream of foul vitriolic words concerning the anatomy of the hostel man's mother gushed out of the reservist's mouth.

"I'm not, I'm not! But please listen!" The hostel man heaved and broke loose from the reservist's grip. The latter was only a lump of fat with nothing underneath. He staggered three steps back and flopped on his rump. When he bounced back to his feet, unexpectedly fast for his bulk, his eyes were blazing murder. His companions came running from their own posts and swarmed upon the defenseless man like a pack of hyenas upon a carcass. The other people who had been marooned on the bridge saw a chance to go past while the wolves were still preoccupied. They ran down the stairs and up Mohale like racehorses. Two other young men who were handcuffed together took advantage of the diversion and bolted down the first street in

tandem, taking their bracelets with them. They ran awkwardly with
their arms bound together, but both were young and fit and they did
their best in the circumstances.

We could not stand the sickening beating that the other man was
receiving anymore.

"Hey! Hey. *Sies,* maan. Stop beating the man like that. Arrest
him if you want to arrest him. You're killing him, dogs!" we protested
loudly from the station. An angry crowd was gathering.

"Stop it or we'll stop you from doing anything else forever!" someone shouted.

The psychopaths broke their rugger scrum and allowed us to see
their gruesome handiwork. The man was groaning at the base of the
fence, across the street where the dirt had gathered. He twisted painfully to a sitting position. His face was covered with dirt and blood
from where the manacles that were slipped over the knuckles had
found their marks, and his features were grotesquely distorted. In
spite of that, the fat man was not satisfied. He bent and gathered the
whimpering man's wrists with the intention of fastening them to the
fence with the handcuffs.

"Hey, hey, hey, Satan! Let him go. Can't you see that you've hurt
that man enough?"

The tension was building up to explosion point and the uniformed policeman sensed it.

"Let him go, boys. Forgive him. Let him go," he said, shooting
nervous glances in all directions.

Then the beaten-up man did the most unexpected and heartrend-
ing thing. He knelt before the one ordering his release and held his
dust-covered hands with the palms together in the prayer position,
and still kneeling he said, "Thank you very much, my lord. God
bless you. Now I can go and see my twins and my people at home."

He would have done it. Only it never occurred in his mind at that
moment of thanksgiving to kiss the red gleaming boots of the policeman.

The miserable man beat the dust off his clothes as best he could, gathered his two parcels and clambered up the stairs, trying to grin his thanks to the crowd that had raised its voice of protest on his behalf. The policeman decided to call it a day. The other unfortunates were shepherded to the waiting *kwela-kwela*.

I tried to imagine how the man would explain his lumps to his wife. In the eye of my mind I saw him throwing his twins into the air and gathering them again and again as he played with them.

"There's still a long way to cover, my friend," I heard Mandla saying into my ear.

"Before?" I asked.

"Before we reach hell. Ha, ha, ha! Maybe there we'll be men."

"Ha, we've long been there. We've long been in hell."

"Before we get out, then."

THE SPEARMEN OF MALAMA

||||||||||||||||||||||||||||||||||||||||||||||||||||||||||||||||||||||||||||||||||||||||||||||||||||||

by Kafungulwa Mubitana

Kafungulwa Mubitana *was educated at Munali School in Lusaka, Makerere, in Uganda and the University of Edinburgh, Scotland. An artist and anthropologist, he is at present deputy director of the Livingstone Museum.*

CHIITA STRETCHED HIS hand and started feeling for his loincloth in the darkness of the hut. Having found it, he stood up and wrapped it quickly around his waist. He stepped out and examined the sky. Clouds of gray and blue raced across. Above the eastern horizon, a strip of clear sky showed. Over this, a yellowish sun floated, radiating some of its color into the neighboring islands of clouds. It was a chilly morning.

Chiita walked to the cattle kraal, stick in hand, humming some tune to himself. His mind was set on getting to the fire in the kraal. He could see even from a distance the smoking from the fire rising in a thin wisp. Having approached the kraal, he wormed his way carefully among the sleepy cattle toward the center where the fire was. He had done this every morning for as far back as he could remember since the cold season began. Here, he could always find company and warmth. It was the practice of the local lads to gather here round a huge fire of smoldering cow dung every morning before they began their daily round of cattle husbandry.

There was only one person already at the fireplace when Chiita got there this time. It was Chibangu, his favorite playmate, who sat there with a very sullen face. All around him were cattle in all sorts of stances and states of wakefulness. Some were sprawled on the ground, dozing away quietly. Others stood on all fours, showing all signs of severe fatigue, but never submitting to this; while yet others chewed the cud noisily as though dissatisfied with their present lot. Almost all the cattle were facing the fire. Chibangu did not seem mindful of the huge ox whose horny head towered above. The ox was evidently enjoying his domination of the situation. He had started to lick Chibangu's left ear when the latter decided that enough was enough, even from an ox. He gave a big yell and punched the ox over its nose with his elbow and the beast retreated unceremoniously, sniffing, and obviously disappointed with his shortlived brotherhood with man.

Chiita had observed all this drama silently. Now he ventured to find out whether his dear friend was angry with him. He could not remember causing any inconvenience to him over the past few days. In any case, he had only seen him the previous night.

"Well now, lion tamer, it can't be that bad?" began Chiita. He had not the least idea what he was himself saying. Yet, by chance, perhaps by intuition, he had taken the right line . . .

"Maybe not to you," retorted Chibangu. "But I could kill him now. Why did he have to do that to me?"

Tears had started to well in Chibangu's eyes. "What," he barked. "What does Malama think he is, taking Miimbi away from me? He will pay for it. Very dearly. Oh, yes!" So saying he became silent, but looked very agitated.

Now it all became clear to Chiita. Indeed, Malama had openly wooed away his friend's girl the previous night. But then Chibangu had appeared not to bother about the whole thing. He had simply remarked that he had always had a secret lover who was so much better and prettier than the bony Miimbi, and that he could now court her openly without any feeling of guilt. So Chiita had taken the declaration as genuine and dismissed the whole episode. But now, his friend must have had second thoughts about the incident and was fighting back.

"You don't really mean to put that useless affair on your mind, baby warrior? You are meant for better things and better women, too.

Besides, Malama can't be a match for you," flattered the diplomatic Chiita. Deep down he never believed his own flattery.

"But that wasn't an isolated incident. Perhaps you, of all people, know that only too well. Didn't Malama take Nanda away from you last year, only to discard her after a short time? You know he did it to hurt you. You did not fight him, whatever your private reasons for not doing so. It is different with me. I will have to fight him . . . that soft-bellied rabbit! He ascends the heights of fame while you and I get washed down the waves of oblivion. No longer do the girls with the milk-white eyes look upon us as the young men of the day. They have—all of them, I mean—their eyes set upon the lionhearted Malama—their idol!"

Chibangu had always been a good and effective speaker. Even when addressing one man, it seemed as if he usually had a score of listeners in mind. Now, the impact of his oratory had had an immediate effect on his friend who suddenly remembered his own humiliation over his girl Nanda a year ago. It was not because he was a pacifist that he had failed to challenge Malama to a duel. No. He had just been scared of the man, although he dare not admit it publicly. But Chibangu's oratory had now somehow broken that fear. Whereas in the past he had been afraid of the man, and even secretly admired him for his prowess, now he was filled with a sense of loathing for him.

"Malama must die," he declared firmly and then walked out of the kraal, leaving his friend quite satisfied with his attempt at incitement. Chibangu had always loved to observe the effect of his little plotting speeches on his friends.

The cold season of the Bwaami area is a time of hardship for the cattle-loving people, for the grass goes dry for lack of water. It takes a period of six months before the rains appear again. The people must drive their herds to the pools on the Mulele Plain every day. Around these pools, fresh grass flourishes, and the herds may graze to their satisfaction. But this daily trek was not without its inconveniences. Once in a while, the herds from the different villages and areas got mixed up and the owners found it difficult to sort them out again. Worse still, herds split up and some disappeared into the tall grass for days on end. When this happened, a party of men had to set out to try to find them before the wild beasts ate them up.

It was in connection with a lost herd that the three young men, Malama, Chiita and Chibangu, had set out one ordinary morning. They looked a fine trio, but for one thing: Malama, knowing *nothing*, appeared cheerful enough, as cheerful as one can possibly be among people one has contempt for. A foreboding silence reigned over the two conspirators. They were fighting battles of final decision within themselves. The great moment had come sooner than they expected and it was a chance they could not let slip through their fingers. They must see their plan to the bitter end.

Malama was a tall, lean youth with a reputation for determination and general ability. The girls even thought him good-looking. But then girls have the habit of calling every man "good-looking" if he excels in some social activity. In fact, Malama's face really reminded those who disliked him of the vulture's face. Chiita was almost as tall as Malama, but was stocky and had a regular face. He was the most gentle of the three. Chibangu was a little fat fellow. Everything about him was vulgar. But he had, in particular, a very persuasive tongue, born of his inability for personal physical action.

The sun had risen high above as the three young men trudged along. The rays beat upon their skins fiercely and they felt thirsty. The Pool of the Lions was still a long way off and they quickened their pace. The sharp blades of their spears flashed in the bright sunshine as they carried them high above their heads.

At last they sighted the green patch of grass surrounding the pool, which was renowned for the lions that lurked there, especially during the night, in readiness for the animals that used it as a watering place. These lions often took their toll of the cattle that were left wandering about around the area at night, in grateful substitution for the more alert wildebeest, impala or waterbuck.

There was a herd of cattle on the other side of the pool, but the young men did not bother to check them for the moment. They waded through the tall, sharp grass toward a clearing in the middle of the pool where the water sparkled most. Malama was leading the way while the other two followed him several paces behind. They had stopped talking and, to Malama's ignorance, were trembling like a pair of frightened old women. They no longer felt thirsty for water. They only wanted to get it over with . . .

Malama stuck his spear into the wet soft mud beneath his feet and stooped to drink, and just at that moment something struck him in the back, just below his left shoulder. A spear blade, which had torn through his lower shoulder muscle, ripped through his left forearm muscle as well and came to rest with the shaft stuck firmly into the two muscles. He fell down in the water, crying: "Mother, they are killing me!" For a moment he sank below the surface of the water, only his right arm, which was free, stuck out, waving defiantly. Then slowly, painfully but resolutely he rose and turned to face his assailants. Chibangu and Chiita stood there wide-eyed and petrified. It was Chiita who had stabbed him, for the little Chibangu still held his spear poised in his hand. As usual his courage had failed him at the last moment.

Malama began to tug at the blade end of the spear with his right hand. Each time he gave it a pull, it moved, but just as he was moving the end shaft through his shoulder muscle, the other two suddenly regained their senses and started to run away, splashing water as they did so. When they came to the edge of the pool, they looked back without breaking their run to see Malama sinking to his feet again. Blood gushed profusely down the left side of his body.

As they walked home, Chiita and Chibangu hoped they would never see Malama again. They felt they had dealt him a fatal blow. That Malama of a thousand sins! There were the hungry vultures to gobble all his flesh, and the scavenging jackals and hyenas to grind the bones. He would never walk out of that pool alive. Indeed, nobody would ever find out what became of Malama.

They concocted a story to the effect that he had parted company with them while they were inspecting the herds and had not joined them again. The people of the area, knowing how independent-minded Malama was, would easily take that. Chiita and Chibangu assured themselves they could have all the girls to themselves—and all the fame, too!

But when they got home and told their story, Chiita began to entertain some private doubts. Had they in fact killed Malama? he asked himself again and again.

The cocks crowed, giving a strange quality of depth to the night. It was almost midnight, but old Umpami still sat by the dying fire, sucking thoughtfully at his long-stemmed pipe. It was always like this, he reflected to himself sadly, always huddled by the fireside smoking, and then going off to bed. Didn't life bear any promise for the aging? The old man's two sons sat with him by the fire. They, too, seemed to be engrossed in their own thoughts. Theirs were, perhaps, thoughts of youth and desire.

Suddenly, old Umpami became uneasy. He shifted about in his stool and occasionally cocked his ears to the wind. His sons looked inquiringly at each other, and then at him. Then in a whisper he said: "Listen! I hear something. Now just listen very carefully and you will hear it, too."

Yes, indeed, his sons heard it, too. From somewhere in the distance, there came an irregular and faint wail. It grew louder and more threatening as the wind changed direction. A man was in agony, a man was calling for help.

Umpami ordered his older son to sound the *indandala*, the war drum. He then disappeared into his hut and emerged a moment later, carrying in his right hand his *impula*, a short, spiked spear, all metal. He had owned this since his youth and had fought against man and beast with it.

There was confusion in Umpami's village as the inhabitants began to shoot out of their huts in the darkness. Dogs barked furiously and caused awkward obstruction to the men in search of their spears and torchwood.

Umpami worked his way toward the meeting place of the elders in the center of the village, there to deliver his finest harangue in many,

||||||||||||||||||||||||||||||||||||||||||||||||||||||||||||||||||||||||||||||||||||||||||||||||||

many years. Words tumbled out of his sunken, toothless mouth like myriad sparks escaping from a tortured, red-hot piece of metal on a dark, starless night. They shot out, rasping and intoxicating, casting a graveyard spell and order upon the people. He began by invoking the powerful spirit, Mwanamaundu, who controlled the dangerous elements of the forests, the plains and the rivers:

> Maaweee . . . *Mwanamaundu!*
> *Unchallenged ruler of mighty forests,*
> *Wide-eyed overseer of the vast plains,*
> *Captain of the water-breaking hippo and the evil-eyed*
>   *crocodile,*
> *Save us from your fury,*
> *And quicken our pace to the battle ground.*
> Maaweee . . . *Mwanamaundu!*

And the warriors answered in reverence:

> *Give us your speed, power and courage,*
> *And quicken our pace to the fighters' paradise.*

This ritual performed, Umpami now addressed his body of warriors, symbolically jabbing his *impula* into the brilliantly illuminated air above him. He told them: "Men of unflinching courage; great sons of Mwanamaundu who resides in the invisible anthill; lionhearted fighters! Tonight, you must defend your honor; it is the honor of your forefathers, and of the great Mwanamaundu himself. You have hunted the lion before, and the buffalo; the leopard, too. Your courage has never been questioned. I heard a voice a short while ago. It was the cry of a man in agony; a dying man. It came from the direction of the river; perhaps from the leopard-infested thicket across the river. He may not be one of us, but we must defend him; we must save him, whether he be friend or foe. And now," shouted the old man, making his occasional spear jab into the air, "now, if you are men, and not women, follow me!"

Umpami led the way. Even at his age, he carried himself admirably well. Yes, age might sap away the greater part of a man's physical strength, but a true warrior's spirit lives eternally, guiding the ideals and aspirations of the rising generations, and forever weaving an intricate legend of the warrior with each generation, each age-set and each age-grade. Death, when it finally comes, only gauges the warrior's exploits against those of his forebears and enshrines them in tribal lore.

The river was not far from the village and the men were soon there. As old Umpami had predicted, the groans of the man in agony issued forth from the carnivore-infested reed thicket across the Mupili River. The water was very deep and, besides, enormous crocodiles lurked there; so the idea of wading through the water was immediately discounted. Two canoes, the only ones available in the area, were soon made ready. Their carrying capacity was limited to four people each. Umpami made his choice of seven men: they were veterans of dangerous ventures.

Umpami entered into the first canoe. The other seven pillars of courage then divided themselves into two groups, the three coming along with Umpami and the other four occupying the second canoe.

Umpami's canoe took the lead as they paddled slowly toward the other bank. The night was pitch-black, but the torches shone high and bright. The men who had remained behind waited tensely.

The river was quite shallow by the thicket and Umpami stumbled out of his canoe into the waist-high water and began to wade through to the edge of the thicket. Only then did he begin to feel the effect of age on his limbs. The others followed suit, dragging the two canoes along. They fastened these to the reeds and then started to work their way through the reeds toward the mystery of the night. By now they were all convinced that the moaning man had been attacked by either a lion or a leopard. But they all wondered why the beast had not finished him off.

They made slow and laborious progress through the dense reeds and bushes. At one time a dove fluffed its wings nearby and everyone started! Suddenly, the thicket cleared and they found themselves out in the open, to their surprise. They thought they had missed the spot. They remade their dying torches and searched along the edge of the thicket. They did not go far. One of the men pointed out at something ahead and whispered in a tense voice: "Look, it is over there!"

With drawn spears and in battle formation, they rushed upon the scene... A man lay face-upward in a pool of blood. He was half conscious and moaned at irregular intervals.

There was nothing around the scene to give a clue to the men as to what might have happened; not until they turned the wounded man over. His left shoulder and his left forearm muscle showed very deep wounds. Blood had clotted round the wounds. They had never seen the man before.

"He has been stabbed," declared the experienced Umpami. "But he will talk when he gets better—that is, if he gets better at all."

They carried the wounded man home.

Several days after Chibangu and Chiita had reported back to the village folk that Malama had parted company with them and gone his own way in search of cattle, Malama's parents started to worry. They could not understand why their son had not returned yet. Search parties were organized, but they had failed to find Malama. So a "funeral" was finally held.

In fact, soon after Chibangu and Chiita had run away, leaving him struggling and bleeding heavily in the middle of the pool, Malama had managed to crawl up to the edge of the water where he had fainted for some time. He was awakened late in the afternoon by huge birds flapping their wings nearby. He had then realized that these were vultures ready to eat him. He had got to his feet and stumbled on. He had not known where he was going, nor had he cared. His one main aim was to walk on, hoping to find help somehow. He had not allowed himself to lie down as he realized that once he did that he would never get up again. He had walked in what must have appeared a trance or dream. His conscious mind had ceased to function properly. It was perhaps his subconscious self that had assumed control.

Then Malama became completely unaware of his own existence. The next thing he remembered was coming to in strange surroundings. The people who surrounded him were strange, too. It took him many, many days before he could piece together and tell his own story. The rest was told him by his hosts.

After many months of convalescing, Malama took leave of his kind hosts and thanked Umpami for saving his life. The latter gave the young man his *impula*, a sign of admiration from the old man for Malama's determination and courage in the worst of situations.

"I give this to you, brave young man, so that you may be even more brave," the old man said, handing him the spear and shaking his hand with unusual fire.

The people of Umpami's village had vaguely heard of the existence of Bwaami village, far away to the west, and a full day's journey from their own village. During the period that Malama had stayed with them, critically ill, they had failed to contact the people of Bwaami to notify them of Malama's whereabouts and condition. Several men had set out for this distant village but had turned back in disappointment, having lost their way. Now as Malama trotted along, he was himself not sure that he was following the right direction.

He at first began to follow cattle tracks and, when these ended abruptly, began to follow wild animal tracks. By midday, he felt he had covered much distance. Late in the afternoon, he came to a village he recognized. His own was not very far now. He did not enter this village as he was afraid he might alarm the inhabitants, since the whole of this area must have been told of his disappearance. They had probably attended his funeral, too!

As the sun was setting he sighted his village. He was tired, after the long illness and the long walk. He was beginning to get angry, too. He had been betrayed by those two cowards. He would now teach them a lesson. But they would never live to learn it. He would kill them both in front of their mothers and sisters!

A beer party was in full swing and a huge group of men and women stood in a circle watching dancers of the *kamatamata* with great enthusiasm. Malama swiftly joined in the crowd and was soon swallowed in it, happy in the thought that he had not been recognized. At one time an old woman opened her mouth in alarm after peering into Malama's face but then thought best not to make a fool of herself in public: Malama was dead, after all, she reassured herself.

Malama turned away from the old woman quickly and drew deeper into the circle of spectators. Among the enthusiastic dancers in the center was Chiita, the man who had hurled the spear that day! Chiita danced, wielding a battle-ax wildly, to a thunderous applause from the spectators. He had a flair for introducing mimicry to all his dancing. Malama watched him with mounting anger and hatred as the famous dancer clutched at some imaginary object stuck in his chest, and sank to his knees as though overwhelmed by the object. He was acting out with great relish the episode at the Pool of the Lions. But he never rose again; for, while he squatted on the ground, with his mouth wide open, portraying a situation of agony, he opened his eyes to stare straight into the eyes of the man he had never hoped or wanted to meet again. Malama drove his *impula* point deep into Chiita's heart. The latter slumped backward. Even in death, he appeared to be acting out his abortive venture of many months back.

Before the people recovered from the shock, Malama had sought out the fiendish Chibangu. The little man had been among the spectators. Malama held him by the back of his neck, flung him to the ground, and hacked his head off with an ax he had snatched off the dead body of Chiita.

Malama's vengeance was over.

A PRESENT FOR MY WIFE

|||||||||||||||||||||||||||||||||||||||||||||||||||||||||||||||||||||||||||||||||||||||||||

by Mbulelo Mzamane

Mbulelo Mzamane *is a joint winner of the Mofolo-Plomer prize for literature, 1976. He has recently written a novel,* The Children of Soweto. *His collection of short stories,* My Cousin Comes to Jo'burg, *was published in 1980.*

WHAT DO YOU DO WITH a nagging wife? She knows very well that I barely earn enough to enable us to rise above *pap* and *morogo*. Yet she expects me to buy her expensive presents of leather jackets, mink coats and evening dresses—which she'll never wear, anyway, since we can't afford to attend balls and shows. She can't even dance, even if we could. What intensifies her nagging is the fact that our next-door neighbor, Mazibuko, is always bringing his wife nice things. She won't believe me when I tell her that the things Mazibuko brings his wife are all stolen, every single item of them.

"*Keng wena o sa dire je ka banna ba bang?*" she asks.

I tell her I can't steal just because everybody's husband is a thief. It's against my convictions.

"*Empa ga o na conscience dicheleteng tsa batho.*"

She's got me there and she knows it. I don't say tomorrow where money is concerned. I've emptied her purse before and denied it flatly, even though we both knew that it could only have been me. On several occasions she's caught me redhanded, disappearing with her handbag into the toilet.

My problems gather momentum with the arrival of the new fridge Mazibuko brings his wife. We're watching from our stoop.

"I want to branch into private business," she says as the stolen fridge is being carried next door. I'm convinced it's stolen. Mazibuko later confirms this himself in a little conversation we have across the fence. "And I need a refrigerator for the business," she adds. Whoever taught her that word!

I know just what "private business" she means. Hasn't she been telling me about that, nights on end? I wish I was like the other fellows who have *dmyatsi* to whom they can escape. My problem is that I'm generally shy with women. She was the first and only girlfriend I ever had so when she proposed we marry or split, we married, of course. But she's not going to steamroll me now. I just don't like this other proposition. Who wants to get to bed, each night, only after all the others have had their fill? Who wants to live in constant fear of police raids? Who would like to be woken up by fellows, demanding drinks at all sorts of unreasonable hours? Her idea of starting a shebeen just doesn't sit too well on my chest.

"It's not as if you were earning a fortune," she says, as if I'd ever claimed to be Oppenheimer's financial equal. "The extra cash would come in handy," she adds.

I must resist that as long as I can. Has she ever gone hungry? Let her name a single day when she's gone to bed without food. Not always decent meals, I must confess. But don't I eat the same meals? I always augment this with fish and chips and half a loaf of brown bread in town, same as she does. Do I ever hide my pay packet from her? She opens it herself, sealed, every Friday. It's true that I sometimes open it with steam before I get home and seal it again. But it isn't as if I did that every Friday.

Mazibuko jumps across the fence and invites me for a drink, to celebrate the arrival of the new fridge.

She dishes him the kind of smile I used to get when we were still courting. I'd like to see that smile on her face again. Directed at me. But I'm not jealous. Mazibuko is a good neighbor. However, I can't be expected to condescend so low as to pick up a dead man's fridge.

She turns and looks at me as though I'd pumped her full of castor oil. "You won't forget we've some business to settle, will you?" she says as Mazibuko and I skip across the fence.

"What have you done?"

"She wants a fridge. How did you get yours?"

Mazibuko has brought the bottle of our special K.W.V. What I like about this brandy is that it really has no hangover to talk of. I often provide this specialty myself. Surreptitiously, of course. My method is simple. After I've doctored my pay packet, I buy one and give it to Mazibuko before we get home. It's then up to him to come and invite me. The trick almost always works. As far as she is concerned Mazibuko can never err. The perfect gentleman, neighborly and all that. She's lectured me more than once about men who parasite on others, because she thinks I drink with Mazibuko. The lecture goes in through one ear and out through the other. Take the bottle we're going to drink, for instance. Didn't Mazibuko and I *gazaat* when we met during lunchtime? Anyway, I'm not too keen to broadcast the fact, especially to her, that I contributed half the amount that went to buying that bottle. What I'm interested in just now is to know how Mazibuko came by his fridge.

'Tell me about the fridge," I say as soon as I'm sure Meisie, that's Mazibuko's burden, is out of earshot.

Strange thing about Meisie. She's got all the comforts you'd think a woman needs. Bedroom suite, kitchen scheme and now a fridge. She's by far the best-dressed woman in our street, the first to wear an Afro wig and all that. She wants it like that, she likes it that way. But she won't hear of Mazibuko bringing stolen goods to her house. She knows very well that not even Mazibuko's life savings could buy her half the things she has in the house. She'll accept anything as long as you tell her you bought it. But don't make the mistake of telling her you stole it.

Don't I know what I'm talking about? The other day Mazibuko and I returned home—we travel in the same train to work and back—laden with liquor, grocery and meat. It's a whole chicken and we ask her to fry it for us, sharp sharp. She obliges. I cannot forget how we got that chicken so I keep on reminiscing and laughing off the event. She comes in from the kitchen and asks how we got that chicken. I'm in my most communicative mood and so I do not see Mazibuko's forbidding frown until it's too late. So I explain that we snatched it off a crippled white woman. It's only when she spits on the floor and disappears into the kitchen that I realize that something's gone wrong.

"*Uyinyovile*, you've damn well spoiled everything," Mazibuko says through clenched teeth.

There's a fierce rattling of pots in the kitchen. She storms out through the kitchen door and walks round the house to the front gate. I watch stealthily through the window. She has a pot which she empties into the rubbish bin. This woman!

She comes back and plants herself across the door, arms akimbo. "Let me tell you one thing straight," she says. "I never harbor any stolen goods in this house. Fancy, asking me to cook you stolen meat! Contaminating my pots with white disease! I'm a self-respecting woman, I must tell you, and I mean to keep my home respectable. *Manifun' ukuphekelwa inyam'entshontshiwe, hambani niyoyipheka kwa-hell.*"

We should have tried my wife. Not that I think she's referring to her when she says we should go fry our chicken in hell.

I've been on my guard since that fateful day. That's why I'm careful not to ask Mazibuko about the fridge in Meisie's respectable presence. The conversation that follows is mainly carried on in whispers.

Mazibuko explains the matter of the fridge this way. At Bradlow's furniture shop where he works, he does deliveries and repossessions. That very afternoon he'd been sent to collect the fridge from a house in the townships whose owner was no longer able to honor the terms of the hire purchase agreement. When he got to this house, he found their property piled outside. They were moving. It was explained to him that the owner of the house had died some three months ago, after a long illness. As it was not permissible by law for his family to occupy the house any longer, they were going to stay elsewhere, with the widow's brother.

An idea was running through Mazibuko's mind. With many apologies he explained his business. The widow responded with such resignation and listlessness that Mazibuko was almost tempted to let them take away the fridge. "After all it's your job, my son," she said.

That was it. After all, it wasn't really Mazibuko who'd be cheating the widow. It was Bradlow's. By cheating the company Mazibuko would be getting in a blow for the old lady. At any rate, whose house could contain all the widow's property on top of what was already in that house?

He collected the fridge and delivered it at his own house.

"What explanation will you give to the firm?"

"I'll tell them the truth. I'll tell them the occupants of the house have left. Forwarding address unknown. They can verify that for themselves, if they like."

"*Nihleba ngani nina lapho?*" Meisie asks when she comes into the sitting room. "Why talk in whispers like two eternal conspirators?"

"Aah! *Izindaba zamadoda nje*, Sisi," I say.

"I didn't know men also gossiped," she says and then passes into the bedroom.

That terminates our conversation. I immediately rise to leave.

Meisie comes out of the bedroom and sees me already on my feet. "*Hayi!*" she says. "*Bengingakuxoshi.*"

"I know you weren't chasing me away, Sisi," I say, "but I was already on my way out." If I stay longer there is the probability she'll come and fetch me in person. Hasn't she said she has a bone to chew with me?

You can resist some people's requests some of the time, but you cannot resist her requests all the time. I was bound to surrender someday. She knew that and I knew it too. So why not make it tonight? As good a day as any. Thus it was that on that evening I gave my consent to her proposal that we start a shebeen.

We bought a fridge. Mazibuko came to my rescue. I'm not telling how.

She left her job at the CNA, where she used to dust books, to look after the business.

Although we haven't exactly prospered—a good deal of the proceeds goes into police bribes and court fines—we've become a very popular spot. The reason for our success lies mainly in her personality. She's very selective about whom she admits into the house, to keep out the township's riffraff. The result is that our patrons come from the ranks of the township's leading businessmen, doctors, lawyers and teachers, and their girlfriends. People call us the Fish Pond because we're like an alcoholic stream that never runs dry.

I won't deny it. I live in constant fear of the liquor squad. On some evenings I can't sleep at all. But the business has certain compensations too. I don't just mean sharing liquor with my customers. That doesn't call for much imagination because drunkards are open-handed by temperament. They'll thrust liquor down your throat even when you're least inclined to drink. I'm not talking about that. There's this other area in which I feel I must act soon, for my own peace of mind. She's been nagging again, about presents.

"You've enough capital of your own," I say. "Why can't you buy yourself whatever you want."

"It's not the same thing," she says. Don't I know that? Using her money and using my own are two different things. She won't part with hers to buy any of the expensive things she's always at me about, precisely because she knows they're worthless. I must find a way of making her contribute, at least in part, toward the realization of her grandiose schemes.

I've devised this method which has been working fine so far. I suppose that's what drives me to make the rash promise I later make. Success sometimes goes to the head. But it's my scheme I'm talking about. In our business it is very difficult to keep an accurate system of accounts. There are ever so many factors involved. For instance, when a chap buys a lot of liquor from your joint, he's entitled to a *gwaqaza*. The extra liquor you offer him as a gift is never accounted for. Then there's what you take yourself, sometimes, to entertain friends and relatives from afar. All of which makes my scheme particularly simple to carry out. Whenever I sell in her absence—she can't always be in the house, can she?—I pocket the money. There's also the occasional slip, when she leaves her purse lying carelessly about. When I combine all these figures, the amount I'm able to raise as a sideline is quite considerable. I could buy her a mink coat, only that's not what she wants.

"Last year you forgot my birthday," she says. "This year you may do the same if I don't keep on reminding you."

"Not likely. When is it?"

"Listen to that. It's on the twenty-eighth of this month."

"I know. I just meant when would you like us to celebrate."

"You could ask a more pertinent question than that."

"All right."

We both know that she's got me cornered. She's been at me about this etiquette or torniquet business, I can no longer remember which, for so long that I feel I must play the game her way, if only for my peace of mind. There's such a thick atmosphere of expectation in the room you could kick it. I brace myself for the big plunge.

"What do you want for your birthday?"

"You don't ask people what presents they want. It's not only embarrassing but it also removes the element of surprise. Anyway, since you've already asked, I want a leather jacket."

"What size?"

I wish I hadn't asked her what she wanted. I should really listen to her sometimes, when she lectures me on civilized conduct. I could tear a page or two from her books on conduct, stolen in the days she used to work at the CNA, and fling them back at her. About this present, for instance. It would have been so simple to have deposited a pair of stockings at her feet, in just the way she says these things should be done.

"You know what size. Forty-two."

That's a fat order, but I'll try to meet it.

Despite the fact that she reminds me on the twenty-seventh, I forget to buy her present. The first reason why I forget is that in all the shops I've been to, the largest size I could get was a thirty-six. These things are not designed for battleships, but I can't very well tell her that. The second reason is that I still haven't raised enough money. I'd have to empty her purse to do that and to augment the amount with part of my life savings. These things are frightfully expensive. I've ransacked her pockets before for a few coins. But to steal her whole purse would prove beyond even me. The only way out is to procrastinate.

"You haven't bought me my present," she says.

"I'll tell you what. I could have bought you a cheaper jacket, but I didn't want to. I didn't have enough money for the one I deposited."

"How much does it cost?"

"That would spoil the element of surprise?" I'm learning fast.

"When will you pop out the rest of the money?"

"Do not look a gift horse in the mouth." It's a proverb I once read from one of her books. I'm not sure whether I've used it appropriately. To cover up, I rise and kiss her fully on the mouth—you can't talk when you're being kissed—and disappear into the bedroom.

You can fool some people all the time but you can't fool her always, to adapt that famous saying again. I'm a glib liar, I know. Survival demands it. But she's my stop station, as they say.

A week passes, two, still no leather jacket.

I've not really made any serious effort for the simple reason that it's impossible to get her what she wants. There were days on which I'd seriously put some money aside, but that money is all gone. I can no longer buy her even the cheapest imitation.

"Oho!" she starts ominously. "Do you think I still don't know you? After all these years. Tomorrow is Saturday. You're not working. You'll take me with you to show me this leather jacket. I don't know what suddenly turned me into such a fool. Where are the receipts that show you paid the deposit?"

"I deposited it backdoor."

"Oho! *Libala mntwan' abantu.*"

Mazibuko descends on us like a godsend. On our way from work I gave him a bottle and asked him to do the usual.

Not even Mazibuko's usual charms will soothe her tonight. "*Akayindawo lowo*," she says.

Mazibuko is a sensible man. Doesn't he row a similar boat? If she says I'm not going anywhere, that's final. He beats an immediate retreat and leaves me more crestfallen than before.

One of the few blessings of our business is company. I don't mean when it's not desirable. But right now it's needed. You can't run business along sulky lines. You must, at least, smile to your customers. And a smile has the power to relieve tension.

Since it's a Friday evening, the house is soon agog with spirited conversation. She's soon herself again, or so I think. One chap with a whole bottle to himself offers me a few stiff tots. I'm on my third when my glass is unceremoniously snatched from my lips. "Don't give this one anything," she says.

I've my tail between my legs. I must do something or say something to restore my dignity. This woman can be green, green, green with rudeness. Does she want everybody to know that she has me by the cock? I could do something terrible. But I must control my anger. My reputation first.

I laugh behind her back and lean forward to whisper to the other chap. "I've been ordered off the bottle," I say. "Doctor's orders. *Maar dit is nie easy nie om te lay off,* especially if you've been raising the elbow for as long as I've been doing."

My companion nods with sympathetic understanding.

Life is such that good weather must follow long spells of miserable weather. There are days when the ancestors seem to direct our every movement.

My fortunes took a dramatic turn the next Friday after work. We were in the train with Mazibuko. On his lap was a huge parcel.

"*Wat het jy daar in, Fana?*" I asked.

"*My vrou se leather jacket,*" he says. "*Ek koop hom esgodini, B.D.*"

What's going to become of me if she sees Meisie in a leather jacket? I must talk to Mazibuko. Can't he pass the jacket on to me?

III

I'll pay him by and by. He can obtain another the same way he obtained this one. I don't mind how much I pay him.

Mazibuko is adamant. He won't part with it. He could arrange for me through the same channels to get another. Not this one. He's spent too many sleepless nights over this already.

I also tell him I'm living in shit street, too, on account of just such a jacket. He nods and says nothing.

There's something I don't understand about this. Is every housewife now after a leather jacket? I'm really puzzled by this, but not for long. Mazibuko leans across his seat and says there are many things he could tell me. I know that's just a preamble so I keep quiet.

"*Hawu! Jy's nie curious nie?*" he asks and leans closer. "*Ek sal jou een ding vertel. Ngizokutshayela ngoba ngiyabona ukuthi awukeni. Jy ken nix. Jy word 'n moomish. Babhedgile*, your wife and mine, to see who gets a leather jacket first."

She can never forgive me for this. For the first time I seriously contemplate sleeping out. No use, she'd send the police after me, that one. And what then?

I should have never succumbed to her request to start a shebeen. My problems backdate to that fateful decision. The business has given her definite airs. I've noticed that she always wants to look better dressed than, or at least as well dressed as, any of the women who come to drink at our house. I must buy her such and such because she's seen so and so wearing it. That's why we're not prospering. Only the other day I watched her deliberately spill beer over her dress just because she wanted to change into her new slack suit to compete with some teenagers who'd come to our house dressed in similar outfits. It didn't matter that slacks don't become her very well. She just doesn't mind displaying her excess flesh to better effect. She won't realize she isn't shaped differently from a sausage. Now she wants to compete with Meisie whose husband does business with every private corporation in town that deals in stolen goods. And I'm expected to . . . But what's the point of taking off like that? Meisie has the leather jacket and she hasn't. That's the salient point I must tackle, with Mazibuko's assistance.

I have a wonderful idea in my head but I need his cooperation. I put my plan to him. He eyes me with a mixture of skepticism and distrust, and shakes his head sadly. That drives me to near-desperation. Mazibuko's essentially a man of action and I'm primarily a man of ideas and very smooth-talking too. Very reluctantly he yields to persuasion, but warns repeatedly that nothing should go wrong, otherwise he'll have to break into my house and retrieve it himself.

When we get off the train I'm carrying the leather jacket. We walk home. Mazibuko is still trying to find a flaw in my plan. But I've already stated that ideas are not his province.

We part company at his gate. He promises he'll join me soon. There are several reasons why Mazibuko has to be with me tonight. First, he's got to keep away from Meisie, to whom he'd promised to bring the parcel today. He also wants to make sure I don't bungle anything. Lastly, I'll need him to lend a hand later.

"What have you got in there?" she asks as soon as I set my toes in the house.

"Hayi, yi-drycleaner yami net," I say and slip into the bedroom where I shove the parcel under the bed, behind some crates of beer. I can't let her see it now. She'd rush straightaway to go and show it off to Meisie.

Mazibuko walks in, as I come out of the bedroom, and joins two men in the sitting room who've already settled down to their beer. I've given him some cash so that he can order himself some beer too.

"That was fast. Did you tell her I'd invited you over for a drink?" I ask when I'm sure the others can't hear.

"Ja, but she wants that thing terribly blind," he says.

"Your ordeal won't last much longer," I say, "while mine is only just beginning."

I play some records on my hi-fi set which I also bought with Mazibuko's assistance. Where would I be without this wonderful man?

Soon the place is packed with the usual Friday evening crowd. Some are dancing while others are talking as if their listeners were a little on the deaf side.

I stuff Mazibuko with beer, some of it bought and the rest stolen straight out of the fridge.

Later in the night we both agree it is time for the presentation. We've been going over the plan again to check for loopholes but, as I've said before, there are none.

I move into the kitchen where she is busy knocking a meal together. I'm used to having my supper after ten. Then I speak of indifferent things to her until Mazibuko appears at the door to announce that he just wants to hop across the fence to collect the key so that he won't have to bother Meisie when he returns later. He promises he won't be long and takes off.

This is when I am supposed to tell her.

"I've a surprise for you," I say with a grin broad enough to harbor a battleship.

"What is it?"

"Come with me to the bedroom and I'll show you."

We go through to the bedroom. I make a dive for the parcel, tear the wrapping off and hand her the leather jacket.

"Whose is it?"

"Yours. Fit it on."

She's hardened herself, this woman. Can no longer let go. But there's no doubt about it, she's deeply affected. I look the other way for I can see her eyes becoming moist. That gives her the chance to dry them with a single, swift sweep of the sleeves.

She struggles into it. It's a size or two too small, and that's an understatement, but I praise her lavishly. My only fear is that she might tear it. Fortunately she doesn't. She looks at herself in the mirror and shakes her head with dissatisfaction. Her discontentment melts when she sees the smile, like headlines to her praise, on my face.

Someone calls for a drink from the sitting room.

I urge her to go and serve them in her new coat, while I remain giggling to myself.

Her entrance is greeted with loud applause and prolonged whistling. What do you expect from drunken chaps and their girlfriends?

They praise her profusely. I'm afraid some of the praise may go to her head.

"*Wu-u-u!*" Each syllable is accompanied by a handclap. "I'm sure it must have cost you a fortune."

"*Bathong!* Some people are lucky."

"I saw an identical coat the other day, *ha*-John Orr's. *Ha ke sa hopola hore ene ele bokae. Maar ene ele over one hundred rand.*"

"*Wu-u-u! Ke ye galela joang. Ke can't get.*"

"Baby you look smashing."

"*Hayi! Suka wena lapha, lesidakwa,*" she says and makes her way back to the bedroom.

She gives me a resounding kiss on both sides of the face and then plants a prolonged one in the center.

"*Awusenzele i-diet, tu,*" I say, helping her out of the jacket. "Make it two, to include no-Mazibuko. I'm sure he's not had a bite. I invited him over as soon as we got back from work."

"He's back already," she says.

Which was as it should have been. He hadn't gone home really. D'you think Meisie would have let him out of her sight again? He'd only given the illusion of going home, for reasons which should soon be clear.

I folded the jacket and placed it on the bed. We steered ourselves back to the kitchen. While she was dishing up I went to call Mazibuko.

"*Uphi uMeisie?*" she asked. "Can you two attend to the customers while I make a quick dash to her. Here's your food."

"She's asleep," Mazibuko said.

"Why so early? I'll go and wake her up. You've got the key, haven't you?"

"Come on, darling, don't be so inconsiderate," I said.

"She's not feeling very well," Mazibuko said. "But what a remarkable coincidence!"

"What coincidence?" she asked.

"Meisie also has an identical jacket. I bought her one today."

"How come she didn't show it to me?"

"Because I haven't shown it to her yet. Maybe I should go and show it to her now."

But Mazibuko didn't go. We hadn't quite finished yet.

"You see," I said, "Mazibuko and I bought the leather jackets together. That's what we're celebrating tonight."

Her enthusiasm had ebbed so considerably that she refused to touch her food, pleading an upset tummy. Mazibuko and I divided her plate between us. She certainly looked sick at heart and lame of will. I knew then that we'd deliver the coup de grace with ease.

"I think you should retire to bed, darling," I said. "Mazibuko and I will attend to the customers."

Just then someone shouted for a drink. I rushed to serve him. When I returned she was ready to give in.

"Put the plates in the sink when you've finished and cover them with the dish towel," she said. "I'll attend to them in the morning. *Ningada-kwa kakhulu, tu, ngiyanicela,* please don't drink too much."

With that she took off. I escorted her to the bedroom. She began to change into her nightie while I sat on the bed, the leather jacket on my lap. Finally she got into bed. I remained seated and chatted to her until summoned to the sitting room, depositing the jacket at the foot of the bed as I walked off.

"Put it in the wardrobe, will you?'

"I'll do that when I come back, darling. Don't worry." I blew her a kiss.

I didn't go back to the bedroom until much later.

We drank ourselves to a near-stupor with Mazibuko, so that when he left he nearly forgot to take the jacket with him.

He later told me that when he got home he immediately woke up his wife and presented her with the jacket. He didn't forget to tell her that my wife had a similar jacket. She forgave him all his drunkenness and even overlooked the fact that he'd left her alone for the greater part of the night.

The real drama came in the morning when Meisie came to compare coats.

She'd woken up before me. I was about to wake up too, with a king-size hangover, when she walked into the bedroom. I pretended to be fast asleep and even snored for effect.

She ransacked the wardrobe for a while.

Then I heard her say to herself: "*Ngabe uyibebe kuphi?*"

The next thing she was shaking me up, not so gently, to ask where I'd put her leather jacket.

I pointed to the lower part of the bed.

"But I asked you to hang it in the wardrobe," she said with a tear-choked voice.

That jerked me up.

We began searching the house. Meisie joined us. I was so bent upon making the search look authentic that I momentarily forgot my throbbing head. We delved into every corner of the house. For a whole hour we searched diligently. I'd even begun pulling out empty bottles of beer from their case, just to make absolutely certain, when she called off the search.

I went to sit on the stoop, a bottle of beer in my hand, and listened to their conversation in the house.

The words were never far from my own mouth, but I wanted her to start condemning them herself. That way she'd come to believe in the truth of her own fancies. Never feed ideas to a wife who can arrive at the same conclusions by independent means. Ideas, even if they may be circulating in her mind, become suspect once you mention them first. I didn't want her to think I was trying to find a scapegoat. So I was greatly relieved when I heard her accuse them herself.

"I'll tell you whom I suspect," she said to Meisie. "*Di-skeberesh tsa maobane*, they must have stolen it. You've no idea how envious those girls sounded last night. One actually said she wished it was hers. They won't get away with it, they'll certainly hear from my lawyers."

"Shame!" Meisie said.

"And do you know how much it cost?" she asked.

"One hundred seventy-five rand. That's what the price tag read on mine."

(I wonder from what article in which shop Mazibuko ripped off that tag. I should go and ask him.)

"Listen to that. And to think that once I never even believed him when he told me he'd deposited it. Poor *skepsel!*"

I crept back to the fridge, pinched two more beers, and hopped across the fence to Mazibuko. Wonderful chap!

THE RAIN CAME

by Grace Ogot

Grace Ogot *was born in 1930 in Kenya. She worked as a journalist and was a delegate of Kenya in the United Nations. Her first novel,* The Promised Land *(1966), shows this gifted writer's interest in the woman in society. In the collection of short stories* Land Without Thunder *(1968), Ogot presents half-folk stories full of fantasies and magic.* The Other Woman *(1967) is also a collection of stories. In* The Land of Tears *(1980) and* The Graduate *(1980) the author pleads to the educated elite of Africa to return to their own countries and serve their own people.*

T HE CHIEF WAS STILL far from the gate when his daughter Oganda saw him. She ran to meet him. Breathlessly she asked her father, "What is the news, great Chief? Everyone in the village is anxiously waiting to hear when it will rain." Labong'o held out his hands for his daughter but he did not say a word. Puzzled by her father's cold attitude Oganda ran back to the village to warn the others that the chief was back.

The atmosphere in the village was tense and confused. Everyone moved aimlessly and fussed in the yard without actually doing any work. A young woman whispered to her co-wife, "If they have not solved this rain business today, the chief will crack." They had watched him getting thinner and thinner as the people kept on pestering him. "Our cattle lie dying in the fields," they reported. "Soon it will be our children and then ourselves. Tell us what to do to save our lives, oh great Chief." So the chief had daily prayed with the

Almighty through the ancestors to deliver them from their distress.

Instead of calling the family together and giving them the news immediately, Labong'o went to his own hut, a sign that he was not to be disturbed. Having replaced the shutter, he sat in the dimly lit hut to contemplate.

It was no longer a question of being the chief of hunger-stricken people that weighed Labong'o's heart. It was the life of his only daughter that was at stake. At the time when Oganda came to meet him, he saw the glittering chain shining around her waist. The prophecy was complete. "It is Oganda, Oganda, my only daughter, who must die so young." Labong'o burst into tears before finishing the sentence. The chief must not weep. Society had declared him the bravest of men. But Labong'o did not care anymore. He assumed the position of a simple father and wept bitterly. He loved his people, the Luo, but what were the Luo for him without Oganda? Her life had brought a new life in Labong'o's world and he ruled better than he could remember. How would the spirit of the village survive his beautiful daughter? "There are so many homes and so many parents who have daughters. Why choose this one? She is all I have." Labong'o spoke as if the ancestors were there in the hut and he could see them face to face. Perhaps they were there, warning him to remember his promise on the day he was enthroned when he said aloud, before the elders, "I will lay down life, if necessary, and the life of my household, to save this tribe from the hands of the enemy." "Deny! Deny!" he could hear the voice of his forefathers mocking him.

When Labong'o was consecrated chief he was only a young man. Unlike his father, he ruled for many years with only one wife. But people rebuked him because his only wife did not bear him a daughter. He married a second, a third, and a fourth wife. But they all gave birth to male children. When Labong'o married a fifth wife she bore him a daughter. They called her Oganda, meaning "beans," because her skin was very fair. Out of Labong'o's twenty children, Oganda was the only girl. Though she was the chief's favorite, her mother's co-wives swallowed their jealous feelings and showered her with love.

After all, they said, Oganda was a female child whose days in the royal family were numbered. She would soon marry at a tender age and leave the enviable position to someone else.

Never in his life had he been faced with such an impossible decision. Refusing to yield to the rainmaker's request would mean sacrificing the whole tribe, putting the interests of the individual above those of the society. More than that. It would mean disobeying the ancestors, and most probably wiping the Luo people from the surface of the earth. On the other hand, to let Oganda die as a ransom for the people would permanently cripple Labong'o spiritually. He knew he would never be the same chief again.

The words of Ndithi, the medicine man, still echoed in his ears. "Podho, the ancestor of the Luo, appeared to me in a dream last night, and he asked me to speak to the chief and the people," Ndithi had said to the gathering of tribesmen. "A young woman who has not known a man must die so that the country may have rain. While Podho was still talking to me, I saw a young woman standing at the lakeside, her hands raised, above her head. Her skin was as fair as the skin of young deer in the wilderness. Her tall slender figure stood like a lonely reed at the riverbank. Her sleepy eyes wore a sad look like that of a bereaved mother. She wore a gold ring on her left ear, and a glittering brass chain around her waist. As I still marveled at the beauty of this young woman, Podho told me, "Out of all the women in this land, we have chosen this one. Let her offer herself a sacrifice to the lake monster! And on that day, the rain will come down in torrents. Let everyone stay at home on that day, lest he be carried away by the floods."

Outside there was a strange stillness, except for the thirsty birds that sang lazily on the dying trees. The blinding midday heat had forced the people to retire to their huts. Not far away from the chief's hut, two guards were snoring away quietly. Labong'o removed his crown and the large eagle head that hung loosely on his shoulders. He left the hut, and instead of asking Nyabog'o the messenger to beat the drum, he went straight and beat it himself. In no time the whole household had assembled under the siala tree where he usually addressed them. He told Oganda to wait a while in her grandmother's hut.

When Labong'o stood to address his household, his voice was hoarse and the tears choked him. He started to speak, but words refused to leave his lips. His wives and sons knew there was great danger. Perhaps their enemies had declared war on them. Labong'o's eyes were red, and they could see he had been weeping. At last he told them. "One whom we love and treasure must be taken away from us. Oganda is to die." Labong'o's voice was so faint, that he could not hear it himself. But he continued. "The ancestors have chosen her to be offered as a sacrifice to the lake monster in order that we may have rain."

They were completely stunned. As a confused murmur broke out, Oganda's mother fainted and was carried off to her own hut. But the other people rejoiced. They danced around singing and chanting, "Oganda is the lucky one to die for the people. If it is to save the people, let Oganda go."

In her grandmother's hut Oganda wondered what the whole family were discussing about her that she could not hear. Her grandmother's hut was well away from the chief's court and, much as she strained her ears, she could not hear what was said. "It must be marriage," she concluded. It was an accepted custom for the family to discuss their daughter's future marriage behind her back. A faint smile played on Oganda's lips as she thought of the several young men who swallowed saliva at the mere mention of her name.

There was Kech, the son of a neighboring clan elder. Kech was very handsome. He had sweet, meek eyes and a roaring laughter. He would make a wonderful father, Oganda thought. But they would not be a good match. Kech was a bit too short to be her husband. It would humiliate her to have to look down at Kech each time she spoke to him. Then she thought of Dimo, the tall young man who had already distinguished himself as a brave warrior and an outstanding wrestler. Dimo adored Oganda, but Oganda thought he would make a cruel husband, always quarreling and ready to fight. No, she did not like him. Oganda fingered the glittering chain on her waist as she thought of Osinda. A long time ago when she was quite young Osinda had given her that chain, and instead of wearing it around her neck several times, she wore it round her waist where it could stay permanently. She heard her heart pounding so loudly as she thought of him. She whispered, "Let it be you they are discussing, Osinda, the lovely one. Come now and take me away. . ."

The lean figure in the doorway startled Oganda who was rapt in thought about the man she loved. "You have frightened me, Grandma," said Oganda laughing. "Tell me, is it my marriage you were discussing? You can take it from me that I won't marry any of them." A smile played on her lips again. She was coaxing the old lady to tell her quickly, to tell her they were pleased with Osinda.

In the open space outside the excited relatives were dancing and singing. They were coming to the hut now, each carrying a gift to put at Oganda's feet. As their singing got nearer Oganda was able to hear what they were saying: "If it is to save the people, if it is to give us rain, let Oganda go. Let Oganda die for her people, and for her ancestors." Was she mad to think that they were singing about her? How could she die? She found the lean figure of her grandmother barring the door. She could not get out. The look on her grandmother's face warned her that there was danger around the corner. "Grandma, it is not marriage then?" Oganda asked urgently. She suddenly felt panicky like a mouse cornered by a hungry cat. Forgetting that there was only one door in the hut Oganda fought desperately to find another exit. She must fight for her life. But there was none.

She closed her eyes, leapt like a wild tiger through the door, knocking her grandmother flat to the ground. There outside in mourning garments Labong'o stood motionless, his hands folded at the back. He held his daughter's hand and led her away from the excited crowd to the little red-painted hut where her mother was resting. Here he broke the news officially to his daughter.

For a long time the three souls who loved one another dearly sat in darkness. It was no good speaking. And even if they tried, the words could not have come out. In the past they had been like three cooking stones, sharing their burdens. Taking Oganda away from them would leave two useless stones which would not hold a cooking pot.

News that the beautiful daughter of the chief was to be sacrificed to give the people rain spread across the country like wind. At sunset the chief's village was full of relatives and friends who had come to congratulate Oganda. Many more were on their way coming, carrying their gifts. They would dance till morning to keep her company. And in the morning they would prepare her a big farewell feast. All these relatives thought it a great honor to be selected by the spirits to die, in order that the society may live. "Oganda's name will always remain a living name among us," they boasted.

But was it maternal love that prevented Minya from rejoicing with the other women? Was it the memory of the agony and pain of childbirth that made her feel so sorrowful? Or was it the deep warmth and understanding that passes between a suckling babe and her mother that made Oganda part of her life, her flesh? Of course it was an honor, a great honor, for her daughter to be chosen to die for the country. But what could she gain once her only daughter was blown away by the wind? There were so many other women in the land, why choose her daughter, her only child! Had human life any meaning at all—other women had houses full of children while she, Minya, had to lose her only child!

In the cloudless sky the moon shone brightly, and the numerous stars glittered with a bewitching beauty. The dancers of all age groups assembled to dance before Oganda, who sat close to her mother, sobbing quietly. All these years she had been with her people she thought she understood them. But now she discovered that she was a stranger among them. If they loved her as they had always professed why were they not making any attempt to save her? Did her people really understand what it felt like to die young? Unable to restrain her emotions any longer, she sobbed loudly as her age group got up to dance. They were young and beautiful and very soon they would marry and have their own children. They would have husbands to love and little huts for themselves. They would have reached maturity. Oganda touched the chain around her waist as she thought of

Osinda. She wished Osinda was there too, among her friends. "Perhaps he is ill," she thought gravely. The chain comforted Oganda—she would die with it around her waist and wear it in the underground world.

In the morning a big feast was prepared for Oganda. The women prepared many different tasty dishes so that she could pick and choose. "People don't eat after death," they said. Delicious though the food looked, Oganda touched none of it. Let the happy people eat. She contented herself with sips of water from a little calabash.

The time for her departure was drawing near, and each minute was precious. It was a day's journey to the lake. She was to walk all night, passing through the great forest. But nothing could touch her, not even the denizens of the forest. She was already anointed with sacred oil. From the time Oganda received the sad news she had expected Osinda to appear any moment. But he was not there. A relative told her that Osinda was away on a private visit. Oganda realized that she would never see her beloved again.

In the late afternoon the whole village stood at the gate to say good-bye and to see her for the last time. Her mother wept on her neck for a long time. The great chief in a mourning skin came to the gate barefooted, and mingled with the people—a simple father in grief. He took off his wrist bracelet and put it on his daughter's wrist saying, "You will always live among us. The spirit of our forefathers is with you."

Tongue-tied and unbelieving Oganda stood there before the people. She had nothing to say. She looked at her home once more. She could hear her heart beating so painfully within her. All her childhood plans were coming to an end. She felt like a flower nipped in the bud never to enjoy the morning dew again. She looked at her weeping mother, and whispered, "Whenever you want to see me, always look at the sunset. I will be there."

Oganda turned southward to start her trek to the lake. Her parents, relatives, friends and admirers stood at the gate and watched her go.

Her beautiful slender figure grew smaller and smaller till she mingled with the thin dry trees in the forest. As Oganda walked the lonely path that wound its way in the wilderness, she sang a song, and her own voice kept her company.

> *The ancestors have said Oganda must die*
> *The daughter of the chief must be sacrificed,*
> *When the lake monster feeds on my flesh.*
> *The people will have rain.*
> *Yes, the rain will come down in torrents.*
> *And the floods will wash away the sandy beaches*
> *When the daughter of the chief dies in the lake.*
> *My age group has consented*
> *My parents have consented*
> *So have my friends and relatives.*
> *Let Oganda die to give us rain.*
> *My age group are young and ripe,*
> *Ripe for womanhood and motherhood*
> *But Oganda must die young,*
> *Oganda must sleep with the ancestors.*
> *Yes, rain will come down in torrents.*

The red rays of the setting sun embraced Oganda, and she looked like a burning candle in the wilderness.

The people who came to hear her sad song were touched by her beauty. But they all said the same thing. "If it is to save the people, if it is to give us rain, then be not afraid. Your name will forever live among us."

At midnight Oganda was tired and weary. She could walk no more. She sat under a big tree, and having sipped water from her calabash, she rested her head on the tree trunk and slept.

When Oganda woke up in the morning the sun was high in the sky. After walking for many hours, she reached the *tong'*, a strip of land that separated the inhabited part of the country from the sacred place *(kar lamo)*. No layman could enter this place and come out alive—only those who had direct contact with the spirits and the

Almighty were allowed to enter this holy of holies. But Oganda had
to pass through this sacred land on her way to the lake, which she
had to reach at sunset.

A large crowd gathered to see her for the last time. Her voice was
now hoarse and painful, but there was no need to worry anymore.
Soon she would not have to sing. The crowd looked at Oganda sym-
pathetically, mumbling words she could not hear. But none of them
pleaded for life. As Oganda opened the gate, a child, a young child,
broke loose from the crowd, and ran toward her. The child took a
small earring from her sweaty hands and gave it to Oganda saying,
"When you reach the world of the dead, give this earring to my sister.
She died last week. She forgot this ring." Oganda, taken aback by the
strange request, took the little ring, and handed her precious water
and food to the child. She did not need them now. Oganda did not
know whether to laugh or cry. She had heard mourners sending their
love to their sweethearts, long dead, but this idea of sending gifts was
new to her.

Oganda held her breath as she crossed the barrier to enter the
sacred land. She looked appealingly at the crowd, but there was no
response. Their minds were too preoccupied with their own survival.
Rain was the precious medicine they were longing for, and the sooner
Oganda could get to her destination the better.

A strange feeling possessed Oganda as she picked her way in the
sacred land. There were strange noises that often startled her, and her
first reaction was to take to her heels. But she remembered that she
had to fulfill the wish of her people. She was exhausted, but the path
was still winding. Then suddenly the path ended on sandy land. The
water had retreated miles away from the shore leaving a wide stretch
of sand. Beyond this was the vast expanse of water.

Oganda felt afraid. She wanted to picture the size and shape of
the monster, but fear would not let her. The society did not talk
about it, nor did the crying children who were silenced by the mention of its name. The sun was still up, but it was no longer hot. For a
long time Oganda walked ankle-deep in the sand. She was exhausted
and longed desperately for her calabash of water. As she moved on,

she had a strange feeling that something was following her. Was it the monster? Her hair stood erect, and a cold paralyzing feeling ran along her spine. She looked behind, sideways and in front, but there was nothing, except a cloud of dust.

Oganda pulled up and hurried but the feeling did not leave her, and her whole body became saturated with perspiration.

The sun was going down fast and the lake shore seemed to move along with it.

Oganda started to run. She must be at the lake before sunset. As she ran she heard a noise coming from behind. She looked back sharply, and something resembling a moving bush was frantically running after her. It was about to catch up with her.

Oganda ran with all her strength. She was now determined to throw herself into the water even before sunset. She did not look back, but the creature was upon her. She made an effort to cry out, as in a nightmare, but she could not hear her own voice. The creature caught up with Oganda. In the utter confusion, as Oganda came face with the unidentified creature, a strong hand grabbed her. But she fell flat on the sand and fainted.

When the lake breeze brought her back to consciousness, a man was bending over her. ". . . . . !!" Oganda opened her mouth to speak, but she had lost her voice. She swallowed a mouthful of water poured into her mouth by the stranger.

"Osinda, Osinda! Please let me die. Let me run, the sun is going down. Let me die, let them have rain." Osinda fondled the glittering chain around Oganda's waist and wiped the tears from her face.

"We must escape quickly to the unknown land," Osinda said urgently. "We must run away from the wrath of the ancestors and the retaliation of the monster."

"But the curse is upon me, Osinda, I am no good to you anymore. And moreover the eyes of the ancestors will follow us everywhere and bad luck will befall us. Nor can we escape from the monster."

Oganda broke loose, afraid to escape, but Osinda grabbed her hands again.

"Listen to me, Oganda! Listen! Here are two coats!" He then covered the whole of Oganda's body, except her eyes, with a leafy attire made from the twigs of *Bwombwe*. "These will protect us from the eyes of the ancestors and the wrath of the monster. Now let us run out of here." He held Oganda's hand and they ran from the sacred land, avoiding the path that Oganda had followed.

The bush was thick, and the long grass entangled their feet as they ran. Halfway through the sacred land they stopped and looked back. The sun was almost touching the surface of the water. They were frightened. They continued to run, now faster, to avoid the sinking sun.

"Have faith, Oganda—that thing will not reach us."

When they reached the barrier and looked behind them trembling, only a tip of the sun could be seen above the water's surface.

"It is gone! It is gone!" Oganda wept, hiding her face in her hands.

"Weep not, daughter of the chief. Let us run, let us escape."

There was a bright lightning. They looked up, frightened. Above them black furious clouds started to gather. They began to run. Then the thunder roared, and the rain came down in torrents.

THE WILL OF ALLAH

|||||||||||||||||||||||||||||||||||||||||||||||||||||||||||||||||||||||||||||||||||||||||||||||

by David Owoyele

David Owoyele *comes from the northern part of Nigeria,*
where he worked as an officer in the information service.
His short stories and papers appear in numerous journals.
In 1969 he published a collection of short stories.

T HERE HAD BEEN A clear moon. Now the night was dark. Dogo
glanced up at the night sky. He saw that scudding black clouds
had obscured the moon. He cleared his throat. "Rain tonight," he
observed to his companion. Sule, his companion, did not reply immediately. He was a tall, powerfully built man. His face, as well as
his companion's, was a stupid mask of ignorance. He lived by thieving as did Dogo, and just now he walked with an unaccustomed
limp. "It is wrong to say that," Sule said after a while, fingering the
long, curved sheath knife he always wore on his upper left arm when,
in his own words, he was "on duty." A similar cruel-looking object
adorned the arm of his comrade. "How can you be sure?" "Sure?"
said Dogo, annoyance and impatience in his voice. Dogo is the local
word for tall. This man was thickset, short and squat, anything but
tall. He pointed one hand up at the scurrying clouds. "You only want
to look up there. A lot of rain has fallen in my life: those up there are
rain clouds."

They walked on in silence for a while. The dull red lights of the
big town glowed in crooked lines behind them. Few people were
abroad, for it was already past midnight. About half a mile ahead of
them the native town, their destination, sprawled in the night. Not a

|||||||||||||

single electric light bulb glowed on its crooked streets. This regrettable fact suited the books of the two men perfectly. "You are not Allah," said Sule at last. "You may not assert."

Sule was a hardened criminal. Crime was his livelihood, he had told the judge this during his last trial that had earned him a short stretch in jail. "Society must be protected from characters like you," he could still hear the stern judge intoning in the hushed courtroom. Sule had stood in the dock, erect, unashamed, unimpressed; he'd heard it all before. "You and your type constitute a threat to life and property and this court will always see to it that you get your just deserts, according to the law." The judge had then fixed him with a stern gaze, which Sule coolly returned: he had stared into too many so-called judges' eyes to be easily intimidated. Besides, he feared nothing and no one except Allah. The judge thrust his legal chin forward. "Do you never pause to consider that the road of crime leads only to frustration, punishment and suffering? You look fit enough for anything. Why don't you try your hand at earning an honest living for a change?" Sule had shrugged his broad shoulders. "I earn my living the only way I know," he said. "The only way I've chosen." The judge had sat back, dismayed. Then he leaned forward to try again. "Is it beyond you to see anything wrong in thieving, burglary, crime?" Again Sule had shrugged. "The way I earn my living I find quite satisfactory." "Satisfactory!" exclaimed the judge, and a wave of whispering swept over the court. The judge stopped this with a rap of his gavel. "Do you find it satisfactory to break the law?" "I've no choice," said Sule. "The law is a nuisance. It keeps getting in one's way." "Constant arrest and imprisonment—do you find it satisfactory to be a jailbird?" queried the judge, frowning most severely. "Every calling has its hazards," replied Sule philosophically. The judge mopped his face. "Well, my man, you cannot break the law. You can only attempt to break it. And you will only end up by getting broken." Sule nodded. "We have a saying like that," he remarked conversationally. "He who attempts to shake a stump only shakes himself." He glanced up at the frowning judge. "Something like a thick stump—the law, eh?" The judge had given him three months.

Sule had shrugged. "The will of Allah be done..."

A darting tongue of lightning lit up the overcast sky for a second. Sule glanced up. "Sure it looks like rain. But you do not say: It will rain. You are only a mortal. You only say: If it is the will of Allah, it will rain." Sule was a deeply religious man, according to his lights. His religion forbade being dogmatic or prophetic about the future, about anything. His fear of Allah was quite genuine. It was his firm conviction that Allah left the question of a means of livelihood for each man to decide for himself. Allah, he was sure, gives some people more than they need so that others with too little could help themselves to some of it. It could certainly not be the intention of Allah that some stomachs remain empty while others are overstuffed.

Dogo snorted. He had served prison sentences in all the major towns in the country. Prison had become for him a home from home. Like his companion in crime, he feared no man; but unlike him, he had no religion other than self-preservation. "You and your religion," he said in derision. "A lot of good it has done you." Sule did not reply. Dogo knew from experience that Sule was touchy about his religion, and the first intimation he would get that Sule had lost his temper would be a blow on the head. The two men never pretended that their partnership had anything to do with love or friendship or any other luxurious idea: they operated together when their prison sentences allowed because they found it convenient. In a partnership that each believed was for his own special benefit, there could be no fancy code of conduct. "Did you see the woman tonight?" Dogo asked, changing the subject, not because he was afraid of Sule's displeasure but because his grasshopper mind had switched to something else. "Uh-huh," granted Sule. "Well?" said Dogo when he did not go on. "Bastard!" said Sule, without any passion. "Who? Me?" said Dogo thinly. "We were talking about the woman," replied Sule.

They got to a small stream. Sule stopped, washed his arms and legs, his clean-shaven head. Dogo squatted on the bank, sharpening his sheath knife on a stone. "Where do you think you are going?" "To yonder village," said Sule, rinsing out his mouth. "Didn't know you had a sweetheart there," said Dogo. "I'm not going to any woman," said Sule. "I am going to collect stray odds and ends—if it is the will of Allah."

"To steal, you mean?" suggested Dogo.

"Yes," conceded Sule. He straightened himself, pointed a brawny arm at Dogo: "You are a burglar, too... and a bastard besides."

Dogo, calmly testing the edge of the knife on his arm, nodded. "Is that part of your religion, washing in midnight streams?" Sule didn't reply until he had climbed onto the farther bank. "Wash when you find a stream; for when you cross another is entirely in the hands of Allah." He limped off, Dogo following him. "Why did you call her a bastard?" Dogo asked. "Because she is one." "Why?" "She told me she sold the coat and the black bag for only fifteen shillings." He glanced down and sideways at his companion. "I suppose you got on to her before I did and told her what to say?" "I've not laid eyes on her for a week," protested Dogo. "The coat is fairly old. Fifteen shillings sounds all right to me. I think she has done very well indeed." "No doubt," said Sule. He didn't believe Dogo. "I'd think the same way if I'd already shared part of the proceeds with her..."

Dogo said nothing. Sule was always suspicious of him, and he returned the compliment willingly. Sometimes their suspicion of each other was groundless, other times not. Dogo shrugged. "I don't know what you are talking about." "No. I don't suppose you would," said Sule drily. "All I'm interested in is my share," went on Dogo. "Your second share, you mean," said Sule. "You'll both get your share—you cheating son without a father, as well as that howling devil of a woman." He paused before he added, "She stabbed me in the thigh—the bitch." Dogo chuckled softly to himself. "I've been wondering about that limp of yours. Put a knife in your thigh, did she? Odd, isn't it?" Sule glanced at him sharply. "What's odd about it?" "You getting stabbed just for asking her to hand over the money." "Ask her? I didn't ask her. No earthly use asking anything of characters like that." "Oh?" said Dogo. "I'd always thought all you had to do was ask. True, the coat wasn't yours. But you asked her to sell it. She's an old fence and ought to know that you are entitled to the money." "Only a fool would be content with fifteen shillings for a coat and a bag," said Sule. "And you are not a fool, eh?" chuckled Dogo. "What did you do about it?" "Beat the living daylight out of her," rasped Sule. "And quite right, too," commented Dogo. "Only snag is you seem to have got more than you gave her." He chuckled again. "A throbbing wound is no joke," said Sule testily. "And who's joking? I've been stabbed in my time, too. You can't go around at night wearing a knife and not expect to get stabbed once in a while. We should regard such things as an occupational hazard." "Sure," grunted Sule. "But that can't cure a wound." "No, but the hospital can," said Dogo. "I know. But in the hospital they ask questions before they cure you."

They were entering the village. In front of them the broad path diverged into a series of tracks that twined away between the houses. Sule paused, briefly, took one of the paths. They walked along on silent feet, just having a look around. Not a light showed in any of the crowded mud houses. Every little hole of a window was shut or plugged, presumably against the threatening storm. A peal of languid thunder rumbled over from the east. Except for a group of goats and sheep, which rose startled at their approach, the two had the village paths to themselves. Every once in a while Sule would stop by a likely house; the two would take a careful look around: he'd look inquiringly down at his companion, who would shake his head, and they would move on.

They had been walking around for about a quarter of an hour when a brilliant flash of lightning almost burned out their eyeballs. That decided them. "We'd better hurry," whispered Dogo. "The storm's almost here." Sule said nothing. A dilapidated-looking house stood a few yards away. They walked up to it. They were not put off by its appearance. Experience had taught them that what a house looked like was no indication of what it contained. Some stinking hovels had yielded rich hauls. Dogo nodded at Sule. "You stay outside and try to keep awake," said Sule. He nodded at a closed window. "You might stand near that."

Dogo moved off to his post. Sule got busy on the crude wooden door. Even Dogo's practiced ear did not detect any untoward sound, and from where he stood he couldn't tell when Sule gained entry into the house. He remained at his post for what seemed ages—it was actually a matter of minutes. Presently he saw the window at his side open slowly. He froze against the wall. But it was Sule's muscular hands that came through the window, holding out to him a biggish gourd. Dogo took the gourd and was surprised at its weight. His pulse quickened. People around here trusted gourds like this more than banks. "The stream," whispered Sule through the open window. Dogo understood. Hoisting the gourd onto his head, he made off at a fast trot for the stream. Sule would find his way out of the house and follow him.

He set the gourd down carefully by the stream, took off its carved lid. If this contained anything of value, he thought, he and Sule did not have to share it equally. Besides, how did he know Sule had not helped himself to a little of its contents before passing it out through the window? He thrust his right hand into the gourd and next instant he felt a vicious stab on his wrist. A sharp exclamation escaped from him as he jerked his arm out. He peered at his wrist closely then slowly and steadily he began to curse. He damned to hell and glory everything under the sun in the two languages he knew. He sat on the ground, holding his wrist, cursing softly. He heard Sule approaching and stopped. He put the lid back on the gourd and waited. "Any trouble?" he asked, when the other got to him. "No trouble," said Sule. Together they stooped over the gourd. Dogo had to hold his right wrist in his left hand but he did it so Sule wouldn't notice. "Have you opened it?" Sule asked. "Who? Me? Oh, no!" said Dogo. Sule did not believe him and he knew it. "What can be so heavy?" Dogo asked curiously. "We'll see," said Sule.

He took off the lid, thrust his hand into the gaping mouth of the gourd and felt a sharp stab on his wrist. He whipped his hand out of the gourd. He stood up. Dogo, too, stood up and for the first time Sule noticed Dogo's wrist held in the other hand. They were silent for a long time, glaring at each other. "As you always insisted, we should go fifty-fifty in everything," said Dogo casually. Quietly, almost inaudibly, Sule started speaking. He called Dogo every name known to obscenity. Dogo for his part was holding up his end quite well. They stopped when they had run out of names. "I am going home," Dogo announced. "Wait!" said Sule. With his uninjured hand he rummaged in his pocket, brought out a box of matches. With difficulty he struck one, held the flame over the gourd, peered in. He threw the match away. "It is not necessary," he said. "Why not?" Dogo demanded. "That in there is an angry cobra," said Sule. The leaden feeling was creeping up his arm fast. The pain was tremendous. He sat down. "I still don't see why I can't go home," said Dogo. "Have you never heard the saying that what the cobra bites dies at the foot of the cobra? The poison is that good: just perfect for sons of swine like you. You'll never make it home. Better sit down and die here." Dogo didn't agree but the throbbing pain forced him to sit down.

They were silent for several minutes while lightning played around them. Finally Dogo said, "Funny that your last haul should be a snake charmer's gourd." "I think it's funnier still that it should contain a cobra, don't you?" said Sule. He groaned. "I reckon funnier things will happen before the night is done," said Dogo. "Uh!" he winced with pain. "A couple of harmless deaths, for instance," suggested Sule. "Might as well kill the bloody snake," said Dogo. He attempted to rise and pick up a stone from the stream; he couldn't. "Ah, well," he said, lying on his back. "It doesn't matter anyway."

The rain came pattering down. "But why die in the rain?" he demanded angrily. "Might help to die soaking wet if you are going straight to hell from here," said Sule. Teeth clenched, he dragged himself to the gourd, his knife in his good hand. Closing his eyes, he thrust knife and hand into the gourd, drove vicious thrusts into the reptile's writhing body, breathing heavily all the while. When he crawled back to lie down a few minutes later the breath came whistling out of his nostrils, his arm was riddled with fang marks; but the reptile was dead. "That's one snake that has been charmed for the last time," said Sule. Dogo said nothing.

Several minutes passed in silence. The poison had them securely in its fatal grip, especially Sule, who couldn't suppress a few groans. It was only a matter of seconds now. "Pity you have to end up this way," mumbled Dogo, his senses dulling. "By and large, it hasn't been too bad—you thieving scoundrel!" "I'm soaked in tears on account of you," drawled Sule, unutterably weary. "This seems the end of the good old road. But you ought to have known it had to end some time, you rotten bastard!" He heaved a deep sigh. "I shan't have to go up to the hospital in the morning after all," he mumbled, touching the wound in his thigh with a trembling hand. "Ah," he breathed in resignation, "the will of Allah be done." The rain came pattering down.

THE NIGHTMARE

|||||||||||||||||||||||||||||||||||||||||||||||||||||||||||

by William Saidi

William Saidi *is features editor of the* Times of Zambia *and was on the editorial staff of the* Central African Mail, *now the* Zambia Daily Mail. *A successful gossip writer, columnist, and journalist, he has published numerous short stories in newspapers and magazines in Zambia.*

T HIS TIME HE HAD TO contend with seven frenzied, weird and indomitable witch doctors. Their myriad feathers, multicolored and multi-evil to his eyes, fluttered in the slight breeze as they danced around him. Occasionally they pointed their bony, sweaty fingers at him, all the time chanting some eerie incantations which seemed to increase in volume with the breeze.

It was a macabre scene, which in other circumstances the sophisticated Mr. Benjamin Chadiza would have carelessly attributed to his rather flamboyant imagination.

But this scene was real. His presence there in the middle of these emaciated skeletal creatures was indisputable. Even his cynical nature could not cast off the nauseating feeling that these people, if such indeed they were, were real and that the danger they collectively constituted to his life was just as real.

The seven came toward him, the eerie music and the breeze swelling in volume. Their fingers were no longer bony; they were stubby, short, nail-broken, sweat-drenched monstrosities which seemed to have evil powers of their own.

Suddenly, only one of the fingers stood out, as if the others were

||||||||||||

out of focus. That one finger came nearer... nearer... until it was pointing straight at his face. He was incapable of motion. His whole being was focused on that finger. It held a mystic power over him. He felt that he could have done anything it commanded him to do. But it did not command him to do anything. It merely touched his nose, ever so slightly. But the effect was fantastic.

Chadiza felt his soul leap out of his body through his mouth and his body go limp, like an emptied sack of potatoes. Death. So this was death. When you stood on a high peak and looked at your own body from a distance. You saw it as if it were near, as if you were using powerful binoculars to look at it. But you knew one thing, that you could never return to it. It had been a strong body, he mused irrelevantly. Now it was no more. Without its life-giving motor, it was nothing.

He found himself crying for his body, crying for his spirit to return to it. When it did not, he cried some more.

"Ben! Ben! Ben!"

He heard the familiar voice from far away. He was breathing very heavily, like a man who had witnessed a great tragedy for the first time in his life and did not believe that he could live to tell about it.

"Ben! Ben! Ben!"

The familiar voice again. Whose was it? Where was he? With a sinking feeling, he realized he was still crying out aloud for his spirit to return to his body. He cried like a small child, monotonously and without any particular desire to be heard.

He stopped crying abruptly but his mouth remained open as if he would resume crying at any moment. The desire subsided and he heaved a sigh. He opened his eyes and looked into the eyes of his wife.

He gave a shrill scream of terror, remembering the macabre faces of the seven witch doctors. His wife put her arms around him and soothed him with her warmth, pressing her breasts to his chest and whispering comfort close to his ear. At last he was quiet, breathing steadily but still afraid of opening his eyes.

"I have never known you to have such wild nightmares. In fact, I have never known you to have any nightmares at all," Maria said when they were seated at the breakfast table. Her husband looked fresh and infused with a new strength that she found rather disconcerting.

He was normally a very energetic man; it had taken a man of his singular energies to change the school from what it had been before he arrived here. But this morning he seemed all too powerful for her.

"There is always a first time, I understand. A man can live up to fifty without having a single nightmare and then bang! he finds himself panting in the night like a six-year-old. It is nothing that I should worry about, if I were you. The fact that I do not recollect quite what it was all about does not make it any more sinister, as far as I am concerned. It was just a bad dream."

A bad dream? Maria did not think so. Not taken in conjunction with what she knew. She thought he was making a great effort to minimize the significance of the experience—for her sake. But he must realize what it means. He must. She cried out to him in her heart.

The little village was about twenty-five miles from Lusaka. You could not call it entirely rural or primitive, because a bus stopped there once a week to deliver the school mail. But even though it was close to modern civilization it retained the aura of mysticism which had pervaded it even before the days of the trousered white man.

Benjamin Chadiza had been born in Chipata, then Fort Jameson. He was a dedicated nationalist and the fact that this little village in the Central Province was not his birthplace did not detract from the formidable fact that it was part of the country in which he lived and which he loved. He was a teacher with exceptional talents. The head of his department in the Ministry of Education, back in Lusaka, had been enthusiastic about his new posting:

"The people are apathetic to the educational advances we are trying to make in this country. They pay their school fees but in most cases a school cannot run entirely on its school fees. It needs the spiritual support of those whose children it is intended to benefit.

They do not give us their spiritual support. No. They are practically indifferent to every effort we have made to teach their children.

"Mind you, the children attend school. But that in itself is not enough for success. The children have no idea whatsoever what they stand to gain by availing themselves of this opportunity. Their parents have, by their indifference, given them the idea that they can do without this education. And that is dangerous. You cannot teach a child anything if that attitude prevails. I hope you will remedy the situation."

Chadiza's presence had changed the situation, probably remedied it. It had changed the situation so much that it had changed his and Maria's lives.

The witch doctor had had nothing to do with it. His had been a personal and entirely materialistic war against Chadiza. The fact that Chadiza had accepted the challenge rather dubiously had not made it seem any more patriotic in the eyes of the villagers. The villagers were indifferent to the feud between teacher and witch doctor. They did not particularly like the witch doctor but it cannot be said that they loved Chadiza either. They feared the witch doctor but they had no sympathy for Chadiza.

The witch doctor was an old man of about seventy-five. His body was withered and he suffered perennially from all the afflictions of senility. But it never seemed to daunt his spirit. He was everywhere in the village, invincible and imperturbable. He moved among the villagers during the day, spoke to few and was spoken to by none. During the night he prowled the village like an unpaid sentry. He had delegated to himself the duties of overseeing the lives of the villagers. He watched over them, but there were those who looked at his philanthropic nocturnal vigils with great skepticism. They thought he was naturally up to no good. Witch doctors' reputations throughout the country were not respected by anyone.

Chadiza understood that the villagers had accepted the witch doctor as something to be feared but something they could do absolutely nothing about. He was there, omnipresent and almost omnipotent, and nobody questioned his presence. Several people had died, according to stories Chadiza had heard. It was not just by coincidence that these men and women had, at one time, crossed verbal swords with the witch doctor. That they had died under the most unusual circumstances also made it difficult for Chadiza to believe that Nature had actually taken her course.

Chadiza was at first indifferent to the witch doctor and his alleged powers. He had settled down to do his job, changing the attitude of the villagers toward the school. He did not wish to disappoint the head of his department in Lusaka. He had never disappointed his masters before. That was why they had sent him to Oxford to take a special diploma in teaching. He was now back with enthusiasm and dedicated to the noble cause for which his profession stood.

He was friendly with the villagers. Maria, who set out to do so, found the womenfolk of the village prepared to accept her as one of them. Slowly, the village's attitude toward the school changed until now, five years later, every child in school was proud to be there. Every parent whose child was at the school was also proud of it.

It was long after the villagers had accepted the school as something beneficial to them and their children that the vendetta between Chadiza and the witch doctor developed in earnest. Chadiza had, of course, foreseen that his presence would not be taken for granted by the witch doctor. You could not expect a man who had held the position of a minor king to accept relegation to second place without any disapproval. But the disapproval, like everything else about the old man's trade, was subtle.

It became apparent one very dark night, so dark you could not imagine that at times the black sky was illumined by a million stars. Chadiza and Maria were asleep in their house. It was a modern house by the village standards. It was the only house built of burnt bricks. And it had proper windows. The interior was even more surprising to the villagers. The furniture was highly polished and the floor was covered with an expensive carpet on which the villagers trod with awe whenever they visited the house.

Maria was loved by practically every woman in the village. She taught some of them the things she had learned while at Chipembi

Girls' School near Lusaka. They were eager to learn from her and soon she was running a small domestic science class for them.

Maria slept peacefully, her head nestling comfortably in the crook of her husband's arm. Then she stirred slightly and made a childish sound in her sleep. Chadiza was fast asleep.

Then Maria woke up. She left the bed carefully and made for the door without bumping into any of the bedroom furniture.

There stood the witch doctor, his aging face wreathed in humorless wrinkles. He stood there immobile and apparently not startled by Maria's sudden appearance. He looked at her with yellow eyes that reflected nothing whatever of the emotions running through his withered body.

It was only after he had turned and walked away, without any change of expression on the old face, that the scream suddenly tore out of Maria's heart and blasted the dark silence of the village.

Chadiza was out of bed and standing beside her before she had finished screaming. He rushed after the receding figure of the old man, but did not catch him up. The old man did not seem to have been in a hurry to get away, but Chadiza lost sight of him in the darkness. He returned to find Maria now surrounded by a group of concerned and jabbering village women.

Chadiza let his anger lie low for three days before he went to the witch doctor's small hut on the outskirts of the village, "to warn him off," as he put it to Maria. On that day two people visited the witch doctor's hut, each at different occasions and for entirely different reasons. The first was Chadiza himself. The second was his wife, Maria.

Chadiza visited the lonely hut one dark starless night. As he strolled to it, the anger he had suppressed during the past three days surged to the surface. He clenched his fists. He made a great effort to steel himself against the seemingly insurmountable desire to smash the old man's face at first sight. The consequences could either be disastrous or downright ridiculous. The witch doctor could cripple him; that would be tragic. Then again the witch doctor could make him the laughingstock of the village—a young man hitting a defenseless old man.

There was no door on the witch doctor's hut. It was dark inside, although Chadiza saw later that an old candle cast lame light in the hut.

"Come in, my son," the strong, faintly sneering voice said from somewhere near the flickering light of the candle. For a moment, a small chill ran down Chadiza's spine. "My son"? Chadiza wondered. Why "my son"?

That voice! It seemed to drip with evil, with multiple innuendoes of wicked intentions. But he could not allow such ridiculous superstitious nonsense to influence him. Here he was, a twentieth-century educated and intelligent African who had no ties with the forgotten past of his people's dark ages. What could the witch doctor do to him? What, indeed, could anybody—the witch doctor or anybody else in the village, except God—do to him that he could not do to them?

Chadiza thought there was nothing. So he stepped into the little dark hut, sensing as he did that it would be very difficult to see the old man in the restricted light. He also sensed, rather than saw, the paraphernalia of the man's trade. They hung from the soot-blackened grass roof, like their master's guardians. They swayed slightly, although the night was still and windless. Chadiza had vague ideas about the wares of the witch doctor in his beloved country. But he had never come face to face with them. Now he consoled himself with the thought that in the doubtful light he was not going to see them at close quarters.

The whole interview was a shambles as far as Chadiza was concerned. Instead of being the aggressor that he had intended to be, he ended up cowering before the vitriolic abuse the old man poured out at him from his old toothless mouth.

"You are not one of us. You do not understand. You are educated. You think you know better. You despise me. You think I cannot harm you. You think I am just a spent old man playing a game that has long become obsolete."

The witch doctor's voice rose. "I am not! I tell you, I am not! I can do things to you that your white people cannot do to you. I am an old man. That is true. But I am only old in my body. Not in my mind. I still have the power bestowed upon me by my forefathers, the powers that have made these people in the village fear me, respect me. And you come here and think you can lower their respect for me. I am telling you here and now that before you leave this village —whether before or after I have joined my distinguished ancestors— you will learn a few things."

He paused. Chadiza could not see him. He himself had not said a word. After that outburst, he had no wish to say anything either. All he wanted to do was to leave the hut.

The old man said, his voice softening imperceptibly: "You would not know about this, but do you know what it feels to be disowned by your own daughter because of the powers bestowed on you by your forefathers? Never mind, it is something you will not understand. You think you are too educated. But I am telling you . . ."

Chadiza could not laugh at the threats. He had intended to take them lightly. But as he walked back to his own house he found it increasingly difficult to do so. And what about the daughter who disowned her father? He was not supposed to understand that. He did not understand it.

The intense feeling with which the old man had infused his voice during the one-sided interview had gone right to his heart. The old man was not to be dismissed perfunctorily like a medical charlatan. There was nothing bacchanalian about him, or about his hut, for that matter. The village did take him seriously. Maybe Chadiza should start taking him seriously too.

But his wife refused to let it worry him. "It cannot be that serious. That old man is just a ranting old weasel with nothing useful to do around here."

Maria said this before she herself went to visit the old man. She thought she would come to no harm. She did not come to any harm at all. But when she left the old man she wished he had cast a spell on her.

She held the secret from her husband, much against her will. She held it until the witch doctor, unable to use his wares to postpone an appointment with his own Armageddon, died.

For five years, she lived with it. And for five years, her husband lived quite happily, with thoughts of the vendetta with the old man carefully shelved into the back of his mind. Occasionally, however, a shadow crossed his mind as he remembered the hate with which the old man had spoken to him. And he was convinced that the reference to the daughter who disowned her father had had nothing whatsoever to do with him.

It was, however, just five years after the witch doctor's death that Chadiza began to have bad dreams. On the day of his first nightmare, Chadiza was unfortunate. He was unfortunate because only his wife knew that he had cried and ranted in his sleep. He had no recollection of the experience whatsoever. It pained Maria to see him so happy, so unaware of the ordeal he was going through. She was disturbed because she knew something that he did not know about the deceased old man. She suggested they leave the village.

"What? Leave all this? All these things we have done for the villagers? You must be out of your mind. Back to the maddening confusion of the town? No. I am afraid I must disagree with you. We shall remain here until we die."

They died. Both of them. They died in a raging inferno which the villagers, watching helplessly from a distance, knew to have been their peaceful and well-furnished house.

"If only they had known. At least, if only he had known . . ."

"But how could he? She obviously never told him. Never told him that she was the witch doctor's granddaughter. You cannot blame her, probably, for she loved her husband. She feared to lose him."

They chatted on about the tragedy. They—the whole village— had known. They had known that Maria had been watched by the old man on the first day she arrived at the village. The old man had boasted quite publicly that his granddaughter—the child of a daughter who had forsaken him because of his sorcery—was going to live among them.

"But he swore he would do her in because his daughter forsook him. And now he has done it. Poor girl. She was such a beautiful and kind woman. And that husband of hers! Such a wonderful man."

The villagers walked slowly away from the charred debris.

"I wonder if she told him that she was born right here in this village," said one villager.

"Oh, I do not think so. They would have left right after they arrived here," another countered.

The smoke rose high in the early morning sky. It faded into nothingness as if signing an epitaph on the lives of the occupants of the house from which it originated.

THE RETURN

||||||||||||||||||||||||||||||||||||||||||||||||||

by Ngugi wa Thiong'o

Ngugi wa Thiong'o *was born in 1938 and is considered
the leading writer of Kenya. He was a university professor
in Nairobi. He is a prolific writer; his works include* Weep
Not, Child *(1964),* The River Between *(1965),* A Grain
of Wheat *(1967),* Secret Lives, *a collection of short stories
(1975),* Petals of Blood *(1977), and* Devil on the Cross
(1982).

*Ngugi is a very committed writer and the political
ideas for which he has been fighting led him to prison. He
described his prison experiences in the novel* Detained: A
Writer's Prison Diary *(1981). His texts written between
1973 and 1976 were published under the title* Writers in
Politics.

Ngugi is also a playwright; his plays include The
Black Hermit *(1968), and he is co-author of the renowned
plays* The Trial of Dedan Kimathi *(1976) and* I Will
Marry When I Want *(1982).*

T HE ROAD WAS LONG. Whenever he took a step forward,
little clouds of dust rose, whirled angrily behind him, and then
slowly settled again. But a thin train of dust was left in the air,
moving like smoke. He walked on, however, unmindful of the dust
and ground under his feet. Yet with every step he seemed more
and more conscious of the hardness and apparent animosity of the
road. Not that he looked down; on the contrary, he looked straight
ahead as if he would, any time now, see a familiar object that

||||||||||||

would hail him as a friend and tell him that he was near home. But the road stretched on.

He made quick, springing steps, his left hand dangling freely by the side of his once white coat, now torn and worn out. His right hand, bent at the elbow, held onto a string tied to a small bundle on his slightly drooping back. The bundle, well wrapped with a cotton cloth that had once been printed with red flowers now faded out, swung from side to side in harmony with the rhythm of his steps. The bundle held the bitterness and hardships of the years spent in detention camps. Now and then he looked at the sun on its homeward journey. Sometimes he darted quick side-glances at the small hedged strips of land which, with their sickly-looking crops, maize, beans, and peas, appeared much as everything else did—unfriendly. The whole country was dull and seemed weary. To Kamau, this was nothing new. He remembered that, even before the Mau Mau emergency, the overtilled Gikuyu holdings wore haggard looks in contrast to the sprawling green fields in the settled area.

A path branched to the left. He hesitated for a moment and then made up his mind. For the first time, his eyes brightened a little as he went along the path that would take him down the valley and then to the village. At last home was near and, with that realization, the faraway look of a weary traveler seemed to desert him for a while. The valley and the vegetation along it were in deep contrast to the surrounding country. For here green bush and trees thrived. This could only mean one thing: Honia River still flowed. He quickened his steps as if he could scarcely believe this to be true till he had actually set his eyes on the river. It was there; it still flowed. Honia, where so often he had taken a bath, plunging stark naked into its cool living water, warmed his heart as he watched its serpentine movement around the rocks and heard its slight murmurs. A painful exhilaration passed all over him, and for a moment he longed for those days. He sighed. Perhaps the river would not recognize in his hardened features that same boy to whom the riverside world had meant everything. Yet as he ap-

proached Honia, he felt more akin to it than he had felt to anything else since his release.

A group of women were drawing water. He was excited, for he
could recognize one or two from his ridge. There was the middle-
aged Wanjiku, whose deaf son had been killed by the Security
Forces just before he himself was arrested. She had always been a
darling of the village, having a smile for everyone and food for all.
Would they receive him? Would they give him a "hero's welcome?"
He thought so. Had he not always been a favorite all along the
ridge? And had he not fought for the land? He wanted to run and
shout: "Here I am. I have come back to you." But he desisted. He
was a man.

"Is it well with you?" A few voices responded. The other
women, with tired and worn features, looked at him mutely as if
his greeting was of no consequence. Why! Had he been so long in
the camp? His spirits were damped as he feebly asked: "Do you not
remember me?" Again they looked at him. They stared at him
with cold, hard looks; like everything else, they seemed to be deliberately refusing to know or own him. It was Wanjiku who at last
recognized him. But there was neither warmth nor enthusiasm in
her voice as she said, "Oh, is it you, Kamau? We thought you—"
She did not continue. Only now he noticed something else—surprise? fear? He could not tell. He saw their quick glances dart at
him and he knew for certain that a secret from which he was
excluded bound them together.

"Perhaps I am no longer one of them!" he bitterly reflected. But
they told him of the new village. The old village of scattered huts
spread thinly over the ridge was no more.

He left them, feeling embittered and cheated. The old village had
not even waited for him. And suddenly he felt a strong nostalgia for
his old home, friends and surroundings. He thought of his father,
mother and—and—he dared not think about her. But for all that,
Muthoni, just as she had been in the old days, came back to his
mind. His heart beat faster. He felt desire and a warmth thrilled
through him. He quickened his step. He forgot the village women as

he remembered his wife. He had stayed with her for a mere two
weeks; then he had been swept away by the colonial forces. Like
many others, he had been hurriedly screened and then taken to detention without trial. And all that time he had thought of nothing but
the village and his beautiful woman.

The others had been like him. They had talked of nothing but
their homes. One day he was working next to another detainee from
Muranga. Suddenly the detainee, Njoroge, stopped breaking stones.
He sighed heavily. His worn-out eyes had a faraway look.

"What's wrong, man? What's the matter with you?" Kamau asked.

"It is my wife. I left her expecting a baby. I have no idea what has
happened to her."

Another detainee put in: "For me, I left my woman with a baby.
She had just been delivered. We were all happy. But on the same day,
I was arrested . . ."

And so they went on. All of them longed for one day—the day of
their return home. Then life would begin anew.

Kamau himself had left his wife without a child. He had not
even finished paying the bride price. But now he would go, seek
work in Nairobi, and pay off the remainder to Muthoni's parents.
Life would indeed begin anew. They would have a son and bring
him up in their own home. With these prospects before his eyes,
he quickened his steps. He wanted to run—no, fly to hasten his
return. He was now nearing the top of the hill. He wished he
could suddenly meet his brothers and sisters. Would they ask him
questions? He would, at any rate, not tell them all: the beating,
the screening and the work on roads and in quarries with an askari
always nearby ready to kick him if he relaxed. Yes. He had suffered
many humiliations, and he had not resisted. Was there any need?
But his soul and all the vigor of his manhood had rebelled and
bled with rage and bitterness.

One day these wazungu would go!

One day his people would be free! Then, then—he did not know
what he would do. However, he bitterly assured himself no one
would ever flout his manhood again.

He mounted the hill and then stopped. The whole plain lay below. The new village was before him—rows and rows of compact mud huts, crouching on the plain under the fast-vanishing sun. Dark blue smoke curled upward from various huts, to form a dark mist that hovered over the village. Beyond, the deep, blood-red sinking sun sent out fingerlike streaks of light that thinned outward and mingled with the gray mist shrouding the distant hills.

In the village, he moved from street to street, meeting new faces. He inquired. He found his home. He stopped at the entrance to the yard and breathed hard and full. This was the moment of his return home. His father sat huddled up on a three-legged stool. He was now very aged and Kamau pitied the old man. But he had been spared— yes, spared to see his son's return—

"Father!"

The old man did not answer. He just looked at Kamau with strange vacant eyes. Kamau was impatient. He felt annoyed and irritated. Did he not see him? Would he behave like the women Kamau had met by the river?

In the street, naked and half-naked children were playing, throwing dust at one another. The sun had already set and it looked as if there would be moonlight.

"Father, don't you remember me?" Hope was sinking in him. He felt tired. Then he saw his father suddenly start and tremble like a leaf. He saw him stare with unbelieving eyes. Fear was discernible in those eyes. His mother came, and his brothers too. They crowded around him. His aged mother clung to him and sobbed hard.

"I knew my son would come. I knew he was not dead."

"Why, who told you I was dead?"

"That Karanja, son of Njogu."

And then Kamau understood. He understood his trembling father. He understood the women at the river. But one thing puzzled him: he had never been in the same detention camp with Karanja. Anyway he had come back. He wanted now to see Muthoni. Why had she not come out? He wanted to shout, "I have come, Muthoni; I am here." He looked around. His mother understood him. She quickly darted a glance at her man and then simply said:

"Muthoni went away."

Kamau felt something cold settle in his stomach. He looked at the village huts and the dullness of the land. He wanted to ask many questions but he dared not. He could not yet believe that Muthoni had gone. But he knew by the look of the women at the river, by the look of his parents, that she was gone.

"She was a good daughter to us," his mother was explaining. "She waited for you and patiently bore all the ills of the land. Then Karanja came and said that you were dead. Your father believed him. She believed him too and keened for a month. Karanja constantly paid us visits. He was of your Rika, you know. Then she got a child. We could have kept her. But where is the land? Where is the food? Ever since land consolidation, our last security was taken away. We let Karanja go with her. Other women have done worse—gone to town. Only the infirm and the old have been left here."

He was not listening; the coldness in his stomach slowly changed to bitterness. He felt bitter against all, all the people including his father and mother. They had betrayed him. They had leagued against him, and Karanja had always been his rival. Five years was admittedly not a short time. But why did she go? Why did they allow her to go? He wanted to speak. Yes, speak and denounce everything—the women by the river, the village and the people who dwelled there. But he could not. This bitter thing was choking him.

"You—you gave my own away?" he whispered.

"Listen, child, child . . ."

The big yellow moon dominated the horizon. He hurried away bitter and blind, and only stopped when he came to the Honia River.

And standing at the bank, he saw not the river, but his hopes dashed on the ground instead. The river moved swiftly, making ceaseless monotonous murmurs. In the forest the crickets and other insects kept up an incessant buzz. And above, the moon shone bright. He tried to remove his coat, and the small bundle he had held on to so firmly fell. It rolled down the bank and before Kamau knew what was happening, it was floating swiftly down the river. For a time he was shocked and wanted to retrieve it. What would he show his— Oh, had he forgotten so soon? His wife had gone. And the little things that had so strangely reminded him of her and that he had guarded all those years, had gone! He did not know why, but somehow he felt relieved. Thoughts of drowning himself dispersed. He began to put on his coat, murmuring to himself, "Why should she have waited for me? Why should all the changes have waited for my return?"

THE POINT OF NO RETURN

||||||||||||||||||||||||||||||||||||||||||||||||||||||||||||||||||||||||||||||||||||||||||||||||||||

by Miriam M. Tlali

Miriam M. Tlali *was born in South Africa in 1930. In 1975 she published a novel,* Miriel at Metropolitan, *after heavy censorship. Metropolitan is the name of a store similar to one in which the author once worked. In 1978, Tlali attended the International Writing Program at Iowa City, her first trip abroad.*

At present, Tlali lives in Johannesburg and writes the "Soweto Speaking" column for Staffrider. *Her second novel,* Amandla *(1980) is about Soweto riots. A collection of short stories,* Mihoti (Teardrops), *is ready for publication.*

Her stories have been published regularly in magazines, and are widely anthologized.

S'BONGILE STOPPED AT the corner of Sauer and Jeppe streets and looked up at the robot. As she waited for the green light to go on, she realized from the throbbing of her heart and her quick breathing that she had been moving too fast. For the first time since she had left Senaoane, she became conscious of the weight of Gugu, strapped tightly on her back.

All the way from home, traveling first by bus and then by train from Nhlanzane to Westgate station, her thoughts had dwelt on Mojalefa, the father of her baby. Despite all efforts to forget, her mind had continually reverted to the awesome results of what might lie ahead for them, if they (Mojalefa and the other men) carried out their plans to challenge the government of the Republic of South Africa.

The incessant rumbling of traffic on the two intersecting one-way streets partially muffled the eager male voices audible through the open windows on the second floor of Myler House on the other side of the street. The men were singing freedom songs. She stood and listened for a while before she crossed the street.

Although he showed no sign of emotion, it came as a surprise to Mojalefa when one of the men told him that a lady was downstairs waiting to see him. He guessed that it must be S'bongile and he felt elated at the prospect of seeing her. He quickly descended the two flights of stairs to the foyer. His heart missed a beat when he saw her.

"*Au banna!*" he said softly as he stood next to her, unable to conceal his feelings. He looked down at her and the baby, sleeping soundly on her back. S'bongile slowly turned her head to look at him, taken aback at his exclamation. He bent down slightly and brushed his dry lips lightly over her forehead just below her neatly plaited hair. He murmured, "It's good to see you again, Bongi. You are *so* beautiful! Come, let's sit over here."

He led her away from the stairs, to a wooden bench farther away opposite a narrow dusty window overlooking the courtyard. A dim ray of light pierced through the windowpanes making that spot the only bright area in the dimly lit foyer.

He took out a piece of tissue from his coat pocket, wiped off the dust from the sill and sat down facing her. He said:

"I'm very happy you came. I . . ."

"I *had* to come, Mojalefa," she interrupted.

"I could not bear it any longer. I could not get my mind off the quarrel. I could not do any work, everything I picked up kept falling out of my hands. Even the washing I tried to do I could not get done. I *had* to leave everything and come. I kept thinking of you . . . as if it was all over, and I would not see you nor touch you ever again. I came to convince myself that I could still see you as a free man; that I could still come close to you and touch you. Mojalefa, I'm sorry I behaved like that last night. I thought you were indifferent to what I was going through. I was jealous because you kept on telling me that you were committed. That like all the others, you had already resigned from your job, and that there was no turning back. I thought you cared more for the course you have chosen than for Gugu and me."

"There's no need for you to apologize, Bongi, I never blamed you for behaving like that and I bear you no malice at all. All I want from you is that you should understand. Can we not talk about something else? I am so happy you came."

They sat looking at each other in silence. There was so much they wanted to say to one another, just this once. Yet both felt tongue-tied; they could not think of the right thing to say. She felt uneasy, just sitting there and looking at him while time was running out for them. She wanted to steer off the painful subject of their parting, so she said:

"I have not yet submitted those forms to Baragwanath. They want the applicants to send them in together with their pass numbers. You've always discouraged me from going for a pass, and now they want a number. It's almost certain they'll accept me because of my matric certificate. That is if I submit my form *with the number* by the end of this month, of course. What do you think I should do, go for registration? Many women and girls are already rushing to the registration centers. They say it's useless for us to refuse to carry them like you men because we will not be allowed to go anywhere for a visit or buy anything valuable. And now the hospitals, too . . ."

"No, no wait . . . Wait until . . . Until after this . . . After you know what the outcome is of what we are about to do."

Mojalefa shook his head. It was intolerable. Everything that happened around you just went to emphasize the hopelessness of even trying to live like a human being. Imagine a woman having to carry a pass everywhere she goes; being stopped and searched or ordered to produce her pass! This was outrageous, the ultimate desecration and an insult to her very existence. He had already seen some of these "simple" women who come to seek work from "outside," proudly moving in the streets with those plastic containers dangling round their necks like sling bags. He immediately thought of the tied-down bitch and it nauseated him.

S'bongile stopped talking. She had tried to change the topic from the matter of their parting but now she could discern that she had only succeeded in making his thoughts wander away into a world unknown to her. She felt as if he had shut her out, aloof. She needed his nearness, now more than ever. She attempted to draw him closer to herself; to be *with* him just this last time. She could not think of anything to say. She sat listening to the music coming from the upper floors. She remarked:

"That music, those two songs they have just been singing; I haven't heard them before. Who composes them?"

"Most of the men contribute something now and again. Some melodies are from old times, they just supply the appropriate words. Some learn 'new' tunes from old people at home, old songs from our past. Some are very old. Some of our boys have attended the tribal dancing ceremonies at the mines and they learn these during the festivities. Most of these are spontaneous, they come from the feelings of the people as they go about their work; mostly laborers. Don't you sometimes hear them chanting to rhythm as they perform tasks; carrying heavy iron bars or timber blocks along the railway lines or road construction sites? They even sing about the white foreman who sits smoking a pipe and watches them as they sweat."

S'bongile sat morose, looking toward the entrance at the multitudes moving toward the center of town and down toward Newtown. She doubted whether any of those people knew anything of the plans of the men who were singing of the aspirations of the blacks and their hopes for the happier South Africa they were envisaging. Her face, although beautiful as ever, reflected her depressed state. She nodded in halfhearted approval at his enthusiastic efforts to explain. He went on:

"Most of the songs are in fact lamentations—they reflect the disposition of the people. We shall be thundering them tomorrow morning on our way as we march toward the jails of this country!"

With her eyes still focused on the stream of pedestrians and without stopping to think, she asked:

"Isn't it a bit premature? Going, I mean. You are *so* few; a drop in an ocean."

"It isn't numbers that count, Bongi," he answered, forcing a smile. How many times had he had to go through that? he asked himself. In the trains, the buses, at work... Bongi was unyielding. Her refusal to accept that he must go was animated by her selfish love, the fear of facing life without him. He tried to explain although he had long realized that his efforts would always be fruitless. It was also clear to him that it was futile to try and run away from the issue.

"In any case," he went on, "it will be up to *you*, the ones who remain behind, the women and the mothers, to motivate those who are still dragging their feet; you'll remain only to show them why they must follow in our footsteps. That the future and dignity of the blacks as a nation and as human beings is worth sacrificing for."

Her reply only served to demonstrate to him that he might just as well have kept quiet. She remarked:

"Even your father feels that this is of no use. He thinks it would perhaps only work if all of you first went out to *educate* the people so that they may join in."

"No, father does not understand. He thinks we are too few as compared to the millions of all the black people of this land. He feels that we are sticking out our necks. That we can never hope to get the white man to sit round a table and speak to us, here. All he'll do is order his police to shoot us dead. If they don't do that, then they'll throw us into the jails, and we shall either die there or be released with all sorts of afflictions. It's because I'm his only son. He's thinking of *himself*, Bongi, he does not understand."

"He *does* understand, and he loves you."

"Maybe that's *just* where the trouble lies. Because he loves me, he fails to think and reason properly. We do not agree. He is a different kind of person from me, and he can't accept that. He wants me to speak, act, and even think like him, and that is impossible."

"He wants to be proud of you, Mojalefa."

"If he can't be proud of me as I am, then he'll never be. He says I've changed. That I've turned against everything he taught me. He wants me to go to church regularly and pray more often. I sometimes feel he hates me, and I sympathize with him."

"He does not hate you, Mojalefa; you two just do not see eye to eye."

"My father moves around with a broken heart. He feels I am a renegade, a disappointment; an embarrassment to him. You see, as a preacher, he has to stand before the congregation every Sunday and preach on the importance of obedience, of how as Christians we have to be submissive and tolerant and respect those who are in authority over us under all conditions. That we should leave it to 'the hand of God' to right all wrongs. As a reprisal against all injustices we must kneel down and pray because, as the scriptures tell us, God said: 'Vengeance is Mine.' He wants me to follow in his footsteps."

"Be a priest or preacher, you mean?"

"Yes. Or show some interest in his part-time ministry. Sing in the church choir and so on, like when I was still a child." He smiled wryly.

"Why don't you show *some* interest then? Even if it is only for his sake? Aren't you a Christian, don't you believe in God?"

"I suppose I do. But not like *him* and those like him, no."

"What is *that* supposed to mean?"

"What's the use of praying all the time? In the first place, how can a slave kneel down and pray without feeling that he is not quite a man, human? Every time I try to pray I keep asking myself—if God loves me like the Bible says he does, then why should I have to carry a pass? Why should I have to be a virtual tramp in the land of my forefathers, why? Why should I have all these obnoxious laws passed against me?"

Then the baby on Bongi's back coughed, and Mojalefa's eyes drifted slowly toward it. He looked at the sleeping Gugu tenderly for a while and sighed, a sad expression passing over his eyes. He wanted to say something but hesitated and kept quiet.

Bongi felt the strap cutting painfully into her shoulder muscles

and decided to transfer the baby to her lap. Mojalefa paced up and
down in the small space, deep in thought. Bongi said:

"I have to breast-feed him. He hasn't had his last feed. I forgot
everything. I just grabbed him and came here, and he didn't cry or
complain. Sometimes I wish he would cry more often like other
children."

Mojalefa watched her suckling the baby. He reluctantly picked up
the tiny clasped fist and eased his thumb slowly into it so as not to
rouse the child. The chubby fingers immediately caressed his thumb
and embraced it tightly. His heart sank, and there was a lump in his
throat. He had a strong urge to relieve S'bongile of the child, pick
him up in his strong arms and kiss him, but he suppressed the desire.
It was at times like these that he experienced great conflict. He said:

"I should never have met you, Bongi. I am not worthy of your
love."

"It was cruel of you Mojalefa. All along you knew you would have
to go, and yet you made me fall for you. You made me feel that life
without you is no life at all. Why did you do this to me?"

He unclasped his thumb slowly from the baby's instinctive clutch,
stroking it tenderly for a moment. He walked slowly toward the dim
dusty window. He looked through into the barely visible yard, over
the roofs of the nearby buildings, into the clear blue sky above. He
said:

"It is because I have the belief that we shall meet again, Bongi;
that we shall meet again, in a free Africa!"

The music rose in a slow crescendo.

"That song. It is so *sad*. It sounds like a hymn."

They were both silent. The thoughts of both of them anchored on
how unbearable the other's absence would be. Mojalefa consoled
himself that at least he knew his father would be able to provide the
infant with all its needs. That he was fortunate and not like some of
his colleagues who had been ready—in the midst of severe poverty
—to sacrifice all. Thinking of some of them humbled him a great
deal. S'bongile would perhaps be accepted in Baragwanath where she
would take up training as a nurse. He very much wanted to break the

silence. He went near his wife and touched her arm. He whispered:

"Promise me, Bongi, that you will do your best. That you will look after him, please."

"I *shall*. He is our valuable keepsake—your father's and mine—something to remind me of you. A link nobody can destroy. All yours and mine."

He left her and started pacing again. He searched hopelessly in his mind for something to say; something pleasant. He wanted to drown the sudden whirl of emotion he felt in his heart when he looked down at S'bongile, his young bride of only a few weeks, and the two-month-old child he had brought into this world.

S'bongile came to his rescue. She said:

"I did not tell my mother that I was coming here. I said that I was taking Gugu over to your father for a visit. He is always so happy to see him."

Thankful for the change of topic, Mojalefa replied, smiling:

"You know, my father is a strange man. He is unpredictable. For instance, when I had put you into trouble and we realized to our horror that Gugu was on the way, I thought that he would skin me alive, that *that* was now the last straw. I did not know how I would approach him, because then it was clear that you would also have to explain to your mother why you would not be in a position to start at Turfloop. There was also the thought that your mother had paid all the fees for your first year and had bought you all those clothes and so forth. It nearly drove me mad worrying about the whole mess. I kept thinking of your poor widowed mother; how she had toiled and saved so that you would be able to start at university after having waited a whole year for the chance. I decided to go and tell my uncle in Pretoria and send *him* to face my father with that catastrophic announcement. I stayed away from home for weeks after that."

"Oh yes, it was nerve-racking, wasn't it? And they were all so kind to us. After the initial shock, I mean. We have to remember that all our lives, and be thankful for the kind of parents God gave us. I worried *so* much, I even contemplated suicide, you know. Oh well, I suppose you could not help yourself!"

She sighed deeply, shaking her head slowly. Mojalefa continued:

"Mind you, I knew something like that would happen, yet I went right ahead and talked you into yielding to me. I was drawn to you by a force so great, I just could not resist it. I hated myself for weeks after that. I actually despised myself. What is worse is that I had vowed to myself that I would never bring into this world a soul that would have to inherit my servitude. I had failed to 'develop and show a true respect for our African womanhood,' a clause we are very proud of in our disciplinary code, and I remonstrated with myself for my weakness."

"But your father came personally to see my people and apologize for what you had done, and later to pay all the *lobola* they wanted. He said that we would have to marry immediately as against what you had said to me—why it would not be wise for us to marry, I mean."

"That was when I had gone through worse nightmares. I had to explain to him why I did not want to tie you down to me when I felt that I would not be able to offer you anything, that I would only make you unhappy. You know why I was against us marrying, Bongi, of course. I wanted you to be free to marry a 'better' man, and I had no doubt it would not be long before he grabbed you. Any man would be proud to have you as his wife, even with a child who is not his."

He touched her smooth cheek with the back of his hand, and added:

"You possess those rare delicate attributes that any man would want to feel around him and be enkindled by."

"Your father would never let Gugu go, not for anything, Mojalefa. He did not name him 'his pride' for nothing. I should be thankful that I met the son of a person like that. Not all women are so fortunate. How many beautiful girls have been deserted by their lovers and are roaming the streets with illegitimate babies on their backs, children they cannot support?"

"I think it is an unforgivable sin. And not all those men do it intentionally, mind you. Sometimes, with all their good intentions, they just do not have the means to do much about the problem of having to pay *lobola*, so they disappear, and the girls never see them again."

"How long do you think they'll lock you up, Mojalefa?" she asked, suddenly remembering that it might be years before she could speak to him like that again. She adored him, and speaking of parting with him broke her heart.

"I do not know, and I do not worry about that, Bongi. If I had you and Gugu and they thrust me into a desert for a thousand years, I would not care. But then I am only a small part of a whole. I'm like a single minute cell in the living body composed of millions of cells, and I have to play my small part for the well-being and perpetuation of life in the whole body."

"But you are likely to be thrust into the midst of hardened criminals, murderers, rapists and so on."

"Very likely. But then that should not deter us. After all most of them have been driven into being like that by the very evils we are exposed to as people without a say in the running of our lives. Most of them have ceased to be proud because there's nothing to be proud of. You amuse me, Bongi. So you think because we are more educated we have reason to be proud? Of what should we feel proud in a society where the mere pigmentation of your skin condemns you to nothingness? Tell me, of what?"

She shook her head violently, biting her lips in sorrow, and with tears in her eyes, she replied, softly:

"I do not know, Mojalefa."

They stood in silence for a while. She sighed deeply and held back the tears. They felt uneasy. It was useless, she thought bitterly. They had gone through with what she considered to be an ill-fated undertaking. Yet he was relentlessly adamant. She remembered how they had quarreled the previous night. How at first she had told herself that she had come to accept what was about to happen with quiet composure, "like a mature person" as they say. She had however lost control of herself when they were alone outside her home, when he had bidden her mother and other relatives farewell. She had become hysterical and could not go on pretending any longer. In a fit of anger, she had accused Mojalefa of being a coward who was running away from his responsibilities as a father and husband. It had been a very bad row and they had parted unceremoniously. She had resolved that today she would only speak of those things which would not make them unhappy. And now she realized with regret that she was right back where she had started. She murmured to herself:

"Oh God, why should it be us, why should we be the lambs for the slaughter? Why should you be one of those handing themselves over? It's like giving up. What will you be able to do for your people in jail, or if you should be..."

She could not utter the word *killed*.

"*Somebody* has got to sacrifice so that others may be free. The *real* things, those that really matter, are never acquired the easy way. All the peoples of this world who were oppressed like us have had to give up *something*, Bongi. Nothing good or of real value comes easily. Our freedom will never be handed over to us on a silver platter. In our movement, we labor under no illusions; we know we can expect no handouts. We know that the path ahead of us is not lined with soft velvety flower petals: we are aware that we shall have to tread on thorns. We are committed to a life of service, sacrifice and suffering. Oh no, Bongi, you have got it all wrong. It is not like throwing in the towel. On the contrary, it is the beginning of something our people will never look back at with shame. We shall never regret what we are about to do, and there is no turning back. We are at the point of no return! If I changed my mind now and went back home and sat down and deceived myself that all was all right, I would die a very unhappy man indeed. I would die in dishonor." He was silent a while.

"Bongi, I want to tell you my story. I've never related it to anyone before because just *thinking* about the sad event is to me a very unpleasant and extremely exacting experience..." He was picking his way carefully through memories.

"After my father had completed altering that house we live in from a four-roomed matchbox to what it is now, he was a proud man. He was called to the office by the superintendent to complete a con-tract with an electrical contractor. It had been a costly business and the contractor had insisted that the final arrangements be concluded before the City Council official. It was on that very day that the superintendent asked him if he could bring some of his colleagues to see the house when it was completed. My father agreed. I was there on that day when they (a group of about fifteen whites) arrived. I had heard my parents speak with great expectation to their friends and everybody about the intended 'visit' by the white people. Naturally, I was delighted and proud as any youngster would be. I made sure I would be home and not at the football grounds that afternoon. I thought it was a great honor to have such respectable white people coming to *our* house. I looked forward to it and I had actually warned some of my friends . . .

"After showing them through all the nine rooms of the two-story house, my obviously gratified parents both saw the party out along the slasto pathway to the front gate. I was standing with one of my friends near the front veranda. I still remember vividly the superintendent's last words. He said: 'John, on behalf of my colleagues here and myself, we are very thankful that you and your kind *mosade* allowed us to come and see your beautiful house. You must have spent a *lot* of money to build and furnish it *so* well. But, *you should have built it on wheels!*' And the official added, with his arms swinging forward like someone pushing some imaginary object: 'It should have had *wheels* so that it may *move* easily!' And they departed, leaving my petrified parents standing there agape and looking at each other in helpless amazement. I remember, later, my mother trying her best to put my stunned father at ease, saying: '*Au, oa hlanya, mo lebale; ha a tsebe hore ontse a re'ng. Ntate hle!*' ('He is mad; just forget about him. He does not know what he is saying!')

"As a fifteen-year-old youth, I was also puzzled. But unlike my parents, I did not sit down and forget—or try to do so. That day marked the turning point in my life. From that day on, I could not rest. Those remarks by that government official kept ringing in my mind. I had to know why he had said that. I probed, and probed; I asked my teachers at school, clerks at the municipal offices, anyone who I thought would be in a position to help me. Of course I made it as general as I could and I grew more and more restless. I went to libraries and read all the available literature I could find on the South African blacks.

"I studied South African history as I had never done before. The history of the discovery of gold, diamonds and other minerals in this land, and the growth of the towns. I read of the rush to the main industrial centers and the influx of the Africans into them, following their early reluctance, and sometimes refusal, to work there, and the subsequent laws which necessitated their coming like the vagrancy laws and the pass laws. I read about the removals of the so-called 'black spots' and why they were now labeled that. The influenza epidemic which resulted in the building of the Western Native and George Goch townships in 1919. I dug into any information I could get about the history of the urban Africans. I discovered the slyness, hypocrisy, dishonesty and greed of the lawmakers.

"When elderly people came to visit us and sat in the evenings to speak about their experiences of the past, of how they first came into contact with the whites, their lives with the Boers on the farms and so forth, I listened. Whenever my father's relations went to the remote areas in Lesotho and Matatiele, or to Zululand and Natal where my mother's people are, during school holidays, I grabbed the opportunity and accompanied them. Learning history ceased to be the usual matter of committing to memory a whole lot of intangible facts from some obscure detached past. It became a living thing and a challenge. I was in search of my true self. And like Moses in the Bible, I was disillusioned. Instead of having been raised like the slave I am, I had been nurtured like a prince, clothed in a fine white linen loincloth and girdle when I should have been wrapped in the rough woven clothing of my kind.

"When I had come to know most of the facts, when I had read through most of the numerous laws pertaining to the urban blacks—the acts, clauses, subclauses, regulations, sections and subsections; the amendments and subamendments—I saw myself for the first time. I was a prince, descended from the noble proud house of Monaheng—the true kings of the Basuto nation. I stopped going to the sports clubs and the church. Even my father's flashy American Impala ceased to bring to me the thrill it used to when I drove round the townships in it. I attended political meetings because there, at least, I found people trying to find ways and means of solving and overcoming our problems. At least I knew now what I really was . . . an underdog, a voiceless creature. Unlike my father, I was not going to be blindfolded and led along a garden path by someone else, a foreigner from other continents. I learned that as a black, there was a responsibility I was carrying on my shoulders as a son of this soil. I realized that I had to take an active part in deciding (or in insisting that I should decide) the path along which my descendants will tread. Something was wrong: radically wrong, and it was my duty as a black person to try and put it right. To free myself and my people became an obsession, a dedication.

"I sometimes listen with interest when my father complains. Poor father. He would say: 'Mojalefa *oa polotika*. All Mojalefa reads is politics, politics, politics. He no longer plays football like other youths. When he passed matric with flying colors in history, his history master came to my house to tell me how my son is a promising leader. I was proud and I moved around with my head in the air. I wanted him to start immediately at university, but he insisted that he wanted to work. I wondered why because I could afford it and there was no pressing need for him to work. He said he would study under UNISA and I paid fees for the first year, and they sent him lectures. But instead of studying, he locks himself up in his room and reads politics all the time. He has stopped sending in scripts for correction. He is morose and never goes to church. He does not appreciate what I do for him!' Sometimes I actually pity my father. He would say: 'My father was proud when Mojalefa was born. He walked on foot rather than take a bus all the way from Eastern Native Township to Bridgman Memorial Hospital in Brixton to offer his blessings at the bedside of my late wife, and to thank our ancestors for a son and heir. He named him Mojalefa. And now that boy is about to sacrifice himself —for what he calls "a worthy cause." He gives up all this . . . a house

I've built and furnished for twenty-one thousand rand, most of my money from the insurance policy my good old boss was clever enough to force me to take when I first started working for him. Mojalefa gives up all this for a jail cell!'"

There were tears in the eyes of S'bongile as she sat staring in bewilderment at Mojalefa. She saw now a different man; a man with convictions and ideals; who was not going to be shaken from his beliefs, come what may. He stopped for a while and paused. All the time he spoke as if to some unseen being, as if he was unconscious of her presence. He went on:

"My father always speaks of how his grandfather used to tell him that as a boy in what is now known as the Free State (I don't know why) the white people (the Boers) used to come, clothed only in a 'stertriem', and ask for permission to settle on their land. Just like that, barefooted and with cracked soles, begging for land. My father does not realize that *he* is now in a worse position than those Boers; that all that makes a man has been stripped from under his feet. That he now has to *float in the air*. He sits back in his favorite comfortable armchair in his living room, looks around him at the splendor surrounding him, and sadly asks: 'When I go, who'll take over from me?' He thinks he is still a man, you know. He never stops to ask himself: 'Take *what* over . . . a house on wheels? Something with no firm ground to stand on?'" He turned away from her and looked through the dusty windowpane. He raised his arms and grabbed the vertical steel bars over the window. He clung viciously to them and shook them until they rattled. He said:

"No, Bongi. There is no turning back. Something has *got* to be done . . . something. It cannot go on like this!"

Strange as it may seem, at that moment, they both had visions of a jail cell. They both felt like trapped animals. He kept on shaking the bars and shouting:

"Something's *got* to be done. . . . Now!"

She could not bear the sight any longer. He seemed to be going through great emotional torture. She shouted:

"Mojalefa!"

He swung round and faced her like someone only waking up from a bad dream. He stared through the open entrance, and up at the stairs leading to the upper floor where the humming voices were audible. They both stood still listening for a while. Then he spoke softly yet earnestly, clenching his fists and looking up toward the sound of the music. He said:

"Tomorrow, when dawn breaks, we shall march . . . Our men will advance from different parts of the Republic of South Africa. They will leave their passbooks behind and not feel the heavy weight in their pockets as they proceed toward the gates of the prisons of this land of our forefathers!"

Bongi stood up slowly. She did not utter a word. There seemed to be nothing to say. She seemed to be drained of all feeling. She felt blank. He thought he detected an air of resignation, a look of calmness in her manner as she moved slowly in the direction of the opening into the street. They stopped and looked at each other. She sighed, and there were no tears in her eyes now. He brushed the back of his hand tenderly over the soft cheeks of the sleeping Gugu and with his dry lips, kissed S'bongile's brow. He lifted her chin slightly with his forefinger and looked into her eyes. They seemed to smile at him. They parted.